Never Good-bye:
The Eternal Nature of Soul

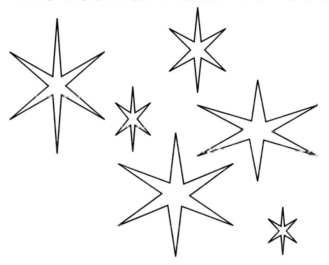

To Connie
Thank you for a
great book discussion.
Much Love Vivian B.

By Vivian C. Beckingham

Note for Librarians: a cataloguing record for this book that includes Dewey Decimal
Classification and US Library of Congress numbers is available from the Library and
Archives of Canada. The complete cataloguing record can be obtained from their online
database at: www.collectionscanada.ca/amicus/index-e.html
ISBN 1-55395-238-3

Printed in Victoria, BC, Canada

TRAFFORD

Offices in Canada, USA, Ireland, UK and Spain
This book was published **on-demand** in cooperation with Trafford Publishing. On-demand
publishing is a unique process and service of making a book available for retail sale to the
public taking advantage of on-demand manufacturing and Internet marketing. On-demand
publishing includes promotions, retail sales, manufacturing, order fulfilment, accounting and
collecting royalties on behalf of the author.
Book sales for North America and international:
Trafford Publishing, 6E–2333 Government St.,
Victoria, BC v8t 4p4 CANADA
phone 250 383 6864 (toll-free 1 888 232 4444)
fax 250 383 6804; email to orders@trafford.com
Books sales in Europe:
Trafford Publishing (uk) Ltd., Enterprise House, Wistaston Road Business Centre,
Wistaston Road, Crewe, Cheshire cw2 7rp UNITED KINGDOM
phone 01270 251 396 (local rate 0845 230 9601)
facsimile 01270 254 983; orders.uk@trafford.com
Order online at:
www.trafford.com/robots/02-0952.html

10 9 8 7 6

Suddenly I bolted to a sitting position; I rubbed my eyes and squinted at the image of a hazy ghost-like waterfall that had materialized about five feet to the left of the stage. An illuminated shimmering blue doorway was half-hidden behind the falling water. I stared in stunned disbelief as I looked around to share my shock with others. No one else noticed this phenomenon; everyone else's attention was riveted on the three performers on the stage.

The blue door opened and a brilliant white light beamed into the room, I was the only person who shielded their eyes, I realized that no one else saw this. A figure of Light stepped through the door and motioned for me, to follow. I pointed to myself; again, the Being of Light motioned for me to follow. I wondered, *is this Light person a member of 'The Brotherhood of Light and Love'?*

I slowly stood up and looked around, no one yelled at me to sit down. I was startled to see my physical body, I looked at my sleeping face; my chin was on top of my folded hands. Patty she was in a different type of dreamland, I stepped in front of her but she did not react, it was as if she could see right through me. I wondered *is this another out-of-body experience?*

I straightened and shielded my eyes as I maneuvered my way towards the figure of Light. I was like Evan, invisible to everyone except for the Being of Light. As I moved next to the waterfall, I felt the misty coolness of the water.

The illuminated figure nodded and although he did not speak aloud I heard the figures say, "If you are a truth seeker, follow," before he turned and disappear through the blue doorway. I looked around the room; everyone was still staring at the stage. I trustingly followed the figure of Light into the unknown.

Table of Contents

DEDICATION:

TO MY SPIRITUAL GUIDE,
FOR YOUR CONSTANT GUIDANCE
AND LOVING PRESENCE,
THANK YOU FROM A GRATEFUL SOUL.

EDITED BY DEBRA HICKMAN

JANET BECKINGHAM

AND MY EDITING TEAM

Acknowledgments

In this book I have incorporated my own spiritual understandings, without attempting to speak on behalf of any spiritual teaching or leader.

The people and events depicted in this novel are fictional, any similarities to actual events and people are strictly coincidental.

There are an endless number of people to thank, for without each and every one of them, this book would not have been completed.

To Harold Klemp, my spiritual guide, teacher and quiet advisor in my life and through out this writing project, thank you. You constantly inspired and guided me to reach beyond my known limitations. I wish I had the words to express my gratitude.

Thank you to the "Institute of Children's Literature" and my writing instructor Karen O'Connor, your course and guidance helped me to not be afraid of self evaluation and editing as I polished my creative efforts and writing skills.

To my first editor, Shari Brown, thank you for your patience with the 1988 first draft; thoughout our short working relationship I valued your insights and suggestions.

To my editor, Debra Hickman, for your priceless advice, encouragement and suggestions, I thank you. You were a gift from the Divine Spirit.

To Jeff Beckingham, my husband and editor, thank you for your directness honesty and unconditional love. Your presence has made my life and the characters in this novel more realistic and honest.

To my cousins Martin and Karen, thank you for your great ideas. The readers can thank you for the added wonderment, spice and romance. Thank you to my Mother in law Norma, for your encouragement and honest evaluation. Thank you to my Mother Lily for the idea of having my niece Kristy read this novel, much all around change resulted from that choice.

Thank you to Dr. Daria Shewchuk-Dann, for your insights and suggestions, the suggestions which were implimented added to the novels authenticity.

To school counsellors Mrs. Ogrodnick and Chris Williams, your insights and suggestions were valuable additions to the reality of the facts of the storyline.

Thank you to my family, your encouragement helped me to never give up.

Thank you to my final editing team Janet Beckingham, Cairol McMorrow and Michelle Shon, your combined suggestions and efforts help to ensure that the finished novel was the best that it could be.

Thank you to Maureen, as the first person to read this novel, your early enthusiasum was greatly appreciated.

Thank you to Sue and Donna for your early evaluation and encouragement, it gave me hope. Thank you to Debbie W. for your insights and attention to details. Thank you to the writer's group, for your encouraging words and evaluation of the first few chapters. Thank you to the life guard, fire fighter, nurse and green house sales person, for your patience on the phone, while I pelleted you with numerous questions.

Lastly, thank you to the Divine Spirit, for helping me to develop determination, persistence and the creative spirit.

Introduction

Fear of the unknown mystery surrounding death, is a common factor in almost every culture on earth. In order to cope with this fear, individual cultures have created rituals to try to appease the mysterious forces behind life and death.

Many scientists and mathematicians, like Albert Einstein have developed scientifically proven theories to explain how the physical universe functions. Einstein had the inspirational idea that, "Energy is never lost; it is just changed or transformed. What becomes of the energy that is the awareness of the individual, after death occurs? There is much speculation and theorizing concerning what happens after death, but for most people, there is no definitive answer.

Can hope and understanding change the fear-filled energy surrounding the unknown reality called death, into a peaceful, relaxed energy?

Perhaps you will find entertainment within these pages, or a few quiet moments to relax and enjoy your creative imagination; or perhaps this story will answer some of your questions and give you hope and move you beyond your boundaries to experience new possibilities concerning death and life on earth and in the heavens.

Chapter 1

The Terminator Never Dies

Everything was moving in slow motion; my lungs were crying for air as I struggle to reach the light. I frantically pulled at the water as if I was pulling on my last link to hope and life. Breaking through to the surface, coughing and sputtering, air filled my lungs; priceless life giving air. I was alive. Blinking, scanning the river bank, I refocused my eyes on the shoreline; people were watching me but he was not there. I repeatedly yelled his name.

I jumped, Mom was shaking my shoulder, she said, "We're here." I looked around and squinted, as my eyes adjusted to the bright midday sunlight. Today seemed like an ideal July day, except for one thing, we were at my brother's funeral.

I am an average 15-year-old, interested in cool clothes and going to the Mall to meet friends. Katy McCall has lived a pretty average, routine life. I remember when I wished for a little excitement in my life, you know, a little spice. There is a saying, "Be careful what you wish for, you might get your wish." Well, I now know that whoever coined that saying was a wise person.

My life changed forever over four days ago. I would have paid anything if someone had given me the ability to turn back the clock. Then I could be the ordinary, bored 15-year-old again. If God could have given me back that one day, I would have been eternally grateful. I had closed my eyes to make this wish over a dozen times, but nothing had changed.

My brother Evan was a typical 17-year-old, royal-pain in the neck brother. Sometimes I would say to him, "Why are you such a royal-pain?" He would say, "I'm your worst nightmare." He would laugh like Dracula, before he would walk away. Now Evan's death has become my nightmare. I repeatedly wondered *why it happened. Is this all there is? You live, you die, is that it?*

These questions are living in my head; they have taken up residence and I do not believe they are going to leave until I can find the answers.

It is strange, the time has come for me to say my last good-bye to Evan and I cannot do it. I look around and stare at all the grieving faces. Their red eyes and raw noses, their quiet pain-filled sobs reminded me of why we are all here. I wish every one would just be quiet.

The minister's voice broke into my thoughts, "Evan will always be remembered as a fine son, brother and friend. Our thoughts are with the McCall family during their time of loss." The minister hesitated before he concluded, "We will always miss Evan." He stepped towards my parents, embracing them in succession; whispering more words of comfort. The minister hugged me and said, "He is safe in the hands of God now."

I remember reading Jack and the Beanstalk to Justine, the little girl I baby-sit. I had visualized Jack running from this massive hand, straining his neck, as he looked back and up into the giant's looming face. I could see Evan sitting on the palm of God's hand, straining to see God's face, if God has a face. It was not hard to imagine God liking Evan. Everyone liked Evan.

People file past my father, mother and me, expressing quiet words of comfort. I look towards my parents as they acknowledge the endless stream of people. They lean on one another to give each other support. People spoke in hushed whispers, as they pay their final respects to Evan. The thought occurs to me, maybe they are afraid of waking him up; I immediately admonished myself for thinking that thought.

It is hard to know what to say to these people. They look so sad. Most of them give me a puzzled glance, as if they expect me to be devastated, but I am not. It does not feel like Evan is gone. As I look at his coffin, I can imagine Evan sitting up and saying, "Hey man, it's all a rotten joke, you can go home now." Evan could come back like Tom Sawyer; I still hope and dream of something different.

"You look tired, Katy." A shudder went through me; Travis's voice brought me out of my daydream. He added, "The tetanus shot did its job. I guess you're not nauseous anymore." I ignored him, but he continued to talk to me. "I was worried about you. . . . Katy, I'm so sorry." Travis grabbed my hand. I tensed and yanked my hand away from his comforting hand.

"Travis, let go!" I ordered. I wrapped my arms across my stomach.

He hesitated before speaking, "Your jaw looks sore." He raised his hand towards the bruise on the left side of my face; I jerked my head away. Travis paused, before slowly lowered his hand. "I'm sorry I hit you, I had no choice."

I laughed in astonishment. How could he stand there and say that to me. "You had no choice? Don't give me that." I was looking up into his eyes now. I struggled to keep my voice calm and under control. "You shouldn't have stopped me from finding him." I clenched my fists and teeth as I spoke. I felt like taking another swing at him. Instead, I controlled that impulse.

Travis spoke in a hushed whisper, "Katy, you were exhausted." He leaned towards me before continuing, "If I hadn't pulled you out of the North Saskatchewan, you would have drowned, or gotten sick. It's not like a clean mountain river."

"You had a choice," I yelled. "You should have helped me find him, instead of stopping me." People were turning to stare at us. "Forget it! Just forget it," I ordered. I did not want to hear about that day. Why was he reminding me of that day?

"I want us to talk before I leave." I put my hands over my ears to try to shut him out. "Katy," Travis yelled, "Listen to me!" I shook my head; I could still hear his muffled voice through my hands.

Mom stepped forward and hugged Travis. She spoke in a quiet, breaking voice. I lowered my hands to listen. "Thank you for coming, Travis. You were a good friend to Evan." Mom's voice broke, as she stopped to compose herself. They both began to cry.

"Mrs. McCall, if we had done something different that day," Travis spoke in a halting voice. "Evan might still be alive." Mom held Travis securely in a bear hug. Travis covered his face with his hands and cried.

Mom quietly whispered, "If you had done something different, what would have happened to the little boy? You both did all you could do that day. When you move to Winnipeg, don't take this pain with you, Evan wouldn't want that."

They cried in each other's arms. I felt like placing my hands over my ears again; I hated the sound of their crying it made Evan's death seem more real. Who needed that reality? I used to think of Travis Abler as my second brother, now; I could barely stand to look at him. I closed my eyes. I imagined the river surrounding me; my voice repeatedly screamed Evan's name.

"Katy, honey," Mom tapped me on the shoulder. Travis had moved by us to stand with some classmates. "Mrs. Cope asked you a question." Mom squeezed my shoulders and motioned to Mrs. Cope.

Mrs. Cope had been Evan's student teacher in English last year, and she would be my English teacher for the up-coming semester. Her quiet disposition and controlled manner lulled students into thinking she was a pushover, that is, until she laid down the law. That is all it took. Evan told me about his first encounter with her.

It was over a year ago during a noon-hour, when Evan, Russ Wilson and Travis were walking through the deserted hallways of Crestmore Senior High. They spotted a small grade-ten student walking towards them. For kicks, they decided to throw her into the boy's john. They figured that would spice things up. It did. The blood-curdling shriek that came out of that small girl sent the three of them running for the hills. At the beginning of English class, their teacher introduced them to that small student. I wish I could have been a fly on that wall day. I would have paid money to see their faces.

Evan said he learned a valuable lesson that day. He said, "If you judge a situation entirely by appearances, you'll get burned." That wee, little student was their new English 10, student teacher. She was also a mother, who lived in the same apartment building where our mother worked, as the maintenance person. After that day Evan was an ideal student, at least in English class.

Evan's attitude towards English really changed a lot, due to the influence and guidance of Mrs. Cope. English was no longer a way to pass an hour's time, for Evan had rediscovered stories. Stories became gateways to magical worlds, worlds of mystery and science fiction. Evan discovered he had a knack for weaving a tall tale, especially when it came to fantasy, or science fiction. This was no surprise to me. Evan loved fantasy fiction. His favorite movies were the different Lord of the Ring movies, the Matrix movies Star Trek series, all the Star Trek movies, the Star Wars Movies, ET, the Terminator movies, the first two Alien movies, The Wizard of Oz and It's a Wonderful Life. If you had to change your concept of reality, or existence for the duration of the movies playing time, then Evan would be interested, oh heck, he would be a die-hard fan.

Evan's Mr. Spock imitation was flawless, and his Terminator imitation was irritating. Evan thought the story line of The Terminator, the movie that had Arnold Schwarzenegger playing a futuristic robot, whose goal was to come back through time to kill the mother of his future enemy, was cool. Evan would pretend to be the Terminator and terminate me with a sound whack on the back.

He would say in his terminator voice, "I'll be back," before he would laugh and walk away.

I once snuck up on him and gave him the same terminating blow. Boy was he surprised, his eyes looked like they would pop out of their sockets.

"Got you, you're terminated," I announced. "How does it feel to be the one who is terminated? Not so great, right?"

Evan made a quick recovery; his mischievous smile told me he was up to something before he spoke. I soon found that I was right, "Pretty sneaky Sis, but you should know that you can't terminate the Terminator." He bent his arm to show me a muscle. I pretended to gag, and then asked him if he was trying to gross me out. Evan just laughed and said, "The Terminator is indestructible."

"What are you talking about?" I asked in exasperation. "In the movie the Terminator's lights were shut off. What makes you so different?" Brothers, they always change the rules of the game.

"I'm the new improved model," Evan stated. Then he terminated me with a similar whack to my back. He laughed, "Ha, ha, foolish human. Don't you know by now that the Terminator never dies?"

When this happened, I was more annoyed at him for changing the rules on me than anything else. Evan whistled, Somewhere Over the Rainbow, as he turned and left the room. At that moment I had wished he was somewhere over the rainbow. Now he is there for good. I wish I had not wished that.

The mourners are gone. My cousins, Aunts and Uncles are climbing into their cars and leaving. Dad hands Uncle Jeff the house keys and asks him to meet visitors at our home. Dad had promised both Mom and I some quiet time with Evan, this was it. Mom and Dad are holding each other; their eyes are red and swollen from all the crying. I am the only one who has not cried yet. I wondered *would I ever cry*.

Dad squeezed my shoulders and said, "Katy, it's time to leave," Mom and Dad had quietly crept up behind me.

I said, in a quiet whisper, "In a couple of weeks a blanket of leaves will cover Evan. A golden blanket will keep him warm." I did not say it to bring Mom more sadness, but that is what I accomplished. Mom began to cry, again. Dad put his arms around Mom's shoulders, she whispered into her ear. He gently turned Mom around and guided her towards the waiting car.

"Let's go Katy, we're going home," Dad stated, as he started to walk a snake-like path around the many cold head stones.

It is tough being fifteen. I want to say mature things, but I seem to end up saying things that make everything worse. To top it off, I was not going to obey my father right away. All day long, I had wanted to say something to Evan; this was my last chance to speak with him alone. I was not going to let this opportunity escape.

"I'll be there in a minute, Dad." I figured I did not have much time. What a stupid time to get tongue-tied. Well, I would say whatever came to mind. I hope that what I wanted to say would be a part of what I would say. I began with, "You missed a nice funeral." I slapped my forehead. I mumbled, "That was a stupid thing to say." I started again. "We all miss you a lot. I know you know this already. I haven't cried yet, but that is not because I don't miss you, or don't love you anymore. It just doesn't seem like you're gone. I can feel you here, and if I think and imagine hard enough, I can see myself talking to you." I turned to see Dad waving to me to come to the car. I waved back at him before continuing to speak, "I haven't got a lot of time left. Mom and Dad are waiting at the car." I knew I had to say something else, what was it?

"You know, you lied to me. You said the Terminator was indestructible. You said you were the new improved model. Indestructible means that you never die. Evan, you lied." In my anger, I kicked the loose dirt surrounding my feet, pebbles and dirt scattered over the coffin. If it were an ideal world, Evan would have woken up and told me to, 'Cool it'.

A quiet voice whispered, "Katy." My face grew hot with embarrassment. I knew he had seen my actions. I turned towards my Father. I stared at the ugly brown dirt around my feet, the same dirt that would soon be covering my brother. Dad calmly added, "Honey, it's time to leave."

I ran into his arms. Dad was like a pillar, proud, strong and solid, but he was also like a blanket, warm and comforting. I had watched the hardships and sorrows of the past few days wear my father down, like weather and time erodes the majestic temple pillars. Watching this had really made me want to cry.

"It's all right to cry. It doesn't make you any less of a person in anyone else's eyes," he whispered.

"I'm not going to cry, Dad. I'm too angry to cry. Why did he die? He was a strong swimmer. He was only seventeen. It's not fair."

Dad said, "I haven't heard too many people say that death is fair. I wish I had some answers for you, but I don't, and I'm not sure if I ever will."

I said, "I feel so empty." Dad looked worried, so I quickly hugged him."

Dad nodded and whispered, "Katy, let's go. Your Mother is waiting," Dad, reminded me. I nodded my head, as he turned too walked towards the car.

"Dad, I have to do one last thing. It will only take a moment," I promised.

Although Dad's patience was wearing thin, he nodded his head. I ducked under his encircling arm and moved towards the gravesite. Then I selected three red roses from one of the wreaths, plucked them from their circular homes and breathed in their fragrance. From this moment on, every time I smelled the fragrance of a rose, I would think of Evan. I wanted to leave him with a gift of beauty, instead of words of anger. I gently dropped two roses on top of his coffin. I dropped the third rose into the pocket of my pin-stripped jacket.

"I love you, Evan. Good-bye," I said. I turned to leave. That is when I heard it. It was a whisper, like a feather on a breeze.

It was Evan's voice whispering, "It's never good-bye". If it had not been so quiet, I would not have heard it at all. I gasped and stared at the coffin in disbelief. I stumbled backwards, then turned and ran towards my Father.

"Dad, Dad, did you hear that? It was Evan's voice. He spoke to me." I was hysterical with happiness.

"It was the wind, Katy. It was just the wind." Dad spoke with a calm assurance.

I laughed and said, "There's no wind, Dad. There's barely a breeze." I wanted him to see. "Dad-,"

My father reached out and shook my shoulders, "Katy, enough of this nonsense," he ordered. "Your mother is waiting and I don't want you to upset her. Evan is dead. Stop this nonsense. You are asking for the impossible. Now, hush!"

I felt like an eight year old. My eyes and throat stung, as I held back angry tears. Maybe he was right, I was asking for the impossible. We walked back to the car in silence.

Chapter 2

Why?

It was two weeks after Evan had passed away. It is hard to explain my feelings. I guess I still felt empty; it felt like I had a hollow heart. When Evan died, it took the stuffing out of me. I spent my days in my room just thinking and sleeping. If Mom did not remind me to eat, I would have forgotten to do that.

Mom and Dad were worried about me. They decided to visit Aunt Emily on her acreage, with me in tow. I did not want to go, I did not want to go anywhere, or see anyone. They said that a little fresh air and a change might do me some good."

Aunt Emily and Brandy, her Irish setter, greeted us with open arms and a wagging tail. We stayed with Aunt Emily over the third weekend in July.

Brandy seems to sense that I was in the dumps. She followed me everywhere, but instead of being her hyper-self, Brandy would quietly sit with her head on my lap, just looking at me with those big brownish eyes. Sometimes she would lick my hands, as if she was saying, "Hey, don't forget me. I am here."

Brandy was a natural when it came to making people feel good. Aunt Emily and Brandy belonged to a group of pet hospital visitors. They made weekly visits to children and terminal patients in different hospitals.

During our visit Mom, Aunt Emily and Dad, did a lot of reminiscing, especially on the day that they baked cookies. They cried a lot, but after a while they even started too laugh. All the stories were about Evan.

Mom remembered all the times that Evan had brought her roses. She had them labeled and stored away in an album; each rose has a little story taped beside it. His little antics would live on as a part of our family's history. It would be up to me to pass the stories down to my children.

They remembered the many times when we would make oatmeal cookies. Mom and Aunt Emily were laughing about how Evan used to hang around at the beginning of our cookie forming chores. For every cookie ball that Mom rolled, Evan seemed to stuff his mouth with the same amount of raw batter; he looked like a chipmunk with stuffed cheeks. Finally, Mom would have to banish him from the kitchen.

Mom remembered how she got Evan to stop swearing when he was 5 or 6 years of age. When his swearing made it to Mom's ears, Mom would brush his teeth with soap. Evan had the cleanest teeth in the whole city.

Dad retold the story of Evan and Dad's first fishing trip together, while Mom eagerly filled in any missing details. Maybe that is where Evan learned the fine art of spinning a tall-tale.

Mom said, "I swear, each time you and Evan told us about the one that got away, that trout must have grown a half a foot. After a while it sounded like you both let a whale slip away." They all laughed. Dad rubbed Mom's shoulder, before he excused himself; he said he was going out to help some of the neighbors fix Aunt Emily's water line.

Finally, Mom remembered how he used to give her a huge bear hug. Evan called his hugs, 'Celebration Hugs'. Evan used to pick Mom off her feet, twirl her around and when he set her, down he would plant a kiss on her cheek. Mom said she would miss his hugs the most. That was when Mom started to cry, and then Aunt Emily hugged her and began to cry. I watched them; I could not think of anything to say, so I tried to escape from the sadness. Brandy and I quietly slipped outside. I found that there was no escape, because I was feeling as sad as they were.

Dad was busy helping the neighbors fix Aunt Emily's well. Aunt Emily and a couple of her neighbors got together and hired the track-hoe operator for the day. Aunt Emily was lucky enough to be the first to use its services. The thirty-year old water line connecting the well to the trailer had cracked. The track-hoe operator had dug a long, deep trench where a pool of water had formed above the leaking pipe. It was strange seeing Dad down in the trench helping the repairperson; Dad is more of a businessperson, than a fix-it person.

I looked into the trench and asked, "What are they doing?"

A burly man wearing a dark, green baseball cap said, "They're cutting out the cracked water pipe and splicing in a stronger section of hose."

Brandy greeted a young Oriental man spinning and prancing as if he had given her a favorite toy; I thought he must be an old friend. The man greeted Brandy by circling his right hand palms facing in, around Brandy's muzzle. Brandy circled and pranced around at double speed. The young man made a slow, calming stroking motion with his hand; Brandy promptly sat quietly on all fours with her tail still wagging.

I studied the young man. He had neatly cropped, black hair and a calm, cheerful expression.

He said, "Pressure builds in the system at the weakest point. When the flow is broken, then silt eventually backs in and muddies the integrity of the flow. The system needs to be repaired, then cleaned and flushed out." He added, "Life constantly up-grades and changes, in order to maintain itself or build strength."

I asked, "Are you a teacher?"

The man in the green baseball cap turned and gave me a curious, questioning look; he slowly shook his head and said, "No."

The young man answered, "I am a student of the Spirit of God."

I gave a polite nod of my head and turned to walk away. I mumbled, "What can God teach anyone?"

The Oriental man followed me and answered, "A thoughtful question." The man was walking beside me as he said, "The Spirit of God has given all Beings the opportunity to learn from their past. Every choice we make is a brick added to the creation of our true selves. From our choices in every present moment, we are laying the groundwork for our future. Imagination and the Spirit of God, flows around and through all existence, for the Holy Spirit is the creative link which holds all elements through out existence together."

I said, "Holy cow is that a mouthful." As I stared at the man, I thought about what he had said. I whispered, "I wish I could change the past, just a few minutes in the past, is that too much to ask?" I sat and leaned back against a big birch tree, a few yards away from Aunt Emily's trailer. Brandy sat beside me and rested her chin on her paws. I watched the repair people for a few seconds; I put my head on my knees and closed my eyes

I heard the young man ask, "What would you change?"

I found myself thinking about Evan's death. I asked, "Why did my brother have to die? He was so young. His death was so senseless and it caused tremendous pain to so many people."

The young man appeared to be thinking, he scratched his jet-black hair and said, "This question has been asked countless times throughout human history. Nothing is without purpose in the Universe of God. Hardships, pain and death are all part of the cycle of existence; they inspire people to strive, to strengthen and to reevaluate. God, the Creator has given every being the capacity to learn and grow, because God loves all of its creations."

I looked up and asked in a hushed voice, "What does God want me to learn from Evan's death? What did God want Evan to learn? Why has God cut off Evan's opportunity to learn and grow? Evan was trying to help someone and God let him die, is that love?" Anger oozed from my words. Brandy sat up, as she felt my anger. I hugged my legs and rested my chin on my knees as I glared at the man; my anger had zapped away my energy again.

The Man smiled and answered, "Existence is a testing ground for all Souls. Man is like a marionette; often his mind and emotions pull and push him through every experience in his life. The awakened Soul will continue to reach for truth, divine love and spiritual freedom, in spite of opposition or hardship." The man paused before adding, "Your questioning serves a purpose; it's a part of your spiritual journey."

I continued to hugged my legs and rest my chin on my knees. I said, "That's nice, but I guess I don't really care about all of this stuff. It's not going to change anything."

The man said, "Even death is not an obstacle to discovering truth."

"If death is the end, then death is the ultimate obstacle," I said in a matter-of-fact manner.

The man said, "If death is not the end, then perhaps your brother can answer some of your questions. Imagine what your brother would say to you, if he was here."

I mumbled, "That's silly."

As I closed my eyes, I could hear the man whispering, "Just imagine, imagine."

I thought I imagined Evan's voice saying, 'Katy, death is an illusion.' That is when the strangest thing happened. I imagined Evan giving me one of his great big bear hugs. It seemed so real.

I heard the man whisper, "The answers to all your questions await you, Kathleen. Will you continue to seek out truth?" I looked up to give my answer the man was gone. Where had he gone?

I asked Brandy, "Hey girl, where did your friend go?" The man's sudden departure did not seem to bother Brandy.

"What did he mean when he said that death isn't an obstacle?" I asked. I leaned back against the birch tree and closed my eyes. Brandy rested her head on my thigh, as I stroked the silky smooth fur on her head.

I must have fallen asleep. I remembered Dad picking me up. I said, "I was talking to a teacher."

Dad said, "Yes dear."

I added, "Evan gave me a bear hug."

Again, Dad said, "Yes dear."

The next thing I remember Dad was waking me up in the spare bed in Aunt Emily's trailer. I smiled and said, "Hi Dad."

Dad said, "I haven't seen that in a long time."

I yawned and asked, "What?"

"Your smile," Dad answered.

"I guess I haven't felt like smiling lately," I said.

"I understand," Dad said, before he added, "You said you were talking to a teacher. Did this teacher say something to help you feel better?" I stared at Dad, as I tried to remember.

I slowly asked, "What teacher? I don't remember any teacher."

Dad said, "When I carried you into the trailer, I thought you said that you were talking to a teacher. You also said that, Evan hugged you."

I tried to remember, "I think I was dreaming. I don't remember a teacher, but I remember Evan hugging me. I remember . . . it felt so real."

Dad brushed the hair away from my eyes and said, "I'm glad."

"How come I feel so good and so bad at the same time?" I asked.

Dad quietly answered, "Katy, I know from experience that one day your good feelings will outweigh your bad feelings. It will happen in time."

We both jumped, when we heard Mom call, "Hey isn't anyone else hungry?"

Dad and I laughed, before Dad called out, "We'll be right there." He said, "I forgot my mission. I was sent to let you know that supper is ready."

As we ate supper that night, I knew that something had changed. We had hamburgers and I actually enjoyed the meal. It felt like it was good to be alive again. Mom and Dad sat quietly smiling at me; we all realized that I did not feel depressed anymore.

Chapter 3

The Same Old Evan

It has been almost two month since the funeral. Mom said that it is time to come out of hibernation. She means that school is about to start and it's time to get with the program. This day will be another first. School was not going to be the same without Evan around to bug me. Most of the time, I would not even think about Evan, unless my friend Patty started talking about him.

Evan did have a knack for showing up when I was annoyed, which would annoy me even more. Making me more annoyed just made his day. On those days, he really earned his royal-pain nickname. As brothers go, at least Evan knew when he had crossed the line. The good side of him bugging me was; Evan cared.

When I was feeling low, he would bring me a rose. A warm, happy, feeling bubbles up inside of me, when I remember the times when Evan gave me a rose. The first time he gave me this gift was when my goldfish Homer, died. Evan brought me a huge bundle of beautiful red roses. They were perfect and I felt terrific.

That night Evan found out what price he had to pay for the roses. He had to weed Mr. Lee's garden for an entire month. Evan had plucked the roses off the bushes in Mr. Lee's front yard. I know it is no excuse, but I have to say, Evan was nine years old when he did this. I felt sorry for Evan; he got in trouble when he was trying to cheer me up so I helped him with his weeding chores.

After that, whenever he gave Mom or me a rose, Evan would buy a lone rose from the florist shop at the local mall. When Evan was short on cash, he would talk the sales woman into giving him a discount price for an older rose. To Mom, the condition of the rose was not important. Mom said the love that came with the rose was the most important part of the gift. It took me a couple of years to understand what Mom meant.

I loved remembering the good times. Beautiful memories would float through my mind, like scenes from a special old movie. Now, when I close my eyes I see Evan's hand reaching for me. I hear him repeatedly calling my name, but when I look for him, he is gone.

"Katy, honey, it's time to get up." My eyes pop open, Mom gently brushed the hair out of my face. "It's the first day of school." I tried my best to push her voice from my ears. The last thing I wanted to do was to go back to school. Mom bent down to whisper in my ear, "I made your favorite, chocolate pie."

I bolted upright and indignantly said, "Mom, I hate chocolate pie."

"I thought that would get you up," Mom's laughing voice was nice to hear again.

I had to ruin the mood by saying, "Evan loved chocolate pie. I'd eat it if it would bring him back." I was still trying to make a deal with God.

Mom's smile slowly melted from her face and tears came to her eyes. "Mom, I'm sorry. That was a real stupid thing to say. I don't know why I said that," I apologized. "Idiot," I chastised myself with a hushed whisper.

The last thing I wanted to do was make Mom feel bad again. Mom composed herself as I tried to find the right words to say. After Evan's death Mom, Dad and I had cried for days. Dad began to distract himself with his work and I guess, so did Mom; she had finally stopped crying and had done her best to get back into her old routine. I on the other hand, was still angry with God and life in general for taking my brother from me. I was even mad at Evan for dying as if he had a choice in the matter. I wondered *will these feeling ever change? Will the pain ever go away?*

Mom put her hands over mine. A labored smile came back to her face. "We all miss Evan, you know that Katy. I feel for you honey, I feel for all of us but life goes on," Mom said in a controlled voice.

"I know Mom, but it's so hard to think of anything else."

"I feel that too," Mom paused to compose herself, then added, "Give yourself a little time, concentrate on school and friends. We'll make it through this together." Mom gave me a hug, then got up and headed for the door. She added, "Now, get moving. Your favorite homemade blueberry waffles will be waiting for you."

I watched the door close. Of course, Mom missed Evan just as much as I did. Why did he die? That answerless question frustrated me. It was always in my mind, waiting to resurface. Evan was a good swimmer, so why did he have to drown? Travis did not drown, and neither did I. If only I had realized that Evan needed help sooner. I did not want to think about all of that again it would not change anything.

I dragged myself out of bed and lightly ran my fingers over the dried rose that rested on my desk. I remembered dropping it into my pocket. Roses are so beautiful. Unfortunately, this rose was a reminder of Evan's death. It reminded me of the funeral. I dropped the rose into the wastebasket and turned to leave. I circled back to pick up my clothes from my desk chair and froze. My eyes stared at the rose that sat on the middle of my desk. Was it my imagination? I peeked into the empty garbage basket. I was sure that I had just thrown it in the-?

I jumped when Mom yelled, "Katy, your waffles are ready."

I answered, "Okay Mom. I'll be right down." I ran my fingers over the rose to make sure it was real, before I headed down the empty hallway. That was so spooky. I decided that I had imagined getting rid of the rose.

I peeked around the bathroom doorway; I was still ready for Evan. I imagined him flying at me from around the corner, needling me by saying, 'You're terminated. You need eyes in the back of your head get with the game Sis.'

"Stop it Katy," I ordered myself, as I moved down the hallway.

The bathroom floor was cold against my bare feet, but I was grateful for the awakening chill. It was obvious that the pale and weary face that stared back at me from the bathroom mirror needed a restful sleep.

"Pull up your socks, Katy McCall," I ordered myself. "Evan, get out of my head. Quit bugging me."

"Do you really want that Katy?" A familiar voice asked.

I stared across the bathroom; I could barely catch my breath as I blinked my eyes. The hallucination was still there. The hallucination was dressed in a white shirt, slacks and sneakers. Evan never dressed in white.

"No, you're not hallucinating, and you're not going crazy either," the hallucination said, in a-matter-of-fact manner.

"You look like Evan," my voice whispered. I closed my eyes, leaned back against the bathroom door and slowly slid to the floor. I was hoping that the ghost would leave, but when I opened my eyes, the ghost was still there. A familiar tilt of the head, and a familiar concerned look, was on the ghost's face.

"Probably the best way to help you understand what's going on is for me to explain why I'm here," it said.

"Are you for real? Is that you Evan?"

"Yes, it's me," he-it answered. It laughed before it continued to speak. "I was going to say, 'In the flesh,' but that wouldn't exactly be true." It extended its hand. "I'd let you touch me, but that wouldn't work either."

This was too much; I shook my head. I felt like I needed some fresh air and space to refocus.

"If you leave before you listen to what I have to say you'll regret it. You'll wonder what I would have said, or why I've come back for a visit." It paused, as if it was waiting for a response from me. I could not say anything; I was still catching my breath.

It reminded me, "Besides, you're not dressed to go anywhere at the moment."

It sure looked like Evan. It sounded like him too, but I saw them bury Evan. What was going on here?

"By the way, I'm not an 'it'. I am a he. Just call me Evan," he instructed.

We stared at one another. If it was Evan, then death had not changed him. He was still telling me what to do. A mischievous smile appeared on his face. Evan had got to me and he knew it.

"I wanted you to come back so badly, but now I'm not so sure that I do, especially if you're going to start to boss me around again."

Laughter burst out of Evan. It was so loud, I wondered, *could Mom hear him laughing.* I glanced towards the door. Again, he sensed what I had been thinking and said, "Mom will be up here after you if you don't get into gear. I suggest that you get ready while I talk. Feel free to jump in, ask me anything. If I have the answer, I'll answer you. Is it a deal?"

"There isn't a chance in Hades that I'll dress in front of you, turn around," I ordered.

Evan's ghost seemed to have this perpetual smile pasted to his face. "That's the old Katy I know and love. I wondered where she had gone. Welcome back. . . . I guess you haven't given me the same welcome, because you're not sure if I'm your brother Evan. Am I right?"

"I can decide who, or what you are on my own," I informed him.

"Fair enough," he answered.

"So, who, or what are you?" I asked.

"That would take a little too long to explain right now." His smile had vanished, and all but the warmth in his eyes become stiff and business like. Evan continued to sit on the toilet seat, as he turned to face the yellow sea shells that decorated the pale blue wallpaper that covered the bathroom wall.

I rose to my feet and silently stared at the back of his head as *I wondered if he could somehow see me.* I made no move to begin to change into my street clothes.

"I can't see you, so hurry up and get dressed. Mom will be up here at any moment. She's already wondering what's taking you so long. I'm looking at the wall," Evan expressed his exasperation. He added, "Will you move it."

"You can read my mind. Stop that!" I yelled at him.

Evan started to turn, but turned back towards the wall. "I can't read your mind. Pipe down before Mom hears you. Man, sometimes you're really a jerk." After he said this, Evan moaned with frustration. "Will you hurry up?" Evan implored.

Evan seemed to be trying to calm himself by deep breathing, and I think he was humming. It must have been my imagination. Evan mumbled something like, "Spiritual Master, she's going to drive me nuts." It made no sense.

"What did you say?" I asked.

Evan took a calming breath before speaking. "Look, I'm sorry I called you a jerk. You are just reacting like most people would, if they were in the same situation. For the record I want to say, I can't read thoughts. When I am tuned in I feel what people are feeling. It's sort of like being psychic, but better. I feel the spiritual essence that flows through every cell in our bodies; it is all around us. I tune into what is called, 'The Soul of life.' Everyone can do this, but most people haven't developed this skill yet.

"Evan-." I started to speak, but Evan cut me off.

"Shh," he put his forefinger against his lips.

Someone knocked on the bathroom door. I dropped my clothes in shock. "Katy. Honey, are you all right?" Mom asked.

I grabbed my head with both of my hands and whispered, "You've done it now. Mom heard me talking to you. I bet she thinks I've gone bonkers. What should I do?" I pleaded with Evan to give me divine inspiration.

"Open the door and let Mom know you're alright." Evan spoke without whispering. I placed my hand over my mouth and shook my head. He was getting me mad. How in the world was I going to explain anything?

"Katy, are you all right?" The tone in Mom's voice rang with impatience and I think, fear. She heard his voice and she was freaking out. How could I open the door? What would Mom do if she saw him?

Evan spoke again in a normal voice. "Mom can't see me, or hear me, only you can." We stared at one another.

Mom knocked on the door and shouted, "Katy! Open this door now!" Grace McCall is a quiet person, calm and laid-back, so when she issued an order, we knew she was serious. If Mom stepped into the role of worried, concerned mother, her entire five-foot-three frame changed into a brick wall of determination.

I opened the door and held my breath. Mom was looking straight at Evan, but she did not react. Evan's ghost was still sitting on the toilet seat, watching the both of us.

I jumped as Evan repeated, "I told you, only you can see me, or hear me."

I covered my mouth and said, "Excuse me. I have the hiccups."

"Mom's looking at me and she can't see me," Evan emphasized.

"Why?" I asked.

"Because I'm here for you," Evan answered.

Mom also answered my question, "You sounded like you were talking to someone." Mom scanned the bathroom. "Maybe my ears were playing tricks on me. You're all right aren't you Katy?" I guessed that Mom was wondering about my reaction to Evan's nonexistent voice.

"Sure Mom. I'm fine," I assured her. "I was just giving myself a pep talk before school, like you suggested. You know, it being the first day and all." I hoped that this explanation would explain my strange behavior.

Evan spoke again and this time I did not jump. "Mom is doing okay, isn't she?" I nodded my head. "You don't have to worry about her coping with my death, do you?"

"I'm not worried," I assured him.

"Honey, it's natural to be a little worried about the first day of the school year. Worrying is just a part of living. I worry about you sometimes. You're my baby," Mom brushed my dark brown locks back from my face and kissed my cheek. "You need to cut your hair," she added, as she fingered my hair before letting it drop down to my shoulder.

"Ah Mom," Mom knew I would react this way. "I'm not a baby. I haven't worn diapers for almost 14 years." Mom saying that always annoyed me. However, today I did not get irritated because I sensed that it made Mom feel good.

I added, "I'm all right Mom. Don't worry about me."

"I know you are, but you'll always be my baby and I'll always be your mother." Mom added in a quiet voice, "We're the "Three Musketeers" now." Mom was thinking about Evan. As a family, we use to call ourselves the 'Four Musketeers'. Mom's thoughts returned to breakfast and school. "Katy, your breakfast is getting cold. I'll reheat your waffles. You don't want to be late on your first day of school." Mom turned to leave.

"Mom, Evan's okay wherever he is. I know it," I whispered. Mom hesitated, and then nodded her head before she closed the door. I listened to her quiet footsteps, as she moved down the hallway.

"I shouldn't have said that," I mumbled. I looked up at Evan and said, "Mom just wants to forget that you're gone, but I keep on reminding her that you're gone. How come I keep doing that?" I wondered aloud.

"Mom's needs time to heal from my death. She has to be ready to give up the pain before that will happen. In the end, that's something she'll need to do for herself at her own pace," Evan concluded.

Although I knew Evan was talking about all of us I said, "You're telling me to put a sock in it, right?"

Evan shook his head and answered, "No Katy, I'm not going to tell you what to say. You have a right to figure out what to say for yourself. It's your life, not mine. I'm just a visitor," Evan added.

"Evan, it's not easy to know what to say. I think I put my foot in my mouth more times, than I can count. Sometimes I'm afraid to open my mouth," I admitted.

"Katy," Evan said as he shook his head, "Do you think the awkward foot in the mouth experiences that you've had, are good for nothing? Sometimes, you don't realize the importance of what you're learning when you're going through an experience. I have a feeling that you'll find that out for yourself, very soon."

"What do you mean? Are you saying that in the future I'll be putting my foot in my mouth a lot more?" I asked, before adding, "Couldn't I just skip that part of my life?"

"What, and miss all the fun," Evan joked. I groaned. Evan quickly added, "Those milliseconds of life are necessary elements, you'll grow to know this."

"They're necessary elements?" I repeated.

"Katy, just follow your intuition. Follow what your heart and Soul is telling you. That's all I'm going to say right now, I've already said more than enough. I'm going to leave you now."

"No!" I yelled.

"Hey, don't worry, I'll be back," he assured me.

"You promise?" I wanted a promise that I could hold.

"I promise. My word of honor on it," Evan promised. "Katy, I'm glad you believe I'm me. Hey, thanks for the rose. Now when you look at your rose you can remember our visits." Evan smiled at my shocked expression and added, "I can still give you roses."

"You put the rose back on my desk?" I asked.

"Yup," Evan answered. "And Katy," As he spoke his image began to fade, Evan and the bathroom wall slowly merged and became one. He was gone from my sight, but I heard him complete the sentence, "You were right, it was a nice funeral."

Chapter 4

A Surprise in Heaven

As usual, Patty Burbick and I would be walking to school together. We met when we were toddlers peering at one another through our adjoining yard fence. Our friendship had endured fifteen years of differences. Patty had loved to play with dolls, she played house and made mud-pies, yuk, I could not stand mud pies. I was happiest when I was building sand castles, and drawing dragons, fair maidens and knights. We finally compromised when playing together, combining Patty's choice of playing house with my make believe worlds.

Patty is a lanky girl; her five-foot-nine frame is thin and straight as a rod. Until we entered junior high, she always towered over most of the boys in our grade. She thought of herself as the tall scrawny one. I saw a different Patty, for I knew that someday, she would be beautiful.

I was the opposite of Patty. Katy McCall had inherited her mother's genes, lucky me. Evan used to say that I was a five-three compact block of energy, a duplicate Mom, a chip off the old block. I think he meant it as a compliment, because Evan thought Mom was the ideal Mom.

One time Evan caught me looking into the mirror, primping, and sucking in my cheeks. I was dreaming about being tall and stunning.

Evan threw this line at me, "So you're not on the cover of Life Magazine."

I said, "Vogue."

He continued, "Right, Vogue. You and about three billion other women are not on the cover of Vogue. You are all in the same boat and the boat is still floating. Go do something else." I think Evan thought that I was scatter-brained.

Evan did not know it, but I had realized a long time ago that I would not make it in the world by riding on my looks. I wanted to do other things. I had dreamed of being an artist. I thought that Evan could write stories that I could illustrate. I am not sure if I want to do that anymore.

Life is confusing. Evan is here, but not here. I guess I have him to lean on after all. I am the lucky one. Patty, poor Patty no longer has Evan in her life. She had this humongous crush on him. On the days that he walked us to school, I swear I could hear her heart beating. If Evan spoke to her, she would almost melt into the sidewalk. I am exaggerating, a little. On those days, I would get jealous. Patty had a crush on him and I think he was beginning to like her too. I felt like I was losing my best friend and my brother in one shot; I was a third wheel.

I am not jealous anymore. I feel sorry for Patty, because she misses him as much as I did. She wept buckets at the funeral, while I did not shed a tear. I was sure I was not going to, considering that I knew that he was still sort-of alive.

"Are you all right Katy?" Patty asked. She peered down at me and waited for an answer.

It seemed like hundreds of well meaning people had asked me that same question and it irritated me. I answered with an 'Oh no, this again' attitude. My answer was short, quick and indifferent. "Sure. I'm fine. How come you ask?"

"You're so quiet. You miss Evan a lot don't you?" Patty was trying to give me support again. Could she not see that I was fine?

I groaned and answered, "Of course I miss him. He's my only brother," I snapped.

"He's gone Katy," Patty whispered.

"No he's . . . I mean, I know he's gone. I'm not stupid," I answered.

"I miss him a lot too. You know I had an enormous crush on him, don't you?" Patty whispered as if this was a great secret.

"I know. You told me enough times, 'He's great looking, he's smart, he's funny, and he's nice.' Please, don't tell me that again." I finished the list with an irritated scowl. I had heard it all so many times before. Patty looked dejected, probably because of my foul mood.

"I'm sorry Patty," I gave a tired apology. It felt like my nine-hundredth and ninety-ninth apology. My bad moods resulted in me making repeated apologies. "It's just that I'm not in the mood to talk about Evan right now." It was a sorry excuse for my mood. We walked without speaking, until we were a block from Crestmore High. That is when Patty broke the silence.

"Evan said I was pretty," Patty reminded me. "It happened when I was waiting for you to finish helping to do the dishes; it was May 23rd, of this year. I will never forget that day. It was the perfect day, warm, with a little breeze." Patty stared into space, all starry-eyed with her memories. "Can you believe that?" Patty asked.

She would never forget that day and neither would I. Patty had repeated that memory to me so many times; it made me want to kick Evan for telling her that. "That's nice Patty," was all I could think to say.

"Oh Katy, how can you stand it? He's not my brother and I can hardly stand it."

I finally realized that Patty wanted to talk about Evan, not to comfort me, but to talk about her own feelings. She was searching for a little comfort for herself. I was getting nervous. Patty looked like she was going to cry. I was inept at talking to people who were crying. I gave her a hug and when she calmed down, I let go. I wondered if I should tell her that Evan was not truly dead. Would she understand what I meant? I stared at Patty's questioning face.

"You can't tell anyone about me," Evan yelled. I screamed and jumped away from Patty. Patty screamed and jumped at my sudden reaction as she clutched her heart.

"Don't do that," I ordered.

"Katy, I didn't do anything," Patty said. "You're the one who yelled, why did you do that?"

"Why? Uh, I thought I saw a spider on your shoulder." I brushed off Patty's right shoulder for effect. This freaked Patty out; she began to twirl around, as she repeatedly brushed at her shoulder.

"Is it gone?" she asked.

"Yeah, it's gone. It was probably a hallucination," I said, as I stared at Evan.

He was sitting on the lawn next to us, holding his stomach, while he cracked up laughing. As he caught his breath, Evan managed to repeat, "You can't tell Patty about me."

"Why?" I asked.

"Why . . . what do you mean by 'why'?" Patty asked.

"Because people will think that you're crazy," Evan answered. "It's better to keep silent about my presence in your life," Evan suggested.

"What's the why question?" Patty repeated.

"Why, why . . . do you hate spiders so much?" I finally asked.

"They're creepy weird looking creatures. Who cares why I hate spiders?" Patty's exasperation voice rang with confusion.

"Why do you miss Evan so much?" I quickly added.

"What's with you, Katy? You ask me about spiders and Evan in the same breath. Are you trying to confuse me?" Patty asked. "You scare the wits out of me and then ask me stupid questions. You know I miss Evan. You know I liked him. You don't listen to me Katy. You don't ever listen to me," Patty emphasized.

Evan interrupted Patty's monologue and instructed, "Tell Patty that I said I liked her and missed her too."

I shook my head and repeated, "No, no, no, do you know who is going to have to answer hundreds of questions? Not you buddy," I concluded.

"What are you talking about?" Patty cautiously asked.

"Evan said he liked you, and so, he probably missed you too," I said in desperation for something to say.

"He did!" Patty's eyes lit-up.

"No, no he didn't. I was trying to make you feel better." I watched the light in Patty's eyes fade as what I said sank in.

"Katy, you don't know how to cheer someone up. Someone should teach you how," Patty yelled.

"I'm sorry," I apologized again.

"Why did you say that?" Evan asked.

"I'll never hear the end of it," I answered. Evan stared at me with a scowl on his face. "I'm not your messenger," I informed him.

"Well excuse me for living," Patty exclaimed before adding, "Who asked you to be? You think I can't speak for myself?"

"Patty I wasn't talking to you. I was talking to, myself," I finally concluded.

"Yeah sure you were, and I have been talking to the man on the moon. Forget it Katy. Just forget it." She began to run, I watched Patty cross the Avenue in front of Crestmore, muttering as she ran.

"Look what you've done," I accused Evan.

"What did I do?" he innocently asked. We both watched Patty, as her long strides quickly added to the distance between us. Patty's anger would increase the length of her stride, because she would be trying to put distance between herself and the thing that got her angry; today, that thing was yours truly, Katy McCall. In a few seconds, she would be entering Crestmore High.

"I'll be lucky if she ever talks to me again and it's your fault, buddy." I pointed an accusing finger at Evan as I said this. "Everything was normal until you showed up." I turned and ran after Patty.

"And normal is good?" Evan yelled after me. A few seconds passed before I heard him scream, "Katy!"

Evan's timely scream prevented me from becoming a pancake under the wheels of Andrew Dover's red VW convertible. My left hand was not so lucky; it bounced off the right head light before I could pull it away. After Andrew's car screeched to a stop, he launched himself out from behind the steering wheel slammed the car door and stood glaring at me over the back of the convertible.

"Are you crazy? I could have killed you. Why don't you watch where you're going?" Andrew yelled.

I rubbed my left hand, as I stared blankly at the car. That was so close. I looked up at Andrew's face. An apology squeaked from my throat and emerged between chattering teeth. The words were barely audible, even to me. I was sure he did not hear my apology. Andrew had a, stunned, shocked look on his face.

"Hey buddy, no one yells at my sister," Evan yelled.

"He doesn't hear you," I whispered a reminder. "Besides, it was my fault."

"You bet it was your fault. Now I know why Mom has grey hair. If I were still alive that stunt would have scared me to death. Don't do that again. You need to watch where you're going. I'm not always going to be around to save your bacon," Evan shouted.

I shook my head and asked, "Are you finished?"

Evan sighed and said, "Yeah, I'm finished."

I whispered, "I'm sorry I scared you."

Andrew must have thought I was talking to him, because he began to apologize to me. "I'm sorry I yelled at you. You just scared the . . . . Are you okay? He asked.

"I . . ." I was going to say that I was not talking to him, but I caught myself. "I'm all right. It was my fault. I wasn't watching where I was going." Andrew noticed me rubbing my hand as he approached me from around the back of his convertible.

He asked, "How's your hand?" He carefully held my left hand in his two hands, and gently massaged the back of my hand with his two thumbs. I watched the expression on Andrew's face with the same concentration he gave my hand, he was truly concerned.

"There is some swelling," he announced, "You should really get your hand checked out," he suggested. I felt pain in my hand, but I hardly noticed it. I pulled my hand out of his grasp.

"It's okay," I assured him. It was getting hot and I was finding it hard to breathe. I had a feeling it wasn't because of the accident. "I've got to get to class," I quickly said. "Sorry about all the trouble. I'm sure my hand is fine." I turned and rushed towards the red brick high school.

Andrew walked beside me and said, "I can think of easier ways to meet people than to almost get run over."

"I know what you mean," I agreed. I smiled up at him, and then quickly turned towards the school. He smiled at me and it made me nervous.

"Hey," he stepped in front of me. "What's your name?" Andrew asked. I stared at him without answering. The question surprised me. He added, "I might need to know for insurance purposes, just in case you dented my car with your hand," he joked.

"Tell him your name," Evan nudged me. Evan had materialized beside Andrew.

"It's Katy, Katy McCall," I stated.

"My name's Andrew Dover."

"I know," I said before I could stop myself.

Andrew smiled and joked, "My reputation precedes me." He hesitated before adding, "I hope you've heard good things."

I nodded my head as I answered, "It's all been good." I groaned. I really had a bad case of *foot-in-my-mouth syndrome.*

"If you know me, how come I don't know you?" he asked.

I stared at Evan standing quietly beside Andrew, before I answered his question. "My brother was Evan McCall. You were one of his instructors during his lifeguard training. I used to sit in the balcony and watch the classes."

"You're McCall's kid sister? Hey, I'm sorry about what happened. I wish there was something I could do to make things all right for you."

"Evan's all right. I mean, wherever he is, he's okay." Oh man, Andrew probably thought I was nuts.

Andrew squinted at me, or maybe he was frowning at me. I do know that he was trying to smile, as he tried to figure out what I had just said. "Evan could get along anywhere, with anyone, so you're probably right," Andrew was trying so hard to be kind and nice. I thought he was the most wonderful guy that I had ever met.

"I always liked the guy," Evan said. It seemed that what Andrew said about Evan had a positive affect on him. "Now I have another reason to like him, he makes you smile a lot," Evan observed.

Evan was right. Andrew was the first person who didn't expect me to play the role of the mourning sister. I liked that. I also liked that he was an all around nice guy. What wasn't there to like?

"What grade are you in? Ten?" he guessed. I nodded my head.

"Don't be a mouse Katy, answer his question," Evan ordered.

"Yes," burst from my lips. I sent Evan an angry frown.

"Hey, there's nothing wrong with that. We all have to go through it." Andrew had misunderstood my annoyance.

"Someone's in trouble," Evan warned. He pointed towards the street. I relayed Evan's warning to Andrew.

"Blast it," Andrew muttered, as he headed back to his car. He turned and shouted, "I'll see you around Katy McCall." Andrew got back to his car just as a second car and then a police car began to move around his VW. He seemed to be apologizing to the officer for blocking traffic. Then both vehicles departed.

"He's definitely a nice guy," Evan repeated.

"You said that already," I reminded him. "You said that just after you were yelling at him, for yelling at me."

Evan laughed before responding, "I guess I still can blow a gasket even when I'm in this body. I'll have to work on mellowing my temper.

"Evan, I would love to needle you about what you just said. You're lucky there isn't any time to do that." I checked my watch. "I've got to get going, or I'll have to wait in line for my class schedule, forever. See you later." I readjusted my backpack and started jogging to class.

Evan was beside me, speaking as he jogged. "Katy, that guy is really a good guy. He has a positive energy, or aura. I can feel it in his vibes, you know, vibrations."

"Evan you don't believe in that stuff. You're the one who said that, 'Auras are figments of someone's colorful imagination', end quote," I finished.

Evan laughed and said, "Boy, you don't forget anything do you. I did say that but now I know better. I see them and I've learned that they represent all our energies, our physical, emotional, mental and subconscious energies. Our aura is a reflection of who we are. Seeing an aura is no big deal. It's like a phenomenon, a child's spiritual toy. There's another more important life energy called Soul. We'll talk about that later. Do you want to know what your aura looks like at this moment in time?"

"Sure," I jumped at the chance.

Evan explained, "An aura is illuminated with different colors, and each color represents a different aspect of you. Bright colors are good. Orange reflects health, green is vitality and growth, blue is for wisdom, indigo for intuition, and red reflects your life energy. You have all these colors, including a little blue and indigo. You also have streaks of muddied red, which means you're holding some anger."

I ignored Evan's last comment and changed the subject. "That blue must be a mistake. I'm not wise Evan."

Evan explained, "Blue isn't a dominant color, but its there. You have a wisdom that you haven't begun to explore. Remember Katy, your aura doesn't lie."

"Where did you learn this stuff?" I asked. The old Evan didn't know all this.

"Katy, there's so much more to life and existence than the average person could imagine with their physical awareness, but right now we both have to get to our classes."

"What do you mean?" I asked.

Evan explained, "I have to get to class." For a second I thought Evan was trying to pull the wool over my eyes, but my inner feelings, the intuition that Evan had just talked about, told me that he was serious.

"There is school in heaven?" I laughed at the idea of Evan still having to go to school. "Finding out you had to go to school must have been a big joke on you," I needled Evan.

Evan slowly nodded his head before answering, "Yeah, at first I thought I had ended up in hell. All it took was to attend one class, for me to know that the class was no hell. It's a privilege and honor, to be able to go to school there."

"You want to go to school? You like it?" I asked.

Evan nodded his head, smiled and said, "School is voluntary and I'm always in school. The key is to be aware of the experiences and the lessons." Evan added, "I really have to go now. Let's meet after school at your home." With that, he waved good-bye and vanished from my sight.

I was feeling very comfortable with this new reality. I loved having Evan back. Until life could prove otherwise, Evan's presence would be part of my accepted reality. At the same time, I knew Evan was right when he said that I couldn't tell anyone about his coming back. Society has a tendency to lock away, or ostracize people who fail to follow accepted ideals. I knew it was not a normal occurrence for a sister to visit her dead brother. He was right. I needed to keep silent in regards to his return.

I walked up the cement stairs and stopped to lean on the red brick and cement guardrails. I stared at the school's double doors, while I wondered what Evan's school was like. I was no longer in a hurry. One thought kept running through my head *school in heaven; imagine that.*

Chapter 5

My Dream Escort

Schools have a distinct smell to them. If you are one of the first people to enter these halls of learning on a Monday morning, a clean, scrubbed down, polished scent floats around us stimulating your olfactory senses. The school seems like a pearl white canvas waiting for an artist to make the first brush stroke; and the students and teachers are the strokes of paint that brings life to this canvas. Each day is a link in the chain that forms this living mural. I wondered, *'Who is the artist?'*

Dozens of students have already passed through the hallways. The scent of perfumes, colognes and 'Mr. Clean'; lingers in the air. A few stragglers stroll down the hallway, for them, summer break is not over until the first class begins. I heard voices; everyone else must be in the gym.

On the first day of classes students are supposed to meet in the large gym to pick up their class schedules. Patty and I had decided to pick the same classes, except she selected Food Sciences, and I chose Woodworking as my option class. We were hoping to have most of our classes together.

Students and teachers packed the gym. Evan had once said that school is a microcosm of the world, he was right. Everyone is trying to find their special groove, the place where they fit in. If you belong to a group of two or more students, you are no longer a loner, and you gain a sense of security and belonging. This makes being in school, a lot easier to experience and live through. We all hope to find our niche.

There are cool kids; at least many kids think they are cool. There are the jocks and their fans. Then you have the brains and the average kids. There are floaters, those who have not found their niche. Each group has the want to-bees. They are the ones who are trying to make it into a certain group. I am an average kid, a kid who just lives life and does her best; maybe we are all average kids.

There are conflicts, clashes and resolutions. Each person and group has his or her own personal space and territory. There are written, unspoken and taken-for-granted rules. We have the peacekeepers, the leaders and diplomats. There are the future teachers, the police officers and political leaders. The little groups in our school were, as Evan had once said, 'A microcosm of the big world outside.' I guess living in this student community is really preparing us for the world out there.

As these thoughts float through my consciousness, I hear a whispered voice, "Celebrate the uniqueness of differences and respect all Souls." I quickly turned and looked around; there was no one else near the auditorium entrance.

I whispered, "Evan?" I waited for an answer. Was it my imagination? This was so strange because I knew that thought was not my thought. I moved into the auditorium.

Most students have already found old friends; familiar groups have formed all over the gym. Students in each grade are lining up alphabetically as they go through the process of picking up their class schedules.

I scanned the gym and searched for Patty. I spotted Andrew, surrounded by a group of his friends, a bunch of them are girls. They're talking and joking with him. He looked in my direction I ducked; there are some advantages to being short. I made my way towards the grade tens and Patty; I could see her even though I was crouching.

Patty doesn't tower over people as she used to in junior high, now there are many people who are her height or taller. Patty spotted me and urgently waved to me. When I reach her, she pulls me into her line.

"Katy, what took you so long?" She points to the next line. "Martha Miller is saving you a spot in line. "Where were you?"

"Patty, guess what happened. I-," Patty was so excited; she could not stop to listen to me.

"Look behind you," Patty whispered her instructions. When I began to turn around, she grabbed my arm and said, "No, don't be so obvious. Be casual; start looking over your right shoulder then turn slowly to your right."

"Patty, just let me be casual in my own way. I'll do it in a way that my neck can handle." I turned my head to the right and then I slowly shift my eyes to look further back.

I whispered, "It would help if I knew what I was looking for."

Patty whispered impatiently, "Don't you notice him?" I glanced around as I shook my head. "Chester Langley, he must have grown at least three inches over the summer, he's a bit taller than I am now. Isn't he a dream come true?"

"That's Chester? He's a dream, no. No, I mean if he was my type, then definitely, but he isn't. I'm not saying that there's anything wrong with him, he's nice. You should go talk to him when you get the chance. Definitely talk to him," I repeated.

"You think so, Katy?"

"Yes. Talk to him."

"But I wouldn't know what to say to him. Do you think he will remember me? What in the world should I say?" Patty repeated.

"Maybe reintroducing yourself would be a good start. Tell him when you first met. Then you could say something about how much taller he seems to be. Ask him about his classes, you might be in the same classes together." Patty seemed to be over Evan, and over her angry feeling towards me. She was moving on with her life.

"That's a great idea," Patty agreed. "Thanks Katy, you're a real pal." Patty was next in line to pick up her schedule. After I picked up my schedule, we ripped open our envelopes and studied the contents. Patty said excitedly, "Katy, I got every class I asked for."

"I got the classes I asked for too," I confirmed. Together we yelled, "All right!" We celebrated with an enthusiastic high-five. I screamed in pain and scared Patty again. I bent over and clutched my left arm to my stomach. Since I held my envelope in my right hand, I used my left hand to celebrate. Tears welled up in my eyes as even though I tried to block out the pain.

"What happened?" Patty asked. I didn't hit you that hard."

When I finally answered Patty, I tried to make a joke out of my reaction. "You just don't know your own strength Patty."

When I looked up into her face, I could tell she was worried. "I knocked my hand this morning. It didn't seem that bad," I explained. My hand was throbbing. Patty was worried about me again and that was the last thing I wanted.

I smiled and said, "Patty, I'm all right. Look Patty, Chester, he is watching us. Now is your chance to go over and introduce yourself." Patty turned and looked at him. "Smile Patty," I instructed. She smiled. "Wave to him," I added. She waved at him. Man, I was as bad as Evan was, even worse. "Patty, he's smiling at you. You have his attention. Go for it," I instructed.

"Patty gave me a panic filled look, before she turned and walked towards him. She had a nervous smile pasted to her face. Patty introduced herself. Once Chester had gotten over his shock, he was laughing at something she had said. I gathered myself together and moved across the auditorium. My schedule was in my right hand, as my right forearm supported my left forearm and wrist.

"Hey McCall, how's the hand?" I looked up into Andrew's smiling face.

"I'm fine; it's as good as new." I flexed it to show him the truth, first hand, so to speak. I caught my breath through clenched teeth.

"Nice touch, do you always wince when you move your hand? Don't tell me. Let me guess, it's a family trait," Andrew joked.

"What are you talking about? I didn't wince." Before I could move, Andrew grabbed my hand. I gasped and yanked my hand out of his grip. "Don't do that," I ordered.

"Holy! I'm sorry. I didn't mean to hurt you." I hardly noticed Andrew's startled reaction.

"Forget it," I managed to say. "I have to go." I picked up my envelope and moved to get around him. If I was going to cry, I was not going to cry in front of him.

Andrew asked, "You're going to get that hand checked out, aren't you?"

"Yeah, sure," I said as I kept on walking. Andrew became my shadow. I turned and ordered, "Stop following me." Pain was definitely affecting my mind.

"I'm not following you. We're just walking in the same direction," Andrew explained.

"Yeah, sure," I said, before turning and resuming my journey.

Once again, Andrew fell in step beside me. He resumed asking his questions. "It's bothering you, isn't it?" I didn't answer him. "You're going to have it checked out, right? . . . You really should get it checked as soon as possible."

I stopped walking and answered him, "You don't have to worry about me. I'm fine." He was smiling at me and I automatically smiled back at him. "What's so funny?" I asked.

"You are," he stated. He shook his head and added, "You're deceptive; do you know that? I never expected you to be such a stubborn little thing."

"I'm not little," I tried to say with conviction.

Andrew's smile grew. He could see that I was not fond of the word 'little'. He laughed before he asked, "Will you do this one little favor for me? It's just a little favor. Get the hand looked at, please?" He put great emphasis on the words, 'little' and 'please'. "It would really ease my little mind," he joked.

"I said before that it wasn't your fault," I reminded him.

"Come on. You're not going to make me beg, are you?" Andrew had these sort-of puppy dog eyes.

"Okay, enough already. I'll go." I laughed even though I tried not to. I added, "You have the same look as my Aunt Emily's dog Brandy. I can't say no to Brandy. Plus," I smiled as I shook my head and said, "You sound like my mother."

"No kidding. I look like your Aunt's dog and I sound like your mother." Laughter burst from me. Andrew cheerfully added, "I'd say that you have a pretty nice sounding mother. You can tell your nice sounding mother that it was my pleasure, when you see her."

Andrew smiled at the curious expression on my face, before I asked, "What are you talking about? Why should I tell my Mom that?"

"Why, for being your escort to the office so you can report the accident and get your hand looked at, of course." With these words, he took my schedule and extended his arm, as if he was going to escort me on to a ballroom floor. I stared at his extended arm for a second before I smiled and placed my hand on his arm. I tried my best to look regal, as we left the auditorium. People were watching us, but the funny thing was it didn't matter.

I looked at Andrew and tried to tally up why girls found him so attractive. His beautiful warm smile and great sense of humor caught their attention. I was sure that after a girl had gotten to know him, his considerate, kind, wonderful goodness held their hearts. His eyes were amazing; they sparkled. It was as if there were yellow highlights in them. I had been trying not to stare into them, but I was not very successful. Our walk ended too soon.

"Thanks for walking me to the office. Maybe I should run into cars more often." I smiled at him. It was hard to do otherwise.

Andrew laughed, but this time it was a nervous laugh. He stared at me for a second before saying, "Do me a favor and make this the last time you do that. You came close to giving me a heart attack. I'd rather not go through that again."

"I was joking," I whispered.

"I wasn't," he whispered back. He was being so serious and as a result, I was at a loss for words. Andrew sensed my nervousness and said, "I'll go in with you and explain what happened."

I shook my head and said, "It's not necessary. I'm fine."

Andrew looked at me and slowly answered, "Okay." He didn't sound convinced. He turned to leave.

I said, "Andrew." He turned around and I looked into those amazing eyes. I said, "Thanks for all your help and concern."

"No sweat," he said. Then he pointed to the office and said, "Remember, you promised."

Extending two fingers in what I hoped was a Boy Scout salute, I said, "Scout's honor."

"I guess I'll believe you, even though I know you've never been a boy scout," he said, as he waved.

"See you around," I called after him.

"You can count on it McCall," he said, before he left.

"You can count on it," I repeated. I had a smile plastered on my face as I walked into the office. I explained the situation to the school secretary, Mrs. Wendle. I think she was wondering why I was so happy.

While I waited for Mom, I relived the morning's events. Evan and Andrew, it was like a fragile dream. If it weren't for the pain in my hand, I would have thought that everything was a dream. The pain kept me focused on the here and now.

I saw this old movie on video titled, <u>Network News</u>. In the movie, William Hurt portrayed a network newscaster. In one scene, the newscaster confides to one of his co-workers and asks, "What do you do when your life exceeds your dreams?" His friend answers, "Don't tell anyone." I felt like that. It's like . . . if I tell anyone about this, then this reality will become the dream. I'm keeping my fingers crossed, just in case

Chapter 6

Imagination or Reality

Mrs. Wendle had called Mom and it took twenty minutes for her to arrive. While I was waiting the school nurse Mrs. Larkin, looked at my injury. She wrapped an ice pack in a towel and had me hold it on my wrist. The secretary notified the school councilor. What a hassle.

Mom must have been working at the apartment building, because she appeared in her bulky, navy overalls. They make her look like a kid playing dress-up. Mom was nervous and fidgety; I thought she must not have had her morning coffee. After I had this thought Mom said she would be right back, she was going to get a cup of coffee. Too much coffee or sometimes not enough coffee made Mom very hyperactive, so she limited herself to a couple of cups a day.

In a few minutes, Mom returned to sign some release forms. Then she taxied me over to the Barfield Clinic to have our family doctor, old Doc Sorenson examine the injury. He had been our doctor for as long as I could remember. I called him 'Doc'. He reminded me of a Santa Claus who had come off a very successful diet. Size wise, the Doc could have given Patty stiff competition in the thinness category. White and gray highlights peppered his hair and beard. His spectacles were constantly sliding down the bridge of his nose and he was constantly nudging them back into place.

Mom said he was a first class doctor. Evan had said he was an okay guy and a great 'Doc'. They were right, he knew his doctoring stuff, but what I really liked about him was his knack for finding a person's funny bone. On the laugh meter, he gave Andrew a run for his money.

When he found out that I had a collision with a car, he teased me and asked, "What were you doing, watching the boys or dreaming about them?" The doctor knew about my reputation for daydreaming. When I was nine years old, I walked into the limb of a tree and cut my forehead just under my bangs. The Doc did a great job of stitching it up; the scar is barely noticeable. On that occasion, the Doc nicknamed me 'The Dreamer'.

After Doc examined my hand and wrist, he diagnosed that I had a bruised hand and a possible hairline fracture of one of my metacarpal bones. The Doc sent me for an x-ray to the diagnostic lab located in the basement area of the building. The x-ray results would be ready in about an hour's time.

Doc Sorenson was right. The second metacarpal bone had a hairline fracture. He also diagnosed a strained ligament in my wrist. Doc had the nurse show me how to place a tensor bandage around my wrist. The nurse also showed me how to put my wrist in a sling, to ensure that the blood would not pool in my hands or fingers. She said to secure my hand slightly above the heart level, this position also made the blood's journey back to the heart easier. The nurse warned me to loosen the tensor if my fingers began to swell. I would be wearing a tensor bandage for at least a week. The Doc gave a final warning, "Do absolutely no strenuous lifting." After that, I would have to be careful for a couple of weeks.

I did not make it back to any of my classes on this day. Both Mom and the Doc thought it was best that I go home and rest.

Andrew had been right to goad me into getting my hand checked. I wondered *what Andrew would say if he saw my arm in a sling*.

"You look tired," Mom said. "Right now, rest is the best medicine for you. Dad or I will drive you to school early tomorrow, so you can get your classes straightened out." I nodded and agreed. There was no way I was going to argue with Mom's logic. Doc had given me a painkiller, so I slept on our ride home; he also prescribed a few extra painkillers to help me survive the next few days.

When we got home, I poured myself a glass of apple juice, while Mom brought out a plate of turkey sandwiches and a bowl of celery sticks from the fridge. "I have to get back to the apartment building, but I'll be back in time to get supper on the table or I'll pick-up a pizza. After you've finished your lunch I want you to head up stairs to get some sleep. Don't drag your feet, just go. Are we reading off the same page?"

"Mom, I'm not totally out to lunch." Mom was not in a joking mood, so I quickly added, "A-okay Mom," as I continued to eat.

As Mom put the dishes in the sink, she asked me a question that caught me totally by surprise, "Katy, who is Andrew Dover?"

All I could say was a stunned, "What?"

"Hold it," Mom said as she held her hands up. "I don't want to know right now. I have a feeling that this will be a long explanation. I have to get back to work. We'll talk when I get back." Mom ended the conversation with a kiss on my forehead. The doorbell rang as Mom was leaving. "I'll get that on my way out," she said as she left the kitchen.

"Mom, how did you . . . Mom, how?" I called after her, but she had already answered the front door. I bit into my sandwich and listened, while Mom spoke to whoever was at the front door.

I heard Mom say, "She's in the kitchen having her lunch, go right in Patty, you know the way." Mom's voice raised a couple of decibels as she said, "Katy has promised to get rest after she finishes her lunch, so don't make it a long visit."

Patty answered in an equally loud voice, "Sure Mrs. M. no problem. I just want to see how she's doing. I'll make my visit short, I promise."

"Oh, Patty," . . . I could hear Mom whispering. I strained to hear what they were saying. Patty answered in a hushed voice. Then I heard the front door close before Patty entered the kitchen.

As she passed under the kitchen archway, Patty gasped and asked, "What happened to you?" Her eyes widened, as she answered her own question. "Holy cow, did I hit you that hard? Wow, I guess I really don't know my own strength." She looked at her hand in astonishment. "Why did you tell me to go see Chester when you hurt your hand so badly?"

I shouted, "Patty, wait!" I explained, "I didn't hurt my hand when we were celebrating. I mean it did hurt, but—"

"I knew it," Patty interrupted.

"No. Wait," I interrupted back. "I mean, that's not when I initially hurt my hand. When you left, I ran after you and I didn't watch where I was going. I ran smack into Andrew Dover's VW convertible. If it wasn't for Evan I," I started coughing.

"You did what?" Patty screamed. "You ran into Andrew Dover's VW convertible?" her astonished voice repeated, "You ran into Andrew Dover's VW convertible, I don't believe it. You couldn't tell me this when we were waiting in line? Why didn't you tell me sooner?"

I was relieved. Patty had not noticed my blunder. My reference to Evan had gone unnoticed. I reminded her, "I tried to tell you about it, remember? You weren't listening, you were thinking about Chester."

"Chester, forget about Chester. Don't change the subject on me," Patty ordered.

Annoyance rose inside of me, as I said, "I didn't change the subject."

"Forget about that. That's not important," Patty instructed. She pulled out a dining room chair, plopped herself down and rested her chin on top of her laced fingers. She looked into my eyes and said, "Details, I want details. Tell me everything and don't spare the—"

"I know, details," I finished for her. I smiled. Telling Patty about everything that happened was going to be fun. I told Patty about running into Andrew's car, and explained how my hand bounced off the headlight of his car.

Patty groaned and said in a wishful voice, "Oh, I wish I could have been there. Gee, I miss all the good stuff. It's just like out of a romance novel." Patty was letting her imagination get the best of her, and I felt the need to give her more of a fact-based reality.

"Look Patty, listen to what I'm saying. The accident wasn't romantic." I hid my crossed fingers behind my back. This was very true. The accident was not romantic. What happened afterwards was definitely romantic. "I could have been badly hurt."

"What did he say to you?" Patty was still swooning, which meant, she had not heard a word that I had said.

"He told me to watch where I was going. He was so mad; I think he almost swore at me."

Patty got excited and gushed, "That's great, Katy."

"Great? You think Andrew Dover almost swearing at me is great. You've lost it Patty."

"Now just listen," Patty began. "Once he gets to know you, the sky is the limit." Patty was thinking. When the windmills of her mind began to turn, there was no telling what ideas she would create. "Did he ask you for your name?" she asked.

"Yeah," I slowly answered. "I had to give him my name because of the accident, he asked me for it."

"He asked you for your name. Oh boy, things are looking better and better. He asked you for your name and he got mad at you. Wow, Andrew Dover's car hitting you was a Godsend. How come you have all the luck?"

I pointed to my arm and asked, "You call this lucky?" I shook my head and added, "Patty, you're nuts. You're out to lunch."

"That's one of my endearing qualities," Patty glowed with genuine pride as she said this. Patty was one person who was very content with herself. "Now, let's get back to you and Andrew. What happened next?" Patty's eyes were like saucers and she had a smile as wide as the West Edmonton Mall beaming from her face.

I looked at her for a few seconds and wondered if I should tell her about our walk to the office. Maybe he was just being nice and I was making more out of it than it was. I could not resist. I wanted to see Patty's reaction. I was sure she would flip out.

"After I picked up my schedule Andrew walked me to the office to report my injury." As soon as I said office, Patty began screaming.

"Uh, holy mackerel, he walked you to the office?" She put her hands over her face.

I started to laugh, then stood up and moved into the middle of the kitchen. I continued with my story. "It was so amazing; he escorted me like I was a princess." I lifted my good arm, and pretended to rest it on an extended arm, just as I did when I had rested my hand on Andrew's arm. I held my head up high and walked with exaggerated nobility around the kitchen.

"I'm Princess, Katy, I'm very glad to make your acquaintance." I nodded to imaginary ball attendees. Patty got up and bowed to me, before we both started laughing. The ringing of the phone shocked us into silence. It was Mom. For a split second, I wondered if I should answer it.

I picked up the phone. "Hello? Yes Mom. I'm heading off to bed right now. Yes, I know. I promised."

Patty got up and waved a quiet good-bye, as she whispered, "I'll see you later." I nodded my head to acknowledge that I heard her. I listened to Mom repeating the fact that I need to rest. I heard the front door close.

"Mom, Patty left already. Yes . . . good-bye Mom, bye Mom." I hung up and yawned. I guess I was tired. The doorbell rang. I went and peeked through the front window, and saw that Patty had returned. We waved at each other. I scurried to answer the door.

"Don't worry Katy, I'm not coming in."

"Thanks Patty. I promised Mom again that I'd be going to sleep right away," I explained.

"I know. I just wanted to ask you one last question. It can't wait." I nodded in agreement before Patty asked, "What did your Mom say when you told her about Andrew?"

"I didn't tell Mom about Andrew. What makes you think I said anything about Andrew?" I asked. A puzzled look came over Patty's face. It matched my own expression.

Patty explained, "Your Mom asked me if I knew Andrew Dover, so I thought you said something."

"Mom asked me about Andrew before she left. How does Mom know about Andrew? How does Mom expect me to get any sleep when I'm wondering how she knows about Andrew?"

"Don't worry Katy. Your Mom didn't seem mad, she just seemed curious, that's all. Ask your Mom how she knows him. Mystery solved," Patty, concluded.

"I won't have to ask. Mom's going to do all the asking when she sees me." I cringed at the thought.

"Katy, tell me everything that happens tomorrow."

I nodded my head and said, "Patty, you'll get every detail."

We said our good-byes. I locked the door and made a beeline for my bedroom. My thoughts were on Mom and Andrew, as I removed the tensor from my arm. 'How does Mom know Andrew?' I wondered aloud. One thing for sure, worrying about that right now wasn't going to give me any answers.

I really was tired. I got comfortable and was immediately off in dreamland. My dreams are usually very vivid, but the dream I was about to have was like nothing I'd ever dreamed of before.

Chapter 7

Walking Into a Dream

It seemed too real to be a dream. The scene was in vivid color. The dream did not contain jumbled images, like the other dreams that I remembered. There was one other thing; the subject matter was different, unusual. Did I imagine it all?

The first thing I remembered was looking at a photographic image, floating on the top left-hand corner of a huge black screen. I squinted at this tiny picture and realized that someone was sleeping in a bed. As I studied the image I realized, 'Hey, that person is, me.' Like Goldilocks in the Twilight Zone, I was the stranger sleeping in my bed. Of course, who else would be sleeping in my own bed? If I was the person in my bed, then how was I the person watching me sleep in my bed? Maybe I was having a near-death experience. That is ridiculous. I mean, who dies from a strained wrist? Somehow, things were not making sense here.

I wished that I could talk to Mom and ask her what was going on. In a blink of an eye, I found myself in the kitchen, watching Mom as she repaired the kitchen sink. She was sprawled on her back tightening, no loosening the drainage pipe with a giant wrench. A determined grimace covered her face; this was Mom's never-give-up look. Mom set the wrench aside and felt around beside her until she found a can of WD-40. She placed the thin red straw that extended from the spout against the stubborn joint and soaked it all the way around. Mom positioned the wrench on the stubborn connection and repeated her efforts to try to loosen the drainage pipe joint, it finally moved.

The phone rang, startling Mom. She set the wrench aside and abruptly rose from beneath the sink. In her haste, Mom smacked the right side of her forehead on the side of the cupboard. She yelped, rubbed her head and mumbled angrily, as she rushed to answer the phone. As Mom rounded the island counter, she made a fist and slammed it on the counter a couple of times. When she answered the phone, Mom's voice was pleasant and calm.

I sat up in bed, blinking my eyes several times, as I tried to refocus them in the dimming sunlight. What a dream, I had never had a dream like that before. It was so real and ordinary. Do people really dream about their mothers fixing kitchen sinks? Mom was not dressed in her usual royal blue coveralls, but in the dark brown pair, the pair she hardly wore. She was not fond of the color.

My stomach rumbled and rumbled again. I figured that I was not dreaming now, unless of course I was dreaming that my stomach was rumbling. Either way, my stomach was telling me to go in search of food.

I quickly rolled the tensor bandage around my injured wrist, grabbed the sling and gently pulled it around my arm. I headed down stairs. The clock in the living room must have been on the blink again because it was chiming eight o'clock. I glanced at my watch, eight o'clock, no wonder I was hungry. My stomach made another thunderous roar; it was like my hunger alarm clock. There was only one-way to stop the embarrassing outbursts, I had to eat.

Someone was in the kitchen; it was Mom. After she put her tools into her toolbox, Mom stepped out of her dark brown coveralls. Holy cow, talk about coincidence.

Seeing Mom fixing something with her tools was normal around our home, if I had walked into the kitchen to see Dad fixing the sink, or anything else that would have been unusual. Around our home, Mom was the fix-it person.

Back when Mom and Dad were first married, finances were tight. When Mom found out how much the repair jobs would cost, she decided to do the repair work. It seemed like she had read every fix-it, or how-to-do book that had ever been written. When any repairperson entered our home, Mom became the repairperson's shadow. Mom loved to watch everything they did. She would bombard them with questions; she even took notes and drew diagrams. Mom did not want to be in the dark about anything. Eventually, Mom enrolled in home repair classes.

"Did the sink back up again?" I casually asked. I thought if Evan were here he would have said, 'You'd better put it in drive.' I smiled as I opened the fridge and hunted for something to fill the emptiness.

Mom placed her toolbox up against the island counter. She went over to the sink, soaped up her hands and scrubbed at the grime with a heavy-duty scrub brush. "I've been putting this project off for too long, there were loads of scraps piled up inside the drainage pipe. From now on when you're washing dishes, please try not to wash the pieces of scrap down the drain," Mom instructed. "It only takes a few seconds to throw out that garbage," she said.

"Mom, I almost always throw the scraps in the garbage," I said.

Mom calmly added, "How about getting rid of that almost."

I mumbled an, "Okay," and changed the subject. "How come you're wearing those brown coveralls? I thought you didn't like them."

"My blue coveralls are at work," Mom answered. Mom opened the refrigerator, removed a plate, put it in the microwave and turned it on.

"Oh. . . . Why didn't you call me for supper?" I added.

"I did. I went upstairs, but you were sleeping so soundly, I decided not to disturb you," Mom explained.

"You and Dad both ate?" I asked. Mom nodded. I went through the process of pouring myself a glass of juice. I mumbled, "Someone is trying to teach me to have patience."

Mom asked, "Did you say something?"

"It's nothing important. Is there anything that I can eat?"

Mom said, "Look in the-."

I found a plate of baked chicken, vegetables and rice, in the microwave, after it rang and Mom was saying that I would. "I found it. Thanks Mom. I'm starved." I began to pull at the plastic wrapping that covered my supper; Mom stepped over and pulled it off the plate for me. "I could have done that Mom," I said.

"You're welcome dear," she said as she handed me a set of utensils. I pulled a high stool up to the island counter, hopped up onto it and wasted no time as I dug into my supper. Mom pulled up another stool and sat adjacent to me. She watched me as I ate. I tried to ignore her as I concentrate on eating my supper.

Finally, I asked, "Do you have to watch me eat?"

"I was just waiting, so we could have a little talk," Mom explained. It was going to happen. Mom was going to ask me about Andrew. "How about telling me about the accident," Mom suggested. "Your father asked me some questions, but since I have a minimal amount of details about the accident, I couldn't answer your father's questions.

"Where's Dad? Is he showing homes?" Dad is a Realtor and he owns a couple of apartment buildings, one of which, Mom manages. When we called Mom, 'Super Mom', it had a double meaning. Mom's apartment building was also the one that Mrs. Cope and Justine lived in. This gave me a powerful incentive to be a model student in Mrs. Cope's English class.

"Who is Andrew Dover?" Mom asked.

I had been expecting this question. I had gone over the possible answers, but I was still startled when Mom popped the question.

"Andrew Dover?" I was not trying to act stupid. It was a stalling tactic.

"Patty knows him and I know he knows you," Mom stated.

"How do you know he knows me? How do you know him?"

Mom leaned forward and stared into my eyes. "I met Mr. Dover in the school hallway, when I was getting a cup of coffee. He told me he was sorry about the accident and all the trouble it caused." My mouth dropped open in surprise. Mom continued to ask more questions, "Why is he sorry about the accident? How do you know this Andrew? He also said he would be glad to help you if you needed help."

"Holy cow, he said that?" I was astonished.

"He's a lot older than you isn't he? He looks a lot older," Mom, answered her own question. She was getting impatient with my lack of answers.

"He's a senior," I quickly answered.

"How do you know him?" Mom repeated her question. I bit into a drumstick. "Katy, if you want me to stop asking questions, I suggest that you answer these questions." All the waiting magnified Mom's impatience. It had been over ten hours since the school had called her. All the patience that she did have, had long ago run out.

"There isn't much to tell," I mumbled. I quietly added, "I didn't see the car coming. I ran into his VW convertible."

Mom yelled, "You ran into a moving car!"

"No Mom. No. By the time I ran into the car, I think it had already stopped. I thought that you knew about this. Didn't you talk to anyone about the accident?"

Mom looked angry, "On the accident report you said nothing about running into a moving car. In addition, you didn't mention who was driving the car. I did ask you about what happened," Mom reminded me. She rubbed the corner of her forehead.

"Right, I forgot," I sheepishly mumbled.

"You forgot? You forgot the car was moving?" Mom was definitely angry.

"Mom, it was my entire fault. I wasn't watching where I was going, so I decided to spare the person any hassle. I was lucky he was so alert. I wasn't trying to leave you in the dark. I just didn't add unnecessary details," I explained.

"You call that an unnecessary detail? Why are you trying to defend this hit-and-run driver?" Mom had definitely misjudged her calling. If she hung up her tool belt and hit the law books, she would be tough competition for F. Lee Bailey, in 6 or 7 years, no sweat.

"Mom, the guy stuck around and made sure I was okay. When he saw me later in the gym, he was the one who got me to report the accident. He offered to stay with me, but I told him it was okay. Mom, don't you blame him, please."

Mom took a moment to calm down before saying, "It sounds like you like this person." Mom watched me. I stuffed a fork full of vegetables into my mouth. "I shouldn't have called him a hit-and-run driver. Will you tell me about him?" Mom calmly asked.

I smiled and swallowed the vegetables, while nodding enthusiastically. I said, "Andrew Dover is a kind, considerate, funny guy." Mom looked unimpressed.

"I see," Mom said. She rubbed the corner of her forehead and tilted her right ear towards me, and asked, "What caused the accident?"

. . . I carefully chose my words before beginning to speak. "I was thinking about catching up to Patty. I didn't see his car," I admitted. "It was carelessness on my part."

Mom's emotions were on a tight leash, as she said, "Katy, every time you have one of your absent-minded accidents I age five years. I need you to daydream while you are sitting down, not when you're moving in any way. Your daydreaming is causing me to go white before my time. If I have to start dyeing my hair before I'm forty-five, you're going to buy me the dye."

"Mom, I'm really going to try hard to make this my last accident. I'll concentrate on what I'm doing," I assured her.

Mom was touching the top left corner of her forehead, as if this small gesture helped her think. She had done this a number of times during our conversation, but I didn't think too much of it until now. Mom look tired. She sighed before saying, "That would make me a lot happier," and then she rubbed her forehead again.

"Do you have a headache?" I asked.

"No. Yes, I suppose I do. I bumped it on that, that idiotic kitchen cupboard. I was thinking about answering the phone, so I was not paying attention to how I was getting out from under the sink. Do I have a bruise?" Mom asked. She moved her hair away from her head.

"Oh wow," was my amazed response. Mom had described what I had witnessed in my dream. A bruise, a faint bluish blot, was beginning to form on her forehead. There was no denying what I saw.

"Is it that bad?" Mom asked.

"No. Uh, no it's not that bad," I quickly responded. "There's only a slight bruise forming. I, bet that hurt, didn't it?"

"Hurt isn't the word for it," Mom said. "If I had bumped it any harder, I would have knocked myself out." Wow, this was amazing. There were too many coincidences between reality and my dream to ignore it. An idea slowly formed in my mind, as I stared at the bruise and remembered my dream. Bingo. I knew what to do.

I said, "Uh, when I hurt my hand," I thought for a second before finishing, "I stomped my foot a couple of times. It sounds strange but it actually helped. Maybe you should have tried that," I suggested.

Mom started laughing and said, "Like Mother like Daughter, I did the same thing. I didn't stomp like a horse, I did something a bit more dignified. I slammed my fist on top of the island counter a couple of times and you're right, it did seem to help." Mom laughed, as she gently rubbed the bruise once again.

I dropped my fork. "Holy cow," I mumbled. This time, when my jaw fell open, it felt like it dropped all the way down into my supper.

Mom added, "It was carelessness on my part, pure and simple." I kept staring at Mom's bruise. "Katy, are you going to eat that drumstick, or bat some cauliflower around with it? Hello, Katy," Mom waved her hand in front of my face.

I began to cover my plate with plastic wrap, as I explained, "I'm not as hungry as I thought I was. I'm kind of tired."

Mom took the wrap out of my shaking hands and said, "I'll do that. You do look pale. How do you feel?" Mom asked.

I nodded my head and said, "I'm fine. I guess I just need some more sleep."

"That's a good idea. Go and get some rest," Mom said, as she placed the back of her right hand against my forehead to check for a fever. "I want you to go straight to bed, no reading or listening to any CDs. Agreed?"

"A-okay," I agreed. "Good night, Mom," I said as I gave her a quick kiss on the cheek.

"Sweet dreams. Now, off to bed with you," she said. With a rhythmic sweeping of her hand, she motioned for me to leave.

When I got into my room, I picked up my hairbrush from the dresser and started brushing. After a dozen strokes, I put the brush aside and sat on my bed. Astonishment, bewilderment, and a touch of nervousness washed over me, I had no explanation for what I had experienced.

I was on automatic pilot as I walked through my bedtime routine. I carefully changed into my long cotton nightshirt. I sat on the edge of my bed placing my sling and tensor bandage on the nightstand beside my bed.

For a long time, I lay staring at the white ceiling thinking about my dream. Was it a dream? Again, I thought about near-death experiences. I had seen many books on the subject. Could it have been a premonition? Isn't a premonition sort of like a warning from God? Why was God warning me about Mom bumping her head? There were questions and more questions, what were the answers? Maybe Evan had some answers. I tried to wait for him to show up but, unfortunately, I was just too tired. I slowly slipped off to sleep.

Chapter 8

A Sore Back Returns

Dad rolled to a stop in front of Crestmore. I climbed down out of our burgundy colored Plymouth Voyager, grabbed my knapsack and stepped away from the door to close it; the door magically closed on its own. I turned to see Andrew's smiling face. I smiled and said a surprised hello.

"How's your hand?" He gently pulled at the sling that supported my hand and wrist.

"It wasn't as fine as I thought, but it hardly hurts anymore," I assured him.

"I won't say 'I told you so'," Andrew joked.

I heard the van door close and looked back to see Dad rounding the front of the Voyager. I introduced Andrew to my father, as he moved to stand by my side.

Andrew shook Dad's hand and said, "Hello sir, nice to meet you."

"Thank you for helping Katy out yesterday," Dad gave a warm greeting. "I understand that your quick reaction was the reason why Katy's injury wasn't more serious."

Dad was eyeing Andrew, sizing him up, and Andrew was doing the same thing back. Most people found Dad's six-foot three-inch frame intimidating when they first met him, but Andrew seemed calmly, unaffected.

"I agree with you, Mr. McCall. If Katy had been seriously hurt I would have hated that, but I can't say that I'm sorry the accident happened." Dad stared at him. His blank expression was unreadable. "What I mean is, if the accident didn't happen, I might not have met Katy," Andrew explained. "I wouldn't have liked that," he added, as he smiled at me.

Dad nodded his head and a smile emerged on his lips. "You have a way with words, Mr. Dover," Dad said. He added, "I hope your words and feelings are sincere."

Andrew and I wondered what Dad meant by this statement, didn't he trust Andrew?

Dad turned to me and instructed, "Katy, have a good day and watch out for moving vehicles." He kissed me on the forehead.

"I've walked into my last car," I promised.

"I'll gladly keep both eyes on her," Andrew joked.

"Why doesn't that surprise me? I'm not sure if that pleases me. Are you older than my daughter is? Katy is fifteen years old, how old are you?" Dad asked.

"Dad, what are you doing?" Was I curious, or trying to ask him to back off? Did Mom discuss Andrew's age with Dad?

"I'll be eighteen next March. I'm in my senior year, sir. Is that important?" Andrew was so, very serious. I wished they were still joking around. I could feel the tension flowing from both of them; this made me nervous. What could I say to change this?

"Time will tell," Dad replied coolly. "I should get home and look in on your mother, before I go to the office."

"Tell Mom that I hope her headache is better soon," I called to Dad.

"Will do," he said, before he climbed into the van.

"Bye, sir. It was nice meeting you." . . . Dad drove away from the curb. We watched the Voyager until it turned out of sight. "Time will tell?" Andrew asked in a questioning tone. "What does he think I'll do, sprain your other wrist? Your Dad's a little hard to please."

"No, he isn't really. Dad is just a little over protective. When you know him better, I mean, the people who know him, view him as an average Dad. He really is a great Dad," I said.

"You call him average? How many guys has he scared away from your door?" I was not sure if Andrew was joking around and I was starting not to care. I was getting angry.

"You don't even know him and you are making him sound like some kind of ogre. He is bigger than the average person is, but he is a gentle person. Dad is an angel, a big angel," I added. Andrew laughed in disbelief.

"I'm going to straighten out my classes," I said. "See you later."

Andrew stepped in front of me. "Hey, I wasn't trying to put your Dad down. I was only letting you know about the impression he made on me. I know he isn't an ogre, but I sure don't see him as an angel. Wings are hard to imagine on your Dad."

I laughed and agreed, "I guess that is pretty hard to imagine. He is more of a down-to-earth person. Let's not talk about my Dad anymore, okay?"

"Well, that's going to be difficult to do. I want to talk about him." Andrew added, "I need your advice about your Dad, because I want him to like me."

"You want him to like you. Why?" I asked.

"I already have a strike against me, as far as he's concerned," Andrew mumbled.

"What do you mean a strike against you?"

Andrew rambled on, "What Dad would like someone who almost ran his daughter over, causing her to strain her wrist? I mean, what do I expect?"

"You barely talked to each other for two minutes. No one gets to know a person in two minutes," I reasoned.

"How do I get him to forget that and see me as an okay guy?" Andrew asked himself, as he stared off into space.

"Hey, who's the dreamer now?" I asked. Andrew did not hear me, so I pushed at his chest with my good hand. Andrew startled me, with lightning speed; he grabbed my hand. When he realized he was holding my hand, he smiled.

"What were we talking about?" he asked.

"I can't remember," I answered.

"We make each other forget things. Do you think that means something? What do you think, Katy?" he asked.

"Now I remember. You said you wanted my father to like you and I asked you why," I reminded him. He was not letting my hand go.

"Saved by the bell," Andrew joked.

I was finding it hard to breathe again. Then I thought, *please don't let go of my hand*. I kept staring at his hand holding mine.

"I guess it's not important that your Dad like me right away, but it sure would make it easier, especially when I come to pick you up." Andrew's smile had expanded into a broad grin.

"Pick me up?" I repeated.

"Sure, the guy usually picks up the girl when they go on a date." I stared at him in astonished silence. Andrew said, "You know, a date, when they go to dinner, or a movie, or both." I kept staring at him. "Okay, it doesn't have to be a movie. We can do whatever you want to do on our date."

"You want to go out with me?"

"Do I hear an echo? Yeah, I want to go out with you. What can I say, I guess I like arguing with you," he joked. "What about Saturday night, does that sound good to you?" he asked. We began to walk towards the school. He was still holding my hand.

"Oh wow," I whispered. I quickly added, "You'll need my address and my phone number."

Andrew put his hand on my shoulder and said, "Don't worry about that. I know that info." Andrew grinned at my surprised expression. "I've been thinking about asking you out since I left you at the office yesterday."

"You told my Mom about the accident outside the office yesterday. You didn't have to do that?" We entered the school and he walked me towards my locker.

"Your Mom told you about our talk, that's how come your Dad thanked me, right?"

I nodded and said, "Yes, that's true. It wasn't necessary."

Andrew explained, "It was the right thing to do. I didn't want her to think that I was a hit-and-run driver. They need to realize that I'm responsible, before they'll let me date their daughter."

"...Date their daughter," I repeated in awe. I assured him, "After Mom and Dad get to know you, I'm sure they'll like you." Andrew stood, silently watching me. "What is it?" I asked.

Andrew smiled at me and said, "So, you're saying that we have a date?"

I returned his smile and answered, "You seem like a nice guy. I guess I'll take a chance with you." Andrew laughed at my answer. He did not let go of my hand until we reached the office. My fingers felt numb and tingly.

He asked, "How does Saturday night sound to you?"

"It sounds great," I could hardly contain my elation.

"I'll call you later to talk about the details. See you around, McCall," he said as he backed his way down the hallway.

"I'm counting on it," I called after him. I mumbled through my frozen smile, "I'm counting on it." I shook my head and added, "Does that sound lame, or desperate, or what?" I turned and entered the office.

It did not take long to get my classes straightened out, which was good, because I had used my extra time visiting with Andrew. It was worth the lost time. I rushed to my first period class, English ten, with Mrs. Cope. I mumbled an, "Excuse me," and squeezed through the door just before Mrs. Cope closed it. I sat in the desk in front of Patty's desk.

"Where were you? I was looking everywhere for you," Patty asked.

"You wouldn't believe it if I told you," I whispered. "I just lived it and I'm having a hard time believing it."

"Katy, tell me and see if I believe you," Patty ordered. "Katy!" Patty was as impatient as Mom was.

"Shh. I'll tell you about it later," I whispered. I was staring at Mrs. Cope's raised brow. I had not taken a class from her before, but because of the many times that I had babysat her daughter Justine, I was familiar with her facial expressions and body language. Mrs. Cope came over to my desk and welcomed me. She handed me my English texts and class outline. I nodded and thanked her.

I listened to Mrs. Cope, as she addressed the class. I could hear Patty fidgeting in the desk behind me. She was dying of curiosity and was tremendously annoyed at me, or at the idea of having to wait for my story. Her fidgeting also caught Mrs. Cope's attention. She walked over, stood beside Patty's desk and rested her hand on Patty's shoulder. This gesture settled Patty down immediately. The rest of the class was rather uneventful.

The ringing of the bell was like a signal to Patty to release her curiosity. She tapped me on the shoulder and asked, "What's your unbelievable news? I've waited long enough. Now let's have it."

"Katy, could I speak with you for a second please," Mrs. Cope motioned for me to come to her desk.

Patty groaned. "I'll be right outside the door," she whispered.

Mrs. Cope waited for the classroom to clear out before she began to speak. "I was talking with your mother this morning. I asked her if there would be any chance that you could baby-sit for me this Friday night and Saturday. She said it was all right with her, if it was okay with you."

"This Saturday, I'm sorry, but I have a date this Saturday night," I explained.

Mrs. Cope explained, "I should have said that the baby sitting will just be until noon on Saturday. My sister will be taking the children to see the Shrine Circus. She'll make arrangements with you to pick Justine up on Saturday, if you're baby-sitting."

"In that case, sure, I can baby-sit. That is if you don't mind having a one-armed baby-sitter. My sling stays on for at least a week. When it comes to tying shoe laces, I don't manage too well yet," I said.

"Katy, don't worry about that. Justine will help you out. She loves to help, just use her runners with the Velcro straps. So, I'll meet you in the school parking lot right after school on Friday?" she asked. I agreed.

Patty was waiting for me by the door. She voiced her frustration and impatience as she followed me, "Why did you take so long? Holy, are you long winded. A person could die of curiosity while waiting for you." I struggled to open my locker. Patty grabbed my books and stuffed them into my locker.

"Patty, we haven't got time to talk right now." I glanced at my watch. "We're going to be late for class if we don't hurry up. I'll tell you at noon, when we're not rushed." I struggled to assemble the books for next class. Mr. Fowler taught Math 10 with an iron hand. The students call him, the dragon man. If anyone was late, the rumor was that he would blow fire at him or her.

Patty grabbed my math textbook out of my locker. "Oohhh, okay. First, tell me one thing. Does what you're going to tell me have anything to do with Andrew Dover?" If we had been in the theater, I would have said that Patty was on the edge of her seat. I just grinned. That was enough. Patty squealed, and I laughed at her enthusiasm.

"I knew it. That will keep me dreaming until noon. I can't wait, waiting is pure agony," Patty gushed.

"You should have taken drama as your option class. Patty, you definitely have a dramatic flare," I said the obvious. We jogged towards Math class.

"Really, you think so Katy? I wonder if it's too late to take drama class. Patty Burbick, star of stage, T.V. and the big screen. Sounds pretty good doesn't it?"

"Patty, when you dream, you dream big."

"Hey, why not," Patty said as we entered math class.

Mr. Fowler greeted us when we stepped into his classroom, "Thank you for gracing us with your presence, ladies. Close the door behind you and find a seat." We had made it just in time.

When the noon bell rang Patty quickly gathered both my books and her own books. "Let's go," she said. Lana Carpenter began to say something to the both of us. Patty cut her off, "Sorry Lana, we have no time to talk right now. Katy has an important promise she has to keep. Come on, let's go Katy." Patty waved good-bye to Lana. She was like a blocker making a hole for a tight end in a football game. You know about stuff like that when you spend a lot of time listening to your older brother and a couple of his friends talk.

"I did promise," I said to Lana, as I squeezed passed her. "Patty that was rude."

"You can sue me later," Patty replied.

"Patty!"

"I'll fix it l-a-t-e-r," Patty enunciated. "If you think I'm going to let anything stop you from telling me what happened, you can forget it." Patty hovered over me as I tried to open my combination lock.

"Okay, I'll tell you. I saw Andrew before school and we talked." Patty waited for the rest, and then disappointment appeared in her eyes.

"You put me through torture for that. He talked to you yesterday. That's nothing," she mumbled. "That's old news."

"Yeah, you're right, there's a little more." I kept my excitement in check, as I put my books in my locker.

"What did he say to you? Keep your hands off my car," she mimicked, as she turned to work on her locker combination.

"No, he just asked me out on a date," I casually announced.

Patty stopped in her tracks. Then she slowly turned to face me. Her eyes were bulging, and her mouth was a gaping tunnel. In the next second, her screams echoed down the hallway.

"You!" she said, as she shook her pointer finger at me.

I laughed and said, "Can you believe it. In my wildest dreams, I didn't think that this would happen."

"How are Mutt and Jeff today?" Laughter closely followed the asking of the question. The voice that pulled both Patty and I back from our romantic trance belonged to Erica Miller. The laughter came from three members of her entourage, Henry, a tall young jock, along with her two giggling twin shadows, Jennifer and Hillary. They were all Erica's constant companions.

Her locker was a few yards away from my own. She was not looking directly at us when she asked the question, Erica was addressing our reflections in a mirror hanging on the inside panel of her locker door. She was checking her lipstick while she waited for a response.

The summer had not changed Erica. She reminded me of my Uncle Hugo's sore back, irritating enough to be a nuisance, but not painful enough to go to the chiropractor for. Uncle Hugo had once said, 'A sore back never leaves you; it might take a vacation, but it always comes back.' I winced at the thought of it.

"Erica, I thought you transferred to a different school?" My words did not express my disappointment.

Jennifer said, "You wish."

"I guess you heard wrong, didn't you," Erica answered.

Patty scowled at me and said, "Oh goodie, Katy, Erica's back."

"Did you say that Andrew asked you out?" Erica asked.

That got our attention. We stared at her. "I didn't mention anyone's name," I answered.

"I thought I saw you walking with him this morning," Erica casually commented.

"He was helping me out," I explained.

"Of course, he's so nice. So, why do you think he's interested in you?" Erica asked.

Patty looked at me and chuckled, as she said, "Duh. I'd say that Andrew liking Katy has something to do with his spending time with Katy."

"I know why Andrew's interested in Katy and it has nothing to do with liking her. It has something to do with your looks, but unfortunately, not in a good way," as she said this, she smiled in an 'of course' sort of way. "I hope you have a thick skin, because you're going to need it. Andrew's going to dump you like that," Erica said, as she snapped her fingers. "You're just too dull for him. If he lost interest in my sister Dawn, how do you think you're going to keep him interested in you?" Erica concluded.

"You're clueless. You have no idea of what you're talking about," I tried to sound convincing.

"Tell her," Patty whispered, as she poked my arm and tilted her head towards Erica.

"What?" I asked.

"Tell her about your date," Patty whispered.

"Patty, no," I whispered a warning.

"He'll let you down easy. Andrew is such a gentleman. He used to date Dawn for a long time, almost six months. They're still friends." Erica was eager to let us know, what she knew we already knew.

"Katy will tell you first hand how nice he is, after their date," Patty blurted out.

Erica was surprised for a few seconds, before she regained her composure. "You might not have to tell me anything. Dawn said that Andrew is coming over Saturday afternoon." Erica knew what buttons to push to get to people, and this time, she out did herself. "Maybe I'll have some good news for you come Monday morning?" She let us fill in the rest. "I've got to run. We are meeting Dawn for lunch. Ta, ta."

Jennifer and Hillary mimicked, "Ta, ta." We watched them strut down the hallway.

"We're meeting Dawn for lunch. Ta, ta," Patty mimicked, as she waved her hands in an Erica fashion.

Erica and Dawn were what most people would consider beautiful, so what she said, got me wondering, *why was Andrew interested in a pint-size, mousy, tenth grader like me? Was he feeling guilty about the accident?* Was I imagining his interest in me or was I reading more into his actions than what was there? He could just want to be friends. There was nothing wrong with that. I was kidding myself; I felt like my magical dream, filled with hope and possibilities had suddenly trickled through my fingers.

Patty tried to cheer me up, "That girl is so shallow, if she didn't have her make-up on she wouldn't have a face. No wonder she has a mirror hanging in her locker." Patty was expecting me to laugh, or at least smile, but her words barely filtered through to me. "Katy, she doesn't know what she's talking about," Patty insisted.

"Doesn't she?" I had to face facts. Erica had not said anything that I did not already know.

Friendship is okay. I would look at the positive side of what happened. I just needed a little bit of time to adjust to this idea. Why does it feel like someone has thrown a bucket of ice water on my life and me? I had been jarred awake. My magical dream date had turned into a disappointing dream called reality. The wrong person had found out about my special dream and with expert precision, she cut it into shreds.

Chapter 9

Soul Never Dies

"Mom, I'm home," I called out as I stepped through the front entrance. There was no answer. Mom was probably still at work. I entered the kitchen, dumped my books on the counter and stuck my head into the refrigerator. I wondered what I was looking for. I was not hungry.

"What's got you down?" I jumped at the unexpected voice. Evan sat casually on the kitchen counter in a cross-legged position, watching me. He smiled and said, "Gotcha."

I said, "I wish you would knock like everyone else." I turned to grab a jug of apple juice, set it down on the counter, opened the cupboard to get a glass, set it down, and finally poured the juice. "I hate this one-armed act. I do everything in slow motion," I said in frustration.

"That's not what's bothering you," Evan said. "You're forgetting that I know you. I've been your brother for a long time."

"Yesterday you said you were going to visit after school. Where were you?" I asked angrily.

"I did visit, but you were sleeping, both times," Evan paused before continuing, "That's not what's bothering you, either. You're not going to solve anything if you deny the real reason for your anger," Evan lectured.

"Thank you, Dr. McCall. Freud couldn't do better," anger churned inside me and exited through sarcasm. My words were all the proof that Evan needed to show him how right he was. Evan sat silently, watching me. I suppose he was answering me with his silence.

"Andrew asked me out," I mumbled.

"That's great," Evan had a puzzled expression on his face. "Isn't it?" he finished. "You like the guy a lot, so why are you angry?"

I told Evan about Dad and Andrew's meeting, and about Erica saying that, Andrew would be going over to visit Dawn this coming Saturday.

"He's going out with me because he feels guilty about the accident. Andrew's just trying to be nice," I said. "I'm too dull for a guy like Andrew. Eventually, he's going to dump me. I'm not going out with him," I repeated Erica's words.

"Real smart Sis, a guy you like a lot asks you out and you're going to break the date." Evan tapped his head with his forefinger. "I think you should have your noodles checked out."

"Haven't you been listening to anything that I've said? Oh, forget it." I grabbed my books from the counter top and headed for the stairs, but Evan materialized in front of me.

"Katy, wait."

"Will you cut that out?" I ordered.

"I haven't finished talking to you," Evan said with equal determination. He stood staring at me with his hands resting on his hips.

"Well, I've finished listening to you. Now move," I ordered. I tried to look as determined as my brother did, but I was not making an impression. "I could walk through you," I warned.

"Do you really want me to leave?" he asked. We stared at each other. We each waited for the other guy to move. I turned and sat at the kitchen table.

"I'm listening," I said impatiently.

Evan came forward, hopped above the dining room table, crossed his legs and in slow motion, like in a silent movie, he floated down onto the table. His face erupted in an enormous smile. I had almost forgotten to be annoyed with him.

"Mom doesn't like feet on the table," I reminded him.

"Yeah, right, I could get some heavenly dust on it," he responded.

"Okay, I forgot. You're not a person anymore." I quickly amended the statement when I saw Evan's shocked expression. "What I mean is you're a ghost person, a dead person. Oh . . . Evan, who in the world are you?" I asked.

"I'm still a human being, an eternal Soul, and I'm your brother," Evan concluded.

I smiled and said, "Evan, I'm just glad you're a part of my life, that is, when you're not bugging me."

"Katy, as long as you remember me, I'll be a part of your life," Evan said this in a calm, sure voice.

Evan stopped talking and we both listened as the front door opened. Someone entered and dropped a set of keys on the front entrance table. I looked at Evan and almost warned him to leave, but I caught myself. Mom can't see him, I reminded myself.

"Hello, Katy. Are you waiting for me?" Mom asked. It must have looked like I was waiting, sitting at the table, facing the doorway.

I stood up and answered, "No, Mom, I was on my way upstairs to finish my homework." I gathered my books, looked at Evan and glanced skyward.

Evan nodded his head and said, "Meet you upstairs."

"How is your arm, Katy?" Mom called after me.

"Great, it hardly bothers me anymore," I shouted from the stairwell. I bounded up the stairs.

"How were your classes?" Mom shouted.

"Classes were great Mom, I'll tell you about them at supper," I shouted my answer. I entered my room to find Evan sitting on the end of my bed, in a familiar cross-legged fashion.

"You move fast." I set my books down on the desk. "You'll have to teach me that trick. I'd be able to make it to class in a blink of an eye," I said as, I flopped down onto the bed.

"You would miss your jam sessions with Patty," Evan reminded me.

I nodded and said, "Yeah, I guess you're right. And walking with Andrew was—," Evan's smile widened. I quickly changed the subject. "I still think your way of traveling could come in handy."

"Maybe I can find someone who can teach you," Evan surprised me with this statement.

"Really, there's someone who can teach me to do that?"

"Sure there is. How do you think I learned this special way of traveling?" Evan casually asked, before adding, "I guess you haven't realized that you already had one out-of-body experience?"

"I did, when?" I asked in astonishment.

"When you saw Mom hit her head under the kitchen sink, that wasn't your imagination, that was an out-of-body experience," Evan explained.

"Hey, how did you know I saw Mom hit her head?" I asked.

"I was there with you when you had the out-of-body experience. I wasn't meant to be a part of your experience, so I watched until I knew you were all right, and then I left. Your dream of that experience was no coincidence. Mom really did knock her head on that cupboard and her headache was no illusion. Your conscious awareness shifted out of your body to that place and time, you saw Mom hit her head, that was real," Evan confirmed.

"Wow, this out-of-body experience stuff is amazing. I also like how you are able to know things so fast. That is amazing. It's like dipping into 'Heaven's Information Net'." Evan was staring at me, as if I had a pimple growing on my nose. "You think that's a weird thing to say, don't you? 'Heaven's Information Net'," I repeated.

"Katy, I like that idea, ''Heaven's Information Net''. You're right. I would say that operating from the heavenly information net would be like tuning into and living life from the awareness of Divine Spirit or God. This is also like tuning into the awareness of Soul, because Soul knows the awareness of God. I'm not operating from the Soul awareness, at least most of the time I'm not. I have a lot more living and learning to do, before I could come close to doing that for any length of time." Evan said this without any regret in his voice. Evan beamed, as he added, "But, that's a goal of mine. You could say that I've accepted the challenge."

"Evan, you said you have a lot more living to do, but you're not living anymore," I reminded him.

"Yes I am, Katy," Evan corrected me. "I'm just not living in the same, how I should put it, dimension, plane, level of heaven that you're living in. I am in a different plane of existence. Haven't you realized by now that I am alive?" I must have looked at Evan with a stunned look on my face, because he quickly added, "Okay, let's not get into an argument over semantics. Will you admit that I do exist?" Evan asked.

"I know you exist, Evan, I didn't say that you don't exist. You're still my brother. For goodness sake, I've known you for fifteen years."

"Okay, now that we're both sure I exist; we can get back to what we were talking about." An impish smile appeared on his face. "What were we talking about?" Evan asked.

"I can't remember," I replied.

"Oh, I remember," Evan said, as the impish smile doubled in size. "You changed the subject. I was wondering if you were going to keep your date with what's his name."

I groaned and answered, "I don't know, I haven't decided."

"If you don't go out with him because of what Erica said, then you're letting her run your life. You would be letting her play with your mind. Do you really want Erica to be the captain of your ship? Why should she be running your life?" Evan was making a lot of sense. I suppose I'd have to admit that to him.

"Evan, I-" Evan cut me off.

"Listen to me, Katy. Think about this, how does Erica know what's going on in what's his name's head?" Evan asked.

"His name is Andrew. You know that," I corrected him. Evan's forgetfulness regarding Andrew's name bothered me.

"Sure I know that, but how do you know that I didn't forget? Maybe we dead people forget things. You can't be absolutely sure of what's in my mind," Evan tapped his temple to emphasize his point, "Or Andrew's mind." He continued, "Erica's guess about what's happening between her sister and Andrew is probably all in her imagination. She knows as much about what is going on in his head as you do. That's zilch, until you talk to him and ask him the right questions. Katy, talk to the guy, open the lines of communication. Do it Katy, just do it," he finally finished.

"It's scary to hear you making so much sense." I looked into Evan's eyes and added, "It's even scarier to feel myself agreeing with you so much." Evan's eyes widened with surprise. "I agreed with you back when you asked me if I wanted Erica to be the captain of my ship." I laughed before adding, "You're speechless; I bet that's a first."

"This is the thanks I get," Evan said in mock exasperation. We both laughed together.

I admitted, "Evan, what you said made a lot of sense. I promise that I will talk with Andrew. I give you my word." I raised my hand, as if I was taking an oath in court. "But right now, I don't want to think about it. So give me a break, all right?"

"All right," Evan agreed. "I'll stop lecturing. I swear it on my honor."

"Evan, you've changed. The old Evan would have needled me until I did what he wanted. You look like the same old Evan, but you sure don't sound like the old Evan."

"Hey, don't look so surprised. I told you I've changed." Evan's smile expanded, as he said this. "Katy, remember I told you that I attended classes in the other levels of heaven?"

"Yeah, I remember. That still seems kind of unbelievable to me," I said.

"Well, one thing I've been taught is to respect the rights and beliefs of other people, and other beings. The spiritual consequences of breaking spiritual laws in the levels of heavens and in the physical worlds are very exact; God is very decisive. The returning consequences of a person's karmic creations in the physical worlds can be delayed for weeks, months, years or for lifetimes; but the consequences do eventually return."

"That's really cool," I added, "I didn't think there would be laws in heaven. I thought everyone in heaven would be pure and nice so you wouldn't need any laws," I reasoned.

"No one is perfect. Every being is evolving in awareness. I am a good example. I am learning all the time. The old Evan has evolved into the new improved Evan," he proudly said.

"Sure, the new improved model like the new improved Terminator, the one that can't be terminated. Tell me another lie," I sarcastically challenged. Evan silently stared at me. I looked away from Evan and mumbled, "I'm sorry Evan. I don't know why I said that."

"Yes you do," Evan quietly said. "I knew you were angry about something, but I thought it had to do with Andrew and your future date. I forgot you were mad at me. Now I remember what you said at my funeral."

I turned back to look at him. I was looking into his eyes when I said, "I'm not ticked-off at you. I know you didn't die on purpose."

Evan's eyes widened with surprise. "So that's it," he said. His voice rose, as he said, "Of course I didn't die on purpose. Do you think I am a quitter? Sis, when a person's time here on earth is up, it is finished, done. I could not have changed that. If I was meant to live, then I would still be alive. I held on for as long as I could. The human part of me didn't choose to die," Evan explained.

I thought of Evan dying and squeezed my eyes tight to hold back the tears. I whispered the question, "Why did you have to die?"

Evan shook his head and slowly answered me, "I don't know, Katy. I didn't have the awareness to know when my time was up, or why it was up. As it was, I'm glad I wasn't a person who knew when his time was up."

I grabbed a tissue from the nightstand, blew and wiped my nose, before I asked, "Are you saying that some people know when they're going to die?"

Evan hesitated before he answered my question, "I believe that people who are working from Soul Awareness would know when their time was up."

"Soul Awareness, you've mentioned that before. You said that Soul knows everything?" I reminded him. "So, tell me more about this Soul Awareness."

Evan beamed with enthusiasm as he answered me, "Katy, life is so simple. People think the universe is complicated, but it really is not. In my classes, I have learned that Soul is the God part of us, the eternal part of us that sees and knows everything. Soul is the creative part of who we are. Do you know what that means?" Evan asked.

I shook my head and said, "I'm not sure what you mean."

Evan continued, "The Soul Aware person can see the whole picture, so the Soul Aware person can figure out the way to handle a situation in the best possible way. Isn't that cool?"

"Is this Soul the same Soul that church people are trying to save?" I asked.

Evan thought for a second before answering, "I don't think so. Soul is the essence of God. Soul doesn't die, so why would anyone need to save Soul? Everyone has that spark of God in his or her hearts. Probably the people who are trying to save Souls are trying to save the human part of a person," Evan speculated.

"Evan, I'm so glad you came back. It's a bonus that you're helping me to understand this stuff."

Evan explained, "They said the love in my heart and my willingness to learn, earned me the right to learn this amazing, stuff."

I popped my pillow up against the headboard and leaned back, before I asked, "So Evan, who are 'they'? Who are your teachers?"

Evan bolted upright. He grinned and his voice vibrated with excitement, as he said, "He's a real cool guy. He's a spiritual teacher who belongs to an ancient brotherhood called 'The Brotherhood of Light and Love'. He teaches in the physical worlds and in other nonphysical worlds. Anyone can learn to visit these other worlds, to learn fascinating truths from this brotherhood of spiritual teachers."

"How do you know that they're good people?" I asked.

"They're good," Evan firmly answered. "They help people who are ready to find truth. They also help people to understand only what they are ready to know. The Spiritual Masters would not tell people to do what would hurt anyone. If someone did that, the person would not be a true

Spiritual Master, because a Master lives by the spiritual laws. One day you will meet them and you'll be able to decide for yourself, if they're good people. You don't have to believe me," Evan added.

"Evan, I don't want to meet them now, I'm not ready to die yet, I haven't even had my date with Andrew."

"What? Did I say you had to die to meet them? I didn't say that." I heard laughter in Evan's voice, as he said this.

"Well, you're dead, so I thought this guy would be dead. Isn't that why you got to meet him?" I asked.

"I got to meet him because I was ready to meet him." Evan shook his head. "The answer to your question is, no, he's not dead. He has mastered the ancient technique of out-of-body-travel, like all the other members of The Brotherhood. He can travel to any place here, or to any level of heaven, by simply shifting his awareness to where he wants to be. Katy, this is just one technique that the Spiritual Masters use."

"Wow, boy is that far out," I whispered, as I tried to imagine this idea.

"It's real cool," Evan agreed. "I guess you could say I'm doing the same thing. I concentrate on being here, and I'm here. I just haven't got the same control over the shifting of my consciousness," Evan acknowledged.

"These Spiritual Masters are alive?" I repeated my question. Evan nodded his head. "These Spiritual Masters can travel like this when they're still alive?" I asked again.

Evan nodded and said, "Yes, yes. A lot of them are alive in the physical world, but some of them are like me. Katy, anyone can learn to travel like this."

"Can I learn this technique?" I asked.

"Sure, anyone can. Most people travel at night in their dreams, but they don't remember or realize that they're traveling. They may not even know where to go, but their Soul Awareness knows where they need to go. A few people can do this while they're awake. I didn't tell anyone, but before I died, you know, when I was still alive in my physical body-"

"I get it Evan. I am clued in I know you are alive. You're just living in a different kind of level of heaven than the rest of us, right?"

"Okay, okay, I know you know. What was I saying?" he asked himself. "Oh, yeah, I didn't tell anyone but," Evan leaned forward. I mimicked his actions and leaned towards him. Evan whispered, "I used to go travelling when I was dreaming."

"Go travelling where?" I asked.

"I'd go travelling to different worlds in my dream state," Evan answered.

"Evan, maybe you were just dreaming," I reasoned.

"No, Katy." Evan shook his head vigorously, as he emphasized, "No, it wasn't just a dream. I could not have imagined what I experienced. I met Sri Hikari Hito, my spiritual guide for the first time in my dreams. You weren't the only one who was helping me to study for my life guard exam."

I started humming the music to the Twilight Zone. "This is really far-out, Evan."

Every answer Evan gave me made me stretch to alter my concept of reality, even more. I thought I was ready for these changes. I was discovering that to accept any type of change requires an open mind and a willingness to learn. This was just what the Spiritual Masters had said was required to learn spiritual truth. I was traveling beyond the safety of the known and accepted, into uncharted territory. I was trying to hang onto the old and familiar. Captain Picard would not have picked me to be a member of the Starship Enterprise crew.

"If he's still alive, where does he leave his body?" I asked.

"What?" a quizzical frown appeared on Evan's face.

"Where does the Spiritual Master leave his body," I pointed to my own body, "Body, when he travels? You know the part that's still alive, the physical body." Our minds finally connected.

"I don't know where he leaves his body. I guess he leaves it wherever he was sitting before he left it. Probably he leaves it in a safe place. . . . I don't know where he leaves his body, I never asked him." Evan held his head between his arms, with his fingers entangled on top of his head. "Katy, I don't care where he leaves it. That's not important to me." It was not important to Evan, but it was important to me.

"Evan, how does he know that his body is safe, if he isn't in it?" I asked.

"Divine Spirit and God are making sure he's safe," Evan answered.

"This is really far out, most people will say that it's science fiction," I reasoned.

"Yeah well, most people thought that flying to the moon or walking on the moon was impossible. Oh heck, people in Chris Columbus's day used to think that if you sailed far enough out into the ocean, they would fall off the edge of the world. Once something is no longer a mystery, then the fear of the unknown disappears. Maybe in a hundred years everyone will accept travelling by shifting his or her awareness, as a learned skill. You never know," Evan hoped.

"Who's the dreamer now?" I jokingly asked.

"I think that everyone's a dreamer," Evan answered. "We each have our own special dreams. Aren't they what we build our lives around?" Evan asked me.

I shrugged my shoulders and smiled, as I agreed. "Okay, Evan, I'm with you. I like dreaming. I'm not saying what you said is impossible." Actually, what Evan said made me feel great. It made me feel like anything was possible.

"Remember Katy, if you want to learn this kind of travel, I really do know someone who might be able to help you. I could ask if you want," Evan repeated his offer. I nodded, as I thought about what he said. "It's your choice," Evan casually added, "Maybe they are already teaching you, but you're just not aware of their help." Evan rose from his seat on the end of the bed. "I've got to take off. Need to practice my traveling technique. See you later."

"You have to go already?" I sat up and tried to think of something that would delay his departure.

"I'm not leaving forever," Evan, reminded me. "I'm just going for a little while." Evan voiced his best Terminator imitation as he mimicked, "I'll be back." He switched back to his normal voice and added, "Katy, I love you." My eyes widened in shock. The Evan who said that was not the same old Evan. With that, he began his fade-out trick.

He had just disappeared when I screamed, "Evan!" I stared at the vacated spot.

Evan reappeared. "Katy, yelling at a new pilot creates a skittish take-off," Evan informed me.

"Sorry, it won't happen again," I promised before I quickly added, "Evan, I want to learn this traveling stuff."

"That's great Katy. I will let my spiritual guide know that you want to learn the technique. Katy, if you can't consciously do the traveling right away, don't worry, you can travel in your dreams. Most people learn in their dream state first. I was doing that before I died. You've already had one out-of-body experience," Evan reminded me. "You're an old pro."

I nodded my head as I remembered. "That wasn't hard to do, but, how do I do it again?" I asked.

"One discipline could help you learn to do this," Evan said.

"What is it?" I asked.

"Keeping a journal of your dreams will help you to remember and connect with Divine Spirit and your Soul Awareness. Each person has their own personal symbolism, based on their own life experiences. One example is, if you dream about breakdowns in your house this could represent, a break down of your physical body. To another person, the same dream could mean something entirely different," Evan said.

"That's so cool. Can you tell me more," I asked.

"Katy, we'll have to talk about this later."

"Why?" I asked.

"Because Mom heard you call me. She'll be up here any second now." Evan smiled, as he faded out of sight. Suddenly Mom was standing in Evan's fading shoes.

"Cool," I whispered. "Mom, hi there, I was just dreaming. I guess I woke myself up," I explained. I smiled and added, "It was a good dream."

Chapter 10

Spiritual Evolution a Personal Journey

Thank God, it's Friday. I have seen Andrew a couple of times since he asked me out, but I have not cancelled our date. It would be rude to cancel. I'm kidding myself, Evan was right; I want to go out with him. I think Andrew cares about me and likes me, a little bit. Right now, I am just glad he asked me out.

"Katy, could you look after old Hilda? I'll be right back."

"Sure, Mrs. Cope, that's all right with me," I replied.

Mrs. Cope's car is an ancient tangerine Vega. She named it Hilda. She is trying to get as much life out of the old girl that is humanly possible. She treats it like a dear old friend.

Mrs. Cope noticed that every time she blew her stack, Hilda's radiator would over heat. At first, she thought this was a coincidence. She also noticed that when she began to control her angry reactions, Hilda's many episodes of coolant leaks and radiator over-heating episodes gradually disappeared. I had jokingly said to Mrs. Cope that her car was relaxing, just like she was relaxing.

I had asked her if her troubles stopped because she had a good mechanic. Mrs. Cope agreed that a good mechanic helped, but she thought her new, calmer disposition turned the tide. She honestly believed that her whole life, including her car reflected her own emotions back to her. Instead of being steamed, she now accepts the car's minor and major breakdowns, as a part of life. She said that everything needs tender loving care.

"How's the old girl doing today?" Evan suddenly appeared in the driver's seat. His sparkling eyes stared at my startled face.

"Who are you calling old?" I demanded.

"Who else, Hilda, of course," Evan gave her an affectionate pat on her dashboard. "Do you know that we took bets on how long she would last? The old girl has lasted a lot longer than anyone thought she would. Evan grabbed the steering wheel and imitated a racecar driver, with the original Starship Enterprise's engineer Scottie's voice.

"Captain, I'm giving you all the power I can. We are pushing the engines as far as she'll go; a warp core breach is imminent." Evan laughed and said, "I thought that even engineer Scottie, couldn't save Hilda from being decommissioned."

"Maybe she lasted because Mrs. Cope doesn't get steamed with Hilda or almost anyone else anymore," I speculated.

"You are kidding; Mrs. Cope gets steamed with her car? That must be a one sided argument." Evan laughed as he imagined such an argument.

I explained Mrs. Cope's theory to Evan. I thought he would laugh, but instead Evan surprised me. He listened to what I said with a focused interest, nodding his head, as his eyes brightened with enthusiasm. When he heard me say, "She believes that her whole life, including her car reflect her emotions back to her." Evan got excited.

"That's right on!" He almost cheered, then added, "You remember in physics class, when we learned that for every action, there is an equal and opposite reaction?"

"I remember," I answered.

"Well, that law applies in all aspects of life here on earth. It also exists in most of the levels of heaven. That's what is called the Law of Cause and Effect, it's also called the Law of Karma," Evan explained. "In the Bible they refer to it when they say, 'What you sow, you shall reap,' it's all the same law."

"I thought karma was an eastern idea. Didn't it come from a belief like Buddhism?" I asked.

Evan shrugged his shoulders and said, "It could be something they believe in. I'm not sure. I first heard about it from my spiritual guide, Sri Hikari Hito. He's been helping me to learn about life on both sides of the transition called death."

"Hikari Hito?" What kind of name is that? It sounds Oriental," I added.

Evan agreed, "It's Sri Hikari Hito, and you're right. He is Oriental, or at least part Oriental."

"So this is an Oriental teaching?" I asked.

Evan shook his head and answered, "No, I don't think you can pigeon-hole it like that. From what I've seen, the members of 'The Brotherhood of Light and Love' come from all racial backgrounds."

"The Brotherhood of Light and Love," I nodded my head, before asking, "What's this thing you said he was teaching you, 'To learn about life on both sides of the transition called death?'

"Evan smiled and said, "It sounds pretty far out, doesn't it?" I nodded my head in agreement before Evan continued, "Do you remember me saying that Sri Hikari Hito isn't dead?" I nodded, before Evan added, "He helps to guide people who are ready to learn in the awakened state, dream state and on the other levels of heaven. I would guess that the out-of-body experience, when you saw Mom hit her head under the kitchen sink, could have happened because the Spiritual Masters are already helping you in your dream state.

"Wow, I want to remember them teaching me," I said.

"As members of the Brotherhood help you learn more about this travelling technique, you'll be able to learn about life on different levels of heaven and earth, when you are awake or asleep. As I said before, they will only help you to know what you are ready to know. The Spiritual Master said that, 'If you sincerely ask for help and guidance, and you have love in your heart, and a willingness to listen and learn, then guidance and help will be given.' You just have to develop the awareness to see it. The Spiritual Master also said that, 'You always have the choice to follow or not to follow the guidance that's given. Your free will is always respected.' End quote," Evan finished.

"These guys seem ultra good and honest," I said.

"They are good and honest. They have a mission and they are dedicated to it. The mission of, The Brotherhood of Light and Love, is to help all who wish to learn to enhance their existing connection with spirit."

"That sounds ghostly," I said before I made ghostly sound effects. Evan ignored my theatrics and continued, "I mean Divine Spirit, or the Spirit of God," he added. "Remember in the 'Star Wars Trilogy', the Jedi Master who taught Luke Skywalker called it, 'The Force that permeates and surrounds all life'. Sri Hikari Hito said that, 'We're all individual Souls, but we are also a part of the whole. Divine Spirit is the connecting Spiritual Essence, or spiritual fluid that ties existence together.' "

"He compared us to pebbles dropped into a vast lake. The ripples that our presence creates have an affect on everything. We just don't recognize all the connections. Sometimes we are in harmony with the ripples that other people and beings make, and sometimes we are not. If we can accept the other person's viewpoint, you know, 'Live and let live,' then we don't create tensions. If we cannot accept that others may believe differently than us, or if someone doesn't respect the personal space of others, the result may be tensions, conflicts or even war. Isn't that a great metaphor?" Evan asked.

"I agree with you Evan, at least for the most part, but if you're saying to let people walk all over you, then I don't agree."

"I'm not saying that, Katy. The Spiritual Masters agree that a person needs to stand up for himself if someone is not respecting his personal space. They also said that all situations and people have individual natures, and it is best to respect that situation's characteristics and individuality. They said that most people respond in kind to a calm, honest, respectful voice. There's an underlying reason for this. The Spiritual Masters gave me this knowledge." Evan paused for dramatic effect, before he said, "Everything has a vibration."

"What do you mean, vibration," I wondered aloud.

Evan smiled and continued, "You're going to like this Katy. Think about this. If objects like Mrs. Copes car react to vibes like anger and frustration and if exposure to prolonged anger causes breakdowns in her car, Imagine how the same angry vibrations would affect people who are open to those negative vibes. Everything vibrates at its own specific rate, and the Holy Spirit or Divine Spirit connects everything together, so . . ." Evan let me connect the dots.

"Evan, why did you think I would like that? That's really a scary thought," I said.

"I understand why you find it scary. Don't worry the creator of existence, God, created safe guards which ensure that everything in the universe is as it should be. The first safe guard is the Law of Cause and Effect, The Law of Karma. If you create something from the positive or negative vibes, like thoughts, words and actions, whatever is created will eventually find their way back to the sender and impact on the sender's life. The Brotherhood of Light and Love, call this law, "The Great Equalizer." It is a great phrase. This spiritual law balances everything out. I really like discovering how all the pieces of existence fit together. It's amazing."

As Evan helped me to become aware of the pieces to the puzzle he called existence, I began to catch his enthusiasm and sense of wonder. I liked what he was saying. I needled Evan, "Evan, remember when you used to terminate me. Were you respecting me and my, what did you call it, personal space?"

"Yeah, well, I didn't understand all that stuff back then. I wouldn't do that anymore. You know that don't you, Katy?"

"I know that, I just wanted to needle you. Evan, what you have been telling me is amazing. I want to know more," I said.

Evan smiled and asked, "What would you like to know?"

"Where does one person's personal space officially end and another person's personal space begin?" I asked.

"There's nothing official about it. As the Spiritual Master would say, it's very subjective. The spiritual guides travel with me to visit different cultures, in heaven and here on earth. I saw that there are many factors, that influence where personal space begins and ends. The situation, environment, culture, and . . . did you know that in some cultures, it's okay to eat dogs? We think of them as pets and friends, but in some cultures it's customary to,-" Evan stopped when he saw me put my hands over my mouth. Evan asked, "Who is the true judge of reality or truth?"

I said, "I don't know, in our country I would guess the judges, juries or the law makers; and I guess each of us decide for ourselves what we believe to be true."

Evan asked, "How about God and the Spirit of God or the Holy Spirit, what kind of say do they have in deciding on what is true?"

"I have no idea," I answered.

Evan said, "As I was saying, in some cultures eating a dog is like us eating beef. Wars have been fought because people have believed or have done things differently."

"Evan, stop talking about eating—. Let's change the subject, please," I requested.

"Okay, no more talking about inviting dogs to dinner," Evan joked.

I gave Evan a warning glance and said, "Evan that was an awful joke. You need to go to joke telling school." I made a half-baked attempt at sarcasm.

Evan smiled, and continued, "You know, in France people greet each other by kissing on the cheek. If I had said hello to Joy Michel like that, she would have belted me one. I would be stepping on her comfort zone."

"I knew it! I knew you liked her and you pretended you didn't," I bugged him.

"Hey, I'm a guy with eyes and feelings." Evan was daydreaming as he said, "The French are lucky," Evan, laughed, before quickly adding, "Don't get me wrong. I wouldn't have kissed her without her say so. I had enough smarts back then, to know how to treat a lady with respect." Evan sighed and added, "Joy didn't know I was alive back then, I wish I'd been able to date her."

"She would have liked you, if she had gotten to know you," I assured him.

"Hey, she missed out," Evan joked. We both laughed and then Evan said, "In the end, it doesn't matter. She has her life and I have mine. Life goes on for all of us."

I asked, "Uh, now that everyone in heaven knows about the Spiritual Laws, like the Law of Cause and Effect, is heaven a lot different from here on earth?"

"Katy, not everyone in the different levels of heaven knows about or even believes in these laws. The people who know about these laws still have the freedom of choice to live by them or not. Everyone, even in heaven, is an individual. They still have the chance to choose their reality, truth and beliefs. In many ways, certain levels of heaven are not much different from life on earth. Each person has the potential to create a heavenly consciousness. Heaven can live in your heart no matter where you go. Katy, if people decreased or eliminated the anger, jealousy, greed or disrespect, if everyone lived with divine love in their hearts, imagine how that would affect relationships, and all of life?"

I tried to imagine the picture that Evan had begun to paint. "That's hard for me to imagine, it's a lot to imagine."

"I've had a lot of time to imagine what it would be like," Evans smile broadened. "And Sri Hikari Hito has spoken about the subject. He said, 'If enough people live with divine love in their hearts this new consciousness could transform existence.'"

"That's a nice thought Evan, but not a realistic viewpoint. Everyone isn't going to do that," I said.

"Katy, that's just it, if people gradually changed in this way then each of their personal universes would gradually transform. It would be like that old shampoo commercial, 'And they told two friends, and so on, and so on, and so on.' The change would be cumulative."

"You watched shampoo commercials?" I asked.

"No, I watched the ladies in the shampoo commercials. It was some show to do with old commercials. Don't change the subject. We were talking about the transformation of spiritual awareness and existence, not hair commercials. Like I said, the change would be cumulative."

I nodded and said, "Evan, a change like that would have to happen over ages and ages. Does the Spiritual Master really think that this can happen?" I asked.

Evan slowly shook his head before answering, "I did ask. The Spiritual Master just smiled and didn't answer me in words." Evan added, "We're talking about possibilities here, it might be possible. Has the future been written yet?"

"I'm not totally sure. I guess I'm a little more skeptical than you are. I still find this hard to imagine."

Suddenly I heard another voice, "Kathleen, have you forgotten the expansive God spark within you?"

I quickly turned to find the source of the voice. A Being of Light, shaped like a big oval of light, seemed to be sitting in the back seat, behind the driver's seat. I opened my mouth to scream.

Evan yelled, "No Katy! It's a Spiritual Being. It won't hurt you."

I moved to the far corner of the car and stared, before saying, "Who are . . . ? What are you?" I asked.

"He's a member of The Brotherhood of Light and Love," Evan quickly answered.

"I am Light; I am a single note in the universal sound. I am one of God's helpers. I am Soul, a piece of Divine Spirit. Everyone is Soul," the Spiritual Master calmly answered, "Remember, God loves Soul." The Being of Light added, "God and Divine Spirit have given individuals the longing to learn and know, in order to reunite with the God Essence. Your growing wish to know the secrets of life has opened the door for more Light to enter your world. If you feel unprepared for further contact, the time line can be delayed."

"No! I mean yes! You shocked me; people don't look like you, except in the movies. I want to learn the things that Evan's learning about," I assured the Being of Light.

The Being of Light seemed to nod, as it said, "The quest for spiritual evolution is a gift to life, to existence, beyond imagination. Many beings are adolescent in nature, but they continually grow and transform into new shoes of self-awareness. Just as Pinocchio proved himself responsible enough to exist as a real boy, so will you, and others like you, prove yourselves responsible enough to exist in the Soul Consciousness, and finally God Awareness. Each experience brings you closer to these noble goals." In an instant, like a light switch turning off, the Being of Light had vanished. I continued to stare in awe and disbelief.

Evan composed himself and said, "Well, that was a surprise."

"You call that a surprise! Now that is an understatement. Did you know that was going to happen?"

Evan shook his head and answered, "No, I had no idea. I mean, I knew you would be meeting the Spiritual Masters eventually, but I didn't know when or where."

I shook my head and said, "Boy, he really made an entrance. I was going to ask you what they were like and when I would be meeting them. That answers that question. When you said Brotherhood of Light and Love, you weren't kidding about the light part," I said.

"They don't always appear as Beings of Light; they come in all sizes, as males, females, from all nationalities and cultures. Some of them are thousands of years old but they are not necessarily old looking or dress in ancient costumes. For the most part, they dress to fit into the culture they live in or travel in. It's not what they wear or what they look like that makes them highly spiritual beings, it's what they have in here," Evan pointed to his heart and continued. "It's their countless experiences and the spiritual wisdom that they've gained through their many life times, that makes them highly spiritual beings. It's how they live, and apply this wisdom in every moment, that makes them Spiritual Masters." Evan stared beyond my head.

"What is it?" I turned to look. Mrs. Cope and Justine were approaching the car. I hoped that they did not think I was talking to myself. I turned to Evan but he was no longer sitting in the driver's seat.

"I whispered, "Evan, I want to learn. I'm looking forward to the next surprise." I did not want there to be any misunderstandings. I wanted to learn and grow.

Chapter 11

A Child's Reality

I stepped out of the Vega to meet Justine as she scurried towards me. Justine did not give me her customary giant bear hug; instead, she avoided my wrist and gave me a gentle hug. Justine's eyes stared as if glued to the tensor bandage that circled my wrist.

"Hello, Justine. How are you little munchkin?"

"Hi, does it hurt?" she asked, as she examined my wrist.

I smiled and answered, "Only when I think about it. Just kidding, my wrist will be as good as new in a couple of days." I stepped back to get a better look at her and said, "Now let me look at you. Justine, you've grown at least a half inch since the last time I saw you." The tiny blonde-haired five year old loved to pretend that she was a grown-up. She was always proud and happy when I noticed how much she had grown.

"I grow everyday, Mom has to buy me new clothes all the time," she proudly announced. She seemed to stand straighter and taller as she tried to prove this to me.

"How about you two growing girls hop into little Hilda, before you grow too big to fit," Mrs. Cope suggested.

"Mom, we don't grow that fast," Justine corrected her mother.

"You fooled me. Okay Justine, into the back seat and show Katy how you can put your own seat belt on."

"A-okay Mom, I can do it." Justine scurried into the back seat and fastened her seat belt like an old pro. Mrs. Cope reached back to check that the belt was secure.

"I'm sorry we took so long in there, for some reason Justine's coat wasn't where she had hung it up. This always seems to happen when I'm in a hurry. I hope it wasn't too long of a wait. " Mrs. Cope was talking at double speed, as if she was trying to make up for lost time.

"That's okay, Mrs. Cope. I wasn't bored. I never knew I could learn so much in just fifteen minutes."

"You learned? What did you learn?" she asked.

I had put my foot in it again. "I, I got inspired and did some geometry homework." I scowled as I said this; I detested geometry.

During the drive back to their apartment building, Mrs. Cope asked Justine to tell us what she had done at kindergarten. Justine dug into the pocket of her lemon-and blue-colored jacket. She extracted a folded piece of paper.

"Guess what, Katy?" Justine asked.

"What?" I asked.

"We're going to get a new car," she announced.

"Wow, no kidding." I glanced at Mrs. Cope's frowning face. I got the impression that this was news to her.

"Justine honey, who said that we are getting a new car?"

"You did Mom."

"I did?"

"Mo-om, you said we would get a new car when pigs grow wings and fly. You always say that Mom," Justine reminded her mother.

"Justine, I haven't seen any flying pigs in the skies, have you, Katy?" she asked.

I shook my head and answered, "No, I would have remembered that. That would be cool to see."

I looked back at Justine just as she passed forward the folded sheet of paper. I unfolded it and burst out laughing. There, before my eyes, flew a smiling, angelic, winged pig. I held up the sheet so that Mrs. Cope had a clear view of the masterpiece. She joined me in a duet of breathless laughter.

When Mrs. Cope could finally speak, she asked, "Justine, I love your happy pig. What is its name?"

"I named her Emily, because she smiles like Katy's Aunt Emily," Justine stated.

"You remember my Aunt Emily?" I asked with astonishment.

Justine nodded with enthusiasm and answered, "I remember her big smile in the picture you showed me."

Mrs. Cope chuckled, before saying, "Oh honey, if you can make a flying pig then maybe after your Daddy finishes school we can make a new car," She quickly added, "But it might take us longer to get a new car."

"After Daddy finishes school is okay." Justine leaned towards me and explained, "A car is bigger than a pig."

I nodded my head in serious acknowledgement, and responded, "Of course, that makes sense."

As we rode the apartment building elevator to the third floor, Mrs. Cope explained the arrangements she had made regarding Justine's care. Tomorrow morning Justine and I would take the LRT to the University Station then transfer to bus #39 for a ride to the largest mall in the world, the West Edmonton Mall.

We would meet Justine's Aunt Sylvia in front of the Orange Julius stand, at the Phase 3 food court, at twelve noon. Justine would miss her Saturday afternoon nap since her Aunt would be taking the children to see the Shrine Circus that afternoon. For this reason, I would be putting her to sleep an hour earlier tonight. My babysitting duties would officially end when Justine's Aunt Sylvia met us at the mall.

"Mom," Justine pulled at her Mother's sleeve. "Can I open the door? Can I, Mom?" Mrs. Cope dug into her purse. "Mom, can I have the key?"

"Honey, wait a second," she pulled Justine's hand out from inside her purse. "I need to find it before I can give it to you and you need to wait." As the keys emerged from the purse Justine dived for them. Mrs. Cope quickly pulled them back out of her reach. "Wait." She held up each key as she said, "This key is for the bottom lock and this key is for the dead-bolt. What do you say?" she asked Justine.

"Thank you, please," Justine answered.

"Close enough," she said, as she smiled and handed her keys to her daughter. Justine grabbed them and squealed as she scrambled towards the door. "I should warn you Katy, you're going to hear the words, 'I'll do it,' a lot this weekend. When I told her that you hurt your hand she informed me that she would be doing the cooking. Mrs. Cope whispered, "You're going to be having peanut butter and jelly sandwiches tonight. Justine insisted on making it for your supper. Don't worry; there is a second supper in the refrigerator. I'll let her know that the peanut butter and jelly sandwiches are the appetizer." We both watched Justine as she struggled to open the door.

I smiled as I imagined Justine making the sandwiches. I felt privileged to witness this process once before and appreciated the effort that Justine put into her creation. I said, "Don't worry Mrs. Cope; I know that they're great because I've tried them."

"I thought your Mother said something about peanut butter not being your favorite food. Did I hear wrong?" Mrs. Cope asked.

"Mom's right, but Mom hasn't seen all the effort that Justine puts into making her special sandwich, she makes peanut butter taste terrific."

Mrs. Cope smiled and said, "Katy, you have the makings of a good mother." Pride burst through me when she said this.

"Thank you," I quickly acknowledged.

"There's another thing I should warn you about," Mrs. Cope added. "I've always encouraged

Justine to be creative and to use her imagination; she has created an imaginary friend called, the Magic Man. Maybe it's because she misses her father. Mike is going to be away for another month. His computer-training course is extremely complicated, it's one of a kind, he's so lucky he got into it. What I'm trying to say is the reason Justine created the Magic Man doesn't matter to me. I've discussed it with Mike and we've decided not to interfere with her imaginings. So if you could go along with it for right now, I'd appreciate it."

"Sure Mrs. Cope, no problem," I agreed.

"Hey, I opened the door already." Justine's sudden announcement startled the both of us.

"Thank you, honey," Mrs. Cope, called to her before adding, "We're being paged."

Immediately after entering the apartment, Mrs. Cope phoned a taxi company and gave the dispatcher the necessary information. She said, "It will be a ten minute wait." It was time enough for her to tie up loose ends.

Mrs. Cope's bags were already packed and stacked in the hallway, and she gave me the phone number of the Marriott Hotel in Toronto, room 720. The hotel was not far from the computer-training center where her husband's courses were taking place. Through sheer luck, she was able to get a last minute seat sale and the computer company got a discount on rooms for their students and their visiting family members.

Mrs. Cope double-checked her list of things to do. "What else do I need to do?" She asked herself. "Oh yes, here's the spare set of keys to the apartment. Give them to Sylvia tomorrow, she'll be expecting them. Justine's over night bag is packed and ready to go. Have I forgotten anything else?"

"You forgot to say good-bye to me, Mom." Justine made a running leap into her mother's arms and received a huge kiss for her efforts.

"I'm going to miss you so much," her mother said. She gave her another kiss and a hug.

"I'm going to miss you more," Justine responded.

"You listen to Katy and help her out. I'm going to ask Katy if you were a lazy bones," she warned. Then she added, "Katy, she needs a bath before she goes out tomorrow."

"No I don't, Mom," Justine stated.

"No arguing," she warned. "Oh and Katy, there's some minestrone soup, salad and chicken in the refrigerator." Mrs. Cope quickly added, "You can have that after your peanut butter and jelly sandwiches. On the other hand, you can take it as a picnic lunch when you go to the mall to meet Aunt Sylvia and little Duncan. You two decide. Just eat it, don't let it go to waste."

After a half dozen more good-byes, Mrs. Cope finally left the apartment. We scurried out onto the balcony. Justine climbed up onto a stool, so she could get a better view of the street. We waited. Mrs. Cope emerged from the building and handed her bags to the cab driver. We shouted more good-byes. She looked up at us, waved and blew us a kiss before she entered the cab. We watched it drive out of sight. I helped Justine as she stepped off the stool.

I said, "Justine, I'm getting hungry. How are you feeling?"

"Me too," Justine agreed.

"How about we fix supper?" I suggested. "By the time it's ready, we'll really be hungry."

"A-okay," Justine shouted, as she scurried into the kitchen. She added, "I'm making dinner."

"Okay. Can I help," I asked.

"No," Justine said a-matter-of-factly.

"You're right, you are the head chef. Can I be your assistant?" I asked. Justine stopped and looked at me. "Your helper," I clarified.

"Okay," she agreed.

"As my first duties as assistant, how about I get the peanut butter down and set the table? Then I'll heat up the soup."

"Okay, you can do that," Justine agreed. She got the whole wheat bread and jelly out of the refrigerator as I did what I had agreed to do. She climbed up onto the small step stool and opened the bread bag. I handed her the butter knife and watched her as I stirred the soup. While trying to spread the crunchy peanut butter on the bread, Justine squashed the slice of bread together in several places. When Justine combined the slices, the matching holes on each slice of bread formed a cute little window. Justine suddenly realized that she had forgotten to spread the jelly on the sandwich.

"It's all right Justine, we don't need any jelly," I reassured her.

"Ka-ty, it's not a peanut butter and jelly sandwich if you forget the jelly," Justine informed me.

"Of course," I agreed, "How could I forget that?"

"That's okay Katy, Mom forgets too." Justine spread the jelly over the surface of the two sandwiches. The raspberry jelly surrounded the windows, like lipstick on a woman's lips.

We carried our plates to the table. I had set the table with cutlery, soup bowls, and two glasses of milk. I ladled the soup into the bowls and warned Justine to let the soup cool for a few minutes. I stared at my sandwich and wondered how to pick it up.

Justine stood up, "I forgot," she said. I thought what she had forgotten was in the kitchen. Justine surprised me. She walked around to the far end of the table and pulled a chair away from the table before returning to sit in her own chair.

I stared at the empty chair and asked, "Justine, why did you move that chair?"

"The Magic Man wants to sit down, that's where he sits until Daddy comes home. Then he'll sit there." She pointed to the chair across from me. "The Magic Man comes here and then he goes away, like magic." She gulped some milk before she went on. "His real name is really big, I can't say it. He said it's okay if I call him, The Magic Man." Justine took a bite of her sandwich.

"Oh, you named him like you named Emily," I reasoned. "I made up a pretend friend when I was a young girl, I named her Mona."

"I didn't make him up!" Justine yelled. Then she pointed to the empty chair and said, "Katy thinks you're a pretend person." The funniest feeling washed over me as I stared at the empty chair, I felt like someone caught with her hand in a cookie jar. "How come everyone thinks you're a pretend man?" Justine asked, before she bit into her sandwich. I copied her lead.

After I swallowed I asked, "Could you tell the Magic Man that I'm sorry that I thought he was a pretend person."

Justine spoke between chews, "That's okay. . . . The Magic Man isn't mad. . . . He doesn't ever get mad."

I tried to concentrate on the sticky meal in front of me. I let Justine know that the soup had cooled and then I continued to eat my sandwich. I put it down and licked my fingers and lips, before wiping them with my napkin. Jelly lipstick had a lot of staying power.

"Thanks for making supper for me, it was delicious Justine."

"You're welcome," Justine proudly answered. Justine's toothy smile beamed up at me. She had built this sticky gift with a lot of care and love, so I felt privileged to be the recipient. What did it matter that I did not like peanut butter. Together we cleaned off our hands, faces, the kitchen and dishes. Justine went to the Magic Man's chair and pushed it under the table.

"He had to go home," she explained.

"Of course, I guess we all have to go home sometime." I tried to tune into Justine's reality.

We spent the rest of the evening watching T.V. and coloring. Justine volunteered to draw me a picture of the Magic Man, I thought that he would look like her step Dad but I was completely wrong. The Magic Man's hair was short, straight and dark, not blonde and medium length. The man wore a robe that ended below his knees. I wondered who she patterned her drawing after.

Later that night Mom called to find out how everything was going, after a short visit with both of us, we bid each other good-bye. I was glad when eight o'clock rolled around.

With a little coaxing and a promise that I would read her an extra bedtime story, I set a record for getting Justine ready for bed. We sat on the sofa together, Justine cuddled up to my side and I read the bedtime stories. She was already half asleep when I picked her up and headed for the bedroom. I was careful not to put a strain my wrist, which was easy because of Justine's lightweight.

Justine mumbled, "Good night, Katy. Good night, Magic Man," and managed a quick wave of her hand. She repeated, "Good night." I figured she was imagining and didn't question her. I carefully tucked her into bed and switched on her night light before I left the bedroom.

I gathered my books and set them on the kitchen table. I had a couple of hours to get some homework done so I began to rewrite my physics notes. I was finding it hard to concentrate, my eyes kept glancing at Justine's drawing of the Magic Man. I shoved it under my binder and leaned back in my chair. A breathless scream burst from my lips, I jumped from the chair sending it toppling to the floor. A man was sitting at the far end of the table watching me.

"If you move, I'll scream," I threatened. The man did not move. "Who are you? How did you get in here?"

The man wore a dark blue robe like an oriental costume; a Japanese kimono with a same colored sash secured the kimono around the waist. He had short coal black hair, cropped neatly around his hairline. A joyful light filled his dark piercing eyes; there was something familiar about this man. I slowly reached under my binder and pulled out Justine's drawing. I glanced under the table, the hem of his navy colored robe stopped below his knees; he had brown, leather sandals on his feet, like the man in the drawing.

I whispered, "The Magic Man."

The man finally said, "I was invited to be here."

"You moved the chair away from the table so you don't need Justine's help to do that," I observed.

The man smiled and answered, "The little one's gift of caring and love is gratefully accepted." He spoke with a slight accent.

I said, "Holy cow, you're real!"

The man asked, "Is the child's reality imagined because the reality is the belief of one so young? Or can this child's reality be clear and uncluttered by the concerns of those around her?" He paused, before he continued. "Most people can only wish to see through the eyes of such a child."

I let out a breath; it was as if I suddenly remembered to breathe. As I stared at the man, a faint recognition began to steal into my consciousness. I had a very strong feeling that I had met this man before, but when and where eluded me?

I repeated the question, "Who are you?"

"I am a seeker of truth," he answered.

My knees and voice were shaky, I was scared but I also felt safe. I had an overwhelming feeling to ask my next question. I asked, "What is truth?"

"Truth can be found in the heart of every being. Each person lives his own truth and this truth is reflected back to the world through one's own thoughts words and actions. In turn, the world will reflect his truth back to the individual."

"So, what's that supposed to mean?" I asked. The meaning of his words seemed to be like the answer to a riddle that waited just beyond my grasp.

"An understanding of truth is individual and always changing, for as you grow, your understanding grows. Spiritual truth is a doorway; it opens to all who have the vision and heart to find it. You will find this doorway via the wisdom gained through your daily life experiences, this doorway of spiritual truth leads to the gem of divine love."

"Who are you?" I asked again in a hushed voice.

"A part of your past present and future," he answered before disappearing.

"The past present and future," I repeated. I was sure that he had said that to me before, but when?"

A couple of years ago I had seen an old 1970's T.V. movie. In the movie, a young man was put in a mental institution as a young child. A doctor discovered that this young man could read. They wondered if he was misdiagnosed and they proceeded to put him through many tests. One test was in the form of two questions. They asked him to define reality. The young man handed the doctor a plastic cup. Then they asked him to define imagination. The young man handed the same doctor an imaginary cup.

The same question popped into my head, had I imagined all of this? How could I have imagined all the things that the Magic Man said? Those thoughts were definitely not mine. I had an unsettling thought; if the Magic Man was not real then maybe Evan was not real. Reality for me had changed so much. I wondered if reality could be truth. Maybe reality and truth was individually unique for each person was that what the stranger tried to tell me. Up until two hours ago, Justine's reality was sure a lot different from my own. I had a feeling that very soon I would be exploring this new reality.

Chapter 12

Who Is the Magic Man?

I passed Justine the plate of scrambled eggs. "You forgot something, Justine," I reminded her.

"Please and thank you," she said, as she scraped the eggs onto her plate.

"No, what I mean is you forgot something else." I pointed towards the end of the table.

"Jam?" she guessed.

"No."

"Peanut butter?"

"No."

"Milk?"

"The milk is in front of you. Hold it Justine; it's not food that you forgot." Justine did not hear me. She kept repeating these three words and giggling after each series of words. I decided to wait until she got tired of her game, in the mean time, I ate my breakfast.

"Don't you want to play anymore?" she asked.

I shook my head. "No," I managed to say, as I chewed a mouthful of toast. "I'm all played out. I was trying to say that you forgot to pull the Magic Man's chair out for him." I motioned to the chair at the other end of the table.

"The Magic Man isn't here; I pulled the chair out for him when he's here. Mike doesn't pull out Mom's chair for her when she's not here," she pointed out.

"He'd have to have really long arms to do that from Toronto wouldn't he?" I kidded her. "Justine, that's not what I wanted to ask you." I asked, "Is the Magic Man Oriental?"

"What's orient?" Justine asked.

"Oriental is an ethnic group," I explained.

"What's ethnic?" Justine asked.

"Wait just a second, I have a dictionary, I'll get the definition." I quickly got up and fished the dictionary out of my knapsack. "Okay, ethnic, ethnic," I said as I flipped through the pages. "Got it, ethnic, here's one definition: of or relating to races, or large groups of people classed according to common traits and customs."

Justine's face told me her feelings before she said, "I don't understand."

"Okay, let me try again." I asked, "Do you remember Mr. Lee, my next door neighbor, the older Chinese man? He is short with thinning silvery grey hair and a beard; he is Oriental. His ancestor, that means his parents and grand parents and their parents and grandparents, lived in the Orient; in countries like Japan, China, Mongolia or Korea. That is where their family originated. I mean, that's where his family started, came from, began," I explained.

"Mr. Lee, he's the man with all the roses. He gave me a red rose when I went to your house," Justine remembered.

"That's right, you're right." I felt like we were making progress.

"The Magic Man's hair is black." She added, "He doesn't have a beard."

"Oohhh," I groaned as I covered my face with my hands. I was not getting through to her. How was I going to get through? I tried once again. "Justine, is the Magic Man five feet six, or seven inches tall?"

Justine thought for a few seconds and said, "The Magic Man is really tall."

I asked my question again. "Is the Magic Man about this tall?" I indicated a height about four inches above my head.

She thought about my question for a few seconds before nodding her head and saying, "I think so."

Inspiration hit me; I pulled a piece of paper out of my binder grabbed Justine's crayons off the kitchen counter, then sat down and began to draw. I asked as I kept drawing, "Justine is it okay with you if I borrow your crayons?" Justine had dragged a chair closer to my seat, perched herself on the chair and leaned over to intently watch the picture that I was creating.

She nodded her head and answered, "Okay."

I drew the Magic Man, with his short black hair and dark blue kimono. Justine was squealing with excitement. At last, I colored his sandals. The picture was finally completed. "There, he's done," I announced. I asked, "Is that what the Magic Man looks like?"

Justine grabbed the picture out of my hands and exclaimed, "Katy, you drew the Magic Man. That is the Magic Man. Can I have the picture, Katy?" she asked.

"Sure," I answered. "How about we exchange pictures? Can I have yours?"

"It's a deal Katy," she agreed.

"Let's shake on it," I said as I extended my hand. After the hand shake, Justine gave me a great big hug.

"I'll clean up," I announced.

"I'm supposed to help you," she reminded me.

"Right, I forgot. Well, how about I start to clean up while you go put your picture away, then you can help me?"

"A-okay," Justine shouted. I had barely finished the sentence before she was off and running, she had returned in a few of seconds. "All done, Katy," she informed me.

As I handed Justine the dishes, we talked about the Magic Man and our itinerary for this morning. I explained that after we completed the dishes, we would brush our teeth and Justine would have her bath.

"Uh, I don't want a bath," Justine informed me.

"You need a bath, remember what your Mom said," I reminded her.

"Can we go swimming?" Justine asked.

"No. No, we are not going swimming. We don't have time to go swimming."

"But Katy, you never go swimming with me anymore. Please, please, can we go swimming," she begged.

"No, you need to have your bath," I repeated.

"I always shower after I go swimming. If I shower then I don't need a bath," Justine reasoned. Justine reminded me of Mom and Mr. Spock on Star Trek. She was a pint-sized logic thinking Vulcan, with enthusiasm mixed in.

"Justine, we just haven't got time. I need to, to, meet a friend at the Mall, so there is not enough time to go swimming. I'm sorry." As I said this, I crossed my fingers behind my back. I could not believe it; I was lying to a child.

"You never go swimming with me anymore." This time when she said this, she folded her arms across her chest to punctuate her angry complaint.

"Justine, I'll promise to go swimming with you sometime, if you have a bath now."

"When can we go?" she asked.

"You need a bath right now, before we meet your Aunt Sylvia at the Mall," I reminded her.

"No. I mean, when can we go swimming?" She impatiently repeated her question.

"We will go someday, when we have time." I gave a vague answer.

"When?" Justine asked again.

"Soon," I answered. Justine made it difficult to be vague, she was like an elephant; she never forgot things especially when they were important to her.

There was a time two years ago; I was babysitting Justine and her little nephew Duncan. Duncan had a slight bout of diarrhea. When her Aunt Sylvia had said slight, I thought, 'No problem.' It was not as if I was a novice when it came to changing diapers. Boy was I surprised. Justine was sitting on the training potty when I peeled the Pampers back.

"Oh my God!" I said, as I held my breath, my nose wrinkled, and I muttered another, "Oh my God." While I tackled the task of cleaning the mess, I repeated those three words. I stopped cold when I heard Justine's voice repeating, "Oh my God. Oh my God." I spent the next hour getting her to repeat the phrase, "Oh my goodness." Many times I have underestimated the quickness of this bright little girl.

"How come you don't go swimming anymore?" Justine asked. Before I could answer, I was literally, saved by the bell, the telephone rang. If Alexander Graham Bell were alive, I would have kissed him.

I smiled and said, "I'll get that. Good morning, this is the Cope's residence."

"Katy, I'm glad I caught you before you left. This is Sylvia Zimmer."

"Hi Mrs. Zimmer . . . No, I haven't forgotten. . . . You want to change the meeting time to 1:00 p.m.," I glanced at Justine. She was listening intently. "Sure, we can do that, no problem. We're planning to have a picnic lunch."

"You're a life saver," Mrs. Zimmer said, before adding, "Thank you so much. I'll see you at 1:00 o'clock." We exchanged good-byes and I hung up.

"We're going to meet Aunt Sylvia and Duncan at the Orange Julius stand near the food court at 1:00 o'clock," I informed her.

"Can we go swimming now," Justine asked.

"Justine, you've asked me that three times. No, we don't have time and I forgot my swimming suit." I thought this would end the discussion. I was wrong.

"You could just watch me, you don't have to swim. Mom sometimes watches me, and she doesn't go swimming," she said. Justine had a huge grin on her face, she was amazing, I was debating with a five year old and I was loosing big time.

Then I remembered my old excuse, "I have to meet a friend at the mall. Remember, I said that before?" I reminded her. "I'm meeting a friend from school. We'll go swimming another time."

"You promise?" Justine asked. I could tell that she did not believe me. Maybe it is true that small children have a sixth sense, they know the feel of honesty. Justine's ability to see the Magic Man showed me that she was very intuitive.

When I said the words, "I promise," they were like magic words. Justine had her bath without further argument.

After Justine had her bath, we tidied the apartment and prepared a picnic lunch to take with us. I combed and braided her long blonde hair and inspected her navy slacks and striped navy and white shirt. This outfit gave Justine the spit and polished look of a young sailor.

I carried the knapsack stuffed with my books and our lunch squarely on my back. I was grateful for the invention of Tupperware. I held one strap of Justine's over-night bag while Justine had placed the second bag strap over her shoulder. I kept my tensor wrapped free hand tucked against my side. Once I locked the apartment door, we were on our way.

The bus ride was uneventful for me, but to Justine it appeared to be like an adventure. She stared at everyone and everything. We arrived at the mall's south side giant bus terminal, just before noon. We walked in the shade of the second level parkade and emerged into the warm sunlight before entering the polished glass doors, near entrance #41.

West Ed. is a shopper's heaven. There are two levels of recreation and shopping that stretch on and on forever. There is a miniature golf course, a huge I-Max theater with a fire-breathing dragon and a massive indoor amusement park, which features a three looped roller-coaster ride. One of the main attractions is a gigantic indoor wave pool accompanied by over a dozen water slides, ranging from toddler size to many giant twisting spirals and mazes plus one heart-stopping slide that was a 60-foot drop.

Before Evan's death, we would have gone swimming on such a day and arrived minutes before our 1:00 p.m. appointment. I had always found it difficult to go swimming, a slight case of nausea and fear would hit me. I would have to calm down and take a few deep breathes before entering the water. Now, the nausea was more intense. The water seemed to magnify painful memories and feelings.

The traffic through the mall was busy, more than a usual Saturday morning. I was glad this was not a holiday weekend that would have meant wading through a sea of wall-to-wall people. I was glad to have a relaxing hour before our scheduled meeting. I asked Justine if she would like to window shop, or eat right now. She shrugged her shoulders. The Orange Julius stand where we were to meet Aunt Sylvia was located at the west end of the mall at the mouth of the largest food court.

"I know Justine. How about I treat you to a strawberry drink and we can sit and make up our minds about what to do?"

"Okay, but can I have a banana drink?" she asked.

"Sure," I agreed. We started walking, and did some window-shopping as we went.

A voice asked, "Hi stranger, run into any red VW convertibles lately?"

I turned and stared into a pair of sparkling light brown eyes. It took me a second to get over my surprise. "My running into car days are officially over, I've retired," I jokingly said.

"I'm glad to hear that," Andrew smiled as he said this. His voice was warm and caring with a touch of laughter mixed in. He would have uplifted anyone's day. Andrew was a magic man in his own special way. "What brings you to the mall?" Are you running away from home?" he joked, as he pointed at all our bags.

"We decided to do a little window shopping before we had our lunch," I explained, as I lifted our lunch bag.

"We?" he asked, as he tried to look behind me.

I looked around to find Justine standing directly behind me, peeking up at Andrew's form. She had been unusually shy and quiet so I had forgotten to introduce her.

Andrew leaned to his right so he could get a better look at Justine. "Who's your little friend?" he asked.

I stepped aside and moved Justine up beside me. "Justine, this is Andrew Dover. Andrew, I would like you to meet Justine Cope. She's Mrs. Cope's little, I mean big daughter."

Andrew nodded his head and extended his hand to Justine. He said, "You look pretty big to me. Glad to meet you Justine."

Justine took his hand and shook it but instead of returning his greeting, she asked, "Are you Katy's friend?"

Andrew knelt to be at eye level with Justine. He answered, "I certainly hope I'm her friend."

What Justine said next startled both of us. "If Katy didn't have to meet you, I could have gone swimming." Justine, the Vulcan child made another appearance.

"No kidding, you could have gone swimming. I'm sorry about that." As he said this, Andrew looked up at me and silently asked me what was going on.

I quickly explained that we could not go swimming because I had to meet a friend this morning at the mall. I felt disgusted with myself. I shook my head and bent over to whisper an explanation in his ear, "I'm sorry Andrew, for getting you mixed up in this. I told Justine that I was meeting a friend at the mall, so I could get out of going swimming with her. It was stupid; I shouldn't have lied to her to begin with. I'll set the record straight right now." I turned to face Justine to tell her the truth, but before I could speak, Andrew stopped me.

He pulled my arm and shook his head when I looked at him. Andrew stood and whispered in my ear, "I'm a friend and you met me here at the mall, so what's the big deal?" He turned to Justine and apologized to her, "I'm really sorry that my meeting Katy for lunch, cut into your swimming time. Maybe I can make it up to you and buy you both lunches." He added, "I think that's the least I can do."

When I got over my surprise, I said, "That's not necessary, you don't have to pretend."

Andrew cut in again, "Hey, who's pretending. Lunch is a serious subject to me. I meant it when I said I'd buy you lunch," Andrew assured us.

"We have our lunch," Justine pointed out our lunch as proof.

"Andrew, it was nice of you to try to help me. That's what you were trying to do, right?" I asked.

Andrew nodded and answered, "Right."

I repeated, "It was nice of you, but I'm going to tell Justine the truth." Andrew nodded his head and stepped aside. I knelt down in front of Justine, and said, "Justine, our meeting Andrew here at the mall was just a wild coincidence; I didn't know he would be here." She continued to stare at me with a puzzled look on her face. I added, "I lied to you about having to meet someone here because I didn't want to go swimming in the pool. Right now, it is hard for me to go swimming. If anything happened to you I would have to go into the water and I don't want to go into the water right now."

Justine nodded her head and said, "Okay. We could go later Katy, when your arm is all better. I'm hungry, can we go eat?" Justine's one-track mind had made a sudden about face. I was going to clarify what I had said but I changed my mind, I had a feeling that a more detailed explanation was not necessary.

"How about you both join me for lunch? I'm buying, remember?" Andrew said.

"We have a picnic lunch. You're welcome to join us," I quickly offered.

"Yeah," Justine added her endorsement to my invitation. This was a sure sign that Andrew had Justine's seal of approval.

"How about I buy something and we can all share?" Andrew asked.

"We'll have a picnic," Justine's voice squealed with delight. "I like picnics," she announced.

"Count me in," I added. "Let's go find a table," I suggested.

"That sounds good to me. Come on Justine; let's race Katy to the food court." He grabbed Justine's hand along with her over night bag and headed west down the mall. "See you in a bit," Andrew called back to me.

"Hey that is not fair, you have a head start," I called after them. I quickly straightened my knapsack and picked up our lunch bag before following.

I heard Andrew's voice shout, "Warp nine, engage, and full speed ahead." He picked Justine up and his jogging pace went into high gear. When I finally joined them, they cheered. It was as if they were waiting, anticipating the arrival of a teammate at the end of a race. I raised my hands to acknowledge their cheers. Andrew was amazing, he had met Justine less than ten minutes ago and already they had a growing friendship.

Andrew asked, "Do you both like Chinese?"

I said, "Sure."

Justine said, "Katy's neighbor is a nice Chinese man, he's orient, and he grows nice roses."

I laughed, before agreeing, "Yes he's Oriental and he does grow beautiful red roses. Andrew was wondering if you like to eat Chinese food, that's what type of food he's going to get if you like it," I explained.

Justine answered, "I like noodles."

Andrew said to Justine, "I know some really nice Chinese people. They don't grow roses but they sure make good Chinese food and great noodles. I'll go get some." After Andrew left, we found our table and started to unpack our lunch.

Justine said, "He's nice Katy. And guess what?"

"What?" I asked.

"He likes Star Trek. I told Andrew that I like Mr. Spock, Tuvok, Dr. Crusher and the Doctor. Guess what?" she asked.

"What?" I asked.

"Andrew likes them too, he said that they are smart and they help people," Justine informed me.

"That's great Justine." I said.

Andrew returned with a huge plate of Chinese food, three bottles of juice and extra plates and utensils. "Time to eat," he announced.

Justine and I carefully helped remove the load of food from his hands. "How in the world did you carry all of that? You must have been a waiter."

"I've been there, done that," he said.

"You were a waiter?" I asked, as we all sat down. We began to dish up our food.

"For a little while I was a waiter. My Uncle and Aunt own 'Jake and Harry's Pizzeria and Spaghetti House'. I helped after school and during a few summer holidays to earn extra money for my college fund. This is the first year that I haven't worked a regular shift there. Dad saw some photos I had taken in my last photography class, we talked, and he asked me to work more hours at Dover Photography. I am building a good college fund. I think Dad is hoping that one day the sign on the shop window might read, 'Dover and Son'. All my photography classes may pay off, it's more than a great hobby but I'm not sure if it will be a career. I have other interests and other irons in the fire," Andrew explained.

"Wow, that's great," I said, as I helped Justine to fill her plate. She selected noodles, broccoli, and her mother's baked chicken. "It's great that you know your dreams and options. I'm still trying to figure out my own dreams," I said. "Dreams are what reality is based on," I quoted Evan.

"Everyone's in a hurry to figure out their lives," Andrew said. "We both have our whole life ahead of us. We will make a lot of our dreams come true in the next 50 or 60 years. It's okay if we don't have everything figured out yet. I figure we are not supposed to figure out everything all at once. I know that I wouldn't be able to handle that," he finished good-naturedly.

You sound like my brother Evan. I think that's what he would have said if he were here," I said.

"Is that your brother that died?" Justine asked.

"Yes," I answered. "He was a cool dude."

"Was he as cool as Andrew?" Justine asked, as she looked at Andrew.

I nodded my head and agreed, "Yes, he was just as cool and special," I quietly added, "He still is a cool dude in heaven."

As we ate our meal we talked about school, Andrew's swimming practices and our other interests.

Suddenly Justine's voice said, "The Magic Man said that we don't die. Daddy's not really dead." We both stared at Justine.

I said to Justine, "Of course your Dad's not dead. He's just at school, but he'll be back soon," I reassured her.

"No!" Justine gave an impatient shake of her head. "I mean my first real Dad. He's alive, but he lives somewhere else. The Magic Man helps me to visit him when I dream and sleep," she said.

I was astonished, it sounded like Justine was travelling by shifting her attention and awareness, just like Evan. I hoped that I would get to meet the Magic Man again.

I whispered an additional explanation to Andrew, "The Magic Man is Justine's imaginary teacher and friend, he helps her understand life." Andrew nodded and smiled.

I gave Justine a hug and said, "You're so lucky to have two Dads, the Magic Man and your Mom. They all care for you."

She nodded her head and reminded me, "You watch me too, Katy."

I nodded and said, "Yes, we all care about you. You aren't ever alone." I gave Justine another giant hug.

Chapter 13

Communication

"Have a good time at the circus," I said to Justine, not that she needed me to remind her to do that.

"Me too," a small voice asked to be remembered.

"Of course, you too Duncan," I said to the little boy who pulled at his mother's hand. His smile broadened and he tugged harder at his mother's arm.

I knelt and gave Justine a hug. "Say hello to the Magic Man for me," I whispered.

Justine smiled, returned a hug and nodded her head. She turned to Andrew and said, "I'm not mad about not swimming anymore, I had fun. I like Chinese food," she added.

Andrew also knelt to speak with Justine. "I'm glad you're not mad. Guess what, I had fun too. How about we do this again sometime soon?" he asked.

"When, tomorrow?" she quickly asked, as she looked at both of us.

I shook my head and said, "Tomorrow, I'm sorry Justine. Tomorrow isn't a good day for me."

"Andrew asked, "How about we do this the next time you and Katy come shopping?" He affectionately rubbed the hair on the crown of Justine's head and added, "Do we have a deal?"

"A-okay," Justine agreed. They shook hands to seal the deal.

"All right kids, lets get going. Thanks again Katy, I needed that extra hour." Andrew and I both watched as Aunt Sylvia gathered Justine and Duncan together.

"Bye, Katy. Bye, Andrew." Justine waved good-bye.

Duncan didn't want to be out done. He mimicked Justine, "Bye, Katy. Bye, Andrew."

In unison, they yelled, "Bye Andrew," as they followed Aunt Sylvia, who was trying her best to exercise noise control. They were chattering like parakeets, both of them did not want the other to have the last word.

"You really made a huge impression on Justine. She doesn't talk about the Magic Man in front of anyone." I wanted him to realize how special her sharing was.

Andrew put his arm around my shoulders and said, "She's easy to like. What a kid. One moment she is a five year old and the next moment she is like a wise old woman. Are there a lot of kids out there like her?"

"I don't know for sure. I suppose all kids are unique but Justine is special," I concluded.

Andrew turned me around as he said, "Come with me, I'd like to do something before I go back to the photography shop. Just promise not to tell my Dad that we did this," Andrew requested.

I stopped and looked into his eyes before asking, "What do you mean, don't tell your Dad?" I wondered what we were going to do. "Why isn't he going to like what we're going to do?"

Andrew smiled and said, "Any owner of a photography studio wouldn't like what we're about to do. Come on," he said, as he grabbed my backpack. He began to jog down the mall with me in tow; I had to scramble to keep up with him. In a few minutes we came to our destination, a photo-booth located just past the dolphin pool.

I laughed and said, "Now I understand," I shook my head and laughed again, "I agree, your Dad probably wouldn't like this."

Andrew said, "I really had you worried. You had images of the police coming after us, didn't you?" he asked.

I shook my head and answered, "No, my imaginings weren't that bad. I just wondered what was up. This I can handle, no problem," I joked.

Andrew placed the required amount of coinage into the machine. Then he said, "Well Ms. McCall, how about we find out what's behind curtain number one?" Andrew pulled the curtain aside, I entered and he followed. There was a small bench in the booth so Andrew sat down and put his arm around my neck. It seemed natural to lean on him. He asked me if I was okay with this and I said yes. I did not mind him holding me. I wondered *what girl in her right mind would not feel okay with this situation.*

We mugged for the camera. First, we did a corny picture with contorted faces, that one I felt like ripping up. The second picture was one where he kissed me on the cheek and I played a girl in shock. Then I kissed him on the cheek and he pretended to be swooning. The fourth, and last picture was one where we were just a couple having a picture taken together. It was my favorite. I found out that it was also Andrew's favorite photo. At this time, he realized how very late for work he was. We began to jog while we talked. I promised to draw a picture of us from the fourth picture, if he gave me that picture. He agreed, as we ran back to Dover Photography.

When we reached the store, Andrew gave me the fourth picture and said, "I'd like you to meet my Dad."

"Meet your Dad, really?" I asked.

"I think when my Dad meets you he'll understand why I took an extra long lunch hour. He may still blow a gasket, but at least he'll understand." I felt glad knowing that in some mysterious way, my presence could help Andrew out. "Let's go meet your Dad," I agreed.

When Andrew's father saw him, he was not pleased. Andrew apologized for being late and said it would not happen again. I waited for him to mention me.

I heard a voice saying, "Mr. Dover, I'm the reason why Andrew's late." The voice was my own. Andrew's father turned to look at me. I continued to speak, "We went for lunch, got talking and lost track of time."

"Dad, this is my friend Katy McCall," Andrew came over and put his arm around my shoulder. That felt so nice.

Andrew's father stared at me. When he noticed my wrapped up wrist, a smile emerged on his face and he said, "You're the one."

"I don't understand," I whispered to Andrew.

"It's a family joke," Andrew said, as he turned me towards the door. "I'd better get back to work while my Dad's in a good mood."

"I'm sorry you were hurt. You take care of your hand and bring my son back to work on time from now on." A huge grin was on Andrew's father face as he said this.

I turned to stare at him and asked, "You know about the accident?"

"Yes. Andrew told me all about you. He worries about your hand," his father added.

"Andrew probably told you what a klutz I was." I winced as I said this.

Mr. Dover shook his head, laughed, then answered, "No, Andrew-"

Andrew cut in, "Okay, that's it, we're gone." He turned me back towards the door. I thought I saw him shake his head at his father, before he added, "Dad, I'll be back in a second."

"Your Dad's nice, you didn't have to worry."

"Yeah, he's great. He's a laugh a minute."

I asked, "What did I just miss here?"

Andrew gave a short, quick answer, "Nothing. I need to get back to work. That's all."

"Okay, I get the message, I'm leaving." I turned to leave and said, "I'll see you tonight."

"Katy wait, I forgot to ask you, could I change the time of our date?"

I had almost forgotten what Erica had said. I realized that he wanted to get out of our date. I had known all along that this was too good to be true.

"Hello Katy! Earth to Katy," Andrew called.

I finally gave a quick, "Sure." I turned to make my escape.

"Hold it. We haven't decided on a time yet. How does Sunday at 11 a.m. sound to you?" he asked.

"Sure," I repeated, as I tried to leave again.

Andrew stopped me again and asked, "What's the matter? That wasn't really a sure."

"Nothing's the matter."

"Will you look at me and say that?" I glanced at him and looked away. An exasperated frustrated groan escaped from his lips before he said, "Sometimes you drive me crazy. Why don't you just say what you are feeling? I'm no mind reader," he said as he rolled his eyes skyward.

I stared at his face. That is what Evan said when he lectured me about communication. "You're right," I quietly said.

Andrew looked me straight in the eyes and asked, "Will you tell me what's bugging you?"

"If you feel like you don't want to date me, you don't have too." There, I said it.

"I changed the time of our date, I didn't cancel it. What's got you spooked?" When I did not answer, he said, "Come on, let's have the truth."

"Erica told me that you have a date with Dawn. It's not that I think you have to date me exclusively, but I know when I'm out of my league. I mean, Dawn always looks like she has stepped off the cover of Vogue so I can't understand . . . why in the world are you interested in dating a plain-Jane tenth grader like me?"

Andrew looked annoyed; he stood staring at me while not seeing me. Maybe staring is not the right word, I think he was in a trance again. Silence has a way of grinding on a person's nerves. I looked down at my hands; they were fidgeting with the zipper of my windbreaker.

I began to ramble. "I like being around you and hanging out with you. You make me laugh, I haven't laughed so much since, I don't remember when. And it's so easy to talk to you, most of the time." I added, "But I know it must not be a great kick for you to hang out with a fifteen year old." I looked up at Andrew and saw that his expression had changed, he was smiling again and the gleam was back in his eyes.

"Andrew!" We both jumped. His father motioned to him to come into the shop.

Andrew turned to me and said, "Don't move from this spot. Promise me you won't move from this spot."

I nodded my head and answered, "I promise."

Andrew went over to his father and soon they were having what appeared to be a deep discussion, at first, it was almost as if they were arguing. His father gave him some kind of warning; Andrew answered and nodded his head. When they began to listen to each other, they began to calm down and quickly reached some kind of compromise. Andrew came back out towards me and his father turned to help a customer.

"I got you in trouble, didn't I? I'm sorry about that. I should go," I said.

"No way," Andrew said as he pulled me along after him. He directed me to sit on a near-by bench. "There's no way that you're leaving until we clear this mess up," he said.

"But, your Dad-,"

"My Dad is a pretty smart guy; he knows what's going on. Forget about my Dad right now, Katy, listen to me." Andrew began his monologue, "How long have we known each other, for about a week, right?" He answered his own question.

"That's right," I agreed.

"Just listen, Katy," he instructed.

"But you asked," I reminded him.

"Shh, just listen. Where was I?" he asked himself. This time I knew better than to answer his question and remained silent. Andrew added, "In that time you've told me that you don't need my help. You have told me that I don't have to feel guilty and that it's not great for me to date a, a fifteen year old. Now it is my turn to tell you how I feel. Who knows better than me how I feel? Not you, I know that for sure."

"Andrew, I didn't say that I-," I began.

"Shh," he said, as he waved his pointer finger to emphasis the 'shh'. Then he continued to speak, "Firstly, I don't feel any guilt. I am sorry that the accident happened, but if it were not for the accident, I would not have met you, so I should really say that I'm only partially sorry that the accident happened. Secondly, I don't ask girls to go out on dates if I don't want to date them. I think that's a good policy. Thirdly, Dawn and I are not dating anymore. We aren't interested in one another in that way."

"But Erica said you have a date with her on Saturday," I reminded him.

"I know, Erica said. Erica the guru of truth has spoken. She should stick her sock in her mouth to go along with her foot." I laughed at that image. Andrew smiled before he continued, "Sure we have a date to meet. It's a date to work on an English presentation. We are partners on a stupid English project; she picked my name. We have no interest in each other at all."

"Uhhh, I Uh," I stammered. I felt stupid, relieved and happy. He was watching me again. "I'm sorry," I quickly apologized.

He knelt down in front of me as he had done with Justine. I could almost see directly into his eyes but I wished that he had sat beside me; it felt like a parent was talking with a child. When he began to speak I forgot about these feelings, "Katy, after today I can't understand why you would believe that I don't want to date you. We had a blast. Since we met, we've gotten to know each other pretty well. I think we like each other and I know that I want to know you better. Do you want to know me better?"

"Yes! Of course I do," I quickly answered.

"Hey!" Andrew raised his arms in victory. "And one way for two people to get to know each other can be to date, right?"

"Right," I answered.

"Are you through with all of your doubting?" he asked.

"Yes," I said with conviction."

"Would you walk me back to the shop? I had better get back there before Dad blows another gasket. Dad is an understanding guy but he has his limits."

As we walked I said, "Andrew, I promise to ask you how you're feeling instead of just thinking that I know what you're thinking and feeling. I also promise to try hard not to make a big deal of things. And-,"

"There's more?" Andrew jokingly asked.

"Yes, there is one more thing, I promise to communicate and say what I'm feeling and . . . could you do the same?"

"What? Do you want me to promise to not to make a big deal of things," he joked again.

"No, no, would you be serious for a minute?" He pretended to wipe the smile from his face and replace it with a serious expression but there was still a twinkle in his eyes.

I asked, "Andrew would you promise me that you'll be honest and say what you're feeling? Don't get angry over what I'm going to say next, okay?"

Andrew stopped and said, "I don't like the sound of this."

"If you ever feel like not dating me, could you be honest with me and tell me your feelings."

"Katy, are you going to try to drive me crazy again?" he muttered.

"Listen," I stopped him. "You want to date me now but people do change, we're both young. If either one of us changes our mind I want us to be honest with each other."

"All right, but I have to tell you, I like the mind I have and I'm not looking to change it." We both laughed at his joke. He said, "See you on Sunday at 11 a.m." Andrew touched my cheek, smiled and left.

I watched him go into the photography shop; he spoke with his annoyed father. His Dad glanced at me and smiled, I hoped this meant that he was not overly annoyed with Andrew. His Dad put his arm around Andrew's shoulders as they walked into the back rooms of the studio.

If I knew how to dance, I would have tap-danced all the way home. My cheek felt tingly. If I could have carried a tune, the song I carried in my heart would have found its way into the world. Now I know why people sang in the movies, they were expressing their feelings.

It took a lot of courage and work to communicate with honesty but it was worth the effort. How else would anyone reach an understanding awareness? I was ecstatically happy; finally, Andrew and I were in tune with each other.

Chapter 14

Destination: A Heart of Love

When I entered the door and saw Mom on the hallway phone, I waved to her and started up the stairs.

"Katy," Mom called. I turned, came back down and rounded the banister. Mom held out the phone to me with her hand over the mouthpiece. I thought Patty was on the phone, I reached for the phone and Mom said, "It's Travis." I jerked my hand away from the phone as if I was trying to avoid a red-hot iron.

I whispered, "No Mom, I don't want to talk to him."

"Katy," her eyes were pleading with me to take the phone, I answered with a shake of my head. "Katy, this has gone on for too long." I shook my head. "He was your brother's best friend and he's your friend," she whispered a reminder.

"He's not my friend. There is no way I'm talking to him, ever! And you can't make me talk to him." I said this with absolute conviction, before I ran upstairs. I entered my bedroom and closed the door, loudly.

Mom knew I did not want to talk to Travis. "Why did she ask me to talk to him?" I asked aloud. "Oh, stupid, stupid, stupid, why did I do that? Why didn't I just say no and leave it at that? Now Mom is going to be mad and ground me. Uhhh," I groaned. "I'll miss my date with Andrew."

"I'd bet on that," Evan stated. Evan was perched on my desk.

I flopped back on my bed, covered my eyes and asked, "You heard that, Evan?"

He answered, "That I did."

I peered at him from under my hand and said, "I blew it didn't I?"

"Yup," he answered.

"I didn't want to talk to him and Mom shouldn't have tried to make me," I said.

"Katy," Evan said, as he shook his head. "Mom asked you to talk to him; she didn't try to make you do it."

I sat up and glared at him, "Two months ago if Mom told you to do something that you didn't want to do, you would have been mad."

"Maybe," Evan calmly answered.

"Maybe, Evan, you would have made a logical argument against doing what Mom wanted you to do."

"Katy, after all we've talked about, I can't understand why you still blame Travis." Before I could answer, Evan raised his hand towards his lips to motion to me to be quiet.

There was a knock on the door. I heard Mom's voice, "Katy, I'd like to talk with you. Can I come in?"

"Uhhh," I groaned before answering, "Okay." I sat up.

Mom came in and sat beside me but she did not say anything. I thought I was doomed for sure, but Mom just sat there.

"Mom, I'm sorry I said what I said," I apologized.

Mom said, "I shouldn't have asked you to talk to Travis before you were ready, but that comment about me making you talk to him was out of line," Mom said.

"I know Mom, that's why I said I was sorry but I'm not sorry for not talking to Travis. Please don't ask me to do it again, because I won't," I assured her.

"It wasn't his fault, Katy. Travis tried to find Evan just like you did. It wasn't his fault,"

Mom emphasized.

I looked at Evan as he quietly leaned forward, intently listening to us. "I never blamed him for Evan's death; I blamed him for stopping me from finding him. Everyday I think that if I had just a minute more . . . oh, it is useless to think about this. It does not matter anymore. I know that Evan would tell me that, if he were here." I was staring at Evan as I said this. Evan's smile broadened and he nodded his head.

Mom was stunned, it seemed like there were tears in her eyes, when she tried to speak. After one false start she said, "Katy, you've been blaming yourself for the last seven weeks? I didn't know. Katy, it wasn't your fault no more than it was Travis's fault."

"Mom I, I just wish that I had more time. I can't forgive Travis for taking that away from me. He had no right to stop me. He had no right to do that."

Mom put her arms around me and squeezed. "Honey, I could have lost both of you that day. Travis's actions prevented that from happening. I'll love him forever for keeping you safe. From where I sit, I would say that Travis saved more than your life that day. Do you really think I would have survived losing both of you?" she asked. I did not answer but what Mom said bothered me, it did not occur to me that I could have died that day. Mom continued, "You don't have to feel as I do, just think about it. Will you do that for me?" Mom asked.

I reluctantly nodded my head and whispered, "Okay, I'll think about it." Mom seemed satisfied with my answer. "Mom-,"

. . . She quietly asked, "What is it, Katy?"

I asked, "Have you ever wondered about death?"

Mom asked, "What do you mean when you say, wondered about death?"

"I've been thinking about what happens after death. Do you think that heaven and hell could be imaginary? Could they be more figurative than literal? I saw a T.V. documentary on 'Near Death Experiences'. Most of the people who had these experiences met a Being of Light in another dimension before they came back. Do you think that people could be wrong concerning the heaven and hell stuff? Maybe what is important is the love and caring in a person's heart and not a destination, or maybe that is the destination. I'm not saying that people are lying about that stuff but maybe they don't know the whole truth."

I glanced at Evan, his eyes were as big as marbles and he kept shaking his head. Then he warned, "Katy, what are you doing? You know what Mom believes. She goes to church each Sunday," Evan reminded me.

"I'm just asking," I answered him.

Mom replied, "I agree with you Katy," she cupped my chin gently in her hand and added. "The love you give to your loved ones and the caring you have for the world, it's very important." She is talking about Travis, I reasoned. Mom concluded, "But if you're asking me about what I believe, I'd have to say I'm happy with my belief system."

"But Mom it's okay to think in a different way. No one thought you could be a maintenance person, a Super, but you did it. You did something different," I reasoned.

Mom tried to remain calm, as she said, "It's not even close to being the same issue."

"Mom, I just mean-,"

"Katy, this discussion is over," Mom's tone of voice and the look in her eyes, helped me to swallow my unspoken words.

Mom left the room. I stared at the door after Mom had closed it. I looked at Evan and said, "Wow, she's really mad."

"I tried to warn you," Evan reminded me.

"I wasn't trying to put down her belief. Do you think I was doing that?" I asked.

"Katy, to most people their belief system is special, it can even be sacred. It gets top billing along with motherhood, family, and, and . . ."

"Freedom of choice," I completed the thought for him.

Evan smiled and nodded in agreement before saying, "Right, freedom of choice. If you question a person's belief system, it's like questioning who that person is. To most people, there is a lot of tradition and pride connected with what they believe. It's their connection to their sense of who they are and to their ancestors. That's Mom," Evan concluded.

I got up off the bed and headed for the door. "I'm going to let Mom know that I wasn't trying to put what she believes down." I stopped at the door and added, "Thanks, Evan."

"Anytime," he said.

"Evan, you must have an amazing teacher, you have changed so much. What's his name again?" I asked.

"I have a lot of teachers, Katy," Evan said.

"You told me the one teacher's name, what is it?"

"Sri Hikari Hito," he said.

"Sri Hikari Hito," I repeated. "Uhh," I said, as I remembered the Magic Man. "Evan, does Hikari Hito wear a, a navy blue kimono and sandals? Is he Oriental or part Oriental?" I asked.

"Yes!" Evan said with excitement. "That's him. How did you know-?"

"Evan, I met him, he's Justine's Magic Man. He's been helping her for, I don't know how long. I thought he was part of her imagination until I met him. I don't know why I could suddenly see him. I had wished that I could meet the Spiritual Masters of Light and Love and now I've met two of them."

A smile beamed from Evan's face. He had a look in his eyes, a twinkle that said, 'I know. I've been there.' Evan added, "Katy, Sri Hikari Hito said that in many cases, wishes are an extension of what already is. Our efforts make them real but reality begins with a wish seed."

"Wow," I said, as the poetic inspiration seed entered my heart. I knew one wish that I would keep close to my heart. I would imagine and wish that I could continue to meet the members of The Brotherhood of Light and Love and Evan, many times in the future. I had no doubt that this wish seed would come true.

Chapter 15

Appreciating the Thorns

Everything was so bright and alive, the flowers were more colorful and the trees seemed to vibrate with life. The grass was a brilliant emerald green, like it came from the movie, The Wizard of Oz. A warm breeze gently brushed past me, it was as if I was back at the lake, where the air was crisp, cool and fresh. A better description of the day was to say, it was just right. If it was not for the tall, tapering ridges running parallel to the shoreline to my left, enclosing what appeared to be a lake, I am sure I could have seen forever. I wondered, *was I in the Rocky Mountains again. If I was, how did I get here and why did I not remember the trip?*

On the shoreline, just out of the reach of the lake water, my sneakers sat with my socks stuffed inside them. I sat on a flat, smooth boulder, ten feet from a pebble-covered beach. I saw that I had rolled the legs on my blue jeans up below my knees and the water encircled my ankles. The lake water was not cold; this was different from my past chilly memory. There were no pebbles under my feet, instead, cool mud oozed around my toes as I curled them in the slippery mush. It felt oddly relaxing; usually I hated the feel of mud.

"Hey! Would you mind some company?" I quickly looked towards the shoreline and smiled. Evan was standing there, smiling back at me.

"Evan, it's so nice to see you. Pick a rock, any rock and sit down. Evan sat on the beach in his off white colored attire. He removed his shoes and socks carefully placing them beside mine.

Evan waded out to me. I frowned as I stared at his pants; they were wet. Why were they wet? If we were together in the physical world, then Evan's pants should not be wet. Evan was like a ghost, earthly water should not affect a ghost.

Evan slowly crouched in front of me and took my hands in his own. I gasped and stared at our linked hands, before looking into his laughing eyes.

"Your hands are warm. You're alive, Evan," I shouted. "You're real." My next thought sent a chill through me. I said, "Or, I'm dead."

"I'm alive and so are you. Congratulations, Katy! You've traveled to another level of existence." Evan hugged me, before he added, "It's like visiting heaven while you're sleeping but at the same time, you're aware of what's happening. You made it," Evan said. Warmth and love radiated from Evan. I felt safe and free in this light, beautiful place.

"You're saying that I'm dreaming all of this, right?"

Evan nodded his head and answered, "Yes. That's right."

"So my physical body is sleeping back in my bed?" Again, Evan nodded. I had an image of me sleeping in my bed and Evan began to fade from my view.

"Katy, if you want to stay here for a while, you need to stop imagining yourself back home. Keep your focus in this world," Evan instructed.

I quickly obeyed Evan's instructions; I wanted this experience to last. I looked around me. Evan, the mountains, the lake, everything came back into focus again. "This is so cool; I'm actually in another dimension. This all seems so real, is this real, Evan?" I asked for his reassurance.

Evan nodded his head. "It's very real," he stated. "Katy, if you were imagining a destination on earth it would still be real, even if you weren't there in your physical body, wouldn't it?"

"Yeah, sure it would," I agreed.

"Well, this place is just as real," Evan, reasoned. "This is the Astral Plane, the plane closest to the physical reality; it is the home of the Emotional Awareness. This means, if you react, or act from your emotions, then your awareness is operating from the astral level of consciousness. The

Astral Plane is a much larger place than the physical universe. The physical universe is the size of a peanut, compared to the Astral Plane and the other dimensions above this are even vaster.

I said, "You're kidding. The physical universe is vast, so the idea of other planes of existence being that size seems unbelievable."

Evan continued his explanation, "But it's true. There is something more incredible, the vibrations are different in each dimension or plane. The vibratory rate is much higher and finer here but as you can see, there are a lot of similarities found in both worlds."

"Yeah, I can see some similarities. This reminds me of the lake we visited two summers ago."

"Lake Louise, in Banff National Park on the B.C., Alberta border," Evan clarified.

"That's I, I loved that place. I remember the wiener roasts, exploring in the canoe, and the hikes. We had a lot of fun there," I said. I'll remember those times for the rest of my life. "It was like heaven on earth to me," I said.

"Those were great times," Evan agreed, as he remembered with me.

I asked, "Evan, if this level of heaven is so vast then why do you think I ended up in a place that is similar to Lake Louise? Why didn't I end up on the Star Ship Enterprise or at the gates of heaven, or anywhere else for that matter?"

Evan said, "I'm not absolutely sure but I have a theory."

"I'm all ears," I said, and I meant it. I didn't want to miss a word he said. More and more I could see that things had changed between us, or perhaps I had changed. The calmness in this place seemed to bring peace and contentment into my heart, I felt confident; it was as if I was safe at home.

Evan explained his theory, "Katy, remember you made a wish to meet and learn from Sri Hikari Hito. I would guess that he has been helping you to have spiritual experiences like this one. Whenever the Spiritual Masters of The Brotherhood help anyone, they help with great care and divine love. The Spiritual Masters will try to make a new experience of conscious dreaming enjoyable, comfortable and even familiar. This is so the dreamer can overcome their fear of the unknown, while they visit these new dimensions. This place is like some place that you love, you're comfortable here; anyone will learn more if their fears are not holding them back. The Spiritual Masters knows this."

I thought over Evan's words for a few moments. Then I asked, "So, what am I supposed to learn here?"

"Beats me," he said as he shrugged his shoulders. "That's between you, the Spiritual Masters and Divine Spirit. Divine Spirit is also referred to as the Holy Spirit. Katy, it doesn't matter if you know why you're here right now. When you are meant to know that, you will know it. Hey, you are here and you know you are here; Katy, that's a giant step just on its own."

I smiled and said, "Evan, when you are right, you're right."

Evan stood and stretched before saying, "How about we get our shoes? My feet are getting cold."

I nodded and said, "Okay, mine are too." I followed him towards our footwear and washed the slimy awful mud off my feet. Then I brushed the sand from my feet, before pulling on my footwear. We sat side by side, looking at the peaceful shimmering lake.

"Evan, I want to know more. Like, how can I be sound asleep at home in my bed and still know that I am here in this place with you?"

"It all has to do with being Soul," Evan answered. "We've talked about Soul before, remember?"

I nodded my head and said, "Yes. I remember most of it."

"Master Hikari Hito said that, 'Soul is the inner, most sacred part of each being, it is the God part of who we are. Soul has the ability to see, know and perceive all things and all places, even in another dimension like this place. Divine love draws Soul to the God Essence, or the Great Creator. And if you're tuned into the God Essence, you will be aware that existence is like an enormous puzzle, waiting for you to see its completeness,' end quote," Evan finished.

"Evan, this is going to take time for me to fully understand, even though it does make sense.

Does that make any sense to you?" I asked.

Evan laughed before he agreed, "I understand why it would. Anything that is far-out would have that effect. Tell me this, in your heart, does all this ring true?"

I thought for a few seconds, before saying, "Yeah, I guess what I understand does. I really hope that it's true."

Evan said, "It is true, but that's something that you're going to have to figure out for yourself."

I said, "I've heard about the Astral Plane, and astral travel before, but I thought it was just science fiction. Now I am living it! If I wasn't living it, I probably wouldn't believe it," I admitted.

"It's not science fiction, Katy, it's real," Evan said.

"So I used astral projection to get here, right?" I asked.

Evan slowly shook his head and answered, "If Sri Hikari Hito is looking after you, I'd say no. He teaches his students to travel in their Soul bodies instead of their Astral bodies, and then the traveler is not limited to traveling only in the Astral Plane. Traveling in the Soul body gives much more freedom to the traveler; you can visit many other levels of heaven beyond the Astral Plane."

"Evan, this is better than science fiction. So, can you tell me more about the mysterious, far-out stuff that these Spiritual Masters teach you about?"

Evan did not speak right away, but when he did, he seemed to speak very carefully. "Sometimes life seems unfair, but it really is unconditionally fair. You don't believe me, I know, but it is true. Often when life becomes difficult and painful and we find ourselves wondering why? Katy, Sri Hikari Hito said, 'All reality is linked together. The fabric of existence, past, present and future forms an endless chain.' Try to visualize that. Most people can only see pieces of their present reality so life doesn't always add up, seem fair, or make sense."

The idea that the past, present and future forms an endless chain seemed strangely familiar. Finally, I waved my hands and said, "Let's back track here. You said that life is fair, that it's unconditionally fair."

"That's right," Evan agreed.

"How is life unconditionally fair?" I asked. "I don't understand how that's true."

"You remember "'The Great Equalizer.'"?" Evan asked.

I nodded my head and said, "I remember you telling me about that."

Evan continued, "Our thoughts, words and actions do come back to us in some form. The good news is, no matter what hardships and lessons we've created for ourselves, over our countless life time of experiences, we can also, learn and create solutions to over come any difficulty," Evan emphasized.

"Evan, what you just said makes me feel as if I am a future super-woman. You make everyone sound like potential super men and women," I said.

"I like the word potential," Evan said. "We all have the potential to continually grow everyday to be the best we can be, because we are on a journey of change. Do something for me Katy, think of yourself before you worked through a difficult situation. Then if you compared that memory of you, to who you are now, you'll probably see that you've grown in strength and smarts," Evan concluded.

I quietly whispered, "I felt like dying when you drowned. Mom and Dad," I stopped to compose myself before I continued, "I'm amazed that Mom and Dad survived those first couple of weeks, especially the first few days." I relived those images and feelings as I said, "I was feeling sick from getting the tetanus shot so I hid in my bedroom. Mom and Dad, they couldn't hide, there were so many people paying their respects, they hardly had any down time. Maybe being busy helped them some how."

"Again I remembered how for weeks after the accident, I heard Mom crying at different times during the day. Then it changed to once or twice a day. Now, I think both Mom and Dad can look at your picture and remember the good times, more than the end. I think they are both coping pretty well, but it's still painful. Will the pain ever end?" I asked. I hoped Evan had a magical answer to this question.

Evan hugged me. . . . He quietly spoke, "Katy, I know that you, and Mom and Dad, have traveled through hell and back in the last seven weeks and you've survived. You're lucky to have each other for support. There is light at the end of any difficult experience; keep looking for Light and Love Katy, it always surround you."

"I'll try," I promised.

"I've got to stretch," Evan said, before he stood and stretched. I also stretched. Our long break, sitting together on the pebbled beach as we watched the breath taking landscape, resulted in stiff tight muscles. Evan selected a number of flat rocks from the beach, with a quick flick of his wrist he sent one rock skipping across the surface of the lake.

Evan said, "Katy, you need to realize, what I've been saying comes from what I'm aware of at this moment. It's all something that I'm still learning to do for myself. I'm being taught the theory, but living the theories to the max is a step that can take many, many life times of practice." As Evan spoke, I search for more flat smooth rocks. Evan did the same and continued to talk as he flicked another rock across the surface of the lake, "Usually, once you think you've got it down pat, that's when you find out how much more you need to learn. The Spiritual Masters know that spiritual growth is a never-ending process, they're still learning."

"I understand Evan," I reassured him, as I flicked a rock across the surface of the lake. I added, "But there's always light and Love, right?" I smiled as I said this.

Evan smiled, chuckled, then said, "Katy, promise me that you'll try to make your own decision about truth and reality, based on how things feel to you. Don't believe anything just because I'm saying that this is so; trust your own heart and intuition. Step back, calm down and take an objective look at things, okay?" Evan asked.

I repeated, "Step back, calm down, and take an objective look at things. Okay. I've got it." What Evan had just said felt like something I had known about for ages but I was not aware that I knew it.

"Sri Hikari Hito said something else to me; if I can remember the wording it goes something like this, 'As we gradually change our attitudes and thoughts towards the positive, then our lives will grow in the same direction. As a plant grows towards the light so can a man's positive attitude draw him towards Light and Love. Light and Love vibrates with the pure God Force.' He also said that, 'Our lives can be a bed of roses, if we learn how to handle the thorns. Our life experiences will teach us how to handle and appreciate the thorns of life.'" Evan sat in silence, thinking.

I stared at Evan and mumbled, "Appreciate the thorns of life?" I shook my head, as I thought about this.

Evan looked at me and said, "Sri Hikari Hito said something else to me. These are his exact words, 'Learn well young friend, for if you do so, the past will cease to cling to you.' I don't totally understand this, but I know it's important," Evan admitted.

I watched my brother and it suddenly struck me, 99% of the time he was smiling. Then I realized, we had both been searching for truth for years and now he was discovering truth in a big awesome way. No wonder he was so happy, he was connecting with truth, light and love.

As we watched the water lapping against the beach with a gentle, rhythmic sway, I asked, "Evan, why do you wear off-white colored clothes all the time. I thought you didn't like wearing white. You said it was a dull color."

Evan answered, "It's just a conscious choice; white reminds me of the Light and I don't want to have to spend time wondering about the little things, like what am I going to wear. I want to focus my attention on more important things. You could say that I've simplified my life." I nodded my head in understanding. Evan was dressing for himself.

Evan turned his attention further down the shoreline. I leaned forward to peer around him. In the distance, I could see a figure, a man, strolling towards us.

"Who is that?" I whispered.

Evan did not seem to hear me. He spoke in an equally hushed voice, "I had a feeling we would be seeing him today."

There was something very familiar about this man. As he drew closer, I could feel the excitement building in Evan. The man had short coal black hair and he had on a navy kimono that dropped just below his knees.

"It's the Magic Man," I exclaimed. Excitement bubbled inside of me.

"Who is the Magic Man?" Evan asked.

I reminded him, "He's the spiritual teacher who has been visiting Justine, Mrs. Cope's daughter. He has been helping her understand her life. I told you about him, remember?"

Evan nodded his head. I was not sure if he remembered our conversation, until he said, "The Spiritual Masters help many people." Evan brushed the sand off his pants. I followed his lead.

Evan and I watched the Spiritual Master as he approached us. This man walked with a quiet, confident stride. As I continued to watch him, a strange feeling came over me. It was as if I was watching the personification of change, as it walked into my life. The word 'Relax' drifted through my consciousness, like God whispering a gentle directive.

Usually, when I see or feel a change entering my life, anxiety and fear come along for the ride, this time things were different. Anxiety and fear were standing on the side of the road just watching me pass by.

Chapter 16

A Healing Memory

"Master Hikari Hito, this is my sister Katy," Evan spoke with great respect.

I looked into Sri Hikari Hito's face. His eyes were dark and direct. When he looked at me, I felt as if he was seeing into my very Soul.

"Kathleen and I have met," he calmly said. Evan nodded.

"Justine calls you the Magic Man," I said. He smiled and nodded his head. I asked, "Why does Evan call you Master?" The title had a feeling of force or power connected to it, even though this man's manner was in no-way threatening or oppressive. Warmth and caring radiated from the Spiritual Master, so I could not understand why Evan's use of the word Master bothered me.

My question embarrassed Evan. "Katy, the word Master isn't negative in the way that I use it. The members of 'The Brotherhood of Light and Love' are Spiritual Masters. That means that they're Masters of their own selves and their own destinies in all situations."

The calm melodious voice of Hikari Hito added, "As a computer can be reprogrammed, so can we reprogram ourselves. The human consciousness often fights to hold on to the comfortable, the known, the tried and true, as if they were a child's security blanket. As you strengthen your connection with the God Essence within you, your vision broadens and you see a more complete picture of your own life as well as all of existence. Thus, changing to move beyond the security of the known and the comfortable gradually loses its partnership with anxiety and fear."

The Spiritual Master added, "Some security blankets are very necessary, parents and teachers are a child's security blanket. They give support and comfort as they guide and protect a child. When this guidance is infused with divine love, wisdom and understanding, then the child has a greater chance of growing to achieve a similar spiritual strength and confidence. Life experiences gradually help each being develop the wisdom and divine love to walk as a self-directed being. The child becomes the adult, and the adult matures to become the Spiritual Master, one of God's conscious helpers."

I said, "That sounds so simple," I added, "Life doesn't seem that simple to me."

"Life and existence is filled with unlimited elements and factors, which confuse the mind. The human mind copes with existence by separating and compartmentalizing these countless elements. The foundation of any equation is simple, what grows from this simplicity has the illusion of complexity. Every aspect of existence is constantly evolving; all aspects of consciousness, including the spiritual consciousness are also evolving."

A far off memory was trying to enter my awareness. I could almost see it. It was a memory of Sri Hikari Hito. I had met him before. He was fixing something. No. He was watching when someone was fixing something.

"I have met you before; it was before I found out that you were helping Justine. There was something being fixed?"

The Spiritual Master, Hikari Hito stood silently, waiting and watching me, while a curious frown covered Evan's face.

"Oh my goodness, I remember, I remember!" I backed up and leaned against a fallen tree trunk. The Spiritual Master smiled. "You were there when my Aunt Emily was getting her water line to her well fixed." Master Hikari Hito nodded.

I explained to Evan, "It was about two weeks after you had passed away. Mom, Dad and I went to visit Aunt Emily. I did not want to go anywhere or see anyone. Mom and Dad were worried about me; they said that a little fresh air would do me some good. I think they really wanted me to commune with Brandy, there is so much love in that dog's heart." I slowly added, as I looked up at Sri Hikari Hito, "You already know that, don't you?" Again, the Spiritual Master smiled.

Evan said, "I missed that visit."

I nodded and said to the Spiritual Master with absolute certainty, "But you were there."

The Spiritual Master asked, "Can you tell us what you remember?"

I said, "Back then I was walking through my life like I was a zombie so I might not remember everything." I wanted to prepare them for this possibility.

"Do your best," Master Hikari Hito encouraged me.

I nodded as I focused on the clear memories. "We stayed with Aunt Emily for a couple of days. They did a lot of reminiscing, Mom, Aunt Emily and even Dad, talked and cried a lot. They even started to laugh at some of their stories. Of course all the stories were about you," I motioned to Evan.

"Oh boy," Evan said in an 'oh no', sort of way.

I explained to the Spiritual Master, "Mom created a memory roses album. She pressed and labeled all of the roses that Evan gave her, to remember every situation that inspired Evan to give her a rose." I added, "Each rose had a little story taped beside it." I needled Evan, "All your little antics will live on in the history of our family."

Evan said, "I don't know how I feel about that."

I smiled before I continued with my remembrance. "One afternoon we were making oatmeal cookies. Mom, Dad and Aunt Emily were laughing about how you used to hang around at the beginning of the making cookie-dough time. For every cookie you made, it seemed that you ate the same amount of raw dough time. Finally, Mom would have to banish you from the kitchen." As I finished I noticed the huge grin on Evan's face.

Evan said, "Cookies are better cooked, back then I was a bit impatient."

"Mom was remembering how she got you to stop swearing when you were a kid. Do you remember?" I asked Evan.

Evan grimaced and said, "Do I remember! I had the cleanest teeth in the whole city." Evan explained to Master Hikari Hito, "Mom brushed my teeth with soap; she only had to do it twice, you could say I learned fast."

"Your Mother is very creative," the Spiritual Master was having a silent chuckle, as he said this.

"Mom also remembered how you used to give her a huge bear hug on special occasions, or when you were just feeling happy. You used to pick her off her feet, twirl her around and plant a kiss on her cheek. She said she would miss your hugs the most. That's when Mom and Aunt Emily started to cry. That's when I snuck outside and left them alone."

"I always thought that Mom was the one doing the hugging," Evan added, "I miss her hugs, big time. Sometimes I close my eyes and imagine her hugging me." I could hear wishful longing in his voice.

"Each time I hug Mom and Dad, I'll give them an extra hug and imagine you're giving them that extra hug," I assured Evan.

"Thanks Katy. I like that idea," he said.

I began to remember more. I repeated, "I went outside. Dad and a few of the neighbors were fixing Aunt Emily's well. The thirty-year-old water line had sprung a leak. Aunt Emily and a bunch of her neighbors got together and hired the track-hoe operator. The track-hoe operator had dug a deep, long trench.

"I remember asking you, 'What are they doing?'

"A man in a green baseball cap said, 'They're taking out the cracked water pipe and splicing in a stronger section of hose.'

"The memory of what you said is becoming clearer now. You said, 'Pressure builds at the weakest point and when the flow is broken, silt is able to muddy the integrity of the flow. Life constantly upgrades and changes in order to build and strengthen.'

"When I asked you if you were a teacher, the man in the green cap thought I was talking to him. He looked at me like I had a screw loose." I stared at Sri Hikari Hito for a few seconds, before I asked, "Could anyone else see you?" The Spiritual Master shook his head. "No wonder that man looked at me like that." The Spiritual Master smiled. I explained, "I thought you were one of the neighbors who had come around to help with the repairs. When I asked you if you were a teacher, I remember you said, 'I am a student of the Spirit of God.'

"I remember asking, 'What can God teach anyone?'

"You answered, 'The Spirit of God has given all individuals the opportunity to learn from their experiences. Every choice we make is a brick added to the creation of our lives.' You also said, 'We learn from the past, live and choose in the present, and prepare for the future.'

"I said, 'I wish God would give me back a few moments to live over again.' "

"Then you asked me, 'What would you change?'

"I told you that my brother had died a few weeks ago. I asked, 'Why did God allow my brother to die when he was helping someone?'

"Master Hikari Hito, I remember you said, 'Nothing is without purpose in the Universe of God, loss, hardships and death are part of the cycle of life. They are elements of the learning process which inspires one to strive, to strengthen and reevaluate.' You also said, 'Because God loves all that It has created, It gave us the capacity to learn and grow.'

"I asked you, 'Why did God cut off Evan's opportunity to learn and grow.' I looked at Evan and said, "I was really angry." "I'm amazed that I'm remembering all this. I asked Master Hikari Hito, "Are you helping me to remember all of this?"

The Spiritual Master smiled and answered, "Divine Spirit assists as needed."

"I remember more," I said, as more memories entered my memory bank. "Master, you said, 'Death is not an obstacle to discovering truth.'

"I said, 'Death is the end so it's the ultimate obstacle.'

"You also asked me, 'If death is not the end, then, what would your brother say to you?'

"I thought that was a weird question, I tried to ignore you. You whispered to me, 'Imagine. Imagine.' "

The Spiritual Master, Hikari Hito gave an acknowledging nod.

"Oh, I remember now. That's when I heard Evan's voice." I looked at Evan and said, "You said, 'Death is an illusion.' That's when I thought you were giving me a bear hug.

"Then I heard you, Master. You said, 'The answers to all your questions await you.' I must have fallen asleep after that because the next thing I remember was waking up in bed, in Aunt Emily's trailer.

"I thought that hugging you had been a dream and for some reason I had completely forgotten about even talking to you, Master. That is until today. The funny thing is, even though I forgot our conversation, I felt better.

"I noticed Mom and Dad watching me eat supper that night, they were smiling at me and at each other, because, they knew that something had changed for me, supper actually tasted great. Life did not feel hopeless anymore.

"Master Hikari Hito, you were right. Death is not an obstacle to discovering truth. The answers to my questions were waiting for me." I added, "Thank you for guiding me to understanding,"

The Master nodded and smiled in acknowledgement.

Chapter 17

Spiritual Mastership and the Secret of HU

The Spiritual Master, Sri Hikari Hito listened and answered our questions as we and continued our discussion while we walked along the sandy shoreline.

"You're the Spiritual Master of yourself, not of anyone else?" I asked. The Spiritual Master nodded. An idea popped into my head, I asked, "Are you Divine Spirit's Master Helper?"

"I am one of Divine Spirit's many helpers," Sri Hikari Hito stated. "I assist as the Spirit of God asks. I do no more and no less."

"Right, you said that before. So, you've reached the end of your journey," I concluded.

Spiritual Master Hikari Hito smiled before saying, "There is always one more step to take on a journey to maturity. If a being believes he can learn no more, he is choosing to live an illusion. As individuals grow in their awareness of divine love and the Light and Voice of God, then so will the universe also grow and expand with these God elements. The universe continues on its journey around those who refuse to learn, it waits for no one."

Suddenly, a brilliant warm light engulfed me and for a few seconds I was aware of the universe moving around me. I held my head as I closed my eyes and awareness; I tried to find my way back to balance and stability. I screamed, in an instant it felt like a giant vacuum cleaner sucked me back into my present reality.

Evan asked, "What happened?" I watched Evan as I slowly composed myself.

I said, "I sensed voices and images flooding into my awareness, I sensed countless life forms experiencing changing and growing. It was like experiencing evolution in action." I looked at the Spiritual Master and added, "So many pieces and I know I could only glimpse a kernel, a fraction of existence, it was over-whelming, talk about information overload. How does God keep track of everything?"

The Spiritual Master smiled and answered, "Existence is an endless living mosaic filled with an infinite number of elements which are expanding in every way, on all levels of what is. If a youthful awareness tries to see and know all elements of existence, it would feel anxiety and over-whelming chaos."

I nodded my head and agreed, "That is how I felt."

Sri Hikari Hito added, "The Great Creator knows the rhythms and patterns of existence. It knows eternal order and eternal justness in all that is. It sees how every piece of creation has affected every other piece, over countless lifetimes since the beginning of existence; each piece to this puzzle is where it is meant to be."

I nodded and said, "The countless pieces of existence were changing so fast, they fit together like puzzle pieces. I couldn't understand it all, to understand it all would be impossible."

The Spiritual Master waved his hand in a circular motion and a large circular screen, similar to a movie screen, magically appeared beside him. The image of a family, a father and mother, with their children, were happily interacting in their daily life.

The Master said, "All Souls who enter our lives, especially our loved ones, are linked to us and one another by karmic threads."

Different scenes flashed on the screen, the people in these scenes came from different eras and cultures. They were dressed in costume, perhaps from the ancient Greek, Roman, Oriental, African and Native people's cultures; they were hunters, farmers, merchants, sailors, tyrants and ordinary people. These images continued to flash across the screen.

The pace of the flashing images slowed as Sri Hikari Hito added, "Souls journey through out the ages." The image changed suddenly. I could see the length of a Viking ship from its stern slicing through the water parallel to a rocky shoreline as the Vikings rowed in unison. The images continued to change but the focus remained on this particular family. There were celebrations and wars. A warrior would send his enemies to Valhalla without remorse, while in that same lifetime there were times when the merciless warrior demonstrated divine love for a son, daughter, or wife.

Sri Hikari Hito added, "Spiritual potential exists in all God's creatures." The Master added, "Each of us chooses the path of power or love. Love is respectful and caring. The immature individual will choose power; thus, his or her will is imposed on others without respect or permission."

As the images continued to change, the Spiritual Master continued with his narration, "Life time after life time, Soul lives through countless life experiences." The images on the screen began to change very quickly now, from lifetime to lifetime and century to century. Funerals, weddings, wars, all aspects of daily living flashed over the screen. "The human awareness is motivated by different needs, desires and goals, but Soul pulls the human consciousness forwards towards higher goals. As was said before, one such goal is to develop the ability to live with divine love in one's heart, no matter what the circumstance, in every moment of existence. This is the key to Spiritual Mastership in all realities."

The images continued to change. "Each step towards understanding life and self takes effort and relentless determination. It takes great courage to confront your fears to live with integrity, truth and divine love, as you become the hero of your own life." The Spiritual Master waved his hand again and the screen disappeared.

"Wow, that was awesome," Evan, exclaimed. "What was that?"

"Both of you experienced many visual fragments of your own past lives. With our choices, we choose the course of our past, present and future. Karmic creations influence their creator through lifetimes upon lifetimes, until the lessons are learned and the debits have been paid in full." The Spiritual Master stared at us for a few seconds before he asked, "If we are all characters in a never-ending play called existence, then who is the play-write and author?" While Evan and I mulled over the question the Master said, "Take this question with you on your spiritual journey."

I asked, "Can you guide me on my spiritual journey, through all the changes and obstacles? Can you guide me, so I can become the Spiritual Master of my own life?"

Evan added, "We really want to understand life and existence."

The Spiritual Master smiled and he nodded as he answered, "You have begun to let go of your fear of change. Most people fear change, for change is associated with instability or insecurity; however, change is a necessary component of spiritual growth." I smiled as the Spiritual Master's words sank in.

The Master added, "Divine Spirit has been unobtrusively guiding you since the beginning of your existence as eternal Soul, through countless life times, towards your final destination. What is your final destination?" the Spiritual Master asked.

"I'm not totally sure. Could it be to become a Spiritual Master?" I asked.

"I think divine love has something to do with our goal, doesn't it?" Evan asked.

"Divine love, I'm not sure if I know what that is?" I admitted.

Sri Hikari Hito explained, "Divine love or unconditional love is a merciful love. It is the same as God's love for all which God has created, just as a loving parent loves its child. Divine love is both a tool and goal in one's quest to be a conscious Helper of the Light and Voice of God. The Light and Voice of God are aspects of Divine Spirit. Divine Spirit is also the Essence of God, the Holy Spirit, or the Creative Force. It is the spiritual fluid that ties all life and existence together."

Evan said, "You just said that all existence and life is connected by Divine Spirit or divine love." The Master nodded. Evan asked, "Then why do some people have so much anger and hate in them when they have this connection with divine love?"

The Spiritual Master smiled and said, "A thoughtful question. As said before, divine love is the spiritual ideal. All individuals have journeyed to different stages of spiritual maturity. The average person has the capacity to give a more intense, warm and respectful love to family, close friends and love ones. Usually, a respectful understanding and caring is given with others. The mature Soul learns to be a reflection of divine love." The Spiritual Master nodded and added, "At times we all are vehicles for Divine Spirit. Even a simple nudge from a pet can hold the gift of divine love."

I thought of Brandy, my Aunt Emily's Irish setter. Her quiet, patient, companionship after Evan's death had helped me to begin to feel again. How could I have forgotten those big doggy eyes sending love into my heart?

The Spiritual Master added, "A heart felt smile or words of encouragement can communicate the essence of divine love; thus an individual could plant the seed of caring, inspiration or divine love in the heart of those who feel lost or desperate."

I thought about who had been guiding me through my life. The Spiritual Masters, Mom, Dad, Evan, Mrs. Cope, Justine, Andrew, Patty and Travis and Erica. Erica? How had she been guiding me? Why did I think of Erica?

Erica and Travis, their purpose in my life was a mystery. I tried to smile as I asked, "What if you get angry because a person stops you from doing something you have to do, or if the person does things just to bug you and put you down? What can that person teach me?"

Sri Hikari Hito said, "One who tears down another, in order to elevate his or herself, is one who lives in fear and anger." The Spiritual Master calmly added, "Kathleen, anyone can choose to understand the issue that anger or fear highlights, instead of adding to the anger or fear awareness. The awareness of understanding is but the first step to reaching the ultimate goal. To reach this understanding of truth regarding any issue or situation, first review all the elements of an entire situation without bias. Do not mull over this question in your mind, for this will hold you prisoner in your lower awareness. Allow your awareness the freedom to wonder about any issue. This technique of wondering begins to link your awareness to the Holy Spirit so you can move beyond the awareness of the mind and intellect. Then surrender and let go of this wondering to the Spirit of God or Divine Spirit. Finally, listen and be aware of insights and understanding from the Spirit of God, which will enter your consciousness like a feathers floating into your awareness."

I asked, "Master Hikari Hito, are you saying that intellect is not a good asset?"

The Master shook his head and answered, "Kathleen, intellect does help an individual to live life in the lower worlds but it does not compare to the awareness of Soul or Divine Spirit, for with Soul Awareness you have the potential to know all."

While the Spiritual Master was speaking, an image of Erica crying flashed through my awareness. I saw a hand picking up a colorful blue and orange scarf, the person handed it to Erica before the image faded.

I nodded and said, "I'll work to do that," I wondered *what that image was.* I had a feeling that Master Hikari Hito somehow knew about Erica and Travis.

Sri Hikari Hito said, "There is a common human saying, 'If you keep doing what you are doing, you will keep getting what you are getting.' "

Evan answered, as we both nodded, "We've heard that saying before, it makes sense."

The Spiritual Master smiled and said, "The wise being is also aware and flexible, he knows when to let go and move with change, for why continue to do what creates negative karma? Such choices invite pain and hardship to enter one's life. Awareness, flexibility and change are 3 essential elements that are needed in order to learn and continue your spiritual growth."

The Spiritual Master added, "When an individual understands the spiritual lesson within any experience, even within his mistakes, then this spiritual student has grown towards an unbiased, thoughtful, viewpoint, which helps to expedite learning."

Evan said, "I'm grateful to have freedom of choice, even if my choices may lead to mistakes. If I'm aware while I'm trying then I'm learning, right?"

The Spiritual Master said, "Be aware that even that which is a mistake, or seems to be negative in nature, is on a journey of transformation. As one experiences the resulting consequences of his actions, his karma, will gradually assist the individual to learn discrimination and gain the awareness to better choose more appropriate thoughts, words and actions in his life."

I said, "I never thought I'd ever be grateful for my mistakes."

The Spiritual Master said, "We grow as individuals on our spiritual journeys. We can inspire new understanding in others but we cannot choose another's attitudes or beliefs, nor can we make another change his or her awareness. Such a change can only grow from one's own heart and mind. Thus, it is best to work to nurture the divine love in your own heart and life.

"There are three simple steps which may help you achieve this goal. First, as said before, try to understand the other's viewpoint, or motivation. Understanding may not equal agreement, but as you stretch to see through the eyes of another, your conscious awareness will broadens in many quiet ways.

"Second, highlight what grows from divine love, truth and respect. Love and respect yourself, while you acknowledge and respect other Souls on their spiritual journeys. Remember, what you focus your attention on highlights the reality in your consciousness at any given moment. This awareness builds within you."

Sri Hikari Hito added with great reverence, "The third element is a very important spiritual exercise. HU is an ancient name for God that has a home in the highest reaches of heaven. It resonates with a pure loving vibration and represents the love of God for Soul. You can sing HU for spiritual inspiration or in times of distress to find spiritual protection, spiritual healing, or spiritual insights. Singing the HU Song can help you identify and hear God's voice and guidance.

"When one sings HU with love and only love in his heart, it is a non-directed prayer. You are not telling God what to do, but you are saying 'Thy will be done'. You are trusting God to know what is best for you and all others.

"These three steps have helped many people open their hearts, in order to recognize the Spiritual Essence of God within the hearts of all of God's creatures."

The Spiritual Master asked, "Would you like to sing the HU Song for a few minutes?"

I nodded and said, "Yes, of course."

Evan said, "I've been practicing the HU song. Katy, once the HU Song helps you to be aware of the guidance of Divine Spirit in your life, life will never be the same for you again."

The Spiritual Master said, "This is one method of doing this spiritual exercise." He slowly motioned with his hand, "Please find a comfortable place to sit." The Spiritual Master sat on a nearby tree trunk. Both Evan and I sat on the sandy beach with our backs against a huge, half-buried, fallen, weathered tree trunk.

The Spiritual Master said, "Close your eyes, take a few deep breaths and gently put your attention on your inner visual screen, where daydreams and images come to you. With your eyes closed, sing HU. We will sing this spiritual healing song for a few minutes."

As we, sang HU, our voices harmonized together and a feeling of peace surrounded me. A high-pitched ringing resonated in my ear, I felt like I was almost floating. Too soon, the HU song ended. We sat quietly in the arms of divine love.

The Spiritual Master asked us what we had experienced. Evan said he saw a blanket of blue light surrounded him, he felt peace and he heard the dancing sound of a flute. Then I related my own experience.

The Spiritual Master said, "Over time, singing the HU song may result in an awareness of many different experiences with the Light and Voice of God. The many inner Sounds of God may be sounds of nature, like the buzzing of bees, a strong wind, or sounds of beautiful musical instruments. You may also experience different spiritual realms of existence. Each Being will see, feel, or hear what they are ready to experience. You were both blessed with a communication from the heart of God.

"If you sing the HU Song daily for approximately 20 minutes a day your spiritual connection with the Heart of God will strengthen. Slowly, your awareness will become a resident, not an occasional visitor to the heart of divine love. Thus, the mysteries of life on all levels of heaven and earth will gradually become clear to you. Clarity of communication with Divine Spirit can empower you to become a conscious helper of the God Essence as you grow in awareness and wisdom."

The Spiritual Master looked at me with a piercing intensity, before saying, "The time to end this lesson has arrived."

I covered my face with my hands, and rubbed my eyes as I said, "You've given us so much information." I looked up into the Spiritual Master's face, and added, "I feel like I have information indigestion."

Evan agreed, "Yeah, I feel the same way and I've already been learning about this."

"We will meet again to continue your spiritual quest. Within you exists all which is essential for the attainment of your golden existence." We continued to walk along the beach.

Finally, Evan said, "Thank you Sri Hikari Hito, for allowing us to be here."

The Spiritual Master nodded and said, "You both have enough to assimilate into your awareness. Your cups are full, sip slowly, savor, and learn. As you make the choices that will create your life, remember to 'Let God's Will Be Done'. Listen to Divine Spirit, for It will always mirror God's will. It waits to be heard." He lifted his hand to stop further questioning and said, "Contemplate on what has been given."

I thought about all the issues that Sri Hikari Hito had spoken of, anger, fear, divine love and the HU Song.

As I focused on the Spiritual Masters words, I noticed the lake water continually washing up over the Spiritual Master's sandals. I heard the distant thunderous sound before I noticed the change in our surroundings. The beach was still sandy, but the bordering rocky embankment, which ran paralleled our path had transformed into a jagged, rocky barrier, climbing to about thirty feet over our heads. I looked back and could see the slow ascent of the rocky wall. We had come so far in such a short time. As we rounded a narrow bend in the shoreline, the sound grew louder and more thunderous.

Evan yelled, "Look!" The embankment slowly climbed as its rocky slope paralleled the sandy beach. "Wow," Evan whispered.

Evan and I discovered the source of the thunderous noise. A beautiful majestic waterfall cascaded over the 'C' shaped embankment. We watched and listened to the thunderous, crashing, churning water; it sent a haunting chill down my spine. Had I been here before?

The Spiritual Master said, "Eternal Spirit's constant flow of Divine love is more powerful and necessary to all existences then the air we breathe."

We walked towards a rocky path that moved up and finally behind the base of the churning sheet of water, a misty light reflected off the water. As I followed Evan and the Spiritual Master I hesitated.

The Spiritual Master asked, "Are you ready to move forward?" I nodded my head and moved towards the churning water. An illuminating mist rose from the trunk of the waterfall and slowly enveloped us, a feeling of comfort and peace permeated my conscious awareness. I groaned as I realized that I was at home, back in my bed.

I groaned and asked, "Why am I back here?"

"Katy!" I recognized Mom's voice. "Hey, sleepy head, do I have to come up there to get you?" Mom's question rang with impatience; it was as if she had been calling me for hours.

I yelled a reply, "Okay, Mom, I'll be right down." I hoisted myself out of bed and pulled on my bathrobe. I ran to the bathroom to brush my teeth and wash up, before I ran down stairs the strangest feeling came over me, for a split second my heart filled with the same comfort and peace that I had experienced when I was with Evan and the Spiritual Master Hikari Hito. Maybe I was with them in my heart and Soul, but in the physical awareness, I was living life here in this reality..

I made a conscious choice to focus on the positive Soul stuff in my life; the Soul stuff had always been there, waiting for me to be aware of them.

I entered the kitchen and greeted my parents with a, "Good morning Mother, Father, isn't it a fabulous day? It makes you want to sing, doesn't it?"

With my good hand, I picked up the jug of orange juice and topped up their glasses of juice. Dad was sitting, peeking up at me from over the top of his morning paper. Mom stood frozen in space, staring at me with a plate of blueberry pancakes in her hand. I gave them the widest brightest smile that I could muster. I took the plate out of Mom's hand and bestowed a kiss on her cheek, before setting the plate on the table. I also give Dad a kiss on his cheek.

Dad said, "You're very chipper today, Katy. I don't know if I'm ready for this chipper Katy, so early on a Sunday morning."

I patted Dad on the back and said, "Sure you are Dad, you just don't know it yet." Dad laughed and asked, "What's got into you this morning?"

Mom placed a plate of fruit pieces on the table, before she said, "I for one, like this very cheerful Katy. I am not saying that I don't like the other Katy, but a little variety adds spice to life. I invite you to visit us often."

I smiled at Mom, dished up a couple of pancakes and passed the plate to my father before saying, "I intend for this Katy to be here a lot. I like her a lot. I'm starving, I feel like I've been walking for hours." I smiled at Dad. He chuckled and returned my smile as he put down the newspaper.

I asked my parents, "Do you think that Evan is alive in heaven?" I shocked Dad, Mom and myself with my question. I wondered *had I said the wrong thing again.*

I was surprised to hear Dad answer, "Evan's probably sneaking cookie dough from some hard working Angel." We all laughed.

Mom said, "I hope Evan's not giving God a hard time." We all laughed again. Mom added, "I hope God appreciates roses."

Breakfast was a blast, what a way to begin a day.

vcb

Chapter 18

Making a Mole Hill into a Mountain

A disorderly stack of freshly washed clothes lay piled on my bed. I must have tried on a dozen outfits; I lost count when number eight or nine hit the rejection pile. He had said regular duds, I wondered, *what does, 'regular duds' mean? Did he mean regular duds for school or regular duds for home?*

I mumbled, "He could not have meant regular duds for going out on the town, I mean; our date was supposed to begin at 11:30 on Sunday morning."

I sat on the bed amid my clothes. I was a nervous wreck before even stepping out of my bedroom. This was awful; I would never make it through the date. I pulled on a pair of white socks and blue sneakers that matched my blue jeans and a royal blue sweatshirt.

"I'll tell Andrew that I'm sick. Why not, I'll tell him that I have an upset stomach and that I can't possibly make our date. He's an understanding person, Andrew will understand," I concluded.

"My spiritual teachers have taught me that truth has an identifiable feel to it. You are letting fear overwhelm you." I knew who had spoken these words before I turned around.

I ignored what he had just said and said, "Evan, I am glad to see you. I think Mom's pancakes gave me an upset stomach," I shook my head. "It looks like I'll be staying home."

"Chicken," Evan said, before he began to cluck like a chicken in distress. "Katy, what are you trying to do, convince yourself? Do you believe that if you say it enough, then it will be true? He's not going to understand." Evan repeated and emphasized, "He isn't going to understand. You will really be sick, I mean literally sick if you chicken out on your date. You've been thinking about this date forever."

"Why do you think that?" I asked.

"Because you're not telling the truth and deep down, he's going to know it," Evan stated.

"Evan, I haven't got a thing to wear."

Evan walked over to my bed, bent over and made a great show of staring at the rejection pile. "What are all these things, a new bed cover? Could it be abstract art? It's colorful, but not too practical. You know, I believe you could wear these things and pretend they are clothes. No one will know the difference except you and me." Evan winked at me.

"I can't wear these, these, clothes. They look awful. Andrew would never ask me out again. These clothes are so dull and plain looking. They're just like me, plain and dull," I explained.

"What you have on is fine. Add a jacket and you're all set."

I stood and began to pace, as I said, "You've got to be kidding!" I was agitated. I thought Evan was making fun of me again. "How can you tell me to wear this? It's," Evan and I finished the sentence in unison, "awful. See, even you admit it's awful."

"Katy, I didn't admit anything. I just knew you were going to say that 'awful' word. I've been your brother for your entire life, remember?" Evan reminded me.

Evan stared at me for a moment, then instructed, "Katy, sit down before you fall down." I hopped onto my desk and propped my feet upon my desk chair. Evan added, "You're working yourself into a giant knot of nerves and for what, for indecision about clothes." I started to think about what Evan had just said. It seemed like Evan was waiting for something, maybe it was inspiration. "Katy, relax, loosen up," Evan instructed.

I felt the muscles in my shoulders loosen up. It was as if I was waiting for permission to relax. "Thanks, Evan. I needed that," I said as I took a deep breathe.

"Katy, what were you wearing when Andrew met you?" Evan asked.

"I can't remember but I do remember what he was wearing. Andrew was wearing an old baggy sweat suit, he was gorgeous." I smiled as I relived that moment.

"He wasn't wearing a tux?"

"Of course not," I answered. "It was the first day of school."

"Andrew didn't even have on a suit, sweater, or a tie?" Evan asked with mock astonishment.

"Evan, I told you what he was wearing."

"You mean you liked him and he was in rags?"

"They weren't rags," I defended Andrew. "They were slightly worn but they were clean, I could tell."

"Katy, why are you going out with him if he dresses like that?" Evan asked.

"He doesn't always dress like that; besides, I'm not going out with him because of the way he dresses. He is the nicest guy, he's considerate, kind and honest and he has an amazing sense of humor. I like him; I don't give a hoot about how he dresses." I gave Evan my, 'that's that' look.

Evan had his exasperating grin plastered across his face. He nodded before he asked, "Do you think he gives a hoot about what you're wearing?"

"I don't know."

Evan repeated, "What were you wearing when he met you?"

"Evan, I told you, I can't remember that detail."

"It must not have been spectacular if you don't remember," Evan reasoned. "So, I guess we can rule out an evening gown. Your diamonds must have been in the vault and you must have loaned your tiara to the British Royalty."

I was laughing by now; this was the old Evan, reincarnated. "Yeah, and I vowed never to wear my mink again because I felt sorry for the poor little animals."

Evan laughed too before he asked, "Andrew didn't say that's an amazing outfit, did he?"

I shook my head and said, "No way, I would have remembered that."

"Then it's safe to assume that you weren't dressed to kill since Andrew is still alive." I laughed again, as Evan concluded, "And he asked you out. Imagine that."

I thought about everything that Evan had said. "You know Evan, Andrew did say that he doesn't ask girls out if he doesn't like them, so he must like me some."

"Since the guy has 20/20 vision, he probably knows who he asked out, right? Katy, why don't you accept the good things that come into your life? Just appreciate them and say, "Thank you God, or Divine Spirit, or Spiritual Master, or whoever, for helping me to have some good stuff in my life?"

"Evan,-" I began, but Evan cut me off.

"Katy, don't you remember what Master Hikari Hito said? He said that the different situations, people and problems are in our life for a purpose. They are all teaching us something. Haven't you been listening to anything that he said?" Evan leaned forward, looked straight into my eyes and added, "Katy, why do you insist on doing things the hard way when you don't have too?"

"Evan," I quickly spoke. "You make sense."

Evan stared at me for a few seconds, then leaned back and said, "Oh."

"You're right, Evan. Andrew being in my life is a Godsend. There are no guarantees in existence, so what if it might be temporary gift; nothing is a for sure in life. Why am I trying to make a molehill into a mountain, before I even start the climb?"

Evan said, "Wow, you have been listening to me."

I smiled and moved to the rejection pile and began to sift through it. "What a mess," I thought aloud. I had created a real mess for myself. "This is a good example of karma, the law of cause and effect, isn't it?"

Evan nodded and gave a short, "Yup."

I grabbed a pile of hangers and placed them within easy reach. "Evan, I don't suppose you could snap your fingers and clean this up for me, could you?"

Evan shook his head and answered, "What would you learn if I cleaned up your mess for you?"

"Right, I knew that." I nodded and added, "It sure is my mess. Evan, I hate to ask you to leave but I'm asking you to leave. I need to concentrate on getting ready for my date, but come back later, all right?"

"I'm glad you've come to your senses." Evan's eyes gleamed, as he said this.

One by one, I began to hang each item of clothing. "I'm glad I've come to my senses too. I know one thing for sure, if I had cancelled my date with Andrew, Patty would have locked me up and thrown away the key. She would have been so disappointed."

"How about you Katy, how would you feel if you cancelled?" Evan asked.

I laughed before answering, "Not good. Not good at all."

"Hey Katy, just relax, you'll be fine." Evan said.

"You really think so?" I asked.

"I know so," Evan said with calm conviction. With a nod of his head, he was gone.

I continued to clean up my mess; it takes a lot more time and energy to tidy up a mess than to make one. Under normal circumstances, I would have hated the job of cleaning up that mess but today I did not mind it, I was cleaning up my own world. In addition, it gave my mind a breather; I was no longer worrying about my date. I was thinking about what Evan had said, he was such a clear thinking dude. Finally, the pile of clothes on my bed now hung in the closet. I heard something in the hallway.

"Katy," Mom's voice accompanied her knock on my bedroom door.

I opened the door and said, "Yes, Mom."

"Andrew is here," Mom quietly informed me.

"He's here already? Thank Mom, could you tell him that I'll be just a minute?" I whispered.

"All right honey, I'll ask him to wait in the living room," Mom said, before she turned to retrace her steps down the hallway.

I whispered loudly, "Mom." She stopped, and turned towards me. I quietly asked, "What's he wearing?"

"He's," Mom paused to lower her voice. "He's wearing faded blue jeans, a gold T-shirt, and a gold and navy school jacket."

"Then he's not dressed up. Thanks, Mom." Evan was right. What I had on would be fine. From this moment on my royal blue sweatshirt and faded blue jeans would be a special outfit. It was going to be what I would wear on my first date with Andrew Dover. I grabbed my royal blue windbreaker.

I made a mental note to myself. *Stop putting negative labels on anything. Do not forget*

I knew that saying and thinking that you are going to do something, was much more different from the doing. I also knew that in the future, through the gift of experience, I would be learning this lesson many times over.

Chapter 19

Thank God for All the Picnics

"Hey!" I gave a startled yelp as Andrew pulled my hand away from the blind fold.

"I feel like I'm keeping a kid away from the cookie jar," Andrew said. I had a feeling that Andrew was waving his hand in front of my face, I was sure I felt something brush past my face several times. "No peeking," he warned.

"I'm not," I assured him. Andrew had stopped the VW convertible, but I was sure, we were at another stop sign. I heard him open his door so I felt for the door handle beside me.

Andrew leaned over and moved my hand back onto my lap. "Man you're impatient; just sit there for a second." He tightened the scarf around my eyes. "I'll come and help you in a second."

I was not used to being such a passive part of my own life. I heard the car door close as he got out of the car. All this waiting was driving me crazy. I tried to peek through the blindfold. "Andrew?"

"Yeah," He opened the trunk and removed something before I heard the jarring thud of the trunk closing. He asked, "What is it?"

"I guess we've reached our destination. We've stopped and there's gravel in this parking lot. I heard the sound of gravel." Andrew was silent. I yelled, "Hey, I wouldn't sit around like this for just anyone, you know."

"That's nice to know," he calmly said, as he opened the passenger door. "Katy, give me your hand and I'll help you out of the car." I followed his instructions. "Watch your step," he warned.

I laughed and said, "That's going to be a little difficult. Do I get to take my blind fold off?"

"No, not yet, give me five or ten more minutes." I heard traffic noises we were definitely still within the city. Andrew moved me away from the car and closed the door. He guided me through a small parking lot, warned me to step up over the curb, before we walked onward. His grip tightened on my arm just before I heard a vehicle pass in front of us. I reached for the blindfold; Andrew stopped me and said, "Just follow my lead. I will talk you around the obstacles, okay?"

"Okay?" I agreed. I guess I really did trust him. I did what he asked me to do without qualms. There was nothing dangerous or odd in his requests. He told me when we would be walking up hill, or down hill. He described the scenery around us. Andrew said the reflecting sunlight made the water seem almost silver, instead of its pale blue color. I relaxed in the warmth of the breezeless day as I listened to Andrew's calm and steady voice.

Andrew thought I was getting impatient and reassured me, "We're almost there." We moved off the path onto a grass-covered area. After another minute of walking, we came to a stop. Andrew announced, "Katy, this is the place. Give me half a minute, Katy."

"I've waited this long. Another minute is a piece of cake," I boasted.

"I'll make it even easier for you," Andrew said. I could hear him moving around me as he prepared some kind of surprise. "Count to thirty," he instructed.

"I can't count that high," I informed him.

"I guess I'll have to take the time to teach you how to count that high. You could have that blind fold on for a very long time," Andrew warned. "It all depends on how fast it takes you to learn to count that high."

I counted, quickly, "1, 2, 3, 4, 5 . . . 28, 29 and 30."

"Man you learn fast," Andrew's voice vibrated with mock astonishment.

"Haven't you heard of spontaneous learning before?" I asked.

"No, I can't say I have," Andrew answered.

"Well, now you have," I grinned as I said this.

Andrew said, as he guided me a few feet to my right, "Sit here." He gently helped me to sit on what felt like a blanket.

I asked, "Can I take the blind fold off now?" I tried to peek underneath the bottom edge.

"Sure," he answered. "Let me help you with,-"

I flipped the blindfold off my face, and squinted as my eyes adjusted to the bright sunlight. As I absorbed our surroundings, Andrew took a picture of me. I squinted again and refocused my eyes. Andrew stood behind a red and white checkered tablecloth, which he had spread over a larger brown wool blanket. Sturdy plastic cutlery and white paper napkins flanked two large white plates. An assortment of juice bottles and bottled water were leaning against the cooler.

My astonished voice asked, "How did you manage to carry all this? This is amazing."

"A good knapsack, cooler and a lot of determination can create miracles. It was no sweat, you can feel my head if you want."

"I believe you, Andrew." I surveyed every detail. "You amaze me," I whispered, as I stared in awe at a dried flower arrangement.

Andrew motioned to the food and said, "I reserved us a good picnic spot. Come see what I've whipped up."

"You cooked too?"

"Hey, you're looking at a pretty versatile guy." Andrew took the lid off the cooler and reached inside. He removed containers of chicken, coleslaw, potato salad, and a large, brown paper bag. Andrew described the hidden contents of the bag as dessert. We dished up our food and started to eat.

"This is great," I mumbled between bites. I can't believe that you made all of this. Are you really Superman in disguise?" I asked. Andrew laughed before I added, "Any minute now I expect you to find a phone booth and transform into the man of steel."

He laughed again and said, "My Superman costume is at the cleaners, you're stuck with mild mannered Andrew Dover. I liked our other lunch date a lot, and I decided not to wait until we bumped into each other again for our second lunch date. And, I remember that you said you liked picnics."

"This was a great idea," I said. I looked at Andrew and imagined, before adding, "It's hard for me to picture you in an apron." I dished up some potato salad.

"I borrowed Mom's." Andrew gave a good-natured warning, "But if you tell anyone that, I'll deny it."

"Andrew, your secret's safe with me. This potato salad is fantastic," I said between bites. "It's almost like the kind my Mom makes."

Andrew looked a little sheepish. Before he spoke, I thought he was feeling embarrassed by all the compliments that I kept dishing out. Then he said, "Katy, I have to tell you, Mom helped me with the cooking. She helped me a lot, it was my first time cooking."

"Andrew, that's okay. We all have to learn to do from someone. Everything still tastes terrific. The chicken is great too," I said as I took another bite out of the drumstick. The chicken was moist and flavorful. I looked around at the scenery; our surroundings looked familiar. I could not quite place where we were but the feeling that I had been here before was very strong.

"Have some more chicken," Andrew said, as he passed me the plate of chicken.

"Thanks. This is so good and moist." I thought I was paying Andrew another compliment when I said, "It's just as moist as Kentucky Fried Chicken and in fact it tastes just like Kentucky Fried Chicken."

"It is Kentucky Fried Chicken." Andrew added, "I should have left it in the box."

"Oh, it is? The coleslaw is great too," I quickly added.

"Now that dish, I helped to make. See." Andrew held up his hand. "I only lost part of one finger in the shredder." When he saw my coleslaw-filled fork suspended on route to my mouth, he extended his bent finger and said, "Just kidding."

I laughed and said, "This meal is so good; nothing's going to spoil my appetite." Andrew smiled and we both continued to eat.

I was dishing up my second helping of coleslaw, when I said, "Andrew, I don't care how much of this meal you cooked. The fact that you did this leaves me speechless. This is wonderful. Thank you. You've made this an unforgettable day."

"You just made my day, Katy, thanks. You know, preparing this meal was a real eye opening experience. I don't think I could ever take a meal that my Mom or anyone else makes for granted again. Preparing all of this takes a lot of hard work and I had help from my Mom and the Colonel. If I had to do it on my own I would have ordered take out. He passed me the plate of chicken and prompted me to, "Have some more."

"I was thinking of having a little bit more potato salad." I motioned to what was already on my plate. "It's so good, but I want to save a little room for the mystery dessert," I explained.

Andrew said, "Good thing you reminded me, I forgot about the dessert."

"Should I close my eyes again?" I asked.

"No, that's okay," he answered. I ended up seeing nothing because whatever the dessert was, remained hidden in the confines of the brown paper bag. Instead of just waiting, I found a plastic bag and put the scraps of garbage inside of it. I could hear him ripping a package open and clanking containers together, he seemed to be having some difficulty.

"Andrew."

"Yeah, what is it?" he asked, as he continued to focus on his task.

"Do you need any help?"

"No, I'm okay. I am almost done. A five year old could do what I'm doing."

"I asked because you seem to be having some difficulty preparing our dessert."

"It's okay," he reassured me. "It could be a lot worse; this bag could be the size of a lunch bag." Andrew proceeded to create our mystery dessert.

Finally, with a grand dramatic gesture, Andrew pulled the plate out of the shopping bag to unveil our dessert. Andrew had arranged a dozen peanut butter and jelly crackers on the white paper plate. I stared from the plate to Andrew's smiling face; I didn't know what to say.

"Dessert is served," he announced.

"Peanut butter and jelly crackers, this is a surprise." I managed a curious smile.

"My secret source said you love peanut butter and jelly crackers." He placed the plate in front of me and said, "Don't be bashful." Andrew added, "Try some."

I took a cracker and nibbled at it. With his urging, I took a second one. I asked, "How come you think, know, that I love peanut butter and jelly crackers?"

He smiled and answered, "Justine told me. When you went to freshen up, she volunteered the information. Justine said that peanut butter and jam is your favorite snack and that you really, really like them."

"Justine said that. Now I understand." I smiled and took another bite while I thought; *this is not going to be too difficult to eat after all.* I even enjoyed the second cracker. While I wiped my fingers on a napkin, I heard a click. Andrew had taken a picture.

"Now don't get mad," he quickly said. "I'm a photographer; I'm just doing my job."

"You could have waited until I was ready; I probably have strawberry jelly all over my face." I rubbed my mouth with a napkin.

"You look just fine," Andrew said. As he put his camera back in its case he asked, "How would you like to go for a walk after we get all this stuff back to the VW? I promise not to take anymore pictures today."

"Sure, if that's what you want to do," I agreed.

"Katy, I'm asking you what you want to do because I want your input. This is a democratic date so cast your vote. What do you want to do?" he asked again.

I thought for a second before voicing my idea. "I've got it, why don't we take this stuff back to the car and then we can go for a nice walk?"

Andrew started to laugh; I liked to hear him laugh. When he stopped, he grinned and said, "You know, I couldn't have thought of a better idea if I tried."

For some odd reason there was pride in my voice when I said, "Thanks. I do have a couple of brilliant ideas, every once in a while."'

"Man, you're modest too." We both laughed. "I'm so glad you're not treating me like a Superman with all the answers, I sure don't like that role."

"I thought most guys like that role," I joked with him.

"Hey, don't paint every guy with the same brush. I'm one guy that doesn't like to make all the decisions in a relationship. Women go around fighting for equality and then they turn around and give their freedom of choice away. Why campaign for something and then give it away, does that make sense?"

"Andrew, I was kidding when I said that most guys like that role. Man, you really do sound like Evan," I said. "He would have said something like that."

"Hey, hold on there, I am not Evan. If you are saying you feel relaxed around me, that is great, but I don't want you to think of me as brotherly. . . . Let's get going." Andrew began to gather up the picnic stuff.

"I don't see you in that way," I said as I helped to tidy up. "To me you're like a dream," I said in an awe struck voice.

Andrew shook his head and said, "I'm not a dream, I'm very real."

"I know you're real. I see you as mild mannered Andrew Dover, the guy who sometimes does super nice things." Suddenly he was giving me an enormous bear hug. I knew that this was the big moment; he was going to kiss me for sure. I thought *I wish I had brushed my teeth.*

When he put me down, he said, "Thanks, I'll have to work hard to live up to 'mild mannered', but I'll take it over brotherly any day. Then he kissed me on the forehead, before he let go of me.

Andrew picked up the backpack and helped me get the straps around my shoulders, saying, "If you carry this, I'll carry the rest." I nodded my head and smiled. I had temporarily lost my ability to speak; all I could think about was the kiss. It was probably lucky that he kissed me on the forehead. The kiss was gentle and caring, that is what made it so special. Andrew was intuitively wise, anything more and I am sure I would have fainted.

At this moment I decided, I would never wash my forehead again. My forehead would become a shrine in honor of my first kiss from Andrew, until I got pimples, or Mom noticed my grimy forehead. Maybe it would be simpler to keep the memory and wash my forehead, yup, that is what I would do.

This was the perfect dream date, I was sure dates did not get any better than this. I was very sure that nothing could go wrong with this date. I forgot that the future was yet unformed. There are no absolutes in life, or in all of existence. Life is not a smooth ride for anyone. There are difficulties, hardships and obstacles, and then there are the times when life is like a beautiful picnic on a warm summer's day.

I knew from what the Spiritual Master Hikari Hito had said that every moment in time had its purpose. He also said that we learn the most from the difficult, hard times. I think Divine Spirit throws the occasional picnic at people to keep them from losing hope and faith while they dodge the potholes and lightning bolts of life. The picnics were like joyous resting points. At this moment, I felt like I would be thanking God and Divine Spirit forever for letting me experience this picnic.

Chapter 20

Digging-Up the Truth

We were walking away from Andrew's VW Convertible when I glanced around and asked, "Where are we? Now that I don't have the blindfold on, I can see that this place looks familiar."

"The river valley is one of my favorite places in the city. I come here when I want to jog or just relax," Andrew stated. "This is the river valley area of Victoria Park. I'm glad you decided we should take a walk next. How about we walk up to the Groat Bridge and then go over to the Hawrelak Park? There is a footbridge not far from here, maybe we could try it out when we're exploring. What do you think of that idea?" Andrew asked.

A knot was starting to form in my stomach, how could I have not recognized this area? The Edmonton's river valley parks almost spanned the entire length of the North Saskatchewan River; this river cut the city in half. There was a time when I loved riding through the parks then seven weeks ago, I swore I would never return to this place, and now I was back.

"Are you cold?" Andrew asked.

"No," I shook my head. "Why do you ask?"

"You're shivering." Andrew removed his coat and placed it on my shoulders. "How does that feel?" he asked.

I smiled and thanked him, it was better to let him think I was cold or I would have to explain my feelings. I was not ready to do that quite yet. We kept on walking, Andrew talked and I listened or pretended to listen. The knot in my stomach was growing at a steady rate. The North Saskatchewan River flowed beside us for every step of our journey. I had the sinking feeling that for the rest of our walk, the river would be beside us. I hugged Andrew's coat around me.

The Spiritual Master had said to appreciate the good things in life, I would think about the good things, like Andrew and our date. What happened here before did not matter, it was the past and I could not do anything to change the past. Maybe someone else could have saved him, but unfortunately, I was the person who was dealt those cards. What was I supposed to learn from all of this?

I was living a dream come true and a nightmare, in one surrealistic experience. The day was still beautiful and warm, I could see the people around us, walking, talking and laughing, but now, it was so hard for me to enjoy the beauty of this day.

"Katy, are you still cold? The way you're hugging the coat around yourself, it looks as if you're freezing."

I shook my head, "No," I answered. "I'm okay. I'm sorry. I guess I'm not very good company."

"Do you want to talk about whatever's bothering you? I've been told that I'm a pretty good listener." He leaned forward and smiled as he looked into my eyes. I smiled back at him.

If I talked to anyone, I would have confided in Andrew. There was only one thing stopping me, I was not sure of what I was feeling; I had been running from these feelings for over a month. Avoiding the memories of that day used to be easy, now reminders of that day kept popping up everywhere in my life. The avoidance was affecting my life, in more ways than I wanted to acknowledge. I no longer went swimming with Justine or anyone else. I avoided the river and Victoria Park. In addition, I could not stand talking to Travis. Every time I relived that day a knot would form in my stomach. It was all so stupid because I knew that Evan was not truly dead, I knew he was happily living and learning in his new home.

Andrew bolted down the path in top gear before I realized that someone was screaming from the river for 'help'. Fear welled up inside of me. Andrew accelerated towards the screaming voice; he was Evan rushing to his death.

A whispered, "No," croaked from my throat. "No!" I screamed. I was chasing him screaming, "No! Don't go! Stop! Don't go!" Andrew was not listening.

Trying to stop a lifeguard from saving someone from drowning was like barring a starving man from food, I knew if Andrew had not gone to help he would not have been able to live with himself. Although I knew this, I could not stop myself from trying to stop him. When I finally caught up with Andrew, I was totally out of breath, I yanked at his hand with focused determination and purpose; I had to get him away from the river.

I managed to speak between gasps, "Don't go in, please, don't go in."

"Katy, it's all right. It's just some kids fooling around; I've talked to them about crying wolf."

I was hardly listening to what he was saying. I thought *sure, but if you go into the river, you will drown.* I kept pulling at his hand.

"Katy, listen to me. Katy!" Andrew sounded frustrated but I was not going to let him talk me out of getting him away from this place. Suddenly I was off the ground; he had picked me up and was carrying me over to a nearby bench. Andrew set me down firmly on the bench before he carefully removed the vise like grip that I had on his hand. He flexed his fingers.

"Did I hurt you," I asked.

He shook his head and answered, "No," Andrew kept flexing the fingers of his right hand as he joked, "I'm sure the circulation will return in a few days. You have quite a grip," Andrew knelt in front of me and gently held my hand as we stared at one another. He added, "Have you ever thought of trying out for the school wrestling team?"

"Don't go into the river." I had meant this to be a request but it came out like an order.

The smile faded from his face, Andrew looked worried and when he spoke, he sounded nervous. "Katy, I'm not diving into anything, there's no need for me to do that." He raised our joined hands, squeezing ever so softly and whispered, "I'm right here."

I was shivering again, my teeth were chattering. Slowly, the bowling ball knot in my stomach began to relax. The warmth of his hands radiated life and energy into my cold fingers.

"I'm sorry," I whispered. "I ruined everything. Show me your favorite place, I'm okay." I smiled at him but he did not smile back at me.

Andrew slowly shook his head and said, "Katy, I'm the one who's sorry I didn't realize that it was a mistake to bring you here." Andrew quietly said, "Sometimes I can be real dense."

I laughed and tried to make light of the whole situation, "No. No it isn't. You are making something out of nothing. I'm fine; really I am, so let's go." I started to get up but he stopped me.

"You're not fine, I know it and you know it. Talk to me, tell me what happened back there," Andrew persisted. "I think I already know but I'd rather hear it from you."

"I'm okay. Quit ordering me around." I pulled at my good hand as he held it firmly in his grasp. My voice grew in intensity; it matched the anger simmering inside of me. I began to realize that Andrew was not going to let me off the hook. "I was worried about you going into the river. That's the end of it," I shouted.

"That's not the end of anything," he shouted back at me. "I've trained as a life guard, if someone's drowning, I try to help them." Andrew's voice softened. "Talk to me, I care about you." I could not ignore the honest concern in his voice.

I was shivering again. I closed my eyes and tried to regain my composure. Andrew was beside me with his arm around my shoulder as he softly asked, "This is about your brother, isn't it? I know what it's like to loose someone you love."

I whispered, "You're always playing Superman."

He whispered back, "You're changing the subject."

I continued, "Superman isn't real, he's imagination, like the Terminator. Real people drown and real people die; sometimes they die before we are ready to let them go. You're mild mannered Andrew Dover under your Superman costume and I'm not ready to let you go." We sat in a silence, as if the whole park was sealed in a quiet room, the sound of traffic was so far away, and even the birds were quietly silent.

Andrew finally spoke in a calm, relieved voice, "I understand." Andrew shifted his weight so he faced me, then he gently clasped my hands. He looked at me with a comforting intense gaze, I should have been used to this by now but I was not.

"I'm not Superman but I'm not always mild mannered Andrew Dover. I guess I just proved that. Katy, I'm plain old Andrew Dover and I'm not going anywhere right now," he stated.

I closed my eyes and squeezed his hands; I could feel the tension drain from my body as if someone had opened a drainage spout. I began my apology, "I can't believe I acted like that, I knew you were not going into the river. I'm so sorry."

"Katy, don't worry about it. We all go through life doing the best that we can do. The best that I can do right now is to help you, will let me help you?"

"I shook my head and spoke, "I don't know. I-"

Suddenly a light went on in Andrew's eyes, his excited voice asked, "Hey, why don't you let me be your Superman?"

I laughed before reminding him, "Andrew, you just said you weren't Superman."

"I mean metaphorically," he explained.

"What in the world are you talking about?" I asked.

Andrew continued, "You know how Superman is able to fly over things so he can see things from above, he has a better over all view of everything, right?"

"I guess," I said as I nodded my head.

"And you know how he sees through things with his x-ray vision?" I nodded my head in acknowledgement before he continued, "Well, maybe I can do that for you. If you talk to me about what's bothering you, I might be able to see things from another point of view or maybe I could give you different insights."

As Andrew waited, I thought about what he just said and wondered if he really was like Superman? Maybe super men and women were just ordinary people, perhaps they were people who took the time to care and help others whenever someone requested assistance. Andrew cared and he offered to help, it was up to me to choose the next step.

"I suppose it couldn't hurt," I reasoned. "It might help."

"That's my point," Andrew enthusiastically agreed.

"All right," I smiled as I agreed. "We can give it a try."

Thus, my task began, I was about to shovel out the dirt which covered this particular memory. Every time I had attempted to bury the memory in its final resting place, something or someone would remind me of the events of that day and disturb the gravesite. The memories would bubble to the surface so the gravesite was always shallow and the soil was always fresh and overworked.

A part of me wanted to shovel more dirt on top of it and another part of me wanted to drop the shovel and run as fast and as far as I could go. However, I knew the time for running had run its course.

I wondered *am I Katy the mouse or Katy McCall the eagle*. I quickly showed Katy the mouse the door and watched her reluctantly leave. That timid little creature would not undermine my resolve. The real Katy McCall stepped forward with a sturdy shovel grasped tightly in her hands.

Chapter 21

Removing the Blinders

I began my story, "Evan, Travis and I were spending Travis's last Saturday in the city visiting his favorite digs. By noon the following Monday, Travis would have been boarding a plane for Winnipeg. During the last week in June, his Dad had completed his transfer to a new managerial job and the time had come for Travis and his Mom to join him in their new home.

Travis was Evan's best friend; they had met during the junior high school swimming team try-outs. Neither one of them made the team that first year but over a year later, after an intense few weeks of studying they met all the requirements and succeeded in getting their Life Guard Certificates. I helped them study. Evan was a good lifeguard; he just didn't do a great job of guarding his own life."

"You're right Katy; he was a good life guard. I know, because I was one of his instructors," Andrew gently reminded me.

"I know," I agreed, before continuing my story. "Later on that same evening, Evan and a bunch of their friends from school were going to take Travis out on the town. Mom was planning a surprise party for Travis; all his friends were going to be there. The party was going to start after they returned home.

Travis was like a second son and brother to our family so his leaving was going to be hard on all of us, his leaving would be especially difficult for Evan. I used to think that they were supposed to be brothers but God made a mistake so God got them together as best friends. You're the first person I've said that too, kind of silly don't you think?" I asked.

"I like your idea. I figure that God makes things work out some how," Andrew reasoned.

I smiled and put my head on his shoulder. He lifted his arm, shifted his sitting position and put his arm around my shoulder. I felt wonderful and safe. I added, "The events for that Saturday were the beginning of our long good-bye. It turned out to be a double good-bye." I closed my eyes and paused for a few seconds.

I said, "I remember that day like it was yesterday; it was a cloudy, hot, muggy Saturday morning in early July. The area to the west of the city had received a freak thunderstorm and the Edmonton area was due to get the aftermath. The North Saskatchewan was unusually high for that time of year, the water was rushing and churning like it was angry."

"We rode our mountain bikes down through Kinnaird Ravine." I had always liked that ravine because for a few minutes it felt like you were in the middle of a forest. I added, "We turned west on the bike trail to follow the river until we found a picnic table. We brought out sandwiches, drinks, and hot dogs from our backpacks."

Andrew nodded and said, "Yeah, I believe I know the place, I've ridden the trails a lot."

I slowly nodded my head and continued with my remembrance, "We roasted hot dogs. Evan and Travis had a hot dog eating contest, together they downed over a dozen dogs and they both had a couple bottles of juice to boot. Evan had a bit of indigestion but he pretended he was fine. He kidded me and said we should have brought a chocolate cream pie for dessert; I hate chocolate pie. I'm sure Evan was trying to distract me."

Andrew nodded, before I continued with my story. "Evan looked pale, he looked down right awful. Evan told us again that he was fine. I figured he would be all right in a little while. We got on our mountain bikes and headed west down the bike path." I pointed at the miniature highway of black asphalt.

"It was hard for me to keep up with them. We biked for maybe five minutes, before we heard the screams for help. It wasn't like the screams we heard today, the screams we heard that day, we knew they were real. Evan and Travis reacted to the screams just as you did today; they were off in a flash. They took short cuts when they could, dodging joggers, bikers and pedestrians. I was pushing myself but couldn't keep up with them.

"I came around a bend in the path, just in time to see Evan and Travis leap off their moving bikes. They dived into the river in unison and angled their way towards a crying little boy. I had guessed that he was six or seven years old. Luckily, the boy had his arms tightly wrapped around a good-sized log so his head was above the water level. I turned my bike around and slowly rode along the shoreline to keep pace with them.

"A number of people ran beside me. One frantic woman in the group was gasping for breath, while she did her best to shout to the little boy, 'Hold on. Hold on.' I figured that this must be the boy's mother. I left my bike and ran with her. She stumbled and I tried to help her up. Her gold colored jogging pants had grass stains streaked across her knees, she stumbled again and I helped her again.

"I asked, 'Has anyone called 911?'

"She nodded and said, 'My husband went to call them.' She pointed to an exhausted, wet man, running towards us.

"He hugged his wife and gasped, 'Help is on the way.' We all scrambled to catch up to the three figures in the river.

"Evan had gotten to the boy first. I could see him talking calmly to him, I imagined Evan telling him that everything was going to be okay. The little boy clung to the three-foot long log, as if it was his last link to life. Travis and Evan flanked the little boy as they swam towards the shoreline. The river was churning along at a good clip, so getting back to the riverbank was difficult for them; they kept correcting their course.

"The boy's father said, 'I tried to get him out but the river was too fast; if I could swim better I might have caught him.'

"As I jogged beside them, I said, 'That's my brother and his friend out there. They are very good lifeguards, your son is safe.' I thought I saw relief on their faces.

"More people came to watch the life saving drama. Everything was just fine, until the boy lost his grip on the log, he grabbed for Evan before being pulled under by the under current. Evan grabbed him and yanked him back to the surface; the rescue had changed into what the lifeguards called a contact rescue. Of course, you know all about that, you taught Evan all that he knew about being a life guard," I said, as I looked into Andrew's eyes.

Andrew said, "Evan was a natural, he would have been the teacher in a couple of years."

"Evan will, I mean, would have been happy to hear that." I paused for a few seconds before continuing with my story. I looked at Andrew and said, "I asked the boys parents, 'What is your son's name?'

"They answered, 'His name's Leon Backman.'

"I turned back to the river and yelled, 'His name is Leon.' I wondered what was going on. Travis was towing little Leon and Evan was lagging behind; he looked like he was struggling with the river. Suddenly Evan clutched his stomach and curled up into a ball, I realized he was having stomach cramps. In the next second the river sucked him under the surface, it happened so fast. I have wondered over and over again, why I didn't go after him sooner."

Andrew gently squeezed my upper arm and said, "Katy, you did all that you could do." He was trying to comfort me. Under normal circumstances, I would have loved his caring, but now I knew I had to focus on the story, I had to get it out of my system. I pushed myself away from Andrew and stood, facing him.

I said, "I'm not a bad swimmer. I got to where I believed the river would have taken him and I yelled Evan's name. I thought that Evan must be caught-up on something or he would have come to the surface by now. I filled my lungs, pinched my nostrils and dived. The silt and pollutants in the water prevented me from opening my eyes, I felt around with my hands. It was like looking for a needle in a haystack but I kept diving, I could not give up. I felt an arm and pulled Evan to the surface, I felt hopeful because he still had a strong grip. Evan seemed to be pulling me to the surface, it was Travis; I was holding his arm He came out after making sure that the boy was all right.

"He asked me, 'Katy, where's Evan,'

"I explained, 'I can't find him. He went under before he reached the shoreline, help me find him.' I pleaded with Travis for help, he nodded and together we kept diving and searching. Sometimes we would meet above water. One time I saw lost hope in Travis's eyes but I did not let it affect me I kept on diving.

"Finally, Travis said, 'Katy, you're exhausted and cold, go wait for the rescue unit on the beach, they should be here any second now.'

"I screamed, 'No!' Up until that second, I had not thought about how cold the water was I floated away from him."

"He yelled, 'Katy, you're exhausted!'

"I yelled, 'No way, Travis. I'm not tired, I'm not cold and I'm not leaving. You go wait for them.' I dived again. When I surfaced, Travis was gone, he was not on the beach but the Rescue Unit was on the beach and the Rescue Launch was circling near us. Travis burst from the water, coughing as he gasped for air; I was glad that he had not given up. I was going to dive again but he grabbed my arm and stopped me.

"Travis said, 'The Fire Department's Rescue Unit wants us to get out of the water.'

"I yelled, 'No!'

"Travis said, 'Katy, they want us out of the river so they can do their job.'

"One of the firemen from the launch ordered over a loud speaker, 'Please leave the river immediately.'

"I yelled, 'No!' You could say I dug my heels in the water.

"Travis tried to reason with me, he repeated, 'Katy, you're exhausted and freezing. You're not thinking straight.' He was right," I whispered. "I tried to hit Travis to keep him from stopping me. Travis finally clipped me on the chin and knocked me out before he got me to the Fire Department's Launch."

"He hit you?" Andrew asked.

I nodded and said, "I guess he had no choice, he was right, I wasn't thinking straight." I finally agreed with Travis.

"I don't think he holds it against you, Katy. He probably feels bad about having to hit you," Andrew observed.

"I hope that's true," I whispered. I added, "Mom said that Travis saved my life and her life that day because she wouldn't have survived losing both of us."

"Your Mom is a smart Mom. . . . Andrew asked, "When did they find Evan?"

"They found him about ten minutes later, about a half a kilometer down the river. Evan's body was pinned under some shrubs and boulders near the shoreline, just below the surface of the river. Ten minutes," I repeated in a whisper. "When Travis socked me, the rescue launch had to rescue both of us." I wondered *does Andrew understand how that affected everything.*

Andrew said, "That's great. It's lucky they were there."

I adamantly shook my head; I stared at Andrew before explaining, "No it wasn't great. Because I didn't listen, the Fire Department's Rescue Launch took ten minutes out of their search to take us to the dock; they could have found Evan ten minutes sooner. Maybe it would have made a difference. The river was cold; sometimes the cold slows down the body's systems. People have been brought back to life long after they should have been dead." Tears were running down my cheeks. I brushed them aside.

Andrew said, "Katy, Travis was right. It wouldn't have made a difference; ten minutes wouldn't have made a difference. From what you described to me, I can tell that you were both searching for him for a long time." Andrew guided me back to a sitting position on the bench; he sat beside me again and put his arm around my shoulders. "You both did all that you could do, everyone knows that except you."

I was sobbing but I managed to ask, "Do you think I'll ever know that for sure?" I asked him.

"Some day I hope you will," Andrew answered, as he handed me a couple of tissues. He added, "They look worn but they are clean and unused."

I took the tissues and blew my nose, before I said, "What I'd really like to know is, when did the Soul part of Evan leave Evan's body for good? That's the real time of death. People who have near death experiences return to their bodies, maybe Evan could have returned if he had the extra few minutes?"

"Katy, that's something only Evan or God, knows for sure. It's too bad you couldn't just ask him, but you can't. Like I said before, you and Travis did your best in a difficult situation."

I sat up and yelled, "That's it Andrew. Oh Andrew, you are so wise. That's it; I'll ask Evan when he really died. Why didn't I think of this before? It's so simple." Elation clouded my awareness; I had forgotten how irrational my reasoning must have sounded to Andrew.

Andrew slowly said, "Katy, Evan's been dead for seven weeks."

"I, I know . . ." I quickly came up with an explanation. "I guess I was thinking that somehow there might be a way to communicate with people who have died." As Patty would say, I thought fast on my feet. "It's kind of silly; you must think I'm an A-1 idiot."

Andrew shook his head and answered, "I think that everyone who has lost some one they've loved has wished that wish. If you figure out a fool proof way of talking with people who have passed on, with no hocus-pocus, crystal ball stuff, tell me about it," Andrew said.

I nodded my head and stared at him, while I made up my mind to be quiet about my talks with Evan. Evan would be happy to know that my resolve was solid.

Instead, I said, "Thanks, Andrew. You really were Superman today. You helped me to see that day in an entirely different way, talking to you about it really did help."

"I'm glad I could help, Katy," Andrew tapped his shoulder and added, "My shoulder is available anytime you want to talk, or rest."

"Is it available now?" I asked.

"It's available now and for always, it's always available for you," Andrew said.

I leaned on Andrew; he lifted his arm and encircled my shoulders in a comforting hug. I watched the river through the line of birch trees. The overwhelming anxiety or was it fear, whatever it was had been replaced by something else. Pain and anger still accompanied this memory, yes, but there was something lighter and brighter inside of me, a hope for tomorrow and a quiet peacefulness had made a home in my heart. Did Andrew's arm around my shoulders help me to believe in this renewed hope for tomorrow?

I could not forget what happened in that river. That would always be a part of me but maybe the pain, anger, sadness and that knot in my stomach would slowly be replaced by this new hope. Maybe someday the river would just be a river again and the anger that I directed towards Travis and myself would someday be a quiet memory, for what we had not been able to change seven weeks ago.

I thought about what the Spiritual Master had been helping me to understand. I remember the Master asking, "If we are all characters in a never-ending play called existence, then who is the play-write and author?" I thought *if the journey is endless then I have time to solve the riddle of this question.*

I whispered, "Who is the play-write and author of our lives?"

Andrew asked, "What did you say?"

I looked up into his face and answered, "I'm just wondering about life."

Andrew smiled and kissed my forehead before he said, "You sure do like tackling big questions. How come I feel like you're the person who will find the answers?"

I laughed and said, "Some how I think I will, maybe we all will."

"Yeah," Andrew said as he hugged me, "Maybe we will."

Hope and peace washed over me and through me. It seemed to reflect back to me from the twinkling surface of the river.

Chapter 22

There Is More to Life Then a Kiss

"Katy, spill the beans," Patty ordered.

"What?" I asked.

"Boy, it must have been amazing, you're still day dreaming about it."

"Patty, what are you talking about?"

"You twit, your dream date with Andrew, how did it go?" Patty asked with exasperation.

I smiled as I remembered our date. "It was great," I explained. "It was everything that I imagined it would be, and more." I turned to gather my English books from my locker. My wrist was feeling a lot better, but I still had to wear the Velcro tensor bandage. That is when something hit me from behind. My head hit the locker beside my open locker.

"Oww!" I felt my forehead; it was tender to my touch.

Patty's agitated voice yelled, "Why don't you watch where you're going, you over grown Neanderthal?" I turned to see Erica watching Patty as she shoved Henry Cookson. Henry put up his hands, as if he was conceding the battle to Patty.

He said, "I'm sorry I didn't see you, you're so short. When I'm looking at Erica I forget to watch where I'm walking." As he turned to smile at her, Henry laughed and added, "Hey, what can I say, I was distracted." Erica beamed a smile back at him.

"You're lying," Patty said, as she pointed an accusing finger at him. You shoved Katy on purpose. I saw you."

Henry amended his last statement, "I didn't mean to shove you that hard."

Patty turned towards me and asked, "Are you okay, Katy?"

I nodded. I looked up at Henry and wondered *did you shove me on purpose?* I moved towards him. Henry slowly backed away.

I thought about what Sri Hikari Hito words, 'Kathleen, anyone can choose to add to anger, or would the better choice be to identify and understand the issue which anger or fear highlight, by reviewing all the elements of the entire situation without bias.' I began to cool down, as I tried to figure out my feelings. I wondered *should I let someone shove me around, or should I stand up for myself? Is Katy the mouse gone?*

I slowly raised my hand to point at Henry but before I could speak, he fell backwards. I spotted Andrew standing behind Henry.

Andrew apologized, "Hey man, I'm sorry, I didn't see you; you're so big. I guess I should watch where I'm walking."

Erica yelled, "Hey, you did that on purpose. Why don't you watch where you're going?"

Andrew said, "Maybe if we all watch where we're going there will be a lot less accidents around here. Henry, what do you think?" Andrew extended his hand to help Henry to his feet.

Henry nodded and agreed, "Yeah sure." Henry and Erica quickly turned and left.

As we watched Andrew approaching us Patty gushed, "Oh Katy, you're so lucky."

I asked, "Andrew, how long have you been there? Did you see all that?"

Andrew answered, "I was around long enough to know that I saved Henry from the wrath of Katy McCall, and I've been here long enough to know that you're lucky." Andrew added, "I thought I was the lucky one." Patty sighed and put her hand against a locker for support.

"Andrew, the person behind you making strange noises is my friend Patty Burbick." I motioned towards Patty.

Patty gave me a cut-it-out stare as she shook her head. Andrew turned to look at her. "I was just clearing my throat," Patty explained. "It's nice to meet you." She shook his hand and giggled.

"Same here," he said. Andrew gave Patty a heart melting Dover smile while he returned the handshake.

"Katy and I never miss a wrestling tournament, we're great fans," Patty smiled at the both of us. It was my turn to give an intense *cut-it-out* stare to Patty; she caught it with a widening smile.

"Patty was just hurrying to leave; she wanted to speak with Mrs. Cope regarding our English project. See you in class, Patty." Patty hesitated for a few seconds, as she decided whether to argue with me about my covert request.

Finally, she said, "Okay, I get the message. Why don't you just ask me to leave you alone?" Patty scowled as she asked her question.

"Patty, could you leave us alone?" I silently sent a combined warning and plea to her to heed my request.

"Okay, okay, you don't have to ask me twice. I'm gone but you're going to miss me," she jokingly warned.

"Yeah," I agreed. "It'll be difficult but I know we'll survive. Good-bye, Patty," I firmly stated.

Patty moved past me "Tell me everything." I nodded an affirmation. With a wave of her hand, she turned and headed for English class.

Andrew diplomatically said, "Interesting friend."

"Patty's one of a kind," I agreed. "We've known each other since we were in diapers, but we aren't always tuned into the same frequency. She thinks she knows what I am thinking and feeling, better than I do and she has a way of putting her foot in my mouth for me. It's aggravating. If Patty was my interpreter, I'd fire her."

"I would say there's something special about your friendship," Andrew observed. He added, "In order for the both of you to be friends for so long, there would have to be something special about your friendship."

"You're right; we're always here for each other. And Patty's . . ." I hesitated, as Andrew stared intently at my forehead, I finished my sentence, ". . . her heart is in the right place and it's filled with caring. My life is never boring with Patty around," I concluded.

"Hey, I didn't come down here to talk about your friend, so why are we talking about her?"

"I have no idea," I answered.

Andrew brushed his fingertips over the tender spot on my forehead, he asked, "How does your head feel?"

"I'm fine," I assured him. I laughed and added, "I guess I have a hard head."

Andrew said, "I came by to ask you how you were surviving after our date. It was pretty intense."

I laughed and nodded my head in agreement. I answered, "Oh yes, you're right it was an intense date, but it was also a freeing experience. I figured out a lot yesterday and you helped me to do that. You were Superman; it was as if you saw the situation with your x-ray vision. You helped me to see an overview, just like you said you would."

Andrew said, "Katy, I was lucky that I was able to do that. It helped that we were in tune with one another." He smiled and his eyes twinkled before he added, "I realized another thing, I would say that you were your own super person. I was like your cheering squad, I was just there so you could talk to someone," Andrew concluded.

I nodded and said, "That could be true but in the end you still helped me, I wanted to thank you again."

"Didn't I say he was a helpful person?" Andrew turned. I looked past him to see Erica.

"Oh no," I whispered

"Erica you're back, and you took your sock out of your mouth," Andrew joked. Laughter burst out of me.

Erica's bewildered look accompanied her glance at her socks, she asked, "What are you talking about."

Andrew looked at me smiled and said, "It's just a joke between friends."

Erica sniped back, "The reason that you're interested in the squirt is the real joke." We both stared at Erica as she faked concern. "Oh, you haven't told her yet, have you?" Again, Erica alluded to the mysterious reason for Andrew's interest in me. I listened intently as I waited for her explanation.

Andrew stepped in front of me and said something quick and direct to her. Andrew moved forward as he spoke and ended the sentence with a firm, "Now get out of here."

Erica backed away and said, "Okay, I'm going," "You're both pathetic losers. Why should I waste my time on you?" She turned and ran into Mrs. Henderson's biology class.

"What did you say to her?" I asked.

Andrew answered, "I just unmasked her and called her bluff, Erica's an insecure bully."

"You think Erica is insecure? She doesn't give me that impression," I said. I remembered Sri Hikari Hito's saying, 'Anyone who tears others down in order to feel good about his or herself, lives in fear.'

"She's very insecure," Andrew said. "For some reason you scare her, I don't know why. That's her problem, I wouldn't give her a second thought if I were you, I sure don't," Andrew concluded.

"Andrew, that's the second time Erica's talked about some mysterious reason behind your interest in me. What was she talking about?"

Andrew seemed to be thinking as if he was trying to decide what to say next. He finally said, "Erica is probably trying to put her own spin on the truth. I had better clear thing up." I held my breath, as I waited. Andrew asked, "Could you come with me to my aunt and uncle's pizzeria after school? I'll answer your questions when we get there, it won't take long."

"Sure, I think I can do that," I said.

"Can you meet me at my car after the last class?" Andrew asked. "I'm parked on the south side of the gym."

I nodded and jumped as a voice boomed from the stair well doorway, "Hey, Dover, the coach wants to see us before gym class. We've got less than 5 minutes." He was one of Andrew's friends, Gus something or other.

"I'll be there in a second," Andrew yelled. "That guy has always had lousy timing," Andrew mumbled. "One more question, would you like to go to an Oiler's hockey game this coming Friday night?"

"Sure, I love hockey. I just have to ask my parents, I'm sure it will be no problem," I enthusiastically answered. Life was getting better and better.

Andrew said, "I'll pick you up around 7 p.m. on Friday night." I looked around us at the almost empty hallway and knew that our visit was over.

"Andrew, I have to get to class, I'll see you later."

We stared at each other before Andrew put his fingers under my chin, slowly bent over and kissed me on the lips. It was so gentle and light, it was wonderful. I had watched his lips moving closer and closer to mine, my eyes had gone cross-eyed just before I closed them; I was dizzy and happy in my heaven. It took my eyes a few blinks and seconds to get back to their natural state. I wondered *would I ever be the same again.*

Andrew walked me to my class and said, "Don't forget to meet me at my car after school." We said our good-bye and then he headed down the stairway.

I made it to my desk just as Mrs. Cope began to give us directions. We were to work in our Macbeth study groups. Donald Howser, the third member of our group was ill so for today, Patty and I were on our own. Patty waited until we had moved our desks together before she began to pelt me with questions.

"What happened?" she asked.

I whispered, "I'll tell you later."

"No way you're not going to do that to me again," Patty, warned me. "I can't wait that long, tell me now," Patty ordered.

I glanced at Mrs. Cope and saw that she was busy helping Terry Harris with his paper, so I decided to take a chance and tell Patty about our picnic. When I finished describing the picnic, Patty was almost speechless.

"Wow," was all she could manage to say.

I was glad to see that she was impressed. I glanced at Mrs. Cope and stared into her focused, patient gaze. I elbowed Patty, whispered a warning and we were both hard at work, making a show of being hard at work.

A half hour went by before Patty asked me her next whispered question. "What did he talk to you about?" I stared at her, as I tried to figure out what Patty had just said. "Andrew, what did he want to talk with you about, in the hallway?" Patty pointed in the direction of the hallway.

"He asked me out," I stated. Patty's eyes widened and I knew that in a second her squealing reaction would fill the room. I quickly clamped my hands over her mouth. "Patty, get a grip," I quietly warned. I removed my hand and glanced at Mrs. Cope to see that her attention was elsewhere, relief seeped through me to replace tension.

"I'm in control, don't worry," Patty assured me. "Maybe on your next date he'll finally kiss you, even if it's just a quick good night kiss."

"Finally, what do you mean, finally? We've only been out on one date," I reminded her.

"Yeah, but you've seen him a lot in school and he really likes you, so what's the next step? Don't deny it, it's obvious. Why doesn't he get a move on and kiss you?" Patty asked.

"Patty, you've got kissing on your brain, there's more to life than kissing," I smiled as I lectured her. It was on my brain too but I was not going to tell Patty that.

"I know that, I wasn't born yesterday, but kissing is so romantic," Patty swooned. "I think it's better than shopping but I need more practice to know that for sure," Patty concluded.

I smiled, nodded in agreement and said, "There are probably a lot of things that are as good as kissing."

I knew that I was not going to get anywhere telling Patty how wrong she was, especially when she was right. I wanted to savor the experience but I also wanted to share my heaven.

"I just wondered when he was going to get around to kissing you, that's all," Patty made light of the whole conversation.

"Patty, Andrew kissed me this morning in the hallway," I blurted out.

"All right, finally!" Patty yelled.

I groaned and covered my face; the room had gone dead silent. I did not have to look at Mrs. Cope, to see what she was doing. I peeked at her and stared into her focused eyes. How were we going to explain this?

Patty had already devised a plan. "Katy just told me that Lady Macbeth has a phobia concerning blood, can you believe that?" Patty asked with mock astonishment.

"Really, I would really like to hear this amazing theory," Mrs. Cope said as she leaned back in her chair. "Please share the theory with all of us." Patty and I looked at one another. Well, maybe glared would be a better description of how I looked at Patty. We both knew that we were sinking into a deep trench of trouble.

"Sure," I agreed. "Actually, Patty knows the theory; I think she could explain–"

"No, no, no!" Patty said. She shook her head and added, "No, I can't remember your theory, I, I,"

I whispered, "My theory, my theory." Patty shrugged her shoulders and gave me a silent apology. I looked at Mrs. Cope and reluctantly stood. "Well, I guess it's up to me. Uh, the phobia that Lady Macbeth developed was not just in the physical consciousness; it had its roots in the emotional, mental and spiritual, or her belief consciousness. It was in her entire being. She had nightmares resulting from emotional and mental stress." I paused before continuing. It was so quiet; when someone coughed, it seemed to echo around the room.

As she impatiently waited, the echo of Mrs. Cope's fingers tapping her desk seemed to fill the room. She said, "Let's hear more."

I said, "You know what is said in the Bible, 'What you sow, you shall reap' and the law in

Physics that states, 'With every action, there is an equal and opposite reaction.' This same law exists in all levels of life. Lady Macbeth didn't know that if she and Macbeth killed those men, that they would have to pay for it in some way. Even if they had not been caught the Law of Cause and Effect would have caught up with them eventually."

"The blood was a symbolic representation of her actions; the imaginary blood on her hands was her subconscious mind telling her that she had done something wrong. If she could have seen from a higher viewpoint, she would have known that it was one choice in her life that would lead to many other difficult choices. She didn't look at the long term; she only saw the short term choice, based on greed." I stopped, looked around at the silent room and quickly sat down. Oh, why was I rambling? Now everyone thought I had a screw loose.

"Thank you Katy, I can see why Patty reacted as she did. I can't wait to see your finished papers," Mrs. Cope shook her head. I had surprised her. No wonder, I had surprised myself.

The bell rang; everyone gathered their books and prepared to leave. Mrs. Cope reminded everyone to move their desks back into their proper places. I moved my desk back and breathed a sigh of relief. Patty sat, staring at me, as the class and Mrs. Cope exited.

"Patty, the bell rang. Let's go."

"Katy, where did you get those ideas from? We didn't talk about that stuff," she said with astonishment.

I shrugged my shoulders and though *what could I say, 'My dead brother and his Spiritual Master have been teaching me about existence?'* No way was that going to happen. Patty had already helped me to put one foot into my mouth, I was not about to see if I could fit my other foot in with it.

I said, "Fear does strange things to a person." I was trying to sound wise. I added, "I guess I had a choice, to face the situation and do my best, or to cop out; I did my best."

"You sure surprised me," Patty shook her head; she was as surprised as Mrs. Cope had been. "Aren't you mad at me?" Patty asked.

I hesitated before I answered her, "Maybe I should be but I'm not mad. Patty . . ."

She cautiously said, "Yeah?"

"Don't ever tell anyone that I know anything about something, when I'm not even sure if I know anything about that something, okay?"

"Okay," Patty agreed. "But you have to admit, my solution was pretty inventive," she said as her satisfied grin widened. Patty moved her desk back into place.

"Patty, it could have been a disaster," I reminded her.

"You've got to admit, I think fast," Patty pointed out.

"Yeah, you're fast, you're fast at getting me in hot water," I said.

"Okay, okay, I promise I'll try not to speak for you again," Patty agreed.

I gave her a quick hug and said, "Thanks Patty, but I'll believe it when I see it."

"You don't believe me?" Patty joked as we left the room.

I think that is why Patty and I had been friends for almost fifteen years. If we did not like what the other person said or did, we were honest with one another. We communicate our feelings. We were like cats, no matter how we fell; we somehow managed to land on our feet.

Chapter 23

Megan

I glanced at my watch as I waited for the long-winded girl to get off the phone. When she turned and glanced at me, I smiled with hope. She knew I was waiting to use the phone so maybe she would hurry her call.

Patty suggested, "Let's go find another phone; waiting for her to finish is going to take forever."

"Shh," I warned, as I shook my head. Patty groaned with disapproval. "Patty, you don't have to wait for me. I told you, I am not going straight home."

Patty walked down the hallway, in a few minutes she came rushing back yelling, "Katy, something is going on outside. There is a T.V. news team outside. Come on Katy."

The girl on the phone said a quick good-bye then hung up the phone, before she ran towards the doorway

"Oh finally," Patty said, as she grabbed the phone and handed it to me. "Here, make your phone call."

I asked, "Don't you want to see what's going on outside?"

"I know what's happening outside, nothing," she stated. The light bulb of awareness finally went on in my head.

"Patty, you're wicked," I said, as I smiled with gratitude before I took the phone from her extended hand. "Thanks," I added. I quickly dialed and waited.

"No problem," Patty said, before asking, "Where are you going? Does this have anything to do with Andrew?" I nodded. "Yes!" Patty gave a short, gleeful cheer.

"Hi Mom . . . yes, everything is fine. I am phoning because I want to, uh; go to, the library before I catch the bus. I won't be there long." Patty's eyes widened with surprise. "Bye Mom."

"Katy," Patty's astonished whisper high-lighted what I had just done. "You lied to your Mom, that's not you."

"I might go to the library later," I said, as I tried to rationalize my story. Patty still had the astonished look on his face. "Patty, if Mom said, 'Come straight home,' I might not find out what Andrew's going to tell me. He is going to answer some questions that I asked him earlier today. I don't want Andrew to think I'm a kid who has to ask my Mom for permission to do everything."

"What questions did you ask him," Patty asked.

"I'll tell you later. I have to go meet Andrew."

Patty said, "Katy, phone me. Phone me," she emphasized.

I agreed and said, "I have to go." I ran towards the parking lot.

As Patty ran beside me she said, "You always do this to me." Patty slowed to a stop and yelled, "Katy, if you don't phone me, I'm going to phone you at 5:30 p.m. sharp. Set your watch alarm."

"Okay. I'll tell you everything," I yelled an assurance.

Andrew was leaning against his VW convertible; he turned towards me and smiled as I arrived. "I thought that maybe you couldn't make it," he said.

"Not a chance," I said. He opened the door for me, before I slipped into the front seat.

After Andrew fastened his seatbelt he asked, "Have you ever been to 'Jake and Harry's Pizzeria and Spaghetti House'?"

I nodded my head and answered, "Yes, I've been there a few times. My parent's are always ordering take-out pizza from that pizzeria. Dad said that he likes how they load up their pizzas."

Andrew smiled and said, "That's nice to know." Andrew put the VW into gear and we were off on what to me was a journey of discovery. Andrew talked about the pizzeria and how his Uncle Jake and Aunt Harriet had purchased the pizzeria over twenty years ago, renovated it and revamped the menu." As he talked, I worked on setting the alarm on my watch.

Andrew added, "Any pizza lover knows how famous their pizzas are in the city. My aunt and uncle sometimes say they are getting old and talk about selling the pizzeria, retiring and moving to a place with a warmer climate. I told them that they would have to fight bugs all year round in a warm climate." He looked at me and added, "Hey, I was just being a realist. I did admit to them that I was biased, I would really miss their pizzas."

"My parents would really miss their 'All Dressed Pizza'. That's their favorite," I said.

Andrew said, "That's nice to know." He stared at me fidgeting with my watch and asked, "Katy, what are you doing?"

"I promised Patty that I would set my alarm to remind myself to do something. I'm almost finished."

Andrew asked, "What do you have to remember?"

"It's a girl thing," I gave a vague answer.

Andrew said, "I have to drop an envelope off at Dover Photography. Could you wait in the car for me? I'll just be a few minutes."

Andrew was true to his word, in ten minutes we pulled up in front of the pizzeria. I stared at the pizzeria's neon sign that read 'Jake and Harry's Pizzeria and Spaghetti House'. The letters were a golden pizza crust coloring surrounded by a black outline, on an olive green background. Painted on the front window in a 1950's style fashion, a smiling waiter served two happy customers their anticipated piping hot pizza.

We entered an outer glass door and in a second, we passed through another glass door. Andrew called a greeting, "Hey, anyone home?" We heard some commotion in the kitchen and then a man and women entered the outer restaurant area. They both were average, middle aged people, sturdy and strong. The man's hair was almost white and the woman had brown, graying hair. Their most noticeable characteristic was that unmistakable cheerful, matching Dover smiles.

The woman was wiping her hands on the white tea towel that hung over her shoulder. I could tell that her cheerful, musical voice would uplift anyone's spirits.

"Where have you been hiding Mr. Dover?" she asked, as she waved a pointer finger at Andrew. Andrew picked her up and swung her around just as Evan would give a bear hug.

"Don't you have eyes woman?" the man asked as he extended his hand towards me. "Can't you see why he doesn't visit us so much? My name is Jake Morris, this is my wife," he said, while he shook my hand.

The woman extended her hand and said, "I'm Harriet Morris, but most people call me Harry." She laughed as she saw my questioning expression and added, "My parents named me Harriet, to honor my Grandpa Harry. My Grandpa Harry began calling me Harry when I was in diapers, the nickname stuck."

Andrew said, "People are always surprised when they meet Aunt Harry, a lot of them say that she's not like any Harry they've ever met before." We all laughed before Andrew put his arm around my shoulder and introduced me. "This is my special friend, Katy McCall." Jake and Harry looked at one another and smiled, as he said this.

Jake asked, "Do you have time to stay and have a pizza? I'll make it especially for you." Andrew and I looked at one another, nodded enthusiastically and both answered by giving a heart felt "Yes, thank you."

Aunt Harry explained, "I have to finish up in the kitchen, I am making salad for a take-out order. I'll make a salad for you, before you have your pizza." Before we answered her, she was heading back into the kitchen.

Andrew said, "Wait a second." He went behind the bar and came back with two small plates and some cutlery.

"When you talked about your aunt before, why did you call her Aunt Harriet instead of

Harry?" I asked.

Andrew smiled and said, "It gets kind of tiresome explaining why my Aunt Harriet is called, Aunt Harry. Now, I wait for Aunt Harry to explain everything when people meet her."

"I understand," I said as I continued to look around the pizzeria. I added, "I've been in the restaurant before but I haven't really taken the time to really look around. Usually I was picking up a take-out order."

I saw red vinyl and chrome bar stools set parallel along a nine-foot snack bar. Red and chrome vinyl chairs surrounded two rows of fake-wooden-topped tables. Old movie posters and old pictures of the city, hung on the walls. Beside the cash register, a framed and mounted newspaper review expounded the pizzeria mouth-watering pizzas.

Andrew explained that, when they first bought the pizzeria, a restaurant critic once wrote a less than favorable review about their pizzas. Uncle Jake found out that the reviewer was not a pizza fan, so he sent the newspaper a half-dozen assorted pizzas, with a note that read, "Let the people review our pizzas." A week later, there was this very favorable article, with a poll from the people at the newspaper giving the pizzeria a resounding thumbs-up. The business took off after that, most of the staff at the newspaper became regular customers.

Andrew finished the story by saying, "Uncle Jake is a lovable bull, who meets issues straight on."

I laughed and said, "That is such a cool story."

I continued to explore the restaurant walls. I noticed a lone picture of a young girl hung above the bar. She had short, light brown hair, like mine. The girl reminded me of me. Her smiling face was full of light. I asked, "Andrew, who is that?" Just as I asked that question, Aunt Harry came through the swinging door with two salads in hand. Andrew shook his head to silence me. The salads were loaded with red and green peppers, feta cheese and black olives on a bed of romaine lettuce. She also carried out a holder filled with assorted dressing.

"Wow, this is an amazing looking salad. Thank you," I said, as I selected a salad dressing.

Andrew agreed with me, "Thanks Aunt Harry, you always make the best salads."

Aunt Harry smiled and said, "You enjoy it. The pizza will be ready in 15 minutes." She went back into the kitchen as we began to eat.

Andrew watched his aunt go back into the kitchen before he said, "You wanted to know about the girl in the picture." I nodded as I chewed. Andrew continued, "That's my cousin, Megan, Uncle Jake and Aunt Harry's daughter. We don't talk about her much because it makes Aunt Harry cry."

"What happened?" I asked.

Andrew answered, "She died last November. Megan was not just my cousin she was my best friend. Megan is the person who introduced me to Dawn."

"Dawn who?" I asked.

"Erica's sister, Dawn." Andrew explained, "I'm pretty sure that Dawn used Megan to meet me. I think that Megan knew what was going on but she was happy to be included in this new group of friends. Dawn and I began to date, at first I tried to fit in with their group. I occasionally made appearances at the parties and the raves to make Megan happy. Gradually, whenever possible, I would tell them that I had to work to raise money for my college fund, to get out of going to those parties.

During this time I noticed that Megan had changed, it was as if she was losing herself. Megan was becoming someone for them to put down whenever they needed a laugh, or an ego boost. If she had been laughing with them, it would have been fine. I could see that she felt belittled, so I tried to talk to her." Andrew rubbed his hands over his face as he sighed. "Megan pretended that it didn't bother her, she was kidding herself. To me, true friendship has a foundation built on respect. We had a couple of arguments about her being their foot-mat. Why couldn't I get her to see that?"

I held Andrew's hand as I said, "Those should haves, could haves and the maybes, they'll drive you crazy. You helped me to realize that."

Andrew nodded and smiled, as he said, "I know. It always seems easier to understand things when you're helping the other person."

"How did Megan die?" I asked.

"Megan went to one of those raves, she loved raves. I knew she was experimenting with drugs, Megan said she didn't worry about anything when she tried them, she said she loved everyone. It was the drugs talking. Maybe Megan thought a pill could help her find confidence and friends.

The night she died was one of the times when I weaseled my way out of partying with them. She tried to get me to change my mind but I refused. We argued, again. Later that night, by the time we reached the hospital, she was already gone. I believe it was an accidental over-dose. After that night, I stopped seeing Dawn. That decision made Aunt Harry and Uncle Jake's day, we were all blaming her for the circumstances surrounding Megan's death."

I nodded my head and said, "I know the feeling. Travis was like Dawn to me." I added, "Anger doesn't help or change anything, does it?"

Andrew shook his head and said, "No, it doesn't," he added, "I was angry for such a long time. You could say that I wore my anger on my sleeves, it wasn't a good way to live."

"You're not angry now, are you?" I asked.

"No, I'm not," Andrew, answered. "Thank God I changed. I guess the turning point came one day when I was working here. It was a steady day. Aunt Harry was keeping track of take-out orders and helping with food preparation. Of course, Uncle Jake was the head cook. I was doubling as an assistant cook and waiter." I tried to imagine what Andrew was describing. Andrew added, "Another waitress looked after the tables, while I look after the bar and helped Uncle Jake."

At that moment, Aunt Harry entered through the swinging door to serve our pizza. Fifteen minutes had just zoomed by. She said, "One special All Dressed Pizza with extra toppings, for two special people." Aunt Harry paused before asking, "Is something wrong with the salad?"

"No, it's a great salad," I said as I took a bite.

"Sorry Aunt Harry, we were just talking so much, we forgot to eat," Andrew explained.

Aunt Harry smiled and said, "Don't worry. You can always take it home." She bent over and whispered something in Andrew's ear. He nodded in agreement. She said, "Enjoy," before going back into the kitchen.

Andrew chuckled before he said, "You have Aunt Harry's seal of approval."

"Really, wow, that's so nice," I said. We each took a piece of pizza. I bit into my piece and immediately began to try to cool my mouth, as I said, "Oh, it's piping hot." I took a gulp of water. I began to cut my pizza up as I said, "I'm going to let my piece cool for a few seconds."

Andrew nodded and wiped his mouth with a napkin before saying, "That's smart but I like the pizza too much to be that smart." We both laughed and took another bite.

As we munched on our pizza, we noticed a woman visiting with Aunt Harry for a few seconds as she paid for her take-out pizza.

Andrew waited for Aunt Harry to go back into the kitchen, before he said, "We were talking about when I let go of my anger relating to Megan's death." I nodded. "I'll never forget that day," Andrew said, as he began to weave his story.

"There was this young looking, middle aged man sitting at the end of the counter; he had been studying the menu for a long time. I had gone over a couple of times to ask him if he wanted to order, but he wasn't ready. When he closed his menu I figured he was finally ready to order.

"Before I could say anything the man said, 'You have much anger in your heart.' I was surprised to hear him say that.

"I said, 'No, I'm just in a hurry. Sorry if I'm rushing you.'

"The man said, 'You are courteous and efficient but anger and grief burns your heart.' Then he asked, 'What angers you?' I was surprised again. I thought about telling the man that my anger was none of his business but I was curious, I wondered *how this man knew how I felt.*

"I pointed to Megan's picture and explained, 'That's my cousin. She died of a drug over-dose last November. Her dying was senseless, that makes me angry.' I thought that would end the conversation.

"The man said, 'You had a great love for your cousin, but your anger overwhelms this love. Love and anger cannot exist in the same space, these feelings and their vibrations are opposite in nature.'

"I said, 'I'm not angry with Megan, I'm angry with the people who led her to the drugs.'

"The man asked, 'Did young Megan not choose her path for herself? Perhaps she will love and respect herself more in her next lifetime? Or, perhaps in her next life time, she will have the strength to make different choices?'

"I said, 'that is crazy stuff, who knows for sure if there are different life times or just one lifetime? This doesn't change anything, so why am I telling you this? Do you want to order or not?'

"The man said, 'Anger doesn't change anything does it? Anger doesn't make anything better, or right.'

"I asked, 'What do you expect me to say? Look, you're right, but anger is a part of me right now, I can't change that.' I turned away and began to fill up a bus pan with dirty dishes. I heard the man say, 'We are unique vessels on individual journeys, we man the helm of our own vessels, because we are both the captain and crew. You have chosen to steer into anger.'

"That is when something strange happened. I saw myself struggling with the wheel at the helm of a great ship, its sail unfurled in a battering wind. The gale force wind turned droplets of rain into stinging needles against the surface of our coats and skin. I saw efficient carbon copies of me followed the lead of the helmsman, as they worked to keep the vessel on course.

"As an observer, I stood to the side of the scene and watched one copy of me repeatedly shouting, 'We have to turn back; I think we'll survive it we turn back now.' Another hysterical copy of me stood at the helm of the boat shouting, 'Oh God, we're going to die! It's all your fault you fool.' The other me told the panicked me to calm down. The hysterical me said, 'What should we do?' It was weird to see me arguing with myself.

"Then I heard the man's whispered voice as clearly as a shouting voice, he said, 'You have chosen to steer with anger in your heart. You continue to create, feed and strengthen the karmic storm of anger; you allow it to live and flourish in your life.' "

I said, "There is a part of you that wanted to steer away from the anger, you realized what your anger was creating in your life. Another part of you feared what your anger created."

Andrew nodded and said, "You're right, I believe that was part of the vision's message to me. It was a shocking realization. There is more, I heard the man saying, 'Andrew, you are the only one who can change what is in your heart, you have a choice.'

"It took a while for me to really hear the man's words. I turned around and asked, 'Hey, how do you know my name?' Katy, the man was gone, but he left something behind." Andrew reached into his pants pocket, removed his wallet and took out a paper. He carefully unfolded a napkin and laid it in front of me. Andrew said, "This letter Q, written on this napkin." It was a fancy, lyrical looking Q.

Andrew took another bite from his pizza, after a few chews he said, "Katy, I turned away for less than ten seconds, I looked all through the restaurant, I asked the other waiter and Aunt Harry if they had seen the man, they both said, 'No'. How could he have disappeared just like that?"

When I listened to Andrew's story, I felt a chill travel down my spine. I wondered *was Andrew talking with Sri Hikari Hito.*

I asked, "Andrew, did this man have black hair? Did he look like he was Oriental or part Oriental?"

Andrew answered, "No, he had short, brown, curly hair. He looked like his heritage was a mixture of many races, African, Mediterranean, white and maybe Oriental. I'm just guessing but that's the impression I got."

"Oh," I said. The disappointment in that one word must have been very evident.

Andrew said, "You sound disappointed, you really wanted him to be Oriental."

I shook my head and explained, "Someone helped me to get over my anger when Evan died. I thought you had met the same person, it sure did sound like him."

"You know Katy, the past life talk distracted me. After the man was gone, I thought about what he had said, he made sense. He knew that Megan didn't respect herself. He knew that she didn't have the strength to walk away from the drugs and from her so-called friends. The more I thought about what he said; I realized that Megan did make her own choices. I couldn't blame Dawn and her friends any more, that was useless. I looked for the man for a long time; I hoped he would visit the restaurant again. I wanted to tell him thanks. And I wanted to apologize for being a bull-headed jerk. If it wasn't for the napkin, I would have thought that I had imagined the whole thing."

When we were talking, we were eating at a snail's pace. I had finally finished my first piece of pizza. I began chewing my second piece as I said, "I have a feeling that you'll meet this man again, maybe it will happen when you least expect it."

Andrew nodded. He looked up at Megan's picture and whispered, as he watched Aunt Harry go to the cash register to serve a customer, before she went back into the kitchen, "I wish you had met Megan, you probably would have been great friends."

"I wish I had met her too," I said.

Andrew added, "On the day of the car accident, you looked up at me and I thought I was seeing a ghost. When I got over the initial shock, I still almost called you Megan. You are shorter than Megan was but the resemblance between the both of you is uncanny. Can you see the resemblance?"

"Yes, I see a bit of a resemblance."

Andrew said, "As I got to know you, your mannerisms, your sense of humor, you seemed like Megan reincarnated."

I did not like the idea of Andrew feeling that I was Megan's reincarnated twin." I asked, "Do you like me, because I remind you of Megan?"

"No Katy, I noticed the resemblance when I met you. Now, when I look at you, I see Katy McCall."

I asked, "Andrew, you don't think of me, as a cousin, do you? I mean, friendship is great, I'm not knocking friendship. Relationships are long lasting when they begin in friendship, at least that's what I have heard. When you say I remind you of your cousin, I was just wondering if . . ."

Andrew covered his face with his hands as he shook his head and said, "Oh no, not this again, we've been through this already." He stood and in a flash, he was beside me, kissing me. This time the kiss was not a feathery kiss, it was the most romantic kiss. It was too perfect to describe. When we finally came up for air Andrew asked, "Now, what were you asking?"

I somehow managed to speak. "It doesn't matter," my voice gasped. We were about to kiss again when my watch alarm started to beep. "Oh no, it's 5:25. I didn't realize it was that late, I have to make a couple of phone calls. Where's the pay phone?"

"It's over in the corner," Andrew pointed to the wall beside the end of the bar. "Who are you phoning?" Andrew asked.

"Mom, Dad and Patty," I added. I found the correct change and dialed.

"What's the crisis? When do your parents expect you home?" Andrew asked.

I looked at Andrew and stuttered, "I, uh, well."

Andrew groaned as he realized what I had done. "Katy, you didn't? Oh no, your parents don't know that you're out with me, do they?"

"I was afraid they would say no, I told Mom I went to the library," I sheepishly admitted. "Hi, Mom, I'm on my way home. I will be home in 15 minutes. . . . It was worth every second." Andrew had run into the kitchen at double speed. "I will explain later, see you in a bit." I hung up and said, "One down, one to go." I quickly phoned Patty and asked her not to phone me because I was just leaving for home. I promised again to tell you everything later.

Andrew came back with a take-out pizza box in hand; he began to load the box. We thanked his Aunt and Uncle when they came out to give good-bye hugs. They invited us back for more pizza, before we left.

Andrew said, "This was going to be a gift for your parents, now it's a peace offering. Let's get you home."

"Andrew, can I tell Mom and Dad about Megan? Maybe that would help them to understand you and our relationship."

Andrew answered without hesitating, "Okay, but make sure they know that Megan was a good person."

"I will," I agreed, before adding, "Andrew, I know I'm not helping you to make a good impression on my parents. I promise you I won't do this again. I am responsible so I will accept the consequences, but I have to admit that I don't care what happens; I would not trade this afternoon for all the gold in the world."

Andrew smiled as he nodded and said, "That goes double for me." Andrew gave me a quick kiss. He added, "Thanks for that promise; I need all the help I can get, to get your parents to think of me as an okay date for their daughter. The truth will be a good starting point. Besides, if you pull this kind of stunt again, I'll have to buy both of us flak jackets."

"Oh no, the hockey game is history, isn't it?" I asked.

"Yeah, I'd say you're right," Andrew agreed.

I repeated my promise, "From now on I promise to help you make a better impression with my parents."

As we left the restaurant, Andrew said, "Let's go face the music together."

Chapter 24

A Gift of Pure Harmony

Mom talked with me upstairs in my bedroom, while Dad had a conversation with Andrew in the living room. First, I promised not to lie to Mom or Dad again. Then I told Mom about how we had helped each other to deal with the death of Andrew's cousin Megan and Evan.

I said, "Mom, Andrew is such a special wonderful person." I told Mom about what had happened at school with Henry. I ended with, "I wish you could get to know him better." I anxiously watched Mom to gage her reaction.

Mom said, "I'm beginning to believe you; however, Katy, I caution you about putting him on a pedestal. No person is perfect."

"Mom, I-"

"Katy, listen. I know you are thinking that your old Mom is just being a Mom. Well, you're right, I am a Mom and that gives me the right to be the Mom." Mom brushed my bangs towards the side of my head. "You're so young, almost sixteen, you have your whole life ahead of you. I see that Andrew is a nice, considerate boy, young man," Mom quickly amended. "I believe that he's a very good first boy friend."

"What do you mean, first?" I asked.

"That's what I mean," Mom answered. "You're thinking like Andrew is the be all and end all of your life. You are both very young; you both have a lot of growing and living to do. You may become much more than friends or your relationship may just remain in the friendship stage."

"I get it Mom. You want me to date a whole lot of other guys. You want me to break up with Andrew. Andrew is the best part of my life, but you still want me to break up with him? I can't do that Mom. I won't do that," I stated.

"No Katy that is not what I am saying. I just don't want you to forget your other friends or other interests. I don't want your life to depend entirely on Andrew; if he goes off to college, you might not see each other for months at a time. You need to be able to live your life without expecting Andrew to be around all the time. You need to develop strength inside your own heart. Do you understand what I mean?" Mom asked.

I nodded and answered, "I understand Mom. You're okay with me seeing Andrew, but you want me to be the Katy who can stand on her own two feet, right?"

Mom gave me a big hug and said, "Thank God, you understand. The Mom in me wants to protect you, which was easier to do when you were a baby. Now, I know that is not possible. You're going out into the world and I can't watch you 95% of the time. What I am saying to you is my way of trying to give you a little bit of that cocoon like protection. Katy, your Dad and I love you very much and we'll always be here for you."

"I know Mom, I love you too."

Mom and Dad brought us together in the living room before they went into the kitchen to talk. Andrew and I faced each other with the coffee table between us.

I whispered, "What happened?"

Andrew whispered back, "I think it went well. I explained everything."

I assured Andrew, "I explained everything to Mom." I added, "I was very honest."

Mom and Dad returned to let us know what they had decided. They were happy that we had told the truth about our afternoon but they had to address my lie. I apologized and promised to tell my parents the truth from now on, so Mom and Dad decided to ground me for only two weeks on school nights. That was my karma, the consequence for telling Mom the lie. I felt lucky that the grounding was so lenient, even though this meant that my Friday night date with Andrew was toast.

Happily, there was a small benefit connected with this karma. They said Andrew could come over and visit me once during the week, as long as either Mom or Dad was at home. The weekends were to-be evaluated later in this week. I think they were starting to like Andrew.

That night Patty phoned, Mom told her she would have to wait to speak with me at school the following morning. The pain of waiting seemed to be Patty's reoccurring karma. When Patty heard my story the following morning, she felt elation and disappointment. She said this was like waiting for the next installment in a continuing soap opera.

Before the weekend arrived I would have to work through a couple of math classes, a mathematician I am not, math was my Achilles Heel. I believed there was no hope for this to change in the near future, let alone in this lifetime. I wanted to make sure that my math homework woes would not interfere with this coming weekend. Math class followed our lunch breaks on Mondays, Wednesdays and Fridays. I usually spent part of my noon hour trying to figure out some monstrous math problems. Luckily, Martha Hiller, who was the class math wiz, usually sat with us during the lunch hour.

The school cafeteria was an average looking cafeteria, a giant, open space located in the basement area of our school, with tables colored in pastel blues, yellows, green and orange hues were positioned around the open area. Seating around the tables varied from four to six seats. Vending machines lined the far wall, opposite to a row of windows.

One element of the cafeteria that was unique to our school was a small stage that measured 3 meters by 4 meters. It was located in the corner opposite to the doorway next to the windows. The stage challenged anyone who was brave of heart, to step up and show his or her wares. It had become a gathering spot. Singers, actors, poets, anyone who could, would take centre stage. During the dinner hour, planned or spontaneous student entertainment was usually something to look forward too.

Today, Andrew made a quick pit stop in the cafeteria. I was focusing my attention on figuring out a math problem when he surprised me. He whispered in my ear, "I'd kiss you, but that might start tongues wagging." I turned to look into his laughing eyes, Andrew added, "You're cute when you're blushing."

I found my voice, "Hi, I didn't expect to see you in here."

"You don't think I eat? Or maybe you think I eat only Kentucky Fried Chicken, pizza, or Chinese food?" Andrew joked.

I laughed and was about to answer, before I noticed Patty's eyes and ears glued on the two of us. There was a huge grin on her face and her eyes were huge sparkling pools of anticipation. Martha, Trudy and every other person's eyes and ears within earshot were staring at us. Andrew also noticed the audience.

"Tongues are already wagging," Andrew whispered. He squeezed my hand; I squeezed his hand back. "I've got to go," Andrew said. He smiled and nodded at everyone at our table before he left.

Everyone began to speak at once. Martha Hiller almost yelled, "You and Andrew Dover, this is beyond real."

Trudy Caster agreed, "You're living my dream. How come you're so lucky?"

"It's real," Patty assured them. "He ki-"

"Patty!" I yelled in time to stop her.

"He bought her pizza," Patty finished.

I added, "He's been helping me out, Andrew's nice."

"Maybe he can help me?" Martha suggested.

"Yeah, whatever he's helping you with, count me in," Trudy added.

"We're just friends, I try not to bug him," I said.

Patty's laugh turned into a series of coughs. "Dry throat," Patty said as she rubbed her throat. "Oohhh, look, it's Chester," Patty shouted. "He said his group would be playing a couple of songs. He sang me a couple of verses of one of his songs; he has a heavenly voice. Wait till you hear it." She enthusiastically waved a greeting to him.

I whispered a quiet, "Thank you," to Divine Spirit, or the Holy Spirit for distracting everyone's attention away from Andrew's unexpected visit.

Chester spotted Patty; he waved and smiled. Patty's excitement level jumped off the Richter scale. She stood, started waving and blowing Chester kisses. "I told him we would be his cheering section, come-on gals, show a little enthusiasm," Patty waved to us to join in. I looked at Martha and Trudy; we nodded, grinned and joined Patty's cheering section.

I asked, "Patty, what's their group name?"

"What?" Patty yelled.

I enunciated, "What is the group's name?"

"Pure Harmony," Patty enunciated her answer, before she began cheering again.

I began to repeat a cheer; both Martha and Trudy added their voices and repeated, "Harmony, Harmony, Harmony." Patty laughed, gave us a thumbs-up, and joined the cheer.

By this time, Chester and the other members of the band had finished setting up their equipment. Chester motioned us to quiet down before he adjusted his mike and tuned his keyboard; his two friends tuned their acoustic guitars.

We all sat and Patty repeated, "Wait until you hear them, they're heavenly." She swooned as she said this. Patty was right; they were dreamy. The audience focused their attention on the three band members.

As I listened to the music, I closed my eyes and relaxed, a peaceful feeling entered my heart; I quietly sang the HU song. Gradually the singing began to fade.

I heard the Spiritual Master's voice quietly ask, "Katy, are you ready to step outside the box?"

Suddenly I bolted to a sitting position; I rubbed my eyes and squinted at the image of a hazy ghost-like waterfall that had materialized about five feet to the left of the stage. An illuminated shimmering blue doorway was half-hidden behind the falling water. I stared in stunned disbelief as I looked around to share my shock with others. No one else noticed this phenomenon; everyone else's attention was riveted on the three performers on the stage.

The blue door opened and a brilliant white light beamed into the room, I was the only person who shielded their eyes, I realized that no one else saw this. A figure of Light stepped through the door and motioned for me, to follow. I pointed to myself; again, the Being of Light motioned for me to follow. I wondered, *is this Light person a member of 'The Brotherhood of Light and Love'?*

I slowly stood up and looked around, no one yelled at me to sit down. I was startled to see my physical body, I looked at my sleeping face; my chin was on top of my folded hands. Patty she was in a different type of dreamland, I stepped in front of her but she did not react, it was as if she could see right through me. I wondered *is this another out-of-body experience?*

I straightened and shielded my eyes as I maneuvered my way towards the figure of Light. I was like Evan, invisible to everyone except for the Being of Light. As I moved next to the waterfall, I felt the misty coolness of the water.

The illuminated figure nodded and although he did not speak aloud I heard the figures say, "If you are a truth seeker, follow," before he turned and disappear through the blue doorway. I looked around the room; everyone was still staring at the stage. I trustingly followed the figure of Light into the unknown.

Chapter 25

Answering the Unanswerable Question

I stepped into a new space; it was like stepping through a movie scene. There was a 6 to 7 foot wide pathway bordered with unusual flowers, which led across a small emerald green meadow to gradually ascend a majestic mountain. I looked back; I felt more than saw the Being of Light smiling at me. The waterfall seemed to shimmer around the light of this Being's body; with a nod of his or her head the Being stepping back through the blue doorway. The door and the waterfall shrunk into a thin horizontal line and blinked out of this reality. I felt wonder and then panic starting to grow inside of me; I was in a foreign dimension and my way home had just disappeared.

"Welcome Kathleen, I have been waiting for you." I turned to see Master Hikari Hito's smiling face.

"Master, I was hoping to find you here. When I didn't see you here and the Being of Light disappeared, I started to get a little scared."

"The Being of Light is one of the Guardians of the many Gates of Heaven," the Spiritual Master explained. He added, "The waterfall is a reminder that the constant presence of the Spirit of God flows around and through all existence. Divine Spirit or the Holy Spirit is the spiritual creative link which holds all elements through out existence together."

"Master, I remember you said that to me when I first met you. The Spirit of God links everything together, that is why I can be here now, right?"

"That is one reason," the Master agreed.

I looked around and asked, "Master Hikari Hito, is this your home?"

"This dimension houses one of the homes of 'The Brotherhood of Light and Love'. Come Kathleen, walk with me," the Spiritual Master said as he turned to walk along the shale and stone covered path, I hurried to walk beside him.

"It's so beautiful. It reminds me of earth just as the other place did, but the flowers here are very unusual looking," as I said this, I brushed my hand by one of the flowers. When I did this, the flowers seemed to chime and make heavenly music.

"Holy cow, what was that?" I exclaimed as I jumped back.

The Spiritual Master laughed and said, "These Crystal Harmony Beings are heart mirrors, they reflect back to all who are fortunate enough to walk over their pathway, the Soul music within each individual being. The music that they help to create is different and unique for each Soul."

The Spiritual Master passed his hand by the Crystal Beings; the heavenly music that the Crystal Beings reflected back from the Master filled the air. The beauty of it was beyond words, beyond anything created on earth.

He explained, "Like the flowers of your world, the Crystal Beings are gifts to life from Divine Spirit. The Crystal Beings are loving beings and each is respected as Soul, a loving spark of God." I wondered *how could anyone leave a place like this, let alone leave this heavenly path behind?*

Master Hikari Hito and I continued to walk over the ancient well-worn stone roadway. As we talked I passed my fingers gently beside the Crystal Harmony Beings; their heavenly music gently accompanied us on our journey. We walked for what seemed to be hours, my watch had stopped so I was not sure of the time. I hardly noticed my own fatigue or my shallow labored breathing.

"I was hoping that I would get a chance to visit with you and Evan again. This place is better than anything I could have imagined, thank you for the opportunity to be here," I emphasized my gratitude.

Master Hikari Hito calmly explained, "You are the person who created the opportunity to travel to this new state of awareness."

My eyes widened with surprise as I said, "I created the opportunity; how did I do that?"

"This area of existence vibrates with Light and Love, only those who are in harmony with these vibrations have an opportunity to enter this world. The events in the last few days have helped you to replace your anger with a positive loving heart."

As the Spiritual Master said this, I looked up at an enormous stonewall, perhaps fifty meters high, emerging from behind the rock face. What stood beyond this wall was even more magnificent. The wall curved slowly to encase a huge castle like structure, tucked inside the three sides of a protective mountain valley. I could see numerous spire shaped rooftops which surrounded a very large, central, translucent shaped doom.

"Holy! This is where you live?" My awe-filled voice repeated my question.

The Spiritual Master nodded his head and answered, "This is one of many Temples of the Brotherhood of Light and Love. Each Temple is a sacred and honored home of Love and Light. What is the true heart of any Temple?" the Spiritual Master's question took me by surprise as I admired this majestic Temple.

I turned to the Spiritual Master and repeated his words, "The true heart of a Temple? I'm not sure." I thought fast and asked, "Could it be the people in the Temple?"

The Spiritual Master smiled and acknowledged, "A thoughtful answer." However, he did not explain further.

We kept on walking until we came upon a massive wooden double doorway. The guardian at this doorway was not a Being of Light like the other guardian; a courteous very tall young man built as solid as the Temple walls, greeted us with a respectful nod and smile. The Spiritual Master and I returned the same greeting before we stepped into a vast courtyard.

I looked around; everything was extra large. I felt like Jack in the Giant's castle, minus the beanstalk. Giant stone blocks formed the floor and the walls of the Temple. In the middle of the courtyard, a circular fountain flowed with glistening crystal-clear water. Men and women filled huge ceramic jugs with this water, as they quietly laughed and visited together.

The Master motioned towards a corner of the courtyard and said, "The art of many ancient crafts are practiced and taught here." Different artisans were busy working; large weaving looms held colorful tapestries; artisans were throwing, drying and firing beautiful works of pottery; jewelers and a quilting team were two other artisan groups who were hard at work.

Master Hikari Hito added, "The loving focus, contemplation and meticulous effort which each artisan put into his creation, provides a perfect opportunity for the craft person to commune with Divine Spirit."

I looked around the courtyard and noticed how quiet our surroundings were. Dozens of people were going about their tasks with a focused efficiency; people spoke with quiet, respectful voices, just as a person would have spoken to the Spiritual Master.

Sri Hikari Hito touched my elbow. I quickly turned to look at him as he spoke to me, "Kathleen, we have an appointment. Please come with me."

As we crossed the courtyard, the Spiritual Master acknowledged the respectful greetings of people in the courtyard. We entered an enormous stone building with a giant solarium garden; it stretched across an indoor greenhouse. The warmth and light in this giant room was perfect for both botanical and human habitants. We entered another solarium area through a side door; the Spiritual Master said that this area was one of over a dozen such rooms. People carefully tended to countless varieties of nourishing, flourishing plants. Each of these rooms contained surrounding rows of Crystal Harmony Beings. They seemed to be humming to the other plants. I guess all beings loved harmonious music.

We entered another area of the Temple, a large central meeting room with theater style seating for several hundred, arranged in a semi-circle around a stage like area. We strolled on a walkway that circled above this theater area. We exited through another side door and after a short walk down a wide corridor; we entered a smaller theater area through a back door. Seven rows of seats circled a shallow stage area. A giant sloping sky light spanned the ceiling of half the room. The nature light was not overwhelmingly hot or bright.

Over a dozen people were listening intently to a speaker who I believed was a Spiritual Master of 'The Brotherhood of Light and Love'. He appeared to be a young fifty-year old man; his wavy, dark brown hair was graying very naturally. The man's heritage was maybe part African, Oriental and Polynesian; I sensed that was just the tip of the iceberg; this man was an old Soul. He fit the description of the man who helped and inspired Andrew to change his life. Master Hikari Hito and I quietly seated ourselves on an observation bench behind the seven rows of seats; we listened intently to the on going discussion.

My heart skipped when I heard a familiar voice. "Master Qualitan," Evan spoke up, "Both you and Master Hikari Hito have used the phrase, 'God Awareness', what exactly is God Awareness? How do you know when you have God Awareness?" I was excited to see Evan and excited to hear Evan ask those questions.

Master Qualitan laughed before he answered, "Ah, the unanswerable question, for how can God be explained to the human consciousness? How can the human consciousness be inspired to strive for something beyond its understanding? Who will tackle this impossible task? Luckily, this journey into the unknown will always inspire man to strive to discover and to understand what is just beyond his understanding."

I hoped that the Spiritual Master would try to answer the unanswerable question. I listened and hoped that a word, phrase, or image, would spark a degree of understanding and greater awareness in me. I hoped for an image to inspire my reaching, a flight plan to help me head towards a destination. For years, I had a feeling that there was a great wisdom with all the answers. There had to be something that created this universe, imperfect as it seemed. To me, this was a given. I needed to know why I was here.

Master Qualitan spoke in a calm, relaxed manner, "It's an innate drive of the human being to strive to evolve in awareness. Many people crave fame, riches, social status, acceptance, power, love, or freedom. They believe the attainment of some or all these goals will satisfy their needs. Eventually, they realized that their need to evolve grew out of their unconscious need to unite with Divine Spirit. What more would any person want or need, than to be aware of and to live in the love of Divine Spirit."

The Spiritual Master continued, "When an individual attains the state of God Awareness, the Spiritual Laws of the Universe are understood, they become a living part of this person's consciousness. Patience, wisdom, truth, spiritual freedom and divine love, also live within that individual's heart. Total spiritual responsibility is given in-trust to this Soul who is now a conscious spiritual helper of Divine Spirit."

"Wow." I whispered. I had caught a misty glimpse of the heart of Spiritual Mastership and God Awareness.

Master Qualitan added, "The journey to God Awareness is an arduous unrelenting quest that has strengthened and broken many a traveler. However, like the phoenix, the traveler returns lifetime after lifetime, to journey forward. This journey is not for the timid or fear filled, only the strongest, those who build great inner strength and divine love within their hearts will attain the ultimate goal. All the riches of earth pale when one's heart knows the Awareness of God. It is beyond imagination. Soul knows this golden gift and whispers to the individual to inspire his creative imagination, to keep on reaching for the purity within his or her own heart. In God Awareness, the reality of truth and existence hold no mysteries, the guidance and the voice of God is clear and pure."

"Sri Qualitan, your words did help me to kind of understand why people strive to reach God Awareness. I'm just not sure if I possess the great inner strength that is needed to reach this goal," Evan admitted.

When I heard Evan ask this question, I thought, 'That goes double for me.'

Master Qualitan nodded and said, "The road to divine love and inner strength is an endless quest. No one has absolute knowledge of their own strengths and weaknesses until they are tested. If immaturity and fear prevails, the tests will return at another time, in another place, until divine love prevails. It matters not how long it takes you or what path you choose. The tests of existence are as eternal as Divine Spirit. The Awareness of God will always exist, thus we will always live within God's Love. It surrounds every aspect of existence, during every step on our journey. It waits for us to develop the awareness to know and to live in the heart of Divine Spirit."

A young woman asked, "Master Qualitan is there anything else we can do that would help us achieve the Awareness of God?"

The Spiritual Master reminded us, "The Spiritual Masters of Light and Love have said many times before that every being, every person, every experience and situation is in your life for a purpose. The most difficult times offer the greatest opportunities for growth, learning and divine love to enter your heart. Watch for these valuable opportunities, they are God given gems. Listen to what Divine Spirit is communicating to you; sing the HU song, it will fine tune your spiritual hearing and knowingness," Master Qualitan calmly instructed before adding, "Ultimately, each individual will choose the path he will walk for himself, his thoughts, words and actions, create his life and awareness."

I nodded and smiled, as I thought, 'Listen to the voice and guidance of Divine Spirit and sing the HU Song, exactly what Master Hikari Hito emphasized. It must be important.'

The Spiritual Master's smile broadened as he gazed at all the spiritual students who intently watched him, "Relax and live life; anger, hate and their likeness, chases love and joy from one's awareness; they tune out and confuse the communications of Divine Spirit. If you ask a question with love and sincerity then Divine Spirit will highlight an answer in some form. Learn to listen and hear Divine Spirit's guidance."

"Master Qualitan," Evan nodded to the Spiritual Master and said, "Thank you for allowing me to be here in your class." Some other students nodded their heads and expressed their gratitude.

I looked at Sri Hikari Hito and thought about going to talk to Evan. The Spiritual Master answered my silent question with a nod of his head, I gave a quiet yelp of glee and scurried down to surprise my brother.

"Evan, surprise," I called out.

"Katy hi, wow, I didn't know you were going to visit." Evan gave me his unique bear hug. "Boy, it's nice to see you." He turned to the Spiritual Master and said, "Sri Qualitan, this is my sister Katy." The Spiritual Master smiled and nodded his head, just as Sri Hikari Hito would have done.

"It's very nice to meet you Master Qualitan," I said.

Sri Qualitan nodded and said, "It's nice of you to visit us."

I looked at Evan then back at the Spiritual Master before saying, "I know that I'm a visitor and not one of your students . . ."

Spiritual Master Qualitan asked, "Are you not a student?"

I hesitated before saying, "I mean I'm not a regular student." The Spiritual Master nodded. I asked, "Master, may I ask a question?"

"Of course," Master Qualitan said.

"A man helped a friend of mine let go of his anger. Before he just disappeared, he left behind the letter 'Q' written on a napkin. My friend's description of the man who disappeared reminds me of you . . . I was wondering if you were the person who helped my friend."

The Master smiled and answered, "Perhaps it was a member of the Brotherhood of Light and Love who gave assistance. All students of Light and Love are given assistance if their hearts are open or if they have asked for help, for they will be open to accepting Divine Spirit's guidance."

"Master Qualitan, the reason I asked you that question was, my friend wanted to thank you, I mean, the man for all his help. My friend is very grateful and he also wanted to say that he's sorry for being rude."

Master Qualitan nodded, "Your friend has a true friend in you."

"Katy," I heard someone call my name, as if from across the giant courtyard; I looked back at the Oriental Spiritual Master.

Master Hikari Hito said, "It seems that your visit with us has come to an end." The illuminated blue doorway reappeared and the Being of Light stepped through it. Everyone in the room shielded their eyes as they watched the door; this seemed to be a normal occurrence in this part of existence. Again, someone called my name.

It was Patty's voice calling me, "Katy, weren't they heavenly."

I mumbled, "You can say that again." I nodded and opened my eyes. Everyone was standing and cheering. Patty joked, "They were mellow enough to put you to sleep."

"Patty, I'm sorry, I was really tired," I tried to explain.

Patty clearly enunciated, "Don't apologize. That love song was supposed to be a romantic ballad, Chester will love that you were off dreaming."

I looked at my watch and put it up to my ear, it was working again. Maybe it had never stopped working. Only a few minutes had passed here in the lunchroom; while in the World of Light and Love I had lived at least six or seven hours.

It was mind boggling to realize that we were just specks in this world and the world is just a speck in the universes of existence. Yet, every single element was in its rightful place, learning what was necessary on its spiritual journey. Existence was awesome.

Chapter 26

The Control Panel of Your Life and the Nature of Truth

I could hear the phone was ringing as I fumbled for my keys; I quickly opened the front door, dropping my jacket and books as I rushed to pick up the phone. I disliked picking up the receiver just in time to hear the caller hang up. I would wonder if it might have been Andrew or Patty.

"Hello," my voice gushed a breathless greeting.

"Katy, I'm glad I caught you."

"Mom, hi . . . what's up?" I hid my disappointment.

"Honey, I left a bag of washers and O-rings on the hall table beside the phone. Do you see it?" Mom asked.

"I found it, Mom." I peeked in the bag.

"Katy, could you bring it to the apartment building as soon as you can?"

"Mom, I don't want to go out right now, couldn't you do whatever you're doing tomorrow?" I had my fingers crossed as I waited for her answer.

"Katy, I wouldn't be asking you to bring the bag if I could wait until tomorrow; Mrs. Cope's kitchen and bathroom taps need immediate repair work done. You must have noticed what condition they were in when you baby sat Justine?"

"Oh right, I was going to mention that to you." I remembered the dripping taps. "Will one more day's wait be so bad?"

"Just run the bag over on your bike, it will take you ten minutes; you'll hardly break a sweat."

"Mom-"

"We'll be by the swimming pool."

"Mom, I'm expecting a phone call."

"Thank you Katy; I really appreciate your help."

"Mom, Andrew might phone me later," I pleaded into the dead phone. I hung up and mumbled a sarcastic, "Thanks, Mom." I grabbed the bag and headed for the garage. I doubled back when the phone rang again.

I yanked up the phone and gushed, "Mom, I'll be there in ten minutes. And don't worry, I won't forget the bag." The line was silent. "Mom, did you hear me?" Still, there was no answer. "Who's there?" I asked.

I was about to hang up when a voice quietly said, "Katy."

The person knew me. I started to ask, "Who is . . . Travis, is that you?"

"Yes," he answered.

The volume of my voice rose when I asked, "Travis, how are you?"

"I'm okay, Katy. How are you doing? How are your parents?"

"I'm okay too, Travis. I really am. And Mom and Dad, it's been difficult but we're all moving forward."

"That's good, Katy. I'm glad to hear that." We were stuck in that awkward pause.

I tried to inject a more casual feeling, I asked, "Are you settled in? How do you like it in Winnipeg?"

"It's not bad; it takes a little getting used too. I guess any change is like that," he answered.

"I understand that," I agreed. Again, we each waited for the other person to speak.

Travis broke the silence and said, "I had a feeling to call and see how everyone was doing. I should get going, I'll call again or you guys call, your Mom has our number."

I yelled, "Travis, don't go, I want to talk."

"Sure Katy, what do you want to talk about?"

I knew what I wanted to put into words. He was phoning long distance and I could not get started; I was tongue tied again. Why did this always happen at the most inconvenient moments? I silently lectured myself, 'Come on Katy, one thought at a time, one word at a time.'

I began my apology, "Travis, I'm so sorry about how I've been treating you. I was blaming you for so many things. You probably saved my life and all I could see was, you stopping me from finding Evan. I wish I could change the things I said and did. I don't blame you anymore. I wouldn't blame you if you never spoke to me again. I'm sorry, Travis, I'm really sorry," I emphasized.

"Katy thanks for saying that. It feels like I have been waiting for ages for you to believe that. I hoped that you would see things differently, one day." I could hear the relief in Travis's voice.

"Oh God, I'm sorry, Travis," I apologized again.

"Katy, don't say that. You don't have to say that anymore, it's over. All I ever wanted to hear you say was that you didn't blame me for Evan's death. I know how you felt that day; I wanted to find him too. I keep reliving that day, wondering if I should have done something different. I know it's a stupid thing to do because it's not going to change a thing, but I do it all the same," Travis said. Travis was as logical as Evan but logic does not always stop emotions, or doubts from surfacing.

"I've been doing the same thing," I admitted. "I think it's because we care and feel so much, that we wish . . . It's just a part of learning to live with that memory. Travis, we have so many good memories; Evan will always be a part of our lives."

Travis sounded like he was gasping for air when his shaky voice said, "Oh man, I really miss the Terminator. Someone will say something and I will find myself imagining what Evan would have said. It's like I can hear him joking around or pulling the wool over their eyes."

While I listened to Travis, I thought again *I can still visit Evan, I am so lucky*. I knew that death was not an absolute end; it was just a new beginning, a doorway into another existence. It was as if Evan had removed a costume, after the costume party in the physical universe had ended. I was so lucky to know this. Travis, Patty, Mom and Dad, and everyone who did not realize this fact would have to go through such a painful grieving process. I wondered *could I help Travis in some way to feel better*.

"Travis," I said, as an idea formed in my head.

"Yeah, Katy," he answered.

"Do you remember any of your dreams?" I asked.

"Sure I do. I remember some of them, they don't always make sense," he said.

"I had a dream recently," I slowly wove a story based on what I knew. "Evan was in it. We went for a walk and talked. He was happy, going to school in heaven and learning about life. He told me not to worry about him; Evan said he is doing fine where he is now. I get the feeling that the dream is true," I finished.

"Evan is learning about life after he died? It sounds like something Evan would do. Thanks Katy, you have made my day. Thanks for telling me that, I hope someday I'll dream a dream like that."

"I'm sure you will some day soon, Travis" I assured him.

"I've got to get going Katy; Mom is calling me for supper. Say hi to your Mom and Dad for me, okay?" Travis asked.

"Will do Travis, call any time. And, pleasant dreams," I added.

"Katy, I'm glad we talked. Bye Katy," he said, before hanging up.

I slowly placed the phone on its cradle. Boy, what a feeling, this was terrific. Travis felt better and I felt great. I was humming as I grabbed Mom's plumbing bag and entered the garage through the adjoining exit. I wheeled my bike out of the garage.

Mr. Lee was wearing a different broad rimmed straw hat while he weeded and nurtured his roses. With his roses bordering one side of our driveway and with Mrs. Burbick's roses on the other side, our surroundings did not lack for color or fragrance.

116

Mrs. Burbick grew Hansas, hot pink roses. She had trimmed back the rose bushes, so that they formed a 2 to 3 foot high hedge. Mom and I loved them, even if they were a bit bright.

Mr. Lee's rose bushes formed small beautiful deep red islands of color that bloomed all summer. To the Chinese, this color represented good luck; it was also an imperial color.

As I passed Mr. Lee I said, "Hi Mr. Lee. Your roses are beautiful." When the man looked up, I was startled to see that the man was not Mr. Lee. "I'm sorry to have bothered you. I thought you were Mr. Lee," I explained. The broad straw hat had prevented me from seeing his face or hair; this man was a thin, wiry, Chinese man of about sixty years of age.

The man smiled and nodded his head. "Oh, you're Mr. Lee's brother, right?" Mom said you were visiting from Seattle. That's quite a drive," I said. The man continued to weed the soil around the rose bushes. I figured I was intruding. I felt that he was busy, and probably wanted some peace and quiet.

I was about to say good-bye when he spoke to me in perfect English, "You have traveled a long way to be here today."

"No I haven't," I corrected him. "My name is Katy McCall," I said as I extended my hand towards him, "I live right there." I pointed to my home next door.

He shook my hand, nodded and said, "You have a very harmonious house. It is no wonder you are a joyful individual. I can see light shining from your being," he smiled as he said this. I stared at him; he seemed to be the one who was beaming. He asked, "What is your secret?"

"What secret?" I asked.

The man said, "How have you discovered the happiness within your heart temple?" the man asked.

I slowly repeated, "Heart temple." There was something different about this man. I added, "I do know why I feel so terrific. I have been blaming a friend for something that wasn't his fault and I finally apologized to him. The special thing was, he wasn't mad at me, he was just happy that I didn't blame him anymore." I wondered *why I told this man this personal info.* As I finished, the man's smile broadened and he nodded his head. He reminded me of the Spiritual Master, Hikari Hito.

He said, "You've proven yourself wise for one so young. People hold to what they believe to be true with the talons of an eagle. When they build their reality upon a false foundation, what do you believe would happen when these truths were found to be partial truths, or entirely false?" he asked.

I asked, "People love truth but truth can make people very angry."

Sri Hikari Hito smiled and asked, "When Archimedes, the famous mathematician discovered a new truth he was elated. Are people angry about discovering truth or are they angry when they are deceived by a false truth?"

I shrugged my shoulders and reasoned, "Then people love truth, they don't like being deceived."

He answered, "It goes far beyond liking or disliking." The Spiritual Master added, "Through out history the journey to truth has often been corrupted and truth has been twisted, manipulated and used to tear down and destroy others. Leadership is entrusted to a few, but many are lead by those who have lost their spiritual focus. Those who violate this trust incur their own karma as well as some of the responsibility for those they mislead. Can we put full blame on those we follow for our choices?" I shrugged my shoulders as I thought about the question. The Spiritual Master answered, "Through our mistakes, we learn discrimination. Each person is responsible for the integrity of truth that one accepts into his heart, this truth builds the foundation of one's life. When faced with indecision the journey to the clarity of truth can begin with keeping this focus in your heart, 'What is truth?'

I asked, "Is truth more important than divine love?"

The Spiritual Master answered, "Truth is strengthened by divine love and divine love is strengthened by truth, so they journey hand in hand, for a structure built on a faulty foundation gives the illusion of strength, a false sense of security. The weakness or falseness gradually makes itself known. Finally, a person will need to make a choice; one could stay within the crumbling structure and accept the circumstances; he could work within the structure to identify the falseness and replace it with truth; or finally, one could leave the structure to seek what fulfills his goals elsewhere."

"Buildings and foundations are a great metaphor for our lives. I have the feeling that you're talking about beliefs, ideals, and people."

It sounds silly but if I said he nodded his head in reverence, I do not believe that I would have been wrong. He spoke in a calm, clear voice, "Perhaps you have touched on another truth. We are constantly changing and rebuilding our heart temple. We can do this by altering something as simple and as complex as our perceptions and attitudes. By blaming your friend, you said, 'You are the cause within my life.' You handed the control panel of your life to another. By realizing that your friend was not to blame for the circumstances within your life, you took back control and responsibility for your own life. One always strives for an unbiased truth that stands on its own merits; it is an outer reflection of one's inner awareness. True change manifests within," he touched his heart, then finished the statement, "before change finally manifests in our physical reality." As he said this, he swept his hand, palm up, in a semi circle.

I touched my heart and repeated his words in a whispered voice, ". . . strives for an unbiased honest truth that stands on its own merits." I nodded and said, "That made total sense. The man's last statement floated through my mind, 'True change manifests within before change finally manifests in our physical reality.'

I quietly whispered, "Who are you?"

The man continued, "You finally allowed yourself to recognize a falsehood and did all you could do to replace it with truth. The result for you has been happiness and added inner strength. We all decide if the goal of God Awareness in the heart of divine love is worth all the fear confronting, ego-smashing moments. The choice to make a change for the sake of truth and divine love is a gift to and from Divine Spirit, which all mature Souls appreciate."

I repeated, "Truth and divine love, wow, who are you?" I asked.

The middle-aged Chinese man unwound his form from his kneeling position as he removed his hat. He moved like a young dancer, with grace and agility. Again, he nodded his head and stated, "Every step you take, every choice you make, brings you closer to truth. But to discover truth you must do your part."

"What do you mean?" I asked.

"You and others in the human consciousness must strive to distinguish truth from falsehood; develop the awareness to recognize truth when it enters your life. Truth feeds on truth. Truth has always existed; it waits to be recognized. You always have the freedom to choose your own reality and your own truth. As you listen to your intuition and gut-feelings you will recognize the importance of the apparent coincidences within your life, for you are learning to listen to Divine Spirit, or 'The Light and Voice of God.' Experiencing the pure Light and Voice of God, is a gift of Divine communication." The man smiled as he said this.

I felt as if this man had given me an inspirational gift, but it was not a gift in the material sense. Evan and the Spiritual Master, Hikari Hito would have referred to it as, a gift from the heart. I intuitively knew that truth surrounds us as it waits for us to discover it, so in time, I would understand everything. The man's eyes gleamed, as if he knew what I had been thinking.

"You are like the rose," the man said, as he gently lifted a deep red rose bud. "As the bud, you were closed to your potential and what your life could be." The man gently closed his fingers around the rose bud. "But by seeing from your friend's view point, you took a giant step into the much larger room of caring and compassion. You have strengthened your sacred Temple." He opened his fingers to reveal a beautiful, blooming, young red rose. I extended my hand, as the man let go of the rose, it fell gently into my hand.

I blinked my eyes in disbelief as I looked into the man's eyes, I could feel and see the man's focused eyes. Although I felt drawn towards his compassionate gaze I had to look away. I bent over the rose and inhaled its fragrance. The man said, "This rose is called the Explorer Rose."

"It's beautiful," I whispered.

"What is the true heart of any Temple?" the man whispered.

My eyes popped open. I turned to ask, "What did you . . . ?" He was gone. I gently let go of the rose.

Our neighbor Mr. Lee came through the front gate waved and strolled towards me. He was heavy-set and a few inches taller than his brother, I wondered *how I could have mistaken them for one another*.

"Mr. Lee, where did your brother go?" I asked.

"Gone home to Seattle," he stated, and raised his hands to motion towards the southeast.

Then I saw him silently watching us. I pointed to him and said, "Mr. Lee, there's your brother." Mr. Lee looked around and then turned back to me, laughing as if he had found something funny.

His brother said, "He has neither the need, nor awareness to see me." Then he added, "My message was for you."

Mr. Lee said, "My brother gone home, to Seattle." He pointed in the direction of Seattle.

I whispered, 'You are another Spiritual Master.' When I whispered this the Spiritual Master smiled, nodded his head and then disappeared. In his place the Spiritual Master Hikari Hito and my brother Evan appeared.

Master Hikari Hito said, "You have been honored to have met the Spiritual Master Kei Lok. He is the guardian of the Subconscious Awareness; he assists individuals to recognize the gift of awareness from that realm of heaven. This is one-step in ones spiritual journey. The members of the Brotherhood of Light and Love are only humble guardians and messengers." He slowly bowed, and he too was gone. Evan had a twinkle in his eyes as he smiled, nodded his head and disappeared.

I stared at the empty space. My heart rate slowly returned to normal. I turned to Mr. Lee and said, "See you later Mr. Lee. Maybe next time your brother visits, I'll meet him?"

Mr. Lee waved his hand and said, "Good-bye." He nodded his head and said, "Too late, my brother gone home."

I nodded my head in acknowledgement and answered, "Yes, I know." As I hopped onto my bike I said, "So did mine."

Chapter 27

Over Coming Fears: The Many Tests of Life

I handed Mom the bag of washers and O-rings. She was eyeing me; I could tell that she was wondering what had taken me so long. However, all she said was, "Thank you, Katy." I knew I needed to do some explaining.

"Mom," She was going through the bag selecting the right washer for the repair job. I added, "Travis phoned." Mom's head jerked upwards, she stared into my eyes.

"How is he doing?" she asked.

"He's doing fine, Mom."

"You talked to him?" she asked in astonishment.

I nodded my head and answered, "We talked quite a bit and I said things that I should have said a long time ago. I apologized, everything's okay." I hugged Mom and said, "See, you didn't need to worry." I paraphrased the Spiritual Master, Kei Lok, "I had to let go of old attitudes and old ways of seeing things; it was that simple."

"Katy hello," Mrs. Cope called and waved as she came towards us.

"Hi Mrs. Cope, mom said you have some plumbing problems. When I baby sat Justine I noticed the dripping, sorry I forgot to mention it to Mom."

"I forgot to mention it to your Mother, so don't feel bad," Mrs. Cope stated. "It's strange how everything has worn out at the same time. Maybe it's a blessing in disguise, I'll only have to bother your mother for one plumbing appointment," Mrs. Cope joked. She took everything in stride; the big and little problems were just a part of her life's journey. Without knowing it, she was living by the Spiritual Master's guidance.

"Katy, watch me," Justine called out to me. "Look what I can do." Justine looked like a tiny canary with her yellow hair and yellow bathing suit. She looked like she was about to try her wings as she stood on the end of the diving board.

"Justine!" Mrs. Cope's classroom voice echoed off the walls of the large room surrounding the swimming pool. "If you're going to jump into the pool, jump in feet first."

"Uh Mom, I can do it the other way," Justine pleaded.

"Honey, if you're not going to abide by the rules you'll have to come out of the pool," Mrs. Cope warned.

"Abide means to follow the rules," Justine yelled to me. To Justine, having to leave the pool before she absolutely had too would have been a disaster. She leaped off the diving board, grabbed her knees and completed the perfect cannonball.

"Wow, I couldn't do that until I was at least six years old," I said, as we watched Justine surface safely.

Mrs. Cope shook her head and said, "I have to watch her like a hawk. She's like a bull in a china shop and the world is the shop." She added, "Justine saw a diving competition on T.V. a few days ago, now she is determined to imitate those divers. I've got to look into diving classes for young children, very soon."

"Speaking of doing things, I should get this repair job done," Mom said.

Mrs. Cope nodded and said, "Of course, Justine has been in long enough. If you'll give me a second to get her out and dried off, we'll be right with you."

Mrs. Cope told Justine that it was time to get out of the pool. Justine balked and said, "You said if I followed the rules I could swim more," Justine's elephant memory resurfaced again, an elephant never forgets.

"Mrs. Cope, I'll stay with Justine. I kind of owe her a swim," I volunteered.

"Thank you, Katy. If you don't mind, I'll add a few ingredients to a stew that's simmering in the crock-pot. I promise I'll be just a few minutes."

"No problem, Mrs. Cope. Just take your time," I said.

She called to Justine, "Katy, said she'll stay with you. You listen to her and remember the rules. I'm going up to the apartment for a few minutes."

"A-okay, Mom," Justine enthusiastically yelled. She added, "Thank you, Katy." After Mom and Mrs. Cope had left, Justine asked me, "Aren't you going swimming Katy?"

"No," I answered. "I forgot my swimming suit that means I'd have to ride my bike home in wet clothes if I went swimming." Justine looked disappointed. "But there is something that I can do, Justine? I can get part way into the pool." I removed my socks and sneakers, placed them near the wall and rolled up my jeans to just below my knees. I spotted a plastic stool near the maintenance room door, I placed the stool by the edge of the pool and perched myself on top of it while I let my feet dangle in the cool water.

This felt like I was back on the Astral Plane with Evan, closing my eyes I could still feel the cool mud oozing between my curling toes. I was amazed to remember that the mud around my feet had not bothered me. The water lapped up against my legs, I could almost feel the mist of a breeze off the waterfall just as I had when I was dreaming. It was so peaceful, I wasn't afraid of the water or the river anymore. This was like a mini-test; the secret to success was simply a matter of changing my attitude. I had to let go of the old in order to let this new awareness into my life. I had journeyed through a wonderful freeing experience, Master Kei Lok had been right.

From somewhere in the distance I heard a dull pop, I came out of my daydream. After this, what happened seemed like a hazy nightmare. I had forgotten how fast a five year old could forget the rules of any game. I saw her floating near the diving board, faced down in the water, with her arms resting in front and to the sides of her head.

"Justine! Justine!" I screamed before I dived in. I could see her clearly, there was no silt or muddy water, and there was no under current to pull her away from me. I came up directly underneath her and turned her on her back. She was dead weight. "Justine!" I yelled again, even though I knew there wouldn't be a response.

If I were Evan, I could have given her mouth-to-mouth immediately but I was Katy McCall and I knew my limitations. I needed to get her out of the water, quickly.

The indoor pool was average sized but the water that separated us from the pool's edge seemed to stretch on for miles. She could not have been twenty-five kilos soaking wet, but it felt as if I was dragging her giant form across the Mississippi. Luckily, her weight and the imagined distance were both an illusion. I rolled her out of the water, jumped out, grabbed her under her armpits and pulled her further away from the edge of the water. While supporting her head I turned Justine onto her side, in order to clear any water from her mouth. I gently placed her onto her back. I needed to focus on her breathing; that was my first priority.

Rescue breathing, what were the steps? I had seen Evan practice the technique dozens of times. I had helped him to memorize the technique. Panic squeezed in around me, I knew I would turn into a blubbering ball of jelly if I allowed this panic to take charge of me. I needed a pep talk and I was the only person around to give me one.

"Come on Katy," I began to lecture myself. "ABC, you know the steps. Remember, Soul knows everything." I closed my eyes and imagined Evan's simulated life saving test. It was like watching an instruction video set on fast forward. "Okay, just do it," I shouted this order to myself. My voice was shaking as its lonesome echo bounced off the poolroom walls. "Clear the airway. Check for breathing. Check for circulation. I've got it."

I gently lifted Justine's neck, while pressing her forehead down with my other hand. The result of this movement caused her head to tilt backwards and her chin to point skyward. I knew this movement would lift her tongue forward to clear her airway.

"I've already cleared the water from her airway," I reminded myself. I put my ear near her mouth to listen and feel for breathing. Oh God, she was not breathing. I checked her neck, directly under the right side of her chin for a carotid pulse; there was no pulse.

"Now, two short gentle puffs to inflate the child's lungs. Remember to breathe, Katy," I reminded myself. I placed my mouth over her mouth and nose and followed my instructions. I was remembering. I knew that this forced the air sack to stay inflated; as a result, the oxygen would saturate the blood. Again, I checked her neck for a carotid pulse. There was no pulse. I land-marked from her sternum and with the heel of my hand, I began gentle chest compressions; the rate was about a 100 times a minute for a child. . . I reminded myself to be careful, I did not want to crack or break her ribs. I thought; *after five compressions give one gentle ventilating breath*. I gave the ventilating breath. *If there is no pulse*, I checked for a pulse and found no pulse, *repeat the sequence, 20 times and then check for a pulse*. I continually repeated these steps.

How much time had passed? I was exhausted. Why was not she responding? I had gone by the book. I was crying. I was starting to give up hope.

I quietly pleaded, "Please not again. Oh, please not again." Tears flooded my eyes as the realization hit me, *she might not wake up*.

I called out to the Spiritual Master, "Sri Hikari Hito, Evan, someone help me. Please help me. . . . Don't panic," I ordered myself. "Relax, breathe Katy." I continued the CPR and began to sing a silent HU song within my heart and mind; this was no easy task. I began to calm down, if I ever needed to connect with God, I needed to right now.

A pair of dark sandals, I saw them out of my peripheral vision. I looked up. "You came," I whispered. "You came. You'll make her well, won't you?" I asked.

Sri Hikari Hito shook his head and said, "The choice of life and death is not my decision. I can only do what Divine Spirit asks of me, no more and no less."

I was shocked, "But she'll die!" The panic and disbelief in my voice did not affect the Spiritual Master. I felt hope draining away. "I've failed again," I moaned.

The Spiritual Master asked, "Did you do everything humanly possible to save her physical body?"

"But I failed. She's dead," I cried out. I stared at Justine's lifeless body.

"Did you do everything humanly possible to save her physical form?" The Spiritual Master Hikari Hito repeated the question. I nodded my head, as tears rolled from my eyes. "What more could you do?" he asked.

"Nothing," I whispered. With this one word, it was as if I opened up my fingers and released the last bit of hope I held so tightly in my grasp. Relief and sorrow churned inside me. I could do nothing else. The decision of life and death was not mine to make, it was not even the Spiritual Master's decision.

"You have opened another door of understanding," The Spiritual Master Hikari Hito said with calm assurance. The compassion in his eyes gave me new hope. "You had not surrendered your wish for Justine's life; that was the only thing that you had not done. You had not said to God, "Thy will be done. We all play an active role in our own lives and the lives we touch, but when every effort has been made, it is time to step aside and let Divine Spirit decide what is best."

"What good does that do?" I shouted my grief. "I did that and she's dead!"

"Child, there is no death," Master Hikari Hito quietly responded. Those words seemed to open a door for a miracle. My breath caught in my throat as Justine's body materialized like a mist suddenly coming to life, she held Master Hikari Hito's hand; she smiled up at him. Her canary yellow swimming suit shimmered; her whole body shimmered.

"Justine," I whispered. She smiled. She heard me.

"Have you forgotten that Soul is eternal?" The Spiritual Master continued, "We discard our bodies as we discard a used set of clothing. When the time is right for the physical being to end its life in the physical field of existence, it exits from this physical universe. Death is a natural part of existence in the worlds of negative and positive matter; if one's life span is at an end then even a Doctor cannot give life. Soul knows when its physical life will end, but the average human lacks the vision or insight to be consciously aware of this fact."

The Spiritual Master added, "Man on his own, without the help of God should not pretend to be God. Death is not a way to escape the lessons of life. If one does play God by ending one's own life—I speak of suicide now—then one finds himself or herself reincarnating immediately, to repeat the lessons which one tried to avoid. There are guidelines that prevent children and adults from playing hooky from school or work in this physical world. Existence is Soul's classroom and the lower planes are like grade school, if we avoid a lesson then the opportunity to learn the same lesson will reappear, repeatedly. Situations and patterns reappear when lessons are unlearned."

I looked at Justine's physical body and asked, "Why did I try so hard to save her?"

Master Hikari Hito answered, "If her time had come, all the effort within this world would not have had an effect; however, if her life's journey is not yet complete then your efforts may have been a key thread in the fabric of God's plan. Your presence here today was not an accident; your efforts could make the difference between life, death and understanding."

I asked, "Do you mean that . . ."

The Spiritual Master said, "Your actions will allow this child to hold onto her life and destiny, you were both here for a purpose."

Justine's shimmering form dematerialized; her physical body began to cough and her eyes fluttered open.

"You're alive Justine," I said as laughter and tears joined inside my heart. I helped her up as she tried to push herself up to a sitting position.

Confusion filled Justine's eyes. She said, "I saw the Magic Man. My stomach hurts."

I said, "I know." I hugged her hard, so that this reality would not slip through my arms and dissolve into the world of past hopes and empty wishes. Justine was alive, thank; God, she was alive.

"Thank-," I tried to say thank you but the words tangled in my throat. I squeezed Justine again and rocked her in my arms. Love, gratitude and joy overwhelmed me. I tried again to speak and this time I was successful, "Thank you so much." These words were so inadequate.

Master Hikari Hito sensed what I was thinking and said, "Those words are an outer expression of the true gift which you have given this day. You gave the gift of caring, love and life. Today, your efforts made the difference, Kathleen. Through you, Divine Spirit poured the essence of life into this small being. It was not her time." Master Hikari Hito added before fading from sight, "You were Divine Spirit's helper."

"Katy, were you talking to the Magic Man?" Justine quietly asked.

"Just lie down and rest," I instructed. "And yes, the Magic Man is my friend, your friend and my brother's friend. He helped me to believe you would wake up."

"He helped me meet my first Daddy," Justine whispered.

"That's so special Justine. Your Dad and the Magic Man are looking after you, just like we talked about."

"I know," she said. Justine looked me over before adding, "Katy, you're all wet."

I smiled and said, "Yeah, I know. Isn't it great?"

"Can we go swimming?" Justine asked in a quiet whisper.

I laughed before answering, "Not right now. I promise we'll go some other time, scout's honor." As I made this promise, I placed my hand over my heart.

By diving into the pool and making this promise, I had confronted a fear and the fear was gone. I was free I was the cause within my own life. I had jumped off the sidelines and had taken back the control panel of my life.

Chapter 28

Insights from the Memory Cards

He quietly stood against the wall out of her line of vision and away from the traffic flow in the emergency room; Evan did not want her to detect his presence just yet. His role in her life would soon be changing. He wanted to stop influencing Katy's life and choices, for now, all he wanted to do was watch his sister.

Katy sat on the waiting room sofa, clutching the beach towel that encircled her shoulders. Mrs. Cope was in the examining room with Justine. Katy's Mother had gone home to get her some dry clothes. On her way back to the hospital, Mom would be stopping at the Cope's apartment to turn off the crock-pot. Katy had refused to leave the hospital until she knew that Justine was totally all right. When Justine's light body had reentered her physical body, Katy had been thrilled. Evan could see and feel the change in her; he knew she was letting her doubts and guilt get the best of her again.

Evan knew that for Katy's spiritual well being, the time was at hand for him to step back and let her stand on her own two feet. More and more he needed to watch from the sideline as she faced the challenges of her life, only then would she maximize her spiritual grow. His purpose for visiting was no longer necessary; Katy had handled herself well during this crisis. She had handled herself well since he had reentered her life. If he had still been alive in the physical universe Evan would have announced, 'That's my sister, the one who saved that little girls life.' He wished that Katy could feel the same pride that he felt.

Katy was getting restless; she stood to flag down a passing nurse, to ask for information concerning Justine. The nurse didn't know anything about Justine but she promised to find someone who did, then she hurried off.

Evan knew that Katy hated to wait. He thought, *that is not true, it is the not knowing that she disliked.* They had both inherited that trait from their mother. Their father was more of a laid-back person, who took things in his stride. Katy's impatience was rubbing off on him, for a second he thought about popping into the examining room to check the situation out but he quickly changed his mind. He realized that, without the patient's permission that would be an invasion of their personal space.

Evan was about to make his presence known to Katy, when Mrs. Cope entered the waiting room area. The smile on her face was a good sign. When Katy saw her she started to stand, but Mrs. Cope motioned for her to sit down. She took the seat beside Katy, put her arm around her shoulder and squeezed.

"Thank you Katy. Thank you for giving me back my daughter." Her grateful voice vibrated with emotion.

Katy shook her head and said, "Mrs. Cope, it was my fault. I wasn't watching her close enough. I should have been more careful. . . . I was day dreaming," Katy admitted.

"Katy, you know Justine," Mrs. Cope reminded her. "She's bull headed. Justine would have tried to dive in head first whenever the opportunity presented itself; she was trying to do that when she did a belly flop off the diving board.

Dr. Greenfield calls Justine a headstrong little girl. When they shined a light in her eyes, Justine's pupils reacted a little sluggish and her physical reactions are a little sluggish, so they are going to keep her over night, as a precaution. Justine was unconscious for a long time; maybe that is affecting her in some way. They'll be giving her a more thorough exam in the morning," Mrs. Cope explained.

"Oh no, I'm so sorry," Katy whispered.

Mrs. Cope shook her head, and stated, "Katy, don't worry. The doctor said she's 95% sure that Justine is all right."

Evan silently listened to Mrs. Cope's explanation; this information had been just theory to him. During his short career as a lifeguard, Evan had only saved lives in practice. He decided not to count the incident that cost him his life because he had not lived through the entire event. He thought it was funny, at least from a human viewpoint; Katy had become the lifesaver. All the simulated life saving practice sessions that Katy had helped him through, had really been Katy's practice sessions. They had helped her to save Justine's life. It was an ironic Divine Plan; it showed him that God had a plan for everything.

Mrs. Cope rubbed Katy's back as she said, "Don't worry Katy; Justine sees this as a great adventure. She has already informed me that she is going to find out how they fix people in the hospital. The poor doctors and nurses don't know what they're in for." She chuckled and shook her head, as she thought of her daughter's inquisitive nature.

Mrs. Cope added, "I wanted to let you know what was going on so you wouldn't worry anymore. Could you let your mother know that I will be staying over night with Justine? Please thank her for all her help, in all the confusion I forgot to thank her myself."

Katy nodded her head, "I don't think Mom noticed that you didn't thank her, but I'll tell her that you said thank you."

Mrs. Cope hugged Katy again. Evan listened, as Mrs. Cope spoke the words that he wanted to say, "Thank God you were there, Katy. Thank God, you were there when she tried that stunt. Your actions made the difference." They stood, silently hugging one another for a few seconds. "I have to get back to Justine. I'm going to accompany her to the children's ward." She let go of Katy and said good-bye.

For the first time since all this began, Evan saw Katy relax and let the tension from her body dissolve. She sank onto the sofa, laid back and closed her eyes; she slowly drifted off to sleep.

I found myself watching my exhausted physical body as it sat sleeping on the sofa, wrapped in the beach-towel. I wondered *is this a dream or an out-of-body experience.* I looked down to see the hands of my light body; they shimmered like millions of stars. My now-heightened consciousness brought an unusual clarity to the activity going on around me. It was as if I was both here and somewhere far beyond what I could comprehend.

"I feel so peaceful, like I don't have a care in the world; it's as if my worries are not worries at all. This is amazing, when I am in this lighter body I can see everyone but I'm invisible to everyone else. Whoosh-that includes that man," I quickly turned in time to prevent a nurse from using me as a door. "Wow, this invisibility is sort of fun."

"Sure, being invisible is fun for a little while but it gets boring fast." I turned quickly to see Evan's smiling face.

"Evan, I didn't recognize your voice." I ran into his waiting arms to experience his special bear hug. I added, "Boy, it's good to see you again." I glanced back at my physical body and said, "Don't worry Evan; I'm not going to ask you if I'm alive, I know I'm just dreaming."

Evan nodded his head and answered, "Yes, you are sleeping in your physical body but you're having another out-of-body experience, while you're sleeping. It should be a piece of cake for you now," Evan joked. Excitement bubbled up inside of me; I could hardly wait to relate my story to Evan.

"Evan, look out." My warning gave him the chance to side step an incoming patient and her mother.

"Come on, Katy, let's get out of here," Evan suggested. "There's too much traffic around this area, I can't focus my thoughts."

"But Mom will be back soon. She'll wonder where I went," I said.

"Katy! Your physical body will be here. If Mom wakes your physical body up, you'll pop back in, like that." Evan snapped his fingers to illustrate his point. "You've already forgotten this?" I shrugged my shoulders. I guess I had. "Let's go," Evan repeated, as he grabbed my hand and pulled me along behind him, he seemed to be in a hurry.

"Evan, I'm right behind you. You can let go of my hand." He let go and slowed down a bit as my pace accelerated. I asked, "Hey, guess what happened today?" I wanted to see the look on his face when I told him what happened.

Evan shrugged his shoulders, "I don't know." He looked like his thoughts were a million miles away.

This I did not like. I wanted to pull his attention back to this reality. "Evan, take one guess. If you can't guess, you're off the hook."

Evan glanced at me and spoke, "Okay, I'll take a guess. I noticed that your physical body had a beach towel wrapped around your shoulders. Your hair and clothes were damp, so I would say that you finally went into the water again. Am I right?" he asked, as he gave me a knowing smile.

"Yes. Yes I did," I said with enthusiasm. "I hadn't planned on going in, but I had to. I had to get Justine out of the pool. There was no one else around to do it, so I did it. I got her out. I tried to revive her. I did all I could do and was losing hope, then I sang the HU song. That's when Sri Hikari Hito came and helped me to surrender the situation to Divine Spirit."

"That's great, Katy. You saved Justine's life and you got rid of your fear at the same time. Katy, look at all the things that you are aware of now. You know that the Spiritual Masters are always around, even if you don't see them. You also know from your own first hand experience that the HU song can strengthen your spiritual awareness and help you get spiritual guidance any time you sing it. You're becoming independent."

"You're right, Evan. I'm doing things and getting to know things that I would never have dreamed of doing, or knowing about, in a thousand years."

"If you do have any questions, Master Hikari Hito and the other Spiritual Masters will be around to help you to figure out life. He is your spiritual guide and teacher, just as he is my teacher. Now, I feel okay about not being around," Evan tried to slip that information by me.

I stopped and spun around to face him. "What do you mean; you're not going to be around? Don't you remember what Master Hikari Hito taught you? Soul doesn't die, so you'll be around forever, remember?"

Evan was silent and he was not smiling anymore, he just stared at me. There was something wrong; I could feel it. The knot in my stomach began to form again; it was a sure sign that something was wrong. I stared back at Evan and waited for him to speak.

When Evan finally spoke, he did not answer my questions, but repeated his original suggestion, "Let's find a peaceful place to talk," was all he said. I could tell that change was on its way. I hoped that all I had learned would help me take whatever Evan was going to spring on me in stride.

We walked through two double doors, which separated different hospital wards, without opening the doors. We just walked through them. The biggest surprise came after we passed through these ghostly doors. I looked back, the double doors were gone, and the hospital was gone. We were in a place that was unlike any place I had been to on earth, or even seen in photos. "Wow, this is just like the Hollo-deck in Star Trek," I exclaimed.

"As above so below," Evan stated.

"What does that mean," I asked.

"The Spiritual Masters say that it means that reality in the physical universe is a reflection of the reality of the levels of heaven and the Light worlds of God, just like one's conscious universe is a reflection of his subconscious universe," Evan answered.

I shook my head and said, "This isn't like any place I've seen on earth."

I could see stacks and stacks of giant massive vertical standing cards; they must have stood ten to fifteen feet in height.

I asked Evan, "What is this place? It's like a forest of cards?"

As we walked along, I noticed that some stacks of cards had no affect on me but I could not wait to move away from other stacks of cards. I was pulled towards one stack of cards; they drew me like a magnet ... some how, I felt like they were a part of me.

There were other people around us, dressed in a variety of styles of clothing from different eras of history; they were all looking at different stacks of cards. One man marched up to a stack of cards and placed his hands on the first card. In an instant, the cards unraveled as if someone pulled apart a long giant accordion. When I recovered from the shock, I noticed that all the cards were blank; I wondered *what was so important about a giant set of blank cards*.

Suddenly, the Spiritual Master appeared. "Master Hikari Hito, did you see that? The cards reacted to that man's touch, like they were alive."

"Kathleen, I am glad you came to visit."

"Oh, of course it's nice to see you Master. I 'm glad I'm able to experience this amazing place. What are these cards?"

Sri Hikari Hito explained, "The cards appear to have energy or a pulse, this is true, each stack has its own discernible vibration. The cards are not lifeless to the individual who awakens them. That man was able to do so because that deck of memory cards is his and his alone." The Spiritual Master added, "Your physical body is on the sofa in the hospital lounge. Your consciousness is now on the Causal Plane, which is also the memory level of heaven. He swept his hands around in a circular motion and said, "Each deck of cards is a memory record of one person's past lives, and one card is a specific past life. Much of what we experience in our present life has a cause seed in a past lifetime," he explained.

"I don't totally understand," I said, as I shook my head in bewilderment.

Sri Hikari Hito said, "Perhaps you would like to see an example within your own memory records." He lifted his hand towards the stack of cards standing before us.

"These are my memory records?" I asked in awe.

The Spiritual Master nodded and explained, "You were drawn to the cards which are a part of you. If you wish to view them, merely place your hand on the surface of the deck."

This was an opportunity of a lifetime and yet I hesitated. I knew that insights would be uncovered to help me on my spiritual journey. I gathered my nerve, before I slowly walked towards the stack of cards. As I placed my hand against them, the cards shot skywards. I quickly jumped back to view them ascending skyward, they rose so high I could not see the top of the deck.

"Those are my past lives? There are so many. I think there are more than 52 cards in this deck," I said in awe. Evan laughed.

The Spiritual Master explained, "Each Soul travels a path of spiritual evolution. As was said before, in each lifetime, we learn our lessons, as we create new karma and resolve the old karma of our own making. The Spiritual Master asked again, "Would you like to see a particular lifetime, which influences your present lifetime?"

Without hesitation, I quickly nodded my head and answered, "Yes please, of course I would." When I completed this sentence, a giant card quickly descended and landed with a quiet thud, it stood before me. I jumped back with a startled gasp, "What happened?" I asked.

The Spiritual Master Hikari Hito said, "The Spirit of God heard your request, it has provided an immediate answer. This card provides a karmic link between the karma of your present life and a past incarnation. Divine Spirit has chosen the viewing of a past incarnation, which will help you in your present situation. Gaze at the card with an open loving heart and be aware of the gift of spiritual insight, which you will receive from the Spirit of God."

I turned towards the card and gazed into it with gratitude. The uniqueness' of this moment was not lost on me. I told myself, 'This is a gift from God and Divine Spirit.' I thought of the people in my life who I loved, I let this love fill my heart.

Chapter 29

It Seems Like Yesterday

Suddenly, it was as if I was watching a movie screen. There was a rocky mountainous landscape, an old dusty dirt road snaked its way around a boulder-filled landscape. It made a slow descent towards a clear lonesome river. There was a group of old Conestoga wagons, a pair of giant oxen lumbered down this dirt road pulling each wagon. Their weight shifted from wheel to wheel, like a giant moving from foot to foot. The dust from the road slowly billowed and expanded to fill the screen. When it cleared, the scene was different.

The last wagon had crossed the river and joined the others to settle in for the day on a ridge above the riverbed. The rapid flow of the river made the crossing hazardous but it had taken place without incident.

I saw a little girl making mud pies in a muddy area near the shoreline. I knew in an instant that I had lived in this small girl's body, in this particular lifetime. A homemade doll was tucked tightly under the little girl's arm while she concentrated on her task. The doll was well used and loved, she repeatedly propped the doll up in a sitting position against a tree branch, or boulder, near the river's edge. Each time she moved Tina, her doll she would say, "The river is danger. Now don't go near the river."

A man shouted to the little girl, "Sarah, stay out of the river." I immediately recognized the girl's father, their physical bodies were different but her father and Evan were both the same Soul. Having Evan and Spiritual Master Hikari Hito explain how Soul reincarnates into different bodies in different life times, was radically different from seeing and knowing the truth for myself. This was really like entering the Twilight Zone.

"I'm only going to get some mud for pies, Papa," she responded.

"See that you keep your word," her father warned. He turned his attention to watering the oxen and checking some reed woven fishing cages.

The little girl had the best intentions when she made the promise to her father but soon the attention of this five year old was on other pressing matters. Sarah waded into ankle deep water and placed Tina on a log, which was securely wedged between some boulders. While she chatted to her doll she washed her mud-caked hands in the cool river, Sarah's doll slipped unnoticed into the murky river.

Sarah's screams pierced the quiet of the day. In seconds, the father caught his hysterical daughter as she scrambled into deeper water after her friend Tina. Tears ran down Sarah's face, she pointed to the small doll's form and said, "She can't swim."

Her father carried Sarah to the bank of the river and ordered, "Sarah, stay here. Stay out of the river. Sarah, do you understand me?"

Sarah nodded her head. She wanted her friend back, but an unexplained fear gripped her heart. She grabbed her father's arm and whispered, "Papa,"

Her father knelt down so he could look into his daughter's eyes and said, "Sarah, I will be back in a few minutes. I promise. Now stay away from the river. Climb the ridge and wait." Her father instructed as he pointed to the top of the ridge.

Sarah nodded her head and answered, "Yes Papa."

"Then go," her father said, before turning her small body and propelling her towards the ridge. He watched her for a few seconds as she climbed the gentle incline leading to the ridge. Then he turned and ran along the rocky shoreline as he tried to get as close to the doll as possible. The doll floated down stream and quickly found its way into a deeper swifter moving section of the river. As he followed the doll, Sarah climbed to the top of the ridge and looked back at the river. She saw her father wade into the river towards her prized possession. Sarah scurried after her father and Tina; she hoped that her father would bring Tina back to her.

By this time, Sarah's middle brother Steven had caught up with her. He was always the one their mother assigned to look out for little sister, Sarah. Katy recognized Steven as Travis in her present lifetime. The little girl pointed towards her father (Evan) as he moved closer and closer to the tiny doll.

Sarah explained, "Papa's saving Tina."

Steven admonished, "Sarah, how many times have I told you to take care of your toys. If you kept care of that doll, Pa wouldn't have to go chasing it."

Sarah promised, "I'll be real careful, when Papa brings her back I won't let go of her ever again."

They continued to run along the ridge after their father, when he finally clutched the little doll, the children gave a triumphant cheer. That is when they heard the noise, Sarah did not know what it was but her brother knew.

Steven cupped his mouth with his hands and yelled, "Pa! Pa! Rapids up ahead." He pointed towards the rapids. "Get out Pa! Get out!" he yelled. Steven anxiously waved to his father to leave the river; they both thought they saw the acknowledging wave of their father's hand.

Sarah asked, "Stevie, what are rapids?"

Steven answered, "It is when the water in the river goes a little crazy for a while. The water acts angry, it moves a lot faster and is a lot more dangerous," her brother explained. Steven (Travis) felt panic and fear building inside of him. He looked at his sister and shook his head, before adding, "I wish you never had a stupid doll."

Sarah felt the sting of tears in her eyes. She whispered, "Papa promised that he would come back fast. Papa promised," Sarah, repeated.

"Sarah, stay here. I'm going to help Pa," Steven instructed.

Sarah shook her head and answered, "I want to help you."

Steven yelled, "No! I don't want to have to worry about pulling you out of the water. Now stay here." Steven turned and skipped, slipped and slid down the ridge. He quickly removed his boots and waded into the river. The river was foaming and churning. It seemed to dare him to over-come his fear. Steven cupped his hands around his mouth and yelled, "Pa! Pa!"

He thought he heard his father yell as he struggled, "Stay back!"

Sarah ran along the ridge as she watched them. "Get out, Papa!" Sarah screamed.

Both children watched the water toss their father around like a rag doll, he struggled and gasped for air; suddenly he disappeared into the deep churning water.

Steven felt anger and helplessness wash through his body. Why had he not gone into the river? He felt like a coward, he should have tried to help his father.

Sarah was crying as she repeatedly called out, "Papa! Papa!"

Steven (Travis) followed along the river's edge moving into deeper waters; he continued to call to his father. He still clung to the hope that somehow his father had survived. Eventually he sat on the shoreline and cried. Steven was not sure how much time had passed before he made his way back to his sister.

Sarah continued to cry out, "Papa promised. You promised," as she rocked herself in her own arms. Steven picked up his little sister and began the long walk back to the wagon train. He felt numb inside, it would be his task to break the news to their mother and the other family members. He tried to comfort his little sister. Sarah continued to repeat, "You promised. You promised," while she cried. The picture faded, in a cloud of rolling mist.

I turned to Sri Hikari Hito, and my brother, Evan. I wondered *had Evan seen the events shown to me on the giant card.* I said, "During that lifetime, you were my father, you drowned."

Evan nodded his head and answered, "I saw that life time on my own set of cards, I've known about it for a while. I know that in that lifetime, you were the little girl and I was your father and Travis's father. I know I drowned while trying to bring back your doll. You and Steven or Travis felt responsible for my death, just as you have blamed yourself in this lifetime for my death. Travis blamed you in that lifetime for your Father's death, just as you blamed Travis and yourself for my death in this current lifetime. It's a loop of karma." Evan paused before adding, "Katy, I chose, to try to go after the doll back then, just like I chose to try to save the little boy in this life time."

I whispered to Evan, "I'm sorry you died while trying to save a lifeless stuffed doll that seems so pointless."

Master Hikari Hito calmly spoke, "During that life time, the brother Steven continued to blame his little sister Sarah for their father's death. At the same time, Sarah directed anger towards herself for asking her father to save her doll; she was also angry with her father for not returning to her as he had promised. Was the doll lifeless to that little girl or was the doll a companion and friend, whom she loved?"

I stared at Sri Hikari Hito for a few seconds before saying, "To Sarah, the doll was alive," I quickly added, "But I wish I, she, hadn't asked her father to save her doll."

Master Hikari Hito shook his head and said, "Know that anger concerning what might have been is of the past, insights from the past can help you to live a wiser more loving life. What perpetuates anger and resentment is best left in the past." As we thought about the Spiritual Master's words, he added, "The child's father made a sacrifice because of his love for his young daughter, was it less worthy than your brother's sacrifice?"

I thought about the Spiritual Master's words before answering, "Thank you Master for helping me to see in this new way." The Spiritual Master smiled and nodded his head. I looked from the Spiritual Master to Evan and said, "Now I know why I've always disliked playing with dolls and this explains why I can't stand to look at or eat chocolate pies. They remind me of mud pies. It also explains why I was so angry when the Terminator died; it was as if you broke your promise again. It also explains why I've always felt apprehensive about going swimming with Justine, or anyone else." I looked at Evan and added, "It was okay to coach you during your life saving training but with this fear, I couldn't have done it myself." I smiled and announced, "But I'm not afraid anymore, so many things make sense now."

Evan gave me the thumbs up sign and said, "Right on, Sis." He added, "I have to tell you, I felt fear in me before I went into the river to try to save the boy's life, I guess it reminded me of this past life. I've always felt anxious about going into the water," Evan admitted. "But ever since I discovered the root of that fear, my fear concerning that situation has disappeared."

I was astonished to hear Evan say this. "Evan, I didn't know you were afraid." I added, "But you became a life guard, and you still went into the river?"

Evan explained, "In my heart I instinctively knew I had to overcome that fear. I don't regret my actions; I chose to jump into the river. Katy, both you and Travis tried your best to save me. We all did our best. What more could we have done on that day or on a day over one hundred and fifty years ago? You tried, I know, I was watching," Evan finished.

"Evan, you were watching us? That means you had already left your physical body. You were already dead," I reasoned.

Evan nodded his head and agreed, "Even if you had found me, I don't believe it would have made a difference. I knew you weren't going to find me; it wasn't as if you were looking in a clear, calm, swimming pool. When you were looking for me it was worse than looking for a needle in a haystack. You both did your best, forgive yourself Katy, you are the only one who can do that. You did your best," Evan emphatically repeated.

"Thanks Evan. I've wanted to know if there was more that I could have done. Thanks for answering my question." I hugged Evan.

Master Hikari Hito calmly said, "This deep seeded anger and blame has held you and your friend Travis, captive for many life times. You have repeated this situation over countless life times, trading anger and blame until your present life. Now you have replaced these dark emotions with love and forgiveness. By doing your best, by realizing that you could do no more, and finally by forgiving yourself and your friend, you have gained your freedom. In addition, you have gained an understanding of the true purpose of life, to give Divine Love to all. Forgiveness is a partner of Divine Love. What is the true heart of any Temple?" the Spiritual Master asked.

The hair on the back of my neck stood at attention. I said, "That's the third time that I've been asked that question." I added, "Please tell me."

"Divine love, which is housed within the loving heart that is the true heart of any Temple" the Spiritual Master answered. "For even the holy of holies is hollow and lifeless without Divine Love."

I heard music; I looked around to try to discover the source of the beautiful melodic sound. The source of the heavenly music was everywhere and nowhere. "What is that music?" I asked. "It's beautiful." It sounded like a heavenly orchestra was all around us.

The Spiritual Master motioned around me and said, "That Sound cannot be found outside of your own spiritual awareness, the Sound you seek is the music of God and Divine Spirit. It is within every Soul. By ridding yourself of this anger and fear, you have allowed more of the music of Divine Spirit to enter your awareness. This music is similar to a dormant seed hibernating within your consciousness. Different sounds of Spirit are at home on each level of heaven. The sound which is dominant in the Causal Worlds, the world of past life memories is the sound of bells."

"You said bells?" I said excitedly. "That's what I was hearing." It was an orchestra of bells. I had never heard anything like it before. I said, "It's amazingly beautiful."

"As said before, this Inner Sound is the voice of God," Sri Hikari Hito said. "The Voice and Light of God uplifts each being that is touched by the Divine aspects of Divine Spirit. The Inner Sound may manifest as an orchestra, a chorus of birds, the music of a flute, or violins, woodwinds, bells, a high pitched ringing, a rushing wind, or buzzing of bees. These are only a few examples of the sounds of Divine Spirit."

"Those are all sounds that are found on the Physical Plane," I said.

The Spiritual Master nodded his head and agreed, "These physical sounds are reflections of existence from the worlds above. The Spirit of God is always within every being."

I gasped and stepped back as the cards suddenly descended into a neat, standing stack of cards. "I guess I should be used to this by now," I said.

Spiritual Master Hikari Hito explained, "For this visit we have concluded your exploration of past incarnations."

"This is so amazing," I whispered. "No one would guess that this could be done in a million years."

Evan added, "It's better than science . . . fiction," Evan's voice tapped off as he watched me move to the cards to study them.

I lifted my hand and slowly ran my fingertips lightly over there surface. "These cards really do vibrate. You're right, they do have a pulse or energy," I said, as I turned to the Spiritual Master and Evan.

Master Hikari Hito nodded his head and said, "Every aspect of existence has a vibration, each individual Soul also carries a vibration. The Inner Sound and Light also vibrate with the Divine Love of God and Spirit. All who experience these two aspects of God find more joy and upliftment in their daily lives."

I asked, "Does that mean that I've changed some because I've heard the bells on the Causal level of heaven?"

The Spiritual Master nodded and said, "The Light and Voice of God can transform one subtly or dramatically, just as it transformed Saul of Damascus."

I said, "I'll try to remember everything you've said. Spiritual Master, I thank you."

The Spiritual Master nodded and said, "It is an honor to serve Divine Spirit. Your time on the Causal Plane has ended. Evan will accompany you back to your physical existence." With a wave of his hand I thought he faded out of sight but I was wrong, Evan and I faded from the Causal Plane.

The next thing I knew, I was back in my physical body again. I rubbed my hands over my face and quickly looked around to see if Evan was with me. I smiled with relief; there he was leaning against a wall to my left. He came over and sat beside me on the sofa.

"Evan, did we just look at some giant memory cards on the Causal Plane?" I asked.

Evan nodded and said, "Yes. It still seems unbelievable, doesn't it?"

I nodded and said, "I'm so grateful to both you and Master Hikari Hito, for all that you've helped me to understand. I'm so lucky to have you around." Evan's smile disappeared and he leaned forward.

"What's wrong?" I asked. I could see and feel the tension in Evan.

"Katy, I can't visit you anymore . . . or, at least for, a long time."

"Why? Why can't you visit? Are you sick?" I asked.

Evan explained, "I've got to go, it's like going away to a spiritual university. I didn't want you to wonder where I had disappeared to." I felt tears welling up in my eyes. Evan quickly added, "The Spiritual Masters and Sri Hikari Hito will visit you, or you can visit them. Katy, please don't cry."

I wiped the tears away and said, "I know you're not dying again. I hate, I dislike good-byes." I laughed and added, "I wish I could tell Mom and Dad that you were attending University in heaven."

Evan looked a little sheepish as he said, "Well, to tell you the truth, it's really more like grade school. I am starting from the ground level and working my way up, I have an endless amount of learning still ahead of me. I'm not complaining; I see it as a great opportunity."

I nodded and said, "I understand, Evan."

Evan added, "Katy, one day you might be able to tell Mom and Dad that I'm in school in heaven; like you said, nothing is impossible. You must know that by now?"

I whispered, "But life is going to be so dull without you popping in to visit me."

Evan laughed and said, "Are you forgetting what Patty said about your life. You said that she said, 'It was like waiting for the next installment in a continuing soap-opera.' Does that seem dull to you?" Evan asked.

I shook my head and answered, "No, I guess a lot of new situations and people have entered my life lately. What was I thinking? Life has been anything but dull."

Evan said, "You had me on the edge of my seat a couple of times in the last two weeks."

I laughed and said, "I guess life has changed a lot for me."

Evan concluded, "Katy, one thing that I've learned from all my experiences has been that life is an adventure filled with endless possibilities and learning experiences. Remember Katy, I will be rooting for you whether you can see me here or not."

Chapter 30

Until We Meet Again

I whispered, "This is the end isn't it, Evan? You're really leaving."

Evan nodded his head and said, "Katy, remember, Soul is eternal so it's never good-bye; let's say see you later or until we meet again. Okay?"

I smiled and answered, "Maybe I'll come visit you at school, I did it once before so why can't I do it again? Nothing is impossible," I mimicked Evan.

Evan agreed, "You're right. We'll work on this goal together."

"Evan, can you give me an idea of how long you'll be gone? Please," I asked.

"I wish I could Katy, I really don't know. There's an old joke that might help you to know why I can't be more definite, I hope I can remember it."

Evan closed his eyes and thought for a few seconds, before he said, "It goes something like this; "There was this man who really loved God a lot and wanted to speak with God, finally he heard the voice of God."

"The man asked, 'God, can you tell me how long a million years is to you?'"

"God answered, 'A minute.' "

"The man thought about this answer, then asked, 'God, can you tell me how much a million dollars is to you?'"

"God answered, 'A penny.' "

"The man thought about this answer, and then asked, 'God, can I have a penny?' "

"God answered, 'In a minute.' " Evan grinned at me as he waited for my reaction.

I shrugged my shoulders and said, "Sorry Evan, I don't get it. I mean, I get the joke but I don't get what you're trying to say."

Evan explained, "What I'm trying to say is, the pace of time is different in the many levels of heaven. A day in heaven can be like a few seconds down in the physical universe. I could be away for a decade or a century, while here on earth a few days or month could have gone by."

"Evan, I could be ninety years old when you get back. What if you don't recognize me," I asked. "What if I don't remember you?"

Evan laughed before answering, "I'll always know you, Katy. In your Soul, you will always remember me. Sri Hikari Hito said that, 'When love and respect links Souls, there's always a golden connection.' He also said that, 'Connections forged in divine love are as eternal as, eternal Soul.' "

I sat up and turned quickly. Mom sat beside me. Dad was standing beside her. They stared at my startled face. Mom asked, "Are you all right, Katy?"

I asked, "Mom, Dad, what are you doing here?" For a second I forgot that we were in the hospital, I even forgot our reason for being here.

"I brought you some clothes." Mom handed me a bundle of dry clothes. I glanced at Evan; it was as if someone was stealing my time with Evan.

Mom said, "I heard a nurse say that the little Cope girl was driving her crazy with questions. Justine is all right, isn't she?" Mom asked.

"Justine is fine Mom." I bent over and gave Mom a hug. "Justine said her mission is to find out how they fix people in here." I smiled, as I said, "The poor medical staff."

Mom smiled and said, "I feel for them."

"Oh Mom, Mrs. Cope wanted me to thank you for all your help. She said she'll be staying with Justine tonight, so she won't need a ride home."

Mom hugged me and said, "I'm so glad that Brenda didn't have to go through what we experienced. Katy, thank God that you remembered Evan's life-guard training."

Dad sat beside Mom, clenched his hands together and stared at the hospital floor. He looked very uncomfortable.

I asked, "Dad, are you okay?"

"Oh, sure," he sighed. Mom and I exchanged questioning looks. Dad added, "It's just that the last time I was here was when Evan passed away. Being here doesn't bring back fond memories," Dad tried to smile as he said this.

Mom quietly said, "We all remember that awful day."

Dad said, "I wish I had talked to him more when he was alive. I wish I had told him that I loved him, a lot more."

Mom put her arm around Dad and hugged him as she said, "I wish that too."

Evan had been quietly watching us; he moved to stand before Mom and Dad. Evan said, "Ask Mom and Dad to close their eyes and imagine that they are telling me the thing they want to say to me." I was wondering how Mom and Dad would take that suggestion.

Evan ordered, "Do it!"

"Uh, Mom, Dad, this might seem like a strange suggestion, but just do it, okay?" They both gave me a questioning look before they both nodded their heads.

Dad said, "All right."

Mom asked, "What do you want us to do?"

Evan began to speak and I repeated his instructions. "Close your eyes; imagine telling Evan that you love him and anything else that you would want to say to him." Evan and I quietly waited. Evan began to sing the HU song; I joined him by singing a silent HU song while we waited. Mom and Dad slowly opened their eyes.

Mom said, "I feel better." Mom stared then repeatedly blinked and rubbed her eyes. She covered her face with both of her hands and whispered, "Oh no."

Dad kept staring, he said, "I'm hallucinating, I don't have to close my eyes to imagine Evan; I see him standing in front of me."

"I see him too," Mom said as she peeked between her hands. "Evan thought white was a dull color, so why am I imagining him dressed in white?"

"I see him dressed in white too." Dad asked, "Why would we both be imagining the same thing with our eyes open?"

Evan answered, "I'm not your imagination, I'm real."

Mom gasped, her eyes were like marbles as she covered her mouth with her hands. She asked, "Am I going crazy?"

Dad just said, "Evan?"

Evan nodded, "You're seeing me because you're ready to see me. Back when you were joking about the cookie dough and God liking roses, I had a feeling that you were almost ready for a meeting. If Divine Spirit, you call it the Holy Spirit," Evan said to Mom. Mom nodded, and then Evan continued, "If Divine Spirit thought you weren't ready to see and hear me, we wouldn't be communicating with each other."

"You heard that conversation?" Mom asked.

"Evan, are you dead?" Dad asked.

Evan nodded and answered, "My physical body is dead; but Soul is eternal. I live in a different level of heaven; I have been visiting here for a while. I wanted you to know that I love you and I know you love me. I am doing fine. Mom if you miss me hugging you, just close your eyes and imagine hugging me. I'll feel the love." Mom started to cry. I moved to hug her before she waved me away and said, "I'm just happy."

"Son," Dad paused to compose himself and then said, "We've missed you." Dad began to cry as he said, "We love you."

Both Evan and I wiped tears from our eyes and faces. "I've missed all of you," Evan said. "I'm so grateful that you are ready to see and talk to me." He explained, "The Spiritual Masters who have been teaching me, have taught me that Divine Spirit, or the Spirit of God, and the divine love in our hearts binds us together; that's because Divine Spirit is divine love. Each one of us will always have a connection to each other, because we love each other. . . . Please don't cry Mom."

Mom sputtered between gasps, as she said, "I'm not really . . . crying. I'm, crying and I'm happy."

Dad said, "I hope we'll be able to see you again?"

Evan said, "It's possible that we'll meet again in your life time."

"Evan's going to school in heaven," I blurted out.

Evan nodded and said, "That's another thing I wanted to tell you. I have to go away to school in heaven. I'm not sure how long my schooling will take or for how long I'll stay in this body. Katy will explain that to you," Evan reassured Mom and Dad.

"I'll do my best," I said.

"Katy, you know about all of this?" Mom asked.

Evan said, "I asked Katy not to say anything, you weren't ready to know about my visits back then."

Dad said, "Evan, we are so proud of what you did to save that boy's life. At the same time, I had wished that you had stayed out of the water but I know that you couldn't have done that."

Evan nodded and said, "I understand Dad."

Dad added, "Seeing you and talking to you is a gift from God, but when I think of you leaving us again I feel like I'm being cheated."

"Dad, you always wanted me to go to university. Just think of my leaving to go to school in heaven, as saying good-bye to me when I'm leaving for university," Evan suggested.

"Can I tell Mom and Dad about our experiences together?" I asked.

Evan nodded and said, "Sure, Mom and Dad are ready to hear your stories, but don't tell anyone else. One day maybe you'll be able too, but not right now."

"We'll see you again, won't we, Evan?" Dad asked again.

"Dad, I don't know for sure," Evan answered, he added. "Maybe you will, there's always hope. I'm sorry, I really have to leave. I love you all." Evan yelled, before he blew us a kiss, and waved a last good-bye.

"Good-bye son," Dad yelled.

"Bye Evan," Mom and I called to him.

I looked around to see if anyone heard us yelling. Some people looked at us for a second. I smiled and shrugged my shoulders. They quickly went back to paying no attention to us.

Mom and Dad were staring at me; their world had changed dramatically in the last ten minutes. I wondered how they would handle this new knowledge.

Mom said, "We just talked with Evan, Evan was really here."

Dad nodded and asked, "He really was Evan, wasn't he Katy?"

I nodded and said, "Yes Dad, we all talked to Evan. I guess we have a lot to talk about tonight. I'll go get changed before we leave for home."

Mom and Dad hugged each other, I heard Dad joke, "If we're going crazy, I guess we're going crazy together."

Mom shook her head and replied, "Evan being alive is real and heaven is real. I knew it."

They began to cry, I knew they were more happy tears. I was looking forward to being able to talk to Mom and Dad about my experiences with Evan. I headed for the hospital bathroom to change my clothes.

When we arrived back home, Mom made some hot chocolate for the two of us. Dad opted for a strong cup of coffee. He said that he had a feeling that he would need to be very alert when he was listening to what I was about to tell them.

When Mom had remembered our conversation in the bathroom, on the morning of Evan's first appearance, she repeatedly laughed at the image of Evan sitting on the toilet watching us. Mom and Dad were both grateful when they found out that Evan's warning had stopped me from running straight into the path of Andrew's VW convertible. I tried to recall as much of our dialogues with the Spiritual Masters as my memory would allow.

Dad was glad to discover that there was something called the Law of Karma, "The Great Equalizer." He said it went hand in hand with the concept of reincarnation and self-responsibility. He hoped that one day he would be able to travel to the Causal Level of Heaven to have his own past life experience.

Mom said, "I'm just thankful that God allowed us to visit with Evan again. It is so nice to know for sure, that death is not the end." Mom added in awe, "I saw it with my own eyes, so I have to believe it."

Dad nodded and repeated, "Evan's going to university in heaven; it is so hard to believe. And this HU Song, I know I'm going to have trouble with singing this HU Song." Dad added, "For some reason, I can't see myself singing this word."

"Dad isn't singing a big part of church stuff?" I asked.

Mom agreed, as she said, "Beautiful, inspirational songs have the ability to uplift the human spirit so that's probably why churches have choirs." Mom said, "To say that certain sounds can give uplifting feelings is not an unbelievable idea to me."

As I yawned I said, "Why don't you try singing it quietly to yourself, before you fall asleep, then just see what happens in your dreams. Evan told me that it might take some time to be aware of any kind of spiritual happening."

Mom glanced at the clock on the kitchen wall, before she said, "Oh, look at the time. We should all get some sleep."

Dad nodded and said, "I agree. It has been a long day. Will you have enough energy to make it to school tomorrow?"

"Yes. Of course," I answered. We all had a group hug before we headed off to bed. "Sweet dreams," I called out.

I heard Dad laugh and Mom said, "Of course, good night."

It was almost midnight and we had gone through two more cups of hot chocolate, before I had recounted my entire story. I was tired but there was no way in the world that I was going to miss school tomorrow. I wanted to see Andrew and Patty and I wanted to have all of my class work done before the weekend.

Chapter 31

Revolution

The doorbell rang early Friday morning. I had just begun to eat what Mom called, a power breakfast of poached eggs, whole-wheat toast and a glass of orange juice.

"Hi Mrs. M., I was wondering if Katy wanted to walk to school with me?"

"Hello Patty, come in. I believe we'll be driving Katy to school this morning."

I tried to yell as I quickly chewed and swallowed a mouth full of toast. I shouted, "Patty . . . Patty, come in."

Mom chuckled, as she said, "Go on in, I'm sure you'll have a lot to talk about."

"Thank Mrs. M." Patty hurried passed Mom. Mom followed Patty back to the kitchen.

As I turned towards Patty, I pushed my plate away from me. "Patty, you won't believe what happened last night."

Mom's mother voice directed, "Katy, finish eating your breakfast. I'm your chauffeur this morning, so there's no rush. There's lots of time for you and Patty to visit."

I pulled my breakfast plate back towards me. "Patty, you won't believe what happened last night." I put a fork full of eggs into my mouth.

Patty asked, "This must be a good thing, right?"

I enthusiastically nodded my head and gulped the eggs down, before answering, "For sure. I went into the pool at the apartment building last night, I had too."

Mom had come over to the table and gave me a one armed hugged before saying, "Katy over came a big obstacle last night. She was wonderful." Mom moved back into the kitchen area.

"What happened?" Patty asked.

"Mrs. Cope's daughter Justine, she knocked herself out when she dived off the diving board."

"Wow, is she okay?

I nodded and said, "The last thing I heard, Justine was shooting questions at the nurses."

Mom said, "She's fine. I phoned Brenda, Mrs. Cope this morning. She said to thank you again and to assure you that Justine is doing fine. Oh, and you're going to have a substitute teacher for this mornings English class, Brenda's going to spend the day with Justine."

Patty and I looked at each other. We yelled, "Party, party, party!" We finished our celebration with a chorus of giggles.

Mom asked, "What do you mean by party?"

I got serious, as I said, "Mom, we were kidding."

"Yeah Mrs. M., we were kidding. It's just that a substitute teacher usually means a slack class, it's like having a mini-holiday."

I asked, "Mom, didn't you have more of a relaxing day on the days that you had a substitute teacher?"

Mom simply said, "I don't want you to give anyone a hard time, you would be creating some bad karma." Mom winked, as we smiled at each other.

I explained to Patty, "Karma is a spiritual law. What you create comes back to you that is the Law of Karma."

"Oh no, I'm in trouble. Maybe I shouldn't play those jokes on my little brother," Patty half joked.

I reassured Mom, "We don't really have a party." I think Mom smiled, before she turned back to the kitchen sink to continue to clean the breakfast dishes. She seemed to be satisfied with our explanation

I gathered my breakfast dishes and asked, as I placed them in the sink. "Mom, can Patty catch a ride with us to class?"

"Of course," Mom answered.

As we left the house I said, "I can't wait to tell Andrew about what happened; he'll be so surprised."

When Mom dropped us off at school, I immediately searched for Andrew. I did not have to search for too long, Andrew was leaning against the red brick and cement guardrails on the front steps of the school, talking to a couple of the guys on the wrestling team. Patty was following me until she spotted Chester; she called his name and head off to talk with him.

I ran towards Andrew jumping, waving my hand and calling his name, "Andrew, Andrew, guess what happened. You'll never guess what happened." Andrew said something to his friends before he moved towards me; I gave him an enormous bear hug.

"Katy, catch your breath and down shift so I can understand what you're trying to say." Andrew said, as he held the school's front doors open for me. He added, as he guided me towards the stairway. "Tell me what happened, while I walk you to your locker." I nodded and ducked under his arm, as I composed my thoughts. Andrew took my backpack and swung it over his shoulder. He put his arm around my shoulders as we climbed two flights of stairs.

Excitement was bubbling up inside of me, as I asked, "Do you remember Mrs. Cope's daughter, Justine?"

"Sure I remember Justine, she's pretty unforgettable." He opened the door to the second floor as he said this.

Again, I ducked under Andrew's arm and said, "Last night, Justine was knocked out when she jumped into the pool at the Cope's apartment building."

"You seem to be happy, so she must be okay, right?"

I nodded with excitement and said, "She's fine. I got her out and resuscitated her. I jumped into the pool and got her out. I'm not scared of going swimming anymore."

Andrew yelped as he picked me up, spun me around and said, "Way to go McCall." He set me down and added, "That's fantastic. Didn't I tell you that you are a super-woman? Hey, this calls for a celebration. How about we go . . ."

I was shaking my head. I reminded Andrew, "I'm grounded. We could celebrate at my house but that is it."

"What are you guys going to celebrate?" Patty asked, as Chester and Patty came up behind us.

"We're going to celebrate Katy's conquering a giant fear. She's Super Women," Andrew said.

"Cool," Chester said.

"Yeah, that's cool. Can we help you celebrate?" Patty silently pleaded with me, as she asked this question.

"Well, Uh, I'm grounded, so the celebration would have to be at my house, I'll try to arrange it with my parents, and they might be a part of the celebration."

Patty and Chester looked at one another. I expected them to gracefully back out of the celebration but Chester surprised us all.

Chester asked, "Will you have food at this celebration?"

Andrew quickly answered, "Some pizzas for sure."

"Hey man, count me in. I'll bring my guitar."

Patty made a gleeful yell, before she hugged Chester.

Then it was my turn to receive a hug. She whispered, "Oh thank you, Katy."

I whispered, "Patty, let me talk to Mom and Dad before you start to celebrate. I'm sure they'll have no problem with a little celebration, but just let me make sure, okay?" We all turned to look down the hallway towards a commotion.

A familiar, agitated voice, yelled, "You're nothing without me, do you hear me? You're a dime a dozen. You're losers, losers!" Erica followed Henry and Jennifer as she yelled these words, Hillary followed the three of them.

Henry directed Jennifer ahead of him. She quickly opened her locker. Henry turned and confronted Erica, "You're the loser; you're nothing without us. Go find yourself another couple of losers." Henry put his arms around Jennifer and they maneuvered their way through the crowd.

Patty's awestruck voice said, "Holy mackerel, I think there has been a revolt."

I chuckled and agreed, "I think you're right. Holy cow, would anyone have imagined this?"

Erica yelled, "You're not worth anything. I hate you!" She was crying as she struggled to open her locker. Hillary tried to speak to Erica then Erica turned and yelled, "Go away! I don't need you! I don't need anyone!" Hillary backed away, before she turned and quickly left.

Patty chuckled and added, "Yup, there has definitely been a major revolt. Life in Ericaville will definitely never be the same again." Patty and I smirked at each other.

I looked back to see Erica's scarf fall from her shoulders. I stared at the royal blue and orange scarf. Deja-vu, I remembered seeing this image. While the Spiritual Master was speaking, the image of Erica crying had flashed through my awareness. I saw a hand picking up a colorful, blue and orange scarf. The person handed it to Erica, before the image faded.

I handed Erica her scarf and said, "Erica, you dropped your scarf." I added, "It's beautiful, you don't want to lose it."

Erica spun around and snapped, "Are you calling me a loser? Do you think I'm losing it?"

"No. No, of course not, I . . . I was talking about you losing your scarf."

Erica was trying hard to control her crying as she grabbed the scarf out of my hand, "You came to gloat, didn't you? Leave me alone!" she yelled. Erica covered her mouth with her hand and continued to cry. She ran, bumping her way through the gathering crowd of curious onlookers, before she disappeared into the Lady's room.

Andrew came up behind me and quietly said, "Maybe we should leave her alone for right now?"

I shook my head and said, "I don't think so, let me make sure that she's okay." He nodded and quietly waited.

Patty and Chester were watching us. Patty said something to Chester, then turned and called, "Katy, wait for me."

I moved through the dispersing crowd and turned to look into Patty's eyes, I needed to make sure she was focusing on what I was about to say.

"Patty, could you guard the door? Tell people that the bathroom is out of order, and let me do the talking." Patty's look of surprise told me that she was going to argue against my request. "Patty, please just do this for me."

"All right, I'll do it, but if you need help then all bets are off."

"Patty, if I need help, I'll ask for help. Wait for me to ask, promise me that you'll wait for me to ask."

"I promise," Patty reluctantly agreed.

I quietly entered the bathroom. Erica was crying as she attempted to steady her shaking hands, while trying to reapply her lipstick.

"Erica, are you okay?"

"Oh sure, I'm just peachy. Do I look okay?" she yelled, before mumbling, "What a ridiculous question. Why are you following me?"

"I'm concerned about you, you seem to be really upset," I answered.

"Upset," she laughed and added, "You think I'm upset. Now why should I be upset? Just because a big ape threw me over for a loser, is that any reason to be upset? If Andrew decided to date some loser, would you be upset?"

I nodded and quietly answered, "Yes, course I'd be upset. That would be devastating but I would survive and so will you."

"Oh sure you would. Someone smashes your world and you are going to whistle a happy tune. It could easily happen to you," Erica warned me. "Men are fickle, they have no staying power. If Henry can dump me for a nothing person like Jennifer, then Andrew could dump you like a day old newspaper."

Patty could not let Erica get away with that one; she came charging to my rescue to set the record straight. "You know that's not true, Andrew really cares about Katy. Did that over grown gorilla care about you?" I pushed Patty back past the bathroom entrance, as she yelled, "You say that because you're just mean and angry."

"Patty, shut up. Did I ask for your help? I'm not in trouble." I ordered, "Now be quiet, stay here and don't move." She wanted to argue with me but I cut her off, "Patty, promise me you'll be quiet, you're just making things worse."

"Don't let her put you down," Patty ordered.

"Patty, promise me."

"Alright, alright, I promise I'll be quiet."

I went back in the bathroom and found Erica crying. Smeared mascara surrounded her red, swollen eyes. She stared at her reflection in the bathroom mirror as she desperately tried to reapply her lipstick with her shaking hands.

"Erica, Patty didn't mean what she said."

"Yes she did. Patty is right Henry never cared about me. He just liked this . . . shell, there's nothing inside me to like. That is why he left me. Look at her," Erica said as she pointed to her reflection, "I don't even know her. I hate her." Erica scribbled out her reflection with her bright red lipstick. Erica began to scream, she repeatedly hit her reflection with her fists.

"Erica, stop! Stop that!"

"I hate her, I hate her," she screamed as she continued to hit the mirror. She looked at her cut and bleeding hands in horror.

"Patty! Patty, help me!" Patty was beside me in a flash. She helped me to support Erica, as she collapsed to the floor. "Go tell someone in the office that there has been an accident, Erica needs a doctor. Hurry, go!" Patty was gone before I finished.

Andrew ran in and knelt beside us. He quietly said, "I heard the screams." He gently examined Erica's shaking hands and added, "There could be shards of glass in the cuts."

I nodded and said, "Erica, why did you do that?"

"I didn't want to look at her face any more," Erica mumbled. She looked at her hands and said, "My hands hurt."

Andrew whispered, "That doesn't surprise me."

Erica squinted at Andrew and said, "You're in no-mans-land, what are you doing here?"

Andrew answered, "I always wanted to see what a lady's bathroom looked like. Well, now I know, my curiosity is satisfied."

We heard a voice of authority giving an ultimatum, "You have 30 seconds to get to your classes or you have all volunteered for two hours of detention. The choice is yours." There was a few seconds of commotion, followed by a silent calm.

Erica looked at her bloodied hands and the pieces of broken mirrors scattered around us. She mumbled, "I made a mess."

Vice Principle Harrison entered the bathroom, followed by the school's nurse, Mrs. Larkin. Mr. Harrison quickly surveyed the situation while Nurse Larkin tended to Erica's hands.

Nurse Larkin asked, "Katy, could you help me bring Erica to my office?"

As we helped Erica to her feet, she repeated, "I really made a mess. I'm really sorry about making such a mess." I looked back to see Andrew and Patty speaking with Mr. Harrison. Erica tried to assure us that she was all right, "I'm really fine. You don't have to hold me up, I won't fall. Really I won't."

I felt a tap on my shoulder and turned to find Andrew stepping in front of me to take Erica's arm. He said, "Mr. Harrison wants to talk with you." I nodded and stepped aside.

Erica's worried eyes looked into my eyes. She said, "Tell Mr. Harrison that I'm okay. I'll pay for the broken mirror. I promise."

I nodded and said, "Sure Erica. I'll let him know."

I slowly walked back towards Patty and Mr. Harrison. I wondered what I should and should not say.

Mr. Harrison said, "Miss. McCall, Miss. Burbick, let's go to my office, so you can tell me what happened here."

Patty said, "Yes Mr. Harrison."

I said, "Yes sir." I was grateful for the additional thinking time. Was Erica okay? Had the crisis passed? What if I tell Mr. Harrison that she is okay and then it ends up that she is not okay? All these ifs would drive me crazy if I let them. Maybe the hardest part of life was to learn to know what to say and do, and what not to say and do.

My Uncle Jeff once said, 'You can play it safe and sit at home in the shade eating organic broccoli, but what would you learn by doing that?' My goal of spiritual mastership was not going to happen if I played it safe.

Suddenly the light bulb flashed on; maybe this idea was what the Spiritual Masters were talking about when he spoke about a gut feeling or intuition. I knew now that I had to stick to the facts; Mr. Harrison would take action based on the facts.

Chapter 32

Walking the Talk

"Brandy, you need to be quiet. Just be yourself, okay girl," I hoped that somehow Brandy would intuitively know what I was saying to her.

Andrew asked, "Do you really think that she knows what you're saying to her?"

"Brandy is a smart dog, aren't you girl?" I said, as I gave her a hug.

Andrew warned me, "Maybe we should have asked your Aunt Emily for permission to do this. You know, you're lucky that your parents let up on grounding you. If we get into trouble, they're going to ground you for life. Is this worth the risk?"

"Andrew, I have a feeling, an intuitive feeling that I have to do this. I don't think it was a coincidence that Aunt Emily and Brandy came to visit today. I was thinking about how Brandy could make a difference and there she was, just waiting for us. This is going to lift someones spirits, so what could be wrong with doing this? I promise I'll tell them we took Brandy to visit a friend when we get home." Andrew was still hesitating.

I asked, "Do you want me to change my mind?"

Andrew smiled and answered, "I like your mind and I don't want you to change it." We both laughed, before Andrew added, "Just promise me one thing."

"Sure," I answered.

"If anyone gets mad, or upset, promise me that we're out of here, pronto."

I nodded and agreed, "Pronto, I promise."

Andrew nodded and added, "Your parents are going to expect you home for supper. We've only got one hour, so let's go." My plan was now put into action.

Andrew asked the receptionist for Erica's room number, he repeated the number loadly, "B410, hey, that's my lucky number." Andrew continued to joke and talk with the hospital receptionist. "I bet there isn't a dull moment on your job?"

The receptionist agreed, "You're right. There's always something going on. Why I remember last week, there was a guy, he . . ." The phone rang, "Excuse me. Hello, University Hospital, how can I help you."

I was waiting in the hospital hall entrance, peeking around the corner as Andrew did his part. He peeked back at me and signaled me to make my move.

"Okay Brandy, we're on. Let's go," I instructed.

"Brandy, is that you?" Air was caught in my throat as I looked up into a nurse's eyes. She rubbed Brandy's neck. "I didn't expect to see you today. Where is Emily?" she asked, as she looked at me.

"My Aunt is going to meet us here a little later."

The nurse smiled and said, "That's wonderful. This program brings a smile to so many faces." She looked at her watch, "I've got to go. I'm getting exercise where I can get it, so I'm taking the stairs. Maybe I'll see you later."

I called after her, "That sounds like a good idea. Can I walk with you?"

"Sure you can. You better put a leash on her. They'll kick you out if they find her unleashed."

"Right. Thanks for the reminder," I said, as I attached Brandy's leash. I looked at Andrew, he nodded and pointed upwards. I also nodded.

Andrew was waiting for me near the fourth floor stairway. He said, "That was easier than I thought it would be."

I reminded him, "Don't celebrate yet, our mission has just begun."

"You're right," Andrew agreed, "Let's go."

I asked, "Uh, which way to her room?"

"Follow me," Andrew instructed. "I checked this out while I was waiting for you." Brandy was more at ease than either one of us. As we treaked through the hospital hallways, I sensed that this journey was like old home week for her.

"B410," Andrew announced. I handed him Brandy's leash.

I bent down and whispered, "Brandy, you sit." Brandy sat down. Her tail continued to swhish, back and forth. Now be good," I added, as I gave her an hug, "I'll come and get you when I need you. Until then, you need to be good for Andrew."

Andrew reminded me, "Two knocks means someone is coming, one knock means your time is up."

"Right. I'll remember," I assured him.

He gave me a quick kiss. Andrew said, "For good luck."

I smiled and nodded, before I quietly stepped through the door. Erica was attempting to flip through a magazine, as she asked, "Nurse, could you pour me another glass of water?"

"Sure," I said. I stepped forward.

"When will I get these bandages off? It's hard to do anything with my hands tapped up like this." Erica looked up, the expression on her face was priceless. I poured her a glass of water. "Katy, what are you doing here?"

"I'm visiting you, of course," I answered. "How are you feeling?"

"I'm fine. The Doctor is sure that he got all the glass out of my hand. It hardly hurts at all." Erica whispered, "They believe that I purposely tried to hurt myself, so if I wanted to go home I had to agree to see a shrink on a regular basis. I agreed. They're keeping me here for an extra day, but come Saturday morning I'm out of here."

"That sounds great Erica. I'm happy for you."

"Katy, why were you so nice to me, when I was so . . . well, I was rotten to you."

I said, "Someone helped me to know that there is goodness in everyone.

Erica winced and said, "You are such a goody-two-shoes, you must be faking it. What do you really feel about me?"

I carefully said, "Erica, I really don't know you that well, but I do know that I want to get to know you better."

Erica said, "Do you know that I wanted you and Andrew to break up? I couldn't stand Andrew liking you the way he did. I wondered why a pint sized squirt like you should be able to keep a guy like Andrew interested. It didn't seem real to me, so I wanted to break you up. I thought that I would feel better about everything if that happened. So, what do you think of those apples? Do you still want to be friends with me?"

I asked, "Do you still feel that way?"

Erica whispered, "I don't know what I feel right now, my life is a mess. I used to feel good when I did stuff like that. Now everything seems to be so fake I need the fake stuff to live out there." Suddenly Erica seemed to realize what she had just said. She laughed and added, "Now I have you feeling sorry for me. Ha, I haven't lost my touch, have I?"

"Erica, you don't have to fake it with me."

Erica put her hands over her face and said, "Stop being so nice to me, I can't stand it. Why are you still being nice to me?"

I quietly answered, "I'm worried about you. You hurt your hands pretty bad and you were feeling so down that you said you hated yourself. That really got me worried, I guess I'm a little bit of a worrier," I joked.

Erica slowly said, "I wasn't myself when I said that, I was really bummed out. I'm not myself right now but I'll be okay soon."

"Will you feel well enough to go back to school on Monday?" I asked.

"No! No. I don't think I'm ready for that yet. I'd have to see Jennifer and Henry again, I just can't do that right now. If a guy like Henry gives up on me, then what does that say about me?" Erica asked.

"Erica, Henry made a choice and now you get to make a choice. You can choose not to be interested in someone who isn't interested in you."

"I'm not really worried about that. I . . ."

"What is it?" I asked.

"I keep thinking, who else is ever going to be interested in me? I'm not like you, I'm not loveable," Erica stated.

"Did you hear that? I think someone's at the door," I said.

"I didn't hear anything."

I reminded Erica, "Well, you didn't know that I walked into the room, so maybe you didn't hear, whatever." I opened the door and ushered Brandy into the room, before I signaled Andrew to wait at the door. Brandy made a bee-line for Erica. Her tail continued it's happy swhishing motion.

Erica was laughing as she said, "Who are you?" She bent over and gave Brandy a hug.

"Erica, meet my Aunt Emily's dog, Brandy. She's been waiting very patiently for a chance to meet you."

Erica and Brandy showered each other with love, before she said, "Aren't you a sweet heart. Wow, she's just bubbling over with love. I wish I could give you a proper hug; with these bandages on my hands I bet this doesn't feel like much of a hug, does it?" As she spoke to Brandy, Brandy happily licked her cheeks.

"It's safe to say that Brandy thinks you're a pretty loveable person and I'd say that you seem like a pretty loveable person. Dogs are very intuitive and people think that I'm very intuitive, and we both think that you're a loveable person, imagine that. If you say that you're not loveable, you would be saying that we are both clueless." I waited, before adding, "Erica, one day you'll find a special guy who cares for you and loves you in the same special way that you care for and love him."

Erica smiled and said, "Right now, I almost believe that what you said is possible."

"Erica, it's possible. What does it matter that Henry and Jennifer are a couple, so they hit it off for some unknown reason. One day you will find that special person," I reiterated.

Erica said, "If I could find a dog like Brandy, I wouldn't have to take a chance on any fickle feeling guy."

I sort of agreed with her and said, "If that's what you want for your life, that would be an okay choice." Suddenly the intuitive idea light-bulb switched on, as I connected it with a memory.

I said, "Erica, I remember something that Andrew once said to me. I said that I was happy that he was figuring out his life so fast. I said that I was still trying to figure out my own dreams. I remember my brother Evan once saying that, 'Dreams are what reality is based on.' Do you know what Andrew said to me?"

Erica said, "I have no idea."

"Andrew said, 'We both have our whole life ahead of us. We'll make a lot of dreams come true in the next 60 or 70 years, it's okay if we haven't got everything figured out yet.' He said that he figures that we're not meant to figure out everything all at once. He also said that he wouldn't be able to handle that. Erica, we're all experiencing and learning about life at a rate that's best for each of us."

"Katy, you're a philosopher. You're making sense, or maybe I should say, Andrew makes sense."

I agreed, "He does, doesn't he?"

"Katy, why are you trying to help me?"

"I'm here because I like you," I answered.

"How come you like me, when I've always tried to put you down?" Erica repeated her question.

"Erica, I figured out that, that person wasn't the real you. Brandy knows that too."

"Katy, I'm sorry I tried to bug you by saying that Andrew might dump you. Patty was right, I was angry and I was being mean."

"Erica, that doesn't matter anymore. That's old stuff. Let's start over. How about it?"

"Okay," Erica agreed.

"Before I forget, I had better relay Patty's message. Patty asked me to make an apology to you. She's sorry that she got angry at what you said and she's sorry that she yelled at you."

Erica laughed and joked, "Wow, I never thought I would ever hear that."

"Patty wasn't kidding when she asked me to tell you this, she meant it."

Erica nodded and said, "Tell Patty, thanks. I know that Patty was just being your friend and body guard. She thought I was going to hurt you, she's always there for you. I wish there was someone like that in my life."

"How about you start thinking of myself and Patty as your friends? Hey Erica, how would you like to come over to my house tomorrow afternoon for a party. It's kind of a celebration of life, please come."

Erica had a distant look on her face as she repeated, "A celebration of life."

"Erica, why don't you come to my party. You can forget about all the stuff that happened. It will be a new experience for both of us. I promise you that Brandy will be there."

"How could I say no to that," Erica said, as she gave Brandy another hug. There was a quiet knock on the door.

Erica laughed and said, "Now that was a knock at the door."

I laughed and agreed, "You're right. That's my signal to leave, times up." I handed Erica a piece of paper. "Here's my address and phone number, come by at noon or so. Your chauffer is welcome to stay and join the celebration. And I should tell you, my parents and Mrs. Cope and her daughter Justine will be there. We're also going to have a band. It's going to be great but different."

Erica said, "Katy, could you get something out of the closet for me?" She motioned to the narrow white door to her right.

I said, "Sure I can." I opened the door.

Erica said, "See the blue and orange silk scarf? Can you take it down?"

I nodded and said, "Yes." I started to bring it to Erica.

Erica stopped me and said, "It's yours."

"What? You're giving this to me?"

"Yes. I remember that you said it was beautiful. I want you to have it, from one new friend to another new friend."

"Erica, I can't take this."

"Yes you can. I want you to have it. It would really make me happy if you would take it, really it would."

I slowly nodded and said, "Okay, but if you ever want it back all you have to do is ask and it's yours, agreed?"

Erica said, "That's not going to happen, but I'll agree if it will make you feel better about accepting the scarf."

"It would," I said.

Erica said, "Then we're in agreement." We hugged each other and said our good-byes.

"Hey Katy, thanks a bunch."

"Your welcome but I should be thanking you Erica, you made me and Brandy feel great. See you tomorrow." Erica smiled and waved as I stepped into the hallway. I gave Andrew an enormous hug.

Andrew asked, "Mission accomplished, right?"

"It was wonderful," I said.

Andrew lifted the scarf and asked, "What's this?"

I said, "It's a gift from Erica to me."

Andrew had a startled look on his face as he said, "She gave you this scarf, that's amazing. I thought that her grandmother gave it to her, I probably got my facts wrong. I do know that the scarf is one of her favorite pieces of clothing, maybe she really has changed."

I carefully folded it and put it in my jacket pocket. "Let's go," I said, as I pulled Andrew down the hallway.

"What's your hurry? Where are we going?"

"We're going to tell Mom, Dad and Aunt Emily what happened, then we can ask them if we can have a party. I know they'll say yes. And then, we have a party to plan."

Andrew laughed and shook his head, before he said, "McCall, you have guts, or marbles in your head, I don't know which." We were both laughing and joking with each other as we left the hospital.

The Spiritual Master Hikari Hito was right when he said, 'Awareness, flexibility and change are 3 essential elements needed in order to learn and continue to grow spiritually.'

Who would have thought that Erica and Katy McCall would end up understanding each other, and liking each other? Not me, that's a for sure.

The Spiritual Masters were right. Singing the HU Song and changing my attitude had made a difference in my life; I was creating a different life and destiny for myself. The fog covering the unknown future was something to look forward too, that obscure fog did not seem so scary anymore.

Chapter *33*

What Will a New Day Bring?

I was so excited, I was going to host my first major party. Mom and I had spent the morning preparing a vegetable plate with different dips, a large baked lasagna, a large Caesar salad and an assortment of snacks. Mrs. Cope brought baked chicken and Andrew brought two large loaded pizzas, Andrew also brought two mystery containers.

Patty opted to be in charge of the entertainment. She talked Chester's group, 'Pure Harmony' into donating their musical talents to our party, in exchange for a pot-luck buffet feast. Chester and Patty arrived early, in order to set up the make-shift stage along with some of their equipment. After they were finished setting up, they came upstairs to visit and sample the snacks.

I told Patty about how Andrew and I smuggled Aunt Emily's dog, Brandy, into Erica's room. Patty was surprised to find out that Erica was not the same Erica, that we had thought we knew at school. When she was not trying to fake being Erica the debutant, she seemed softer, more like an average girl.

Patty asked, "Did you tell Erica that I was sorry for saying what I said?"

I nodded and said, "Erica said she knew you were trying to be my body guard. She actually respects you, she wished that she had a friend like you."

"You're kidding," Patty asked.

"No kidding, Erica said that," I reassured her.

We continued to prepare our buffet. I even created a special punch, it was filled with cranberry juice, gingerale, concentrated orange juice, water and strawberries. Patty and I loved the punch, we were about to have our second sample.

Mom finally said, "Katy, the punch is fine, so let's move on to setting up the rest of the brunch."

"Okay Mom. I'll get the napkins."

The phone rang. I dropped the napkins on the counter and yelled, "I'll get it. Hello!"

Aunt Emily shocked voice said, "Hey, you just about shattered my ear drum."

"Sorry Aunt Emily. Where are you? You and Brandy are coming to my party, aren't you?"

"We're going to be a little late. I'm sorry Katy."

"How late? I promised a friend that Brandy would be here."

"What's your friend's name?" Aunt Emily asked.

"Her name is Erica, Erica Miller," I answered. "Why do you ask?"

Aunt Emily did not answer my question and said, "We will be late but we'll be there. I have to go, see you later."

Mom asked, "Who phoned?"

"It was Aunt Emily, she said that they will be late but they will make it to the party."

"Don't worry Katy, it will still be a fine party," Mom assured me.

"I know Mom. It's just that I promised that Brandy would be here."

Mom repeated, "She'll be late but she'll be here, don't worry. Now, I need your help." I nodded and continued to help Mom.

Gradually our guests arrived. Everyone who entered the house was asked to sample and evaluate my punch creation. Each person gave the same answer, 'Great punch.'

When Justine spotted Andrew, she gave him a great big hug. She informed him that, "Katy said that this is my party."

Andrew said, "Really, you're kidding."

Justine nodded and said, "Yes, really."

Andrew smiled and said, "Well, I think the guest of honor should have something special to eat, do you think that's a good idea?"

Justine gave a squeal of glee and said, "That's a really good idea."

Andrew asked, "Ms. Copilot, do you want to start with noodles or beef and broccoli?"

Justine gleefully said, "You remembered that I like noodles,I like broccoli too."

Andrew dished Justine a generous helping of both. He was quietly guided by Mrs. Cope's head nods and shakes.

Andrew also brought his camera. He wanted to document everything that happened during my first party. People were either hamming it up or being totally bashful. Andrew said that, "When people get over their initial reaction to the camera, they gradually start to be themselves. That's when a photographer can get the best photos."

Trudy and Martha were the last to arrive. There was no sign of Aunt Emily, Brandy or Erica.

Patty and Chester introduced the three other members of his band. She said they got spruced up just for my party. The band ate first, so they could have time to get their show ready. They were almost finished their second helping, before we were half way through our first. I've never seen people eat that fast, I guess that is not quite true. Evan and Travis could wolf down food at a good clip, when they were racing time.

Later, after the band had played a couple of songs, Mrs. Cope discovered that Josh Bishop had written the lyrics to one of the songs. She gave him a friendly warning saying, "Josh Bishop, you can write beautifully. Now, don't you tell me that you can't write, ever again."

I went upstairs to get a pitcher of punch. I stopped to phone Erica, maybe she just needed encouragement to attend our party. There was no answer at her home, I knew she should have been home by now. I phoned the hospital to ask if she had been discharged, I was told that she had been readmitted. The receptionist asked me if I was a member of her family. When I said I was a friend, I was told that she could not release any more information.

I hung up the phone and asked, "Why was she readmitted?"

"Who was readmitted?" Andrew asked.

"I was trying to find Erica. There was no answer at her home, so I called the hospital to see if they sent her home. The receptionist said she had been readmitted, they wouldn't tell me anything else. Andrew, why would they readmit her."

Andrew shrugged his shoulders and said, "I have no idea. Hey, don't let this spoil your party. We'll find out what's going on with Erica later. Let me help you take the punch down stairs. Katy, don't worry, I'm sure Erica is fine."

"Yeah, you're probably right. I guess it might not be a good idea for Erica to go to a party on the day she gets out of the hospital, she's probably tired."

Andrew said, "If you don't see her today, you'll see her later or in school." As we went back to join the party, we passed Mom and Mrs. Cope on our way down stairs.

Mom explained, "The music is starting to get a little too loud for us. Why don't you tell the others that there is a last call on the food, we're going to start to clean up."

In less than a minute, everyone was upstairs. Andrew and Justine raced me upstairs again and of course they won. Mom and Mrs. Cope were laughing in disbelief.

Mrs. Cope joked, "Chester, I never thought you could move that fast."

As Chester dished up the last of the lasagna, he said, "When you're in a group with three other guys, a lot of times you have to move fast if you want some food."

Mom said, "Eat up, there is less to clean up if you eat everything." Mom did not have to repeat those words, the leftover disappeared, they were extinct, a thing of the past.

Finally, Brandy and Aunt Emily arrived, they finally finished their volunteer work at the hospital. Luckily for Aunt Emily, Mom thought to save her a plate of food. The second Justine saw Brandy, she focused her attention solely on that good natured old girl. The rest of us could have been carrying a gallon of her favorite ice cream and we would have been invisible.

The party ended soon after the food disappeared. Patty and Justine helped me clean up, while Andrew helped the band pack up their equipment and take down their stage. Aunt Emily, Mrs. Cope and Mom were huddled together talking in whispers. Aunt Emily must have told them some bad news, I think Mrs. Cope was crying.

Mom came and gave me a hug, before saying, "Katy, will you go and tell Justine that her Mother is ready to leave."

"Sure Mom. Is Mrs. Cope okay?"

Mom hesitated, before answering, "We'll talk about it later. Go get Justine." I knew that asking more questions would not get me any answers. I went to get Justine.

After Mrs. Cope and Justine left, Patty and Andrew helped me bring the last of the dishes to the kitchen.

I said with total amazement, "This was such an awesome party. Did you see Mom and Mrs. Cope rocking to 'Pure Harmony'. They loved them. They were like us."

"Get real, our parents aren't like us," Patty's astonished voice stated. Then Patty added, "They just like some of the same music. Chester even noticed that they liked their music, he said," Patty mimicked Chester as she said, 'If the old guys rap to our music, maybe we're going to have a giant audience.' Andrew and I laughed at her imitating abilities.

When we entered the kitchen, Mom and Aunt Emily were standing at the kitchen sink. I asked, "Mom, would you buy one of Pure Harmony's CDs?" Something was wrong, Mom rubbed her face as Aunt Emily gave her a hug.

Mom's shaky voice answered me without turning around, "I don't know, I would have to hear it first before I would know."

I turned to Patty and Andrew, they also sensed the tension and stress in Mom's voice. Aunt Emily turned and moved to lean on the island counter, she stared at us for a few seconds.

Finally, Aunt Emily said, "I took Brandy to the hospital this morning to do our volunteer work. I thought it would be a nice surprise to take Brandy and drop in on your friend, Erica."

I said, "I phoned the hospital about an hour ago. They said something about readmitting her. I thought, if she's not feeling well, Brandy would cheer her up."

Aunt Emily nodded and said, "Yes, I know. I saw her parents and sister."

I got excited, as I asked, "Did you see Erica? Do you know why they readmitted her. Is she okay?"

Again, Aunt Emily nodded her head, before she said, "When she got home, Erica took some pills. Katy, I'm sorry, I was at the hospital when she passed away."

"No! That's not true. She was fine. No! No! No!"

"Katy, I'm sorry." Andrew said, as he hugged me.

As I cried I said, "Andrew, she was fine when I saw her. She was fine."

Patty whispered, "Oh no, it can't be. Katy said she was fine, she was happy when she saw her. How can she be dead? I don't understand."

Mom came forward to hold Patty. Patty asked, "Mrs. M., why did she . . . I don't understand." Patty was crying as she hugged Mom.

Mom whispered in a raspy voice, "I don't know why she did this, I just don't know."

Aunt Emily suggested, "Why don't you all sit in the living room and I'll make you all some tea and we can talk?"

Patty wiped her eyes and said, "I don't want tea, I'm going home."

Mom said, "I will be phoning your mother to let her know that your friend passed away."

"She wasn't my friend, at least not yet. Maybe she would have been a friend if she had given herself more time," Patty added, "She was Katy's friend." Patty walked through our front door, then ran home.

I repeated Patty's words, "I don't want any tea. I'm going to my bedroom."

Andrew said, "Katy, maybe if we all talked then-."

"No. I'm sorry, I can't talk right now." I ran upstairs. I needed some thinking and crying time, it felt like Evan had died all over again.

Chapter 34

Two Steps Forward and One Step Back

What day was it? I had not left my bedroom for . . . for five days; so it was Thursday morning. I continued to rest in bed and stared up at the ceiling hoping to have a flash of divine inspiration. I had even missed Erica's service and funeral.

There was a knock at my bedroom door, Mom entered; she was still dressed in a simple black dress and jacket. She scanned my breakfast tray and found it untouched, I could tell that this worried and bothered her.

Mom said, "I saw Andrew at the funeral, he ask how you were doing." Mom picked up the tray of food and shook her head.

I mumbled, "I'm not hungry, I don't want to eat."

"Katy, you have to eat. Do you remember our agreement? if you don't eat your Dad and I will have to get the Doctors to feed you through an I.V. tube."

"But I'm not hungry."

"Katy, if you eat half your breakfast, I won't bother you with food until supper," Mom negotiated.

"I'll probably get sick," I warned.

Mom reminded me, "If the food you eat doesn't get digested, then it doesn't count as you eating it."

I sat up and said in a disgusted voice, "I'll eat the stupid food." Mom set the tray of food down next to me. I took a gulp of juice and said, "There, are you happy?"

"Keep on eating," Mom instructed.

I shoveled another spoon full of eggs in my mouth and chewed, as I said, "Mom, why don't you put some spice on this food, it tastes like cardboard."

Mom nodded, "I'll work on adding more spice for supper."

I kept on eating and found it difficult to keep the food down. I wondered *why is Mom making me eat this junk?*

Mom repeated, "Andrew was at the funeral and he asked about you."

I took another bite, I wanted to get the eating stuff over with. "That's nice." I tried to give an adequate response.

"Erica's funeral was very nice," Mom said, as she watched me eat.

I repeated, "That's nice." I continued to eat. I felt like gagging. . . .

Mom said, "Erica's mother asked about you, Erica told her mother about you bringing Brandy to see her."

"That doesn't matter," I mumbled between chewing. "There, I'm finished."

Mom picked up the food tray. "Erica's mother wanted me to thank you for trying to cheer Erica up."

"It doesn't matter anymore," I mumbled.

"What do you mean, it doesn't matter?" Mom asked.

I yelled, "It doesn't matter! It made her happy but she still took the pills." Mom looked shocked. I closed my eyes and said, "It doesn't matter, it didn't make a difference. How could she do that?" I laid down and pulled up the bed covers around my chin.

I stared at Mom and whispered, "Leave me alone."

As Mom backed out of the room she said, "I'll leave you to get your rest."

Later that morning, when I was on my way to the bathroom, I heard Mom and Dad whispering in the dining room. I sat on the stairway and listened to them talk.

Mom said, "She has given up again, I don't know what else to do. I can barely keep it together long enough to talk her into eating."

Dad said, "She smiles at me and just repeats, 'Don't worry about me Dad, I'm fine."

Mom said, "Maybe we should ask Emily to bring Brandy for a visit. It helped her when Evan left us."

Dad shook his head and reasoned, "No, that's not a good idea, Brandy reminds Katy of her visit with Erica."

Mom agreed, "You're right. I reminded Katy of her visit with Erica and she screamed, 'It doesn't matter. It didn't make a difference.' I could see Mom's reflection in the china cabinet's glass doors, she leaned back in her chair and put her hands over her face. She sighed and said, "I'm so tired, I can't think straight. What are we going to do?"

Dad leaned forward and said, "I have an idea. Remember when we talked to Evan, he said to sing that word."

"Yes I remember," Mom nodded and added, "It was . . . what was it?"

"It was the HU Song, that was it." Dad added, "Maybe we could sing this HU Song and ask for help from the Spiritual Masters and what did Katy call it?"

Mom said, "It's the Holy Spirit, Katy called it Divine Spirit."

Dad said, "Let's sing the HU song now and see what happens. Right now I'll try anything." Mom and Dad sat up in their chairs and closed their eyes.

Mom said, "I feel silly."

Dad said, "So do I, but you remember the saying, 'Nothing ventured, nothing gained.' Let's just try it and see what happens?"

Mom nodded and said, "Let's close our eyes and relax, just as we did before we met Evan." . . . They closed their eyes and Mom said, "We are addressing the Holy Spirit and the Spiritual Masters, we ask that you help our daughter Katy, in any way possible, if it is Thine will. Thank you in the name of the Holy Spirit." Both Mom and Dad sang the HU Song. While I listened to the both of them, I also closed my eyes and quietly sang the HU Song. My physical body slowly relaxed, but my mind was filled with questions; the same questions that I had thought I had found the answers to already. When they stopped the HU Song, I quietly turned to go back to my bedroom.

I heard Dad say, "I've got an idea; I'm going out for a few hours. I'll let you know what I've figured out when I get back."

Mom asked, "Where are you going?"

Dad said, "I'm going to find some answers."

I turned and left. I crawled into bed and fell asleep without effort.

Someone knocked on my bedroom door. Mom came in and said, "Hi sleepy head."

I mumbled, "What time is it?"

Mom said, "It is 4:00 p.m., you slept for over four hours. Katy, Andrew is downstairs, will you see him?"

I thought *does it matter if he sees me like this?* I said, "Sure Mom, I would like to see him."

In a minute, there was a knock on the door and Andrew, Mom and Dad came in.

Andrew looked me over and said, "Hi, you look well," Andrew added, "You do look a little thin, have you been eating enough?"

I asked, "You know who you sound like?" Mom laughed at my question.

Andrew smiled and said, "I remember who. Hey, I brought a large All Dressed pizza, it's down stairs. I'm invited to supper."

"That's great," I said.

Mom said, "We're going to have an early supper. Your Dad and I are going to make the salad."

Dad added, "We'll go and get it started, we'll call you when it's done." Dad guided Mom out of the bedroom.

Mom said, "Just call us if you need anything." Dad smiled and closed the door.

"They're kind of worried about me. I haven't been myself for the last few days. I'm okay now," I assured Andrew. I added, "Please, sit down."

Andrew sat on the bed and said, "I've missed you. I've been worried about you."

I said, "I'm sorry for worrying you."

"No problem," Andrew said, "You missed the school assembly. A lot of students had a lot of questions. I guess the teachers wanted to correct the rumors about Erica's suicide. All the teachers and counsellors said they were available if anyone wanted to talk. They're going to be busy; Erica's friends are going through a ton of anger and pain."

I nodded and said, "I know how they feel, I get so angry with Erica for giving up and for making me feel this pain again; and then I get angry with myself for getting angry with her. Sometimes I think I'm over it and then that feeling is back again. It's all so stupid but I don't know how to make it stop." Andrew gathered me into his arms and hugged me.

When we both let go I laughed and said, "Your hugs always help me to feel better."

Andrew smiled although he looked very uneasy. I noticed that he had something in his hand, hidden behind his back.

"Do you have some kind of surprise for me?"

Now Andrew was even more uncomfortable as he said, "I've been wondering if I should give you this today. Katy, your Mom, Dad and Dawn, and her Mom and Dad have seen it."

"Seen what, what have they seen?"

"Erica left you a note."

"Erica left me a note?"

Andrew nodded and brought it forward, as he said, "It's yours, if you want it. In one way it will probably going to make you sad." He placed it on the bed in front of me.

I looked into Andrew's eyes and asked, "Andrew, did you read it?" He nodded. "Do you think I should read it?"

Again, he nodded and said, "My gut feeling is yes."

I slowly unfolded the paper and began to read aloud.

Dear Katy,

You made my day when you and Brandy came to visit me. I wanted to go to your party. I'm sure it will be a great party. With how I am feeling, I knew that I won't be going anywhere. I made up my mind that I was going to do this weeks ago. Henry leaving me was kind of good timing. Your visit just about talked me out of doing this. For a little while you made me believe in me. I almost decided against doing it. Thanks for trying to help me and thanks for caring. I'm sorry I let you down. I'm sorry I gave up.

YourFriend ERICA

I hugged Andrew as I cried. I managed to say, "I know . . . that it was her choice . . . to, to end things. She had her . . . whole life ahead of her. She would have met someone else. . . . She didn't give herself a chance."

Andrew said, "I don't know what anyone could have done to change what happened. Dawn said that she seemed to be happy. No one in her family knew that she was planning to do this, she fooled everyone. What a waste of a life."

I moved back to look at Andrew's face, as I said, "Erica seemed so confident. I had no idea that she worried . . . or had concerns about anything, before what happened with Henry and the broken mirror. She always seemed so strong. . . . I guess I didn't know her at all," I concluded.

Andrew said, "You're beating yourself up over this."

I mumbled, "I know it's a stupid thing to do."

Andrew said, "Then don't do it anymore." I nodded.

Mom called up to us, "Supper will be ready in five minutes."

"Mom is really saying that supper will be ready in ten minutes. She's trying to get me to

152

hurry up and get ready. Andrew, could you tell Mom and Dad that I'll be down in a few minutes. I need to freshen up and get dressed."

Andrew hugged me and said, "Take all the time that you need."

After he left my room I laid back in bed and stared up at the ceiling. I had been staring at that ceiling for hours at a time each day. Again, I remembered Uncle Jeff's words, 'You can play it safe and sit at home eating organic broccoli, but what would you learn by doing that?' I was at home in bed and there was not a piece of organic broccoli in sight.

I joked, "Maybe that's why I haven't figured anything out."

I thought I knew what I believed. I thought I was confident. I thought I was ready to face life. I closed my eyes and sang the HU Song.

Chapter 35

Waiting for Inspiration from Heaven

"Are you going to hide in your room forever?" Master Hikari Hito asked.

I bolted up to a sitting position with lightning fast speed. "Sri Hikari Hito, you came." The Spiritual Master was sitting on my desk as he quietly watched me. I explained, "I've been thinking about life and death; I have been wondering about why people choose death instead of life."

The Spiritual Master smiled and asked, "And, what wisdom has all this thinking uncovered?"

I shook my head and said, "I don't understand why a person would do something negative and harmful to herself?"

The Spiritual Master answered, "No one can fully understand the despair and pain in another's heart unless you have walked in that person's shoes. In one person these feelings will create the determination to overcome this despair and a need to find answers; while in another the will to believe, discover and to live is lost."

I almost started to cry as I said, "Her family and friends are going through so much pain."

The Spiritual Master nodded and said, "To grieve goes hand in hand with a heart felt loss. There is a time to grieve and there is a time to move forward, everyone lives by their own time line. Time eventually soften the pain in one's heart."

"Why did she do it?" I repeated my question.

Master Hikari Hito said, "We are all characters and props in a never-ending play. We are eternal Souls, creative beings with divine love in our hearts; we created our lives with every choice we make. One day we will realize that we are and always have been the scriptwriters and directors of our own plays."

"Oh, so that's the answer to that question." The Master quietly watched me as I watched him. I asked, "Who wrote the end of Erica's earthly play?"

The Master asked, "Who writes your role in this play?"

I thought for a long moment before I answered, "I think I do."

The Master asked, "Who was the play-write in Erica's play?"

I answered, "Erica." I quickly asked, "Could I have helped my friend in some way?"

He asked, "How would you answer your question?"

I said, "I thought I could make a difference if I was positive and was the best that I could be. I thought that if I helped my friend to see the future possibilities, then I could make a difference. My friend was positive and upbeat when Brandy and I visited her and she still ended her life. Why did she do that, she had her whole life ahead of her, why would a person choose to end her life? Could I have made a difference?" I repeated before adding, "I still don't know the answer."

The Spiritual Master said, "You may think that the gift of divine love that you gave to your friend had no effect; because in the end you lost someone you cared for. Kathleen, answer this question, did your visit to your friend help your friend in any way?"

"I don't know what good the visit did."

The Spiritual Master asked, "Did your friend thank you for your visit? Did your visit uplift your friend's heart? Did she say that you almost helped her to choose another course of action?"

I nodded and said, "Yes, she did write that in her letter but,"

"What is this 'but'?" the Master asked.

I shrugged my shoulders and said, "There are so many pieces to life and so many ways that they can fit together. I guess the 'but' is my indecision, my lack of understanding."

The Spiritual Master smiled and nodded before he said, "In your friend's next incarnation, the body will not remember your kindness, **but**," Sri Hikari Hito emphasized, "Your gift of divine love lives within the heart of the Soul awareness from lifetime to lifetime; this love cannot be wasted or lost. Kathleen, the letter you received from your friend showed evidence of the difference that your caring and divine love made in your friend's life. For this lifetime, your friend has made her final choice; can your present actions change that choice?"

"Anything that I say or do will not bring Erica back." Suddenly I remembered the Master saying to Evan and me, 'We grow as individuals on our spiritual journeys. Although we can inspire new understanding in others, we cannot choose another's attitudes or beliefs, nor can we make another change his or her awareness; such a change could only grow from ones own heart and mind. Thus, it's best to work to nurture the divine love in your own heart and life.' " The Master nodded before he added, "The divine love within you will shine from your heart to the world." He knew what I had remembered.

Sri Hikari Hito added, "If one chooses death before death has chosen you, then you have wasted the God given gifts of life and opportunity. Your friend's next lifetime will provide another chance to learn the spiritual lessons from repeating situations and missed experiences; no one escapes his spiritual lessons."

The Spiritual Master asked, "Have you seen the movie <u>Ground Hog Day</u>?"

I nodded and said, "Yes, I loved that movie."

The Master explained, "In this spiritual movie, the weatherman was repeatedly committing suicide in order to escape his present reality." Sri Hikari Hito added, "This frustrated man finally changes his attitudes and actions, thus he begins to learn from the challenges that each situation offered; these changes gradually altered his world and reality."

I asked, "Do you think that Erica will have the same realizations."

The Spiritual Master said, "The choice to learn or not to learn is in your friend's hands. When the opportunity to learn and grow is wasted then the hardships and challenges of a situation will reoccur, until the lesson is fully learned. The weatherman had one advantage over your friend; this man remembers his past-experiences. When your friend relives the situation she escaped from; she will retain her present life memories in the Soul body but most likely have no conscious memory of her past life experiences. The opportunity to choose a path of spiritual growth and divine love towards others and towards ourselves is always available. For choosing to throw away this gift an individual will need to make a karmic repayment in one of his or her future incarnations."

Sri Hikari Hito emphasised, "Please remember, the negative karma which returns to one's life is not a punishment or the wrath of God, an individual's karma is a personal creation, it is a consequence of present and past choices. The Spiritual Masters have said many time that karma is a teaching tool which inspires and motivates a group or individual, to learn and grow in awareness."

I asked, "Spiritual Master, if you were me what would you have done differently?"

Sri Hikari Hito answered, "I would always follow the guidance of Divine Spirit."

"I don't hear the guidance of Divine Spirit as clearly as a Spiritual Master so what should a person like me do?"

The Spiritual Master asked, "Should you do as your uncle suggests and sit at home eating organic broccoli? What would you learn from such an experience?"

I joked, "I would learn to dislike broccoli." I quickly added, "I was joking."

"Kathleen, how can you learn to hear the voice of Divine Spirit?"

I thought about what the Spiritual Masters had taught me and Evan over the last couple of week. I said, "We practice the HU Song to open our hearts to the love and guidance of Divine Spirit." The Spiritual Master nodded in agreement. I added, "We also learn from our experiences and our mistakes."

"Kathleen, you are learning." The Spiritual Master said before he asked, "Now answer this question, can you do anything else in your physical awareness to answer your questions?"

"Do something in the physical awareness, I don't know what you mean," I answered.

The Master said, "Divine Spirit waits to give guidance to those who have the awareness to hear; but the Essence of God will not choose for anyone or live life for anyone. Spiritual mastership embodies the spiritual characteristics of self responsibility, discrimination, compassion, truth and divine love. These and other character traits all grow and mature from one's life experiences. Knowledge and knowingness which originates from any level of heaven or the physical awareness, can also help anyone make informed choices or decisions. We all can strive to turn ignorance into knowledge. As one moves towards a clarity of truth and knowledge one also strives to bring inspiration, divine love and creativity into his awareness, for this combination can lead to wisdom and enlightenment. There is a saying in your culture, 'Think outside the box,' to do this opens the gift called possibilities. The people who do this are not afraid to think of the positive possibilities, they ask, 'What if? or Why not?' That is what you did when you visited your friend in the healing institution."

"Now I understand what you are saying, you are saying to investigate any subject, gather information and to remember my experiences. Maybe I can find some answers by doing this."

The Master nodded and said, "You have the ability to find your own answers. Your experiences, your intuition and Divine Spirit's guidance will help you to recognize the merit of your discoveries."

. . . I thought about what the Spiritual Master had just said to me. For five days I had been laying in bed waiting for divine inspiration to drop from heaven; I did not do anything to try to find answers; I did not sing the HU Song to try to tune into Divine Spirit's guidance; I just lay in bed feeling sorry for myself and Erica. The only productive thing to come from those five days was, what? . . .I thought *at least one good thing came out of my five days in bed, I stopped feeling sorry for myself.*

I quietly asked, "Will I ever be able to live so positively?"

The Spiritual Master stared at me for a few seconds before he asked, "Will you hibernate every time life seems to be unfair or unkind?"

Mom called to me, "Katy, we are almost ready to eat."

Master Hikari Hito asked, "How will you live your life?"

I called to Mom, "I'll be down in a minute Mom." I turned back to the Spiritual Master, he was gone.

"Thank you Master," I whispered.

I quickly got dressed and went to the bathroom to wash up. I remembered how startled I was when I saw Evan's ghostly body sitting on the toilet cover; I had no idea how change was about to creep and crash into my life.

I went downstairs to share a meal with my parents and Andrew. After days of nibbling on my meals this supper of pizza and salad seemed like a buffet. Unfortunately, my stomach had shrunk in the last 5 days and I could not eat too much. Andrew suggested that I save my appetite for our next picnic and asked if next Saturday was a good tentative date. Mom countered his suggestion and said we could celebrate with a picnic when I got caught up with my classes, my karma was rearing its ugly head again.

I groaned and said, "Mom, I promise that I'll get caught up with my school work. Us going on a picnic for a few hours isn't going to hurt anything."

Dad said, "How about we compromise and say that Andrew can visit you here at the house while you are getting caught up with your studies?"

Andrew quickly jumped into the conversation and said, "That sounds like a fair idea; don't you think that's fair, Katy?"

"You think that's fair?" I asked.

Andrew tried to warn me, as he said, "Katy, we still get to see each other, don't look a gift horse in the mouth."

Mom said, "Horse, who are you calling a horse?"

Andrew quickly said, "It's just an expression, Mrs. McCall. I meant the idea is a gift horse, I'm not calling you or Mr. McCall a horse."

Mom laughed and said, "I know what you meant, I was joking." Both Dad and Mom began to laugh, then Andrew joined them and finally, I added to the laughter.

I decided to take Andrew's advice. I would have to work on creating some good karma for a change and I would start by getting caught up on my class work.

After Andrew left, there was a knock on the door, it was Patty; she looked as if she had not slept for a week.

Patty said, "Hi Katy. I saw Andrew leaving, he said that you had come out of hibernation. I was wondering how you were doing."

"I'm fine now but you look aweful. How are you feeling?"

Patty said, "I'm feeling not great, I keep thinking about Erica. Can I come in and talk with you?"

"Oh yeah of course, come in, I am sorry for making you stand out there."

"Katy, can we go up to your room?"

I shook my head and said, "I've been in my room for the past 5 days; I would rather not go to my room again until I sleep tonight. Do you mind if we go into the livingroom?"

"That's fine with me," Patty answered.

We both sat on the same chesterfield and faced each other; I hugged my legs and rested my chin on my knees as I watched Patty. Just when we got comfortable Dad walked through the front door, he did a double take as he stared at me.

Dad said, "Katy, you're here, you didn't go back to your bedroom." Dad came over and gave me a hug. "I mean it's nice to see you up and about. Hello Patty."

"Hi Mr. M."

"I figured it was time that I came out of hibernation." Dad had a huge grin on his face; he held my hand and kept on staring at me.

"Dad?"

Dad suddenly seemed to wake up, "Yes. Oh yes, I'll leave you girls alone. I'm sure you have a lot to talk about." Dad gave my hand a squeeze and said, "We'll talk later." Dad was whistling as he went into the kitchen.

I said, "Dad was more than a little surprised to see me."

"You can say that again," Patty agreed.

I studied Patty, she seemed tired. Patty said, "I missed being able to talk with you at school. I've been thinking of Erica a lot."

I said, "I have been thinking about Erica too, she was all I had been thinking about for the last five days."

Patty said, "You said your visit with Erica went great."

I nodded and agreed, "That's true, our visit went great, at least, I thought it went great."

"So why did she take the pills?" Patty shook her head and added, "I don't understand, why?"

"Erica wrote me a letter before she took the pills, it kind of explains things."

"She did?" Patty's astonished voice had a hint of hopefulness mixed in.

"Erica said she had been planning to take the pills for a while, but Brandy and my visit almost changed her mind."

Patty said, "I still feel bad about yelling at her; I wish I could change that one moment."

"Patty, I know what you're feeling. Last October or November Evan told me about a *Life Management/Well Being Class* he took at school, during one of the classes they focused on suicide and depression. He said one sign that a person might be thinking of commiting suicide is, that person may give away their possessions; I guess they think they don't need them anymore. At the hospital Erica gave me a scarf, Andrew said the scarf was her favorite scarf, he even said it might have been her grandmother's scarf. I thought she gave me the scarf as a gesture of friendship."

"Wow," Patty shook her head before she pointed at me and said, "That's exactly what I have been feeling, that 'I wish feeling.' Katy, you were nice to Erica; I just thought she was the queen of nasty, I didn't even try to think of her as a person who had pain in her life and now it's too late to make a difference."

"Patty, right now I don't have enough information about suicide to really know how to try to make a difference; or what to look for to make a difference." I sat up and added, "I have an idea to help us change that, maybe we can do something."

Patty asked, "What's the idea?"

I jumped up and moved around the coffee table as I said, "Follow me." As we entered the kitchen I said, "Mom, Dad we're going to do some research on the Internet, do you need the computer for anything?"

Dad wiped his hands off on a tea-towel and said, "I've got to check my e-mail and print off some notes, then the computer is all yours." Dad moved down the hallway towards the study.

Mom was mopping the kitchen floor. She asked, "What research are you doing?"

I looked at Patty's curious expression and answered, "We're going to research suicide on the Internet." I added, "We won't be long."

Patty asked, "We are?" She added, "Katy, that's a fantastic idea."

Mom said, "That is a fantastic idea, I'm going to join you."

Patty and I asked in unison, "You are?"

Mom answered, "Yes I'm hoping that knowledge will help me get rid of the helpless feeling inside of me. Do you mind if I look over your shoulders?"

Patty and I looked at each other and we both shook our heads and I said, "We're okay with you joining us. I didn't know you felt that way, Mom. Patty and I both were wondering if we could have done anything to help Erica."

Patty agreed, "Yeah Mrs. M., I guess we all are asking the same questions."

Mom said, "Maybe we can all help each other find some answers. I have to dig up some writing paper."

I said, "Me too."

Patty agreed, "Me three."

"Girls, I have a suggestion." Dad was standing in the hallway entrance. "I heard you talking about your plans. Today during the noon hour I went to talk with your school counsellor, Mr. Bennet about Erica and how we were all feeling. We did touch on the Internet as a source of information. He said there was some good information on the Internet and he also said there was some misinformation; he said it is best not to treat the Internet like an all knowing God. He said he hoped that anyone who felt troubled or depressed would talk to one of the teachers, counsellors or their parents."

As I tried to figure out what to do I asked, "So you think that the Internet idea is a bad idea?"

Dad answered, "No, I don't think it's bad, I just think there might be a better way to look for information. Mr. Bennet gave me some information and I got an information package from *The Support Network: The Edmonton's Distress Centre.* Maybe we could start with this information; I would like to be a part of your research team, if that's okay."

"Sure Dad."

Patty nodded and said, "Sure Mr. M." She added, " I'll be right back, I've got a new note book that I want to use." Before Patty exited through the back door she looked at me and said, "This is so great, it's like we're all special agents on the same mission."

Mom laughed and said, "Knowledge and action can empower anyone."

I nodded and said, "Yeah, it sure beats laying in bed and wondering about life for five days."

Dad said, "It will only take me a few minutes to get my office work done." He hurried into the office.

Mom said, "Patty is right this is so exciting; it's like we're all working together on a school project."

I hugged Mom and said, "Thanks Mom."

"Thanks for what?" Mom asked.

"Thanks to Dad and you for being my parents and thanks for caring, I guess we're more alike than I thought."

Mom gave me a hug and said, "Thank you Katy, that's the nicest things you have ever said to me."

Mom picked up the mop and bucket and said, "I had better get rid of this before we begin our special mission." I followed Mom into the bathroom and watched her dump the water down the toilet. She put some water in the bucket from the tube tap, rinsed the bucket before dumping the water out and began to wash her hands.

I said, "Mom, I saw you and Dad singing the HU Song this morning."

Mom's head snapped up and her eyes widened with surprise, she asked, "You did?" I nodded. Mom added, "Your Father and I felt a little silly singing that word, I don't know if it helped the situation."

"Mom, it did help." I took a piece of paper out of a small change purse in my pocket, unfolded it and read aloud, " 'HU is an ancient name for God that has a home in the highest reaches of heaven. It resonates with a pure loving vibration and represents the love of God for all Souls. You can sing HU for spiritual inspiration or in times of distress to find spiritual protection, spiritual healing and spiritual insights. Singing HU can help you identify and hear God's voice and guidance.' Mom had an astonished look on her face. I added, "Mom, look at how things were before you sang the HU Song, now look at how things have changed. I sat on the stairway and sang the HU with you, afterwards, I went upstairs and sang the HU some more."

Mom asked, "Katy, did Evan teach you about this word, HU?"

I shook my head and said, "Evan and I have been learning from different Spiritual Masters, remember we talked about that after we saw Evan. The Spiritual Master Hikari Hito, came to visit me after Andrew showed me Erica's letter. He is one of the Spiritual Masters who have been teaching Evan and me."

Mom's eyes widened again, she said, "Let me sit down to listen to what you're going to tell me." Mom moved to the dining room table and sat down.

"Sri Hikari Hito said that—As I closed my eyes, I could hear the Spiritual Master speaking to me as if he was standing beside me—I repeat his words "If one chooses death before death has chosen you, then you have wasted the God given gifts of life and opportunities.' He also said, 'Your friend's next lifetime will provide another chance to learn the spiritual lessons from repeating situations and missed experiences; no one escapes his spiritual lessons.' "

Mom shook her head and said, "You're a smart girl . . . but I don't believe that you thought all that up on your own."

"Of course I didn't think that up on my own, I told you, Sri Hikari Hito said that to me."

Mom nodded and said, "I was reasoning out loud." Mom added, "This Spiritual Master is really real."

I smiled and said, "The Spiritual Master also said,"—Again, I could hear the Spiritual Master's words—" 'Knowledge and knowingness from the levels of heaven or the physical awareness can help anyone to make informed choices or decisions.' The Spiritual Master also said, 'You have the ability to find your own answers.' The Spiritual Master believes in the merits of human creativity and awareness; he is a very smart man."

"My goodness that is practical," Mom whispered.

I nodded and said, "That's why I decided to investigate the subject of suicide; maybe the information will help all of us find some peace and hope again; maybe the wondering will stop popping into my mind. I'm choosing to take control of my awareness and my life."

Mom got up and hugged me she said, "I'm proud of you, you're becoming a young lady before my eyes."

Someone knocked at the front door, Patty entered and said, "Hey Katy! Mrs. M., Mr. M., are you ready?"

I called back, "I've got to run and get a note book." I ran upstairs.

This was exciting. I would not have imagined that I could be excited about doing research with my Mother and Father. Patty was right, we were all on a mission of discovery and change.

Chapter 36

Experience: A God Given Gifts of Life and Opportunity

The ladies sat on the pastel floral patterns covering the burgandy chesterfield that faced the office window. We scanned the information package high lighting and sharing what needed to be discussed; if Patty wanted a copy of the information Dad photocopied the selected pages, in all Dad copied over a dozen pages of information.

Patty said, "Thanks Mr. M., I guess I didn't need my note book. Here is another page with some more good info." She began to read the copy, "They said that suicide spans all age groups. Listen to this, 'More teenagers and young adults die from suicide than from cancer, heart disease, AIDS, birth defects, stroke, pneumonia, influenza and chronic lung disease combined.' Can you believe that?"

Mom leaned forward to sit on the edge of the couch as she flipped through the information pages on the coffee table; she shook her head and said, "That is astonishing and yet, wasn't there a statement in the literature that said each incident should be treated as an individual incident? That means that each of these many incidents could have similarities but the incidents are also different and individually unique."

"Yeah," I agreed, "There are so many outside influences like," I flipped throught the same pages of copy, found what I was searching for and read, 'Suicide is influenced by the individual as well as peers, ethnic, cultural, religious and political groups.' And even the country can influence a persons view of suicide. Listen to this, 'Attitudes towards suicide can range from a personal choice to a condemnation to hell.' "

Dad got up and said, "I think we need a break; I'll go get us something to drink." Mom and I started to get up to help him, Dad waved us off and said, "I've got it covered, I'll be back in a minute." As Dad moved passed Mom he affectionately squeezed Mom's shoulder.

Patty said, "I wish I had known the stuff about how to react when someone say they are thinking about committing suicide." Patty read aloud, "Take it seriously, listen non-judgementally and help them to get professional help."

I reminded Patty, "We didn't know that Erica was even thinking about suicide."

Patty nodded and said, "You're right."

I shook my head and said, "So many people giving up on life☐I know that life can get you so down that you loose hope and you don't feel like living, but that's not a forever feeling☐you do begin to care again and you begin to feel again."

Mom put her arm around my shoulders and gave me a hug as she said, "That's wisdom born out of experience."

Patty said, "Maybe the people who write happy ending know a secret something about life." Patty covered her face with her hands and sighed before she look up at us and said, "Erica didn't have a happy ending, I wonder where she is now? What happens after a person dies? Do we become food for worms or is there something more?"

Mom said, "Everyone wonders about death and the hereafter, especially after death touches your life."

I said, "There is life after death." Mom and I stared at each other, I added, "I mean I believe there is life after death. I believe our bodies, I mean our body is a container for Soul until death; then Soul the eternal part of us leaves and travels to a different level of existence. Where ever Erica is, maybe she will be able to figure out what she couldn't figure out here in the physical reality. We all have to figure things out sooner or later." Patty just stared at me. I added, "That's just what I figure."

Dad stuck his head around the side of the door and said, "Hey, I smell wood burning in here."

Patty startled voice said, "What!" She quickly looked around the room.

I said, "Dad you're scaring Patty."

Dad said, "It must be from these three busy minds rubbing their heads together." Dad laughed and added, "Sorry Patty."

Patty laughed and said, "That's okay Mr. M., I kind of knew you were joking."

Dad came into the room and said, "Ladies, would you like some juice?" He held up four bottles of cranberry juice and a bunch of straws. He added, "Come and get it." Three ladies were up and moving together.

I said, "Thanks Dad." I sat in the gray cushioned, swivel office chair. Dad sat on the arm of the couch beside Mom.

Patty said, as she sat back onto the couch, "Yeah, thanks Mr. M."

Mom added, "I love being waited on." Mom and Dad lightly clinked bottles together before they opened them. Not to be out done, I rolled the chair towards Patty so we could copy their toasting motion.

I opened my bottle, inserted the straw and said, "To hope."

Patty agree and said, "Ditto."

Dad said, "Here, here."

Mom said, "Good toast."

After Mom sipped her juice then asked, "So Ben, when did you pick up this information package."

Dad said, "I first started to research depression after Evan's death. We were all suffering from grief and depression, especially you, Katy." Dad nodded towards me and added, "I thought I could help you if I understood the subject better. This information package on depression came with some information on suicide."

Mom asked, "Why didn't you tell me you were doing this research?"

Dad shrugged his shoulders and said, "When Katy got over her original depression and we were all starting to get back to living our lives again, it didn't seem so important." Dad looked at me and hesitated; it seemed like he was trying to decide whether to add to what he had already said.

He said, "I didn't know that you were blaming yourself for Evan's death. If your Mother and I had known this we would have tried to help you in some way, instead of waiting for you to stop feeling bad."

"Dad, you make me sound like I'm a helpless person," I stated.

Mom said, "We never saw you as helpless in any way."

Dad nodded before he added, "I didn't realize that you would become depressed over Erica's death. Katy, you are our little girl and you were in pain and we didn't know how to stop the pain. Do you remember that I said I went to talk with the school counsellor, Mr. Bennet.?"

Mom said, "You said you went to speak with him this morning."

Dad nodded and said, "Mr. Bennet gave me one idea to help people cope with grief and pain." Dad took a gulp from his juice bottle.

"Dad, don't keep us in suspense, what's the idea?" I asked.

Patty said, "Yeah Mr. M., tell us what you found."

Dad said, "Mr. Bennet's suggestion regarding coping with grief or suicide was that the survivors of suicide could write about their feelings; he said that this has proven to be helpful.."

Mom said, "I'm glad that we are sharing and listening to each other's concerns; airing out my concerns has been helping me to let go of sadness, maybe this is similar to writing."

I nodded and agreed, "You're right Mom, I feel the same way. And I am going to try the writing exercise."

Mom asked, "Did the school counsellor say anything else that you would highlight?"

1.   Dad nodded and said, "I asked him what advise he would give to parents. He gave 5

points. I wrote them down." Dad took his wallet out of his pocket and removed a folded piece of paper☐Mom and I smiled at each other, father like daughter☐Dad unfolded the paper and read, "The 5 points are:

Do not label anything as good or bad.

Be open to whatever comes.

If depression or suicidal thoughts go on for too long, seek intervention. It is best to talk to an knowledgeable adult, or counsellor.

2. Do not judge how people grieve.

3. The grieving process is a journey that can move from disbelief to anger: 'How could they make me hurt so bad?'before reaching healing and accepting.

The phone rang, I swiveled the desk chair around to reach for the phone. "Hello. Hi Mrs. Burbick. Yes, Patty is right here."

I handed Patty the phone. "Hi Mom. Oh yeah I forgot, I'm coming home right now. Okay, bye." Patty hung up the phone and said, "I'm suppose to look after my little brother this evening, I forgot."

"Have a good . . . good luck," I finished as I thought about what Patty was in for, her little brother Harvey, was a hellion.

Patty repeated in disbelief, "Yeah luck, I'll need it." She laughed, then paused before adding, "I'll try to find something good about tonight. The little twerp going to try to make that hard to do but after today, I guess anything is possible, right?"

I laughed and said, "Right."

Patty said, "This is a wow moment. I'm glad I was part of this research team."

Patty got up and gave me a hug. She said, "Thanks Katy, this is the first time that I've felt like laughing since I heard about Erica. Thanks."

I nodded and agreed, "I feel the same way."

Patty said, "See you later." She turned to Mom and Dad and said, "Thanks a whole lot Mrs. M., Mr. M., you're the best."

Mom said, "So are you Patty." Mom stood and gave her a hug.

"Patty," Dad emphasised as he said, "Have a good, time."

Patty laughed and said, "Thanks Mr. M." She turned to me and asked, "You want to walk to school tomorrow?"

I nodded and answered, "Sure, see you at the usual time."

Patty answered, "Right, don't get up, I know my way out." Patty waved as she left the room. We listened to Patty's light footed steps as she ran down the hallway and through the front door.

Dad said, "I think this was a productive day." Dad looked at his watch, "I should say, evening."

Mom was glancing at a page in the information package as she arrange them into a neat stack, she said, "It is nice to see that the different sources of information are very similar in content."

Dad said, "I totally agree."

I jump into the conversation, "This whole experience was an amazing. We followed the Spiritual Master's suggestion; we all traveled from ignorance to knowledge."

Dad asked, "What Spiritual Master said this? When did you see him?" Dad was startled, just as Mom had been when I said this to her.

I answered, "After Andrew left my room I visited with him, that's why I took so long to get ready." I could tell that Dad still had his doubts.

Mom said, "Tell your father what the Spiritual Master said."

I nodded and said, "Sri Hikari Hito said, 'If one chooses death before death has chosen you, then you have wasted the God given gifts of life and opportunities.' He also said that Erica would get another chance in her next life time to learn the spiritual lessons from the experiences which will soon be repeating.' The Spiritual Master also said, 'No one escapes his spiritual lessons.' " I saw surprise on Dad's face.

I smiled and said, "The Spiritual Master also said something that is kind of common sense, he said, 'Clarity of truth and knowledge from the levels of heaven or the physical awareness can help anyone to make informed choices or decisions. You have the ability to find your own answers.' He also said, 'Experience will help you to recognize the merit of your discoveries.' That's what we did today; we tried to figure out how we could make a difference; we moved from ignorance to knowledge."

The look on Dad's face was priceless. He was realizing the same thing that Mom had realized; his daughter was not the creator of these ideas. Dad said, "I guess it's my turn to say, this is a wow moment."

I said, "The Spiritual Master gave us a spiritual way to look at suicide in relation to a person's spiritual journey."

Mom nodded and agreed, "I felt the same wow reaction."

I laughed and added, "Wow, listen to another one of the bullets under, 'Common Clues to Suicide'. 'Giving away possessions, putting affairs in order.' " I whispered, "I told Patty about one of *The Life Management/Well Being Class* that Evan told me about a year ago last October or November; during that class they focused on suicide and depression. Evan said when a person gives away their possessions that could be one sign that the person might be thinking of commiting suicide.

"Remember Erica gave me a scarf; Andrew said the scarf was her grandmother's scarf. If I had remembered this point, if I had known about all these warning signs, maybe I would have been able to put two and two together. I kept on thinking of Erica as a strong person, inspite of what she did to herself in the bathroom. If I had been more aware maybe I could have made a difference, maybe I could have helped her."

Dad was staring at me as he took the same piece of paper out of his pocket, unfolded it he said, "In my research I found that," he read aloud, 'Suicide is like an epidemics that is common to all age groups, social, economic, religious and cultural back grounds. People in the upper class have higher suicide rates; it's believed that this has something to do with people not being able to live up to the expectations that they place on themselves." Mom was staring at Dad, it seemed like they were communicating through their eyes as they watched each other.

Dad looked up at me and said, "Katy, I said before that I started researching suicide when you were going through your bought of depression."

I quickly said, "I wasn't depressed, I was just thinking and just . . . I don't think that I was depressed."

Dad asked, "Can I see that info. package?"

"Sure," I said, as I handed it to Dad.

Dad found a page with a corner turned down, he read aloud, "Sudden changes in behavior; mood swings; despondency, anxiety, depression; changes in sleeping or eating habits.' " Dad repeated, " 'It is believed that this has something to do with people not being able to live up to their own expectations.' "

I asked, "You both think that I was suicidal?"

Dad said, "No Katy, it is just that Erica's parents had no idea that she was thinking about taking her own life."

Mom agreed, "They said that she was sometimes a little moody but that was normal for Erica, what teenager isn't moody sometimes?"

Dad added, "I just know that in the future I don't want to regret not having this conversation with you. Katy, you have set up such high standards for yourself; you think you could have changed Erica's mind and stopped her from killing herself; now you are talking about living by the ideals of the Spiritual Masters. I am not saying that high ideals are bad, I am saying that these Spiritual Masters went through a lot of training to become Spiritual Masters; they sung this HU song and tuning into the . . . what is it?"

Mom finished Dad's sentence, "The Holy Spirit, or the Divine Spirit."

Dad nodded and agreed, "Yes, tuning into the guidance of the Holy Spirit is very natural, probably automatic for these Spiritual Masters. These Spiritual Masters have been in training for a life time or more. You're just beginning to be aware of your spiritual journey, you're still learning."

I said, "I understand that Dad. The Spiritual Master said the same thing, he said that mistakes are a part of the learning experience. I guess I forgot. He also said that flexability was an important part of self-mastery. I started to focus on making a difference. I had the idea in my mind that if I was the best that I could be, then I could make a difference and everything would work out."

Dad said, "Katy, if life doesn't work out the way you want it to work out, it doesn't mean that you've failed. Give yourself a break when things end up different than you imagined; don't close the door that may lead to other opportunities."

I nodded and said, "I guess I was depressed because life didn't meet my expectations but I never thought about commiting suicide, I'm sure of that." I studied Mom and Dad's faces then asked, "You believe me don't you?"

Mom quickly answered, "Yes we do, don't we?" She looked at Dad.

Dad said, "You had me worried, especially after Erica's death. I know now that you're a lot stronger than I would have ever believed." Dad gave me a hug. Mom wrapped her arms around the both of us, like she was a mother bird putting her wings around her little chicks.

I said, "Dad, when you were talking you kind-of sounded like the Spiritual Master." As I thought about what the Spiritual Master said, I added, "Sri Hikari Hito said, 'Knowledge, when combined with inspiration, divine love and creativity, can lead to wisdom and enlightenment.' Did I tell you that already?"

Dad said, "You've told us a lot about what the Spiritual Master said but I don't think I've heard you say that before."

I said, "We were thinking outside the box." Both Dad and Mom gave me a questioning look. I explained, "That's something else that the Spiritual Master spoke about." Again, it was as if I could hear him saying the words that I repeated. "He said, 'If one thinks outside the box, this change opens the gift of awareness to possibilities beyond our immediate reality. Such people are not afraid to ask, 'What if? or, Why not?' as they work towards a creative, solution to any problem, or question.' "

Mom said, "I am glad the Spiritual Master is a part of your life."

Dad nodded and agreed, "It seems that these Spiritual Masters are trying to help you to become the best person that you can be so you will be able to handle the difficult times."

I nodded and agreed, "That's true Dad the Spiritual Masters are trying to help us to aware of the guidance of the Spirit of God or Divine Spirit."

Dad looked at Mom and they both smiled, as Mom said, "If you ever forget about what the Spiritual Masters have been teaching you and life gets a little overwhelming for you, promise us that you'll talk with either your father or me; talk to us any time you feel like talking."

I said, "I'll always talk with you both, I'll try hard to keep that promise."

I realized that Evan's shampoo commercial was a metaphor for life. Maybe the little changes that one seemingly insignificant person makes are not really so insignificant; the changes in life could add up, and so on, and so on, until the small changes became a catalyst for much bigger, far-reaching changes. The Spiritual Master was right, each experience was a God given gifts of life and opportunities.

Epilogue

There was a slight chill in the September air, so we both had light jackets zipped to keep out the cold.

I said, "I hope this weather lasts until the last of October, knock on wood."

"Me too," Patty agreed.

"I won't be able to enjoy this good weather for a while; I'm going to be working double time for the next two weeks to get caught up on all my homework. I'm not looking forward to that." I sighed at the thought of it.

Patty put her arm around me and gave me a hug before she said, "I'll help you get caught up; you can borrow my notes."

"Thanks Patty," I smiled with gratitude. How different this walk to school was from our walk together on the first day of this school year. Again, we smiled at each other; I could tell that Patty also felt the change.

Patty asked, "What's wrong?"

I shook my head and said, "I was just thinking, so many things have changed in the last three month but even with all the pain I'm standing here feeling grateful. Can you believe that?"

Patty gave a hesitant chuckle before she said, "I kind of feel the same way, sort of."

I felt like I was walking on air for the rest of our way to Crestmore. Maybe I was ready to face life with all its challenges and mysteries. Well, if I was not ready now, I knew that one day I would grow into being ready through living and experiencing life, this was the road to spiritual mastership. Two-steps forward and one-step back; it was a part of life, from now on, I was not going to give up when fear or grief blocked my path.

I said, "I just realized that I am going to miss Erica bugging me, just like I missed Evan bugging me." Patty looked so sad, I quickly said, "Patty, I didn't mean to make you feel bad."

Patty shook her head and said, "Don't worry you didn't, not really; it's just, well, I feel the same way. I thought that after last night I would feel different when I thought of Erica because I felt a lot better," Patty shook her head and added, "I still feel the same way."

I put my arms around Patty as we walked, I said, "I guess healing takes time. We'll get through this together, we always have."

Patty laughed and said, "Right, together." We walked for a while before Patty asked, "Katy, could you do me a favor."

I nodded and said, "Sure, what is it?" We could see the school now so I was half listening as I scanned to see if I could spot Andrew. He had phoned before we left for school and said he would be waiting for me.

Patty said, "I'm going to ask Mr. Bennet for a counseling session; I'll try to make an appointment for a noon hour, Katy, could you come with me?"

I looked at Patty; she looked so serious and hopeful. I nodded and said, "That's a great idea Patty, of course I'll go with you." We hugged. When I looked back at the school I spotted Andrew on the front steps; he was not alone. It felt like something grabbed me around my throat and cut off my breath, that something was fear There were a couple of girls and a guy talking to him, one of the girls was Erica's older sister, Dawn.

Patty punched my arm. I said, "Ouch," but I continued to stare.

Patty called, "Katy, earth to Katy, come-in please." Then Patty saw what I saw, she simply said, "Oh wow." Patty tried her best to cheer me up, she said, "Katy, now don't jump to any conclusions, you know that your relationship with Andrew is solid." We both stared as Andrew hugged Dawn. Patty added, "That doesn't mean anything, from the look of what I saw I would say that he seemed to be comforting her, that's Andrew, I mean it makes sense; she just lost her sister. Katy, you can see that can't you.

Finally, something that Patty said got through to me, 'she just lost her sister.' I felt selfish being jealous of Andrew comforting someone who had just lost her sister. The fearful mouse of a Katy was still waiting in the wings, just waiting for me to allow her to make an entrance.

I looked at Patty, nodded my head and said, "You're right, let's go and say hello to Andrew and his friends."

As we moved towards Andrew, we moved around the students in front of our school. I kept my eyes glued to Andrew's face; wondered *what will he feel when he sees me*

I was standing at the base of the stairs when he saw me. His eyes widened in surprise and he smiled as he called out, "Katy!" I moved towards him; Andrew hugged me before he saw Patty, he grabbed both of our hands and pulled us after him to the landing. He turned me as he put his arm around my shoulders. I looked at Patty and found her to be as surprised as I was to find that we stood in the middle of, what? She was staring at Dawn. I also stared, Dawn was beautiful, like a model beautiful and she had been crying.

Andrew asked, "Dawn, you know Katy McCall and her friend Patty Burbick don't you?" I extended my hand to shake hers and was surprise again when she hugged me.

"Katy, I want to thank you for visiting Erica in the hospital. Erica was so happy when she talked about you sneaking your Aunt's dog into see her; that is all she talked about when we were bringing her home. Thank you for being her friend."

I said, "I was just getting to know her better. I wish . . ."

Dawn let out a stuttering sigh, squeezed me in an extra hug and said, "If wishes were gold, I would be the riches person in the world. I'm going to try not to think of things that I can't change, just as a friend advised," Dawn smiled at Andrew as she said this, she added, "I have to get going, I have an appointment with Mr. Bennet."

Patty said, "Katy and I were going to make an appointment with Mr. Bennet." Dawn had turned to leave, then stopped and stared at Patty. Patty began to fidget.

Dawn asked, "You're Katy's friend Patty, aren't you?"

Patty nodded and tried to muster up a smile as she said, "Yeah, that's me."

Dawn nodded and said, "Erica talked about a Patty, I guess that Patty was you."

Patty winced and said, "Oh boy."

"Erica said you were always there for Katy through thick and thin. She said she wished she had a friend like you."

Patty's eyes widened as she said, "Erica said that?"

Dawn nodded and said, "That's what she said."

Patty shook her head and looked down at her feet before she whispered, "I wish I had gotten to know her better, Erica wasn't at all whom I thought she was. Oh no, it's back again, I can't get over feeling rotten."

Dawn said, "Walk with me to Mr. Bennet's office. You said you wanted to make an appointment with him, you can do that before my appointment."

Patty eyes widen as she asked, "Really?

Dawn nodded and said, "Yes, really."

"That would be great, thanks. Katy, I'll let you know about the time," Patty said as a smile beamed from her face.

Dawn said, "Thank you again for everything," and gave both Andrew and I a hug before they left.

As we watched Patty leave with Dawn and her friends, I said, "Dawn's actually nice, she just made Patty's day."

Andrew said, "Yeah, I think you're right she has changed; or maybe she has always been nice but I was focusing on a not so nice memory so I didn't see that part of her.

I asked, "Was she crying because of Erica?"

Andrew nodded and said, "Yeah, she was trying so hard to put on a happy face when she's feeling so much pain. I know what she's going through, I guess we both do." Andrew added, "I apologized to Dawn for blaming her for Megan's death."

"You did?"

"Yeah, I had to let her know sooner than later. She was so happy when I told her; she hugged me and cried even more."

"That's why you hugged each other."

Andrew looked at me and asked, "You saw that?" Andrew squinted at me, as if he was trying to see right through me before he asked, "You wondered why we were hugging each other?"

I looked up into Andrew's eyes, nodded and smiled as I said, "I was jealous and I couldn't breathe for a few seconds, then Patty helped me to know the truth."

Andrew asked, "Does that mean you're over feeling jealous and scared?"

I nodded and said, "I believe that now I am; plus your hugging Dawn helped me to realize something else."

Andrew smiled and asked, "And what's that?"

"If you ever did get interested in someone else, that would probably be devastating and painful, but I know I would survive. I realized that when I started to breath again after you hugged Dawn." Andrew looked like he was not sure if he was happy for me or not. I quickly added, "Don't get me wrong, I'm not saying that you should test my feeling out by hugging every girl in school. I am just saying that I am glad that jealousy and fear are not bottled up inside of me; I would rather say good-bye to those feelings and focus on a guy with a good and kind heart." I hugged Andrew and added, "You helped Dawn to start to heal and let go of some pain." I looked up at Andrew's face again."

Finally, Andrew smiled, he said, "Talking to Dawn helped both of us let go of some pain. She said I made her day; and she passed it on and made Patty's day; and Patty helped you see that hug in a different way; we've all changed in a good way."

"We have all changed," I repeated as I smiled up at Andrew. The school's warning bell rang. I sighed and said, "Five minutes before class time."

Andrew made an exaggerated sighed and said, "Time waits for no man or women." We entered the school.

I had journeyed from grieving, anger and pain to understanding, hope and healing. It was as if I had lived a lifetime in the last two month and I am only fifteen years old; I hoped I had years of living ahead of me. Hope, hope was a strong part of my life again.

Of all the wisdom that the Spiritual Master helped me to find, one thing gave me the most hope. Master Hikari Hito had said, "We are all characters and props in a never-ending play; we are eternal Souls, creative beings with Divine Spirit in our hearts; we created our lives with every choice we make. One day we will realize that we are and always have been the scriptwriters and directors of our own plays."

Now what would I choose to create in my life? Could my choices change the world in any way, or would my choices change mainly myself? Over a lifetime, each of our lives touches so many different lives. How do we know what effect our interaction, our smiles and words will have on those around us?

I had survived the crisis of Erica and Evan's death, of Justine's near drowning and the imagined crisis of loosing Andrew. I was learning to accept, adapt and change. The magic of possibilities had always been a part of my life but now I was fully aware of this fact. We all have the power to care, to create, to choose, to change, to be aware; but the best power that God gave us was the power to learn to live with divine love in our hearts, this helps us to be the best that we can be. I realized what the Spiritual Master had been trying to teach me that divine love was the key to becoming aware of all the gifts from Divine Spirit.

I remembered our Sunday morning pancake breakfast as we even joked about Evan bugging the God in heaven. What a difference an understanding of the truth about death, the hereafter and divine love made in our lives. What kind of healing would this understanding bring to all people and all the beings in all the worlds?

Sri Hikari Hito was right when he said, 'A life filled with challenges and spiritual growth can manifest into the wisdom to use the God given elements with self responsibility and divine love. This is a life well lived.'

What is HU?

HU–"The Most Beautiful Prayer" is also an nondirected, nondenominational prayer, an ancient name for God and a spiritual exercise. When you sing HU, it is a love song to God.

"You can sing it. And in singing it or holding it in your mind in times of need, it becomes a prayer. It becomes a prayer of the highest sort. ... It becomes a nondirected prayer, which means that we are willing to let the Holy Spirit take care of the affairs in our life according to the divine plan instead of our personal plan."
The Slow Burning Love of God–**by Harold Klemp**..page 183

"Each of us is like a power station. We generate energy all the time, energy that either builds or destroys. If we let unworthy thoughts or desires leave our power station, they pollute everything around us. That is bad karma. ... To avoid making karma, while either awake or asleep, sing HU. It is an ancient name for God that people from any walk of life can sing. Sing it when you are angry, frightened, or alone. You can do this quietly within yourself or out loud. HU calms and restores, because it sets your thought upon the highest spiritual ideal."
A Modern Prophet Answers Your Key Questions About Life–**by Harold Klemp**..page 35

"HU can protect. HU can give love. HU can heal. It can give peace of mind. That doesn't mean forever. It just means that if you face a crisis of some kind or another, remember to chant HU. Sing HU to yourself, or sing it out loud if no one's around."
The Slow Burning Love of God–**by Harold Klemp** page 188

"The word HU is an ancient name for God that has the unique ability to lift one into a higher state of awareness. ... One way to open yourself to the wisdom of your dreams is to sing HU (pronounced hue). Sing it either softly or silently for a few minutes before bedtime. This sacred name for God will charge you spiritually. Then go to sleep as usual."
The Living Word Bk. 2–**by Harold Klemp** page 42

"But don't expect HU to work as you want, because God's love, as it comes down and heals, does things its way. Not my will, but thine be done–the nondirected prayer. You have to have confidence and love in your heart. And you must sing HU for all you do."
The Slow Burning Love of God–**by Harold Klemp** page 192 & 193

"You can find the path to love, wisdom, and spiritual freedom by singing HU every day, until HU becomes a part of you and you of it."
The Living Word Bk. 2–**by Harold Klemp** page 89

More books by Harold Klemp and books about the HU Song and related topics can be found at Barnes & Noble book stores, Chapters Book stores and at other bookstores or some public library.
Excerpts from the following books by Harold Klemp; *The Living Word, Book 2; The Slow Burning Love of God, Mahanta Transcripts Book 14; A Modern Prophet Answers Your Key Questions About Life,* are used with permission of ECKANKAR, P.O. Box 27300, Minneapolis, MN 55427 U.S.A.